Reilly's Walk

This book is provided courtesy of the Amelia Island Book Festival's Authors in Schools literacy program, made possible through the generosity of donors and sponsors listed below.

William L. Amos, SR. Foundation–AEL Family Foundation–Rod & Betsy Odom –Rayonier, Inc.–Pierce & Charlotte Roberts–Amelia Island Periodontics: Dr. Darryl Fields–First Federal Bank–Rick and Hollie Keffer–Marie Billings–The Book Loft–Paul & Kathleen Bosland–Ron & Dorothy Cheeley–Debonair: Jerry and Steve Sell– Sylvia Derrick–Giro di Mondo Publishing: Mark & Marie Fenn–Barb & Bruce Heggenstaller–Institute for Enterprise–Miller Family: Clara, David, & Kathy–Revelation Design–WestRock–Arts & Culture Nassau– Joelle Crahay & Dr. Andrew Weinstein–Davis Chrysler Dodge Jeep Ram–Focus Investment Brokers: Fran & George Shea–Amelia Indie Authors–Golf Club of Amelia Island Book Club–Kiwanis Club–Anonymous

Jack Graystone
• Mysteries •

Reilly's Walk

Freshman Trilogy: Book One

SAT Vocabulary Edition

Will Andrews
Streamline Book Publishers, LLC

To the memory of my dog, Reilly, my faithful companion.

You will never be forgotten, little buddy.

REILLY'S WALK Copyright © 2019 by Streamline Book Publishers, LLC

This is a work of fiction. All the characters, organizations, and events portrayed in this novel are either products of the author's imagination or are used fictitiously.

All rights reserved. No part of this publication may be reproduced, distributed, or transmitted in any form or by any means, including photocopying, recording, or other electronic or mechanical methods, without the prior written permission of the publisher, except in the case of brief quotations embodied in critical reviews and certain other noncommercial uses permitted by copyright law.

Streamline Book Publishers, LLC
P.O. Box 282
Orange Park, Florida 32067

Streamline Book Publishers, LLC
ISBN 978-1-7336222-0-2

jackgraystone.com

Printed in the United States of America

First Edition

10 9 8 7 6 5 4 3 2 1

Cover Design and Layout by Stockton Eller Design
Stocktoneller.com

Front Cover Artwork by Sumo Design Studio
SumoDesignStudio.com

Back Cover Artwork by Steve Dunwell Photography
SteveDunwell.com

From the Author

Welcome to the Jack Graystone Mysteries series, SAT Vocabulary Edition. The goal of this book series is to offer exciting stories for young adults that are believable, yet with an air of fantasy. Jack Graystone Mysteries will consist of four trilogies: The Freshman Trilogy, The Sophomore Trilogy, The Junior Trilogy, and The Senior Trilogy. Each trilogy will generally follow the high school years of protagonist Jack Graystone. As the stories progress, Jack will grow into someone who is part James Bond, Sherlock Holmes, MacGyver, and Robin, The Boy Wonder. If you are looking for an alternative to tales about wizards, vampires, aliens, and ghosts, search no further. I look forward to providing readers of all ages with many more entertaining adventures in the future.

Sincerely,

Will Andrews

SAT Vocabulary Words - Reilly's Walk

Each Jack Graystone Mystery, SAT Vocabulary Edition, will contain approximately 300 vocabulary words, which are potentially found in the current SAT's. These words come from several sources, including Vocabulary.com, Majortests.com, and Quizlet.com. Since many words have multiple meanings, some words may contain two or more definitions. In most cases, the first definition listed is the definition utilized within the story. Merriam-Webster.com, Vocabulary.com, and Wordsinsentences.com were the primary sources for the definitions provided.

Each vocabulary word is in bold print and has a corresponding number. A chronological glossary of these words starts on page 271. Additionally, these definitions can be found on the Jack Graystone Mysteries' website at jackgraystone.com.

PROLOGUE

While the summer sun ducked behind the buildings on Manhattan's Lower West Side, the air grew quiet and stale. The muggy evening settled over the city, concentrating the sounds of this particular Friday's mass exodus. Horns beeping, tires screeching, engines revving—all echoing through the massive stone and glass structures.

Through the chaos of these crowded streets rode a black Rolls Royce Phantom. When it could move, it darted between the swarms of yellow taxis jockeying for position between the **barrage (#1)** of red traffic lights. With a flick of his wrist, the driver glanced at his watch every time he came to a stop. He tapped his fingers on the steering wheel while he waited for the light to turn green. His passenger fidgeted in the seat behind him. It was not until they reached the Hudson Parkway that they made any headway.

"Finally," mumbled the passenger as the car picked up speed and headed for the George Washington Bridge. Once they crossed into New Jersey, it did not take long to get to Teterboro Airport.

The sleek, black car came to an abrupt halt near an awaiting plane. The back door flung open, and the well-dressed passenger—a man in his early fifties—emerged from the rear seat and then scampered across the tarmac. While he juggled his briefcase between both hands, he removed his suit jacket and loosened his tie. Although the creases in his starched shirt remained crisp and there were no signs of perspiration, he appeared to be physically exhausted. His face wore the burdens of this world.

Once seated, the exhausted man sat across from the only other passenger in the eight-seat plane—a handsome, dark-haired male who appeared to be in his late twenties. He wore a linen shirt, designer jeans, and Italian leather loafers, all of which cost more than the older man's tailored suit. The men exchanged no handshakes or pleasantries. They had only a moment of brief eye contact followed by a nod. With a loud thunk, the attendant slammed shut the door and closed the latch. Shortly after, the engines roared and the plane taxied to the runway.

"You're late," the younger man said with a Colombian accent.

"We hit every light on the way here."

The younger man looked up from his laptop. "How'd we do this week?"

"About 2.2 million," the older man replied while he stared out the window.

The engines revved and the vibrating plane began to take off. It ascended at a steep angle and banked abruptly away from the setting sun. After the plane gained altitude, the older man reached into his briefcase for his *Wall Street Journal* and started to read. No other words were spoken.

CHAPTER ONE

The final bell snapped sixteen-year-old Jack Graystone back to reality. Images of numbers and symbols stopped racing through his head. With both elbows resting on the desk, he closed his eyes, leaned forward, and dropped his face into the palms of his hands.

"Time's up. Bring your exams forward and place them on the corner of my desk. For those of you who passed, have a nice summer. For those of you who didn't, see you next September."

There was a pause before the screech of twenty-two chairs sliding across the terrazzo floors filled the classroom. Jack's body remained tense as he rose to his feet and joined the other students walking toward Mr. North's desk. A bead of sweat ran down the left side of his chest. It made him shiver.

Mr. North, a gray-haired, **antediluvian (#2)** teacher who should have retired a decade ago, smiled and nodded at each student. As they delivered their tests, he said one of two things: an **enthusiastic (#3)** "Have a nice summer!" or a **crestfallen (#4)** "See you next fall." The smart students got the "nice summer." The ones having trouble got the "next fall." This was typical behavior for Mr. North. Jack often wondered if this was the teacher's **warped (#5)** sense of humor or if he was just plain mean. Most of the time, Jack thought he was just plain mean.

"Mr. North, you're killing me here." Jack placed the Algebra exam in the pile. "This was the hardest test I have ever taken." He faked a smile and pleaded, "My father is going to send me to a military school if I don't get an A."

While Mr. North sat behind his desk compiling the students' tests, he pulled his glasses toward the end of his nose, looked up at Jack, and in his deep voice said, "Have your father call me. I know several I can recommend."

Jack let out a quick laugh and then walked away. *I'm sure glad that's over*, he thought.

Working his way through the mass of students, many of whom looked as if they were about to cry, he headed toward his locker. The main staircase was always a bottleneck. His head bobbed back and forth from students pushing and shoving on his slow descent to the first floor.

Jack made it to his locker with only one slap to the back of his head from an upperclassman. For the next ten minutes, he filled his backpack with books and removed a school year's worth of papers that had accumulated on the locker's floor. Finally, he took down the half dozen pictures of his girlfriend, Courtney, taped to the inside of the locker's door. Jack's locker was as messy as his bedroom. It took two trips to a nearby trashcan to clean out everything. On the last trip, he found the permission slip he was sure the school had lost. He chuckled to himself. *I guess Mr. Henderson was right. I didn't turn it in.* With one last look inside, he shut his locker, closing the door on his freshman year at Worthington Preparatory School.

A sharp pain shot up Jack's neck when he slung his backpack over his right shoulder. He leaned forward and began his trek to the student parking lot. He talked to no one while he quickly made his way to the far side of campus. A slight breeze did little to prevent beads of sweat from forming on his face.

The student parking lot consisted of spaces along both sides of a road that served as the back entrance to the school. The school assigned these spaces by grade level. The seniors were the closest, followed by the juniors, and then the sophomores. Since Jack was the only freshman old enough to drive, they assigned him the farthest space. Today, it seemed farther than ever.

Jack tossed his backpack into the backseat of his aging Ford Explorer and then jumped on the hood. He leaned with his back against the windshield, hands behind his head, and his eyes closed. The warm glass soothed his tense muscles. *I hope every day this summer's like this.* His mind wondered while he listened to the sounds of classmates talking and laughing, radios blaring, and the occasional honk or yell from a passing car. Several minutes passed before he glanced at his iPhone. *Ollie, it's been ten minutes. Where the hell are you?*

Ollie was Jack's best friend. Ollie's full name was Oliver Hamilton Culver IV—a name he greatly despised. Similar to Jack, Ollie was a day student, although a grade ahead. The day students made up half of the student body at Worthington Prep, an **elite (#6)** private high school in New England. The other half were boarders who came from all around the world.

As far as Worthington Prep students went, Jack and Ollie were about as opposite as they could be. Jack was the only child in a family with highly-educated parents. His father, Thomas Graystone, was a real estate attorney. His mother, Doctor Elizabeth Graystone, was a dentist.

Ollie was one of four children in a family that viewed education as a status symbol, not a means to make a living. Both of Ollie's parents had attended Ivy League schools. His father had earned a prestigious degree in psychology. A degree he only used during arguments—which happened quite often. His mother never finished her **anthropology (#7)** degree. The surprise arrival of Ollie's older sister put an end to her college career.

The differences continued with their attitudes toward school. Jack was mostly an A student who strived to get the best grade possible while making time for several sports. Ollie took pride in being an average student and not much of an athlete. The only sport he played was croquet—if you can even call that a sport.

Ollie's lack of study skills or desire to sweat was the result of his upbringing in an **affluent (#8)** family. His great-grandfather had started a successful munitions company several decades ago. Many years later, his grandfather sold the company and dispersed the profits into trust accounts for each family member. When Ollie was thirteen, he overheard one of his trust managers say, "That's one rich little bastard. He'll never have to work a day in his life." That was probably the worst thing for Ollie to accidentally overhear. Instantly, he developed a new philosophy regarding schoolwork. Since a C average was the minimum required for Worthington Prep, he would study no more or no less to maintain that average. Ollie did not want to get D's, because the school would expel him. But he also did not want to get B's, and certainly not

A's, because that meant he had studied too much.

Jack was not so lucky. There was no old family money. One grandfather was a butcher, the other a barber. Although his father made a comfortable living, supplemented by his mother's part-time job, the Graystones' **prosperity (#9)** paled in comparison to the Culvers'.

One of the few similarities the two shared was they were both a year behind in school. Jack started school late due to living out of the country for a year when he was younger. Ollie was a year behind because, as he had said many times, he was "unfairly held back." Ollie, however, would never explain why.

The sound of Ollie's voice made Jack open his eyes. You could hear him halfway across the parking lot. As he approached, the differences between the two became more apparent. Both were of the same approximate height and weight, but their overall appearances were at both ends of the spectrum. This was especially noticeable in the way they each wore the school uniform—a white shirt, gray pants, blue blazer, and maroon school tie. Jack's starched white shirt remained tucked into his pants, his tie was not loosened, and his short hair was perfectly combed. Ollie, on the other hand, had the right front side of his wrinkled shirt untucked, his tie unloosened and thrown over his left shoulder, and his shaggy hair was in desperate need of a brush.

"'Sup?" Ollie asked.

"Not much. Just trying to recover from Mr. North's Algebra exam. Man, was it hard."

"Well, you don't have to see that old fart or another math problem for the next three months."

Ollie's **irreverence (#10)** toward Mr. North made Jack chuckle. "Yeah, I guess you're right. Unless I have to go to summer school."

"Come on. If I can pass Algebra, I don't think you'll have any problems."

Jack laughed. "Let's go to McDonald's. I'm starving."

"Okay, but we have to wait for Lip."

"Why do we have to wait for him?"

"I told him I'd give him a ride home."

Jack sighed. "Why'd you do that?"

Ollie looked at the ground. "He asked and I couldn't say no."

Ollie had a few **idiosyncratic (#11)** habits. But the inability to say "no" was the one that frustrated Jack the most. "You really need to learn how to say no to people."

"Well, he's my friend."

"Well, you really need to learn how to say no to your friends."

Ollie paused. "*No*, I will not learn to say no to my friends. See, I just said no to a friend."

Jack's forehead wrinkled while he pondered Ollie's **vacuous (#12)** comment. "You're an idiot."

Ollie countered with an exaggerated smile.

Lip, whose actual name was Phillip Simpson, was in the same grade as Ollie. He got the nickname, Lip, two years ago on his first day of school. When his homeroom teacher asked what name she should call him, he said "Phillip." Without thinking, the teacher commented that she overheard his mother call him "Lip." His reply was, "Only my mother calls me Lip. I want everyone else to call me Phillip." Try telling that to a bunch of teenagers. From that point on, everyone called him Lip.

Jack, however, would call him "Mr. Negative" behind his back. The reason? Lip viewed everything negatively. If someone said, "That's a nice car," Lip would say, "It probably gets bad gas mileage." Or if they said, "Let's go to the beach tomorrow; it's supposed to be a nice day." Lip would respond with something like, "I bet it's going to rain." No matter what you said, he had a negative response.

"You need to stop calling him Mr. Negative, Jack. One of these days you're going to say it in front of him, and he's going to throat-punch you."

"Ollie, you ever heard the saying, positive people see the glass as half full, negative people see the glass as half empty? Well, Lip sees the glass as half empty and containing poison."

"I'm just saying. If he hears you, he'll throat-punch you."

Lip, a tall, good-looking, muscular kid, was one of the few students at Worthington Prep who was on an academic scholarship. Not only was he brilliant, but he was also an excellent athlete. He was the **embodiment (#13)** of a student-athlete and had everything going for him, except for one thing. He was shy and lacked self-confidence. He was especially **diffident (#14)** when he had to talk to girls.

Jack glanced at his iPhone. "Where is he? School's been out for a while. He should've been here by now."

"He said he had to talk to Mr. Monroe."

Jack shook his head. "Great. Who knows how long that'll take? McDonald's will be packed by the time we get there."

McDonald's was the only fast-food restaurant in the coastal New England town of Worthington. The town council had fought hard to keep them out. They said these types of restaurants detracted from the town's 'quaint New England charm.' Besides the Worthington Diner, McDonald's was the only place teenagers could afford. The other restaurants were tourist traps with big prices for small portions.

Another ten minutes passed before Lip jogged up to the Explorer. "Sorry, guys." Lip paused to catch his breath. "That took longer than I thought."

"We're going to McDonald's. Wanna go, or do you want me to drop you off first?"

"I'll go, but I need to ride with Jack. I have to talk to him about next year's football team."

The three jumped in the cars and headed out the back entrance. The Ford Explorer led the way, followed by Ollie's new BMW 640i. This was Ollie's second 640i. He had totaled the first one when he hit a telephone pole on Oceanside Drive. Ollie never told anyone exactly how he wrapped the car around the pole. His only explanation was, "I had to swerve to miss a dog."

Jack wasn't thrilled to have Lip as his passenger. It wasn't that he disliked him. He just wasn't in the mood to listen to Lip's complaining. The ride was silent at first. Finally, Jack asked, "What did you want to talk to me about?"

"Nothing. I didn't want to ride with Ollie. His driving scares the crap out of me."

Jack nodded in agreement.

By the time the three arrived at McDonald's, Ollie had already changed his clothes. He was out of his school uniform and into his typical attire—a tie-dyed T-shirt, khaki shorts he had made by cutting off the legs from a perfectly good pair of pants, and leather sandals he referred to as his Air Jerusalems.

"Ollie, how'd you change your clothes so fast?" Jack asked as they walked to the restaurant.

"Magic, my friends. A simple wave of my magic wand, and poof, my clothes were changed."

Ever since Ollie was a child, magic had fascinated him. He constantly studied magicians and their tricks and **aspired (#15)** to be world-famous. Ollie even had a routine. He called himself *Oliver the Magnificent*. If Ollie studied a fraction of the time he spent practicing magic, he would have straight A's.

"Ollie, did you change your clothes while driving?" asked Lip. "No wonder why you ran your first car into a telephone pole."

Ollie grinned. "Lip, I have another magic trick for you." Ollie placed his balled fist in front of his mouth and blew into it several times. Each time he blew, he raised his middle finger.

Jack shook his head. "You're an idiot."

Again, Ollie countered with an exaggerated smile.

The three brought their trays to the back of the restaurant. For the next two hours, they sat at the table laughing and discussing their plans for the summer.

"So, Ollie, do think you passed this year? asked Jack. "Or, are you going to be 'unfairly held back' again?"

"Unfortunately, I studied too much. Mr. Taylor's history exam was so easy I stopped seventy-five questions in. I left the last twenty-five blank so that I wouldn't ruin my C average."

Lip rolled his eyes. "You're full of crap."

Jack nudged Lip under the table and then gave Ollie a serious look. "Hey, you've never told us what grade you were in when you were unfairly held back. Was it kindergarten? A lot of kids' parents hold them back if they don't think they're ready to start school. I actually went to kindergarten twice. Once in Russia, then again in the United States."

"It really doesn't matter," Ollie said in an attempt to change the subject. "Why don't we go to the movies tonight?"

"Seriously, Ollie, what grade was it?" asked Lip.

After a pause, Ollie reluctantly said, "Second grade."

"Second grade," Jack blurted out. "How do you fail second grade? What? Were you still eating paste?"

Lip could barely contain his laughter. "Or were you still peeing your pants?"

Obviously **miffed (#16)** by the conversation, Ollie said in a raised voice, "I was too smart. I got bored in class and didn't pay attention. So, I got bad grades. Also, my teacher told me that she liked me so much, she wanted me in her class for another year."

Jack shook his head. "Let me get this straight. You were too smart. So, instead of moving you ahead a grade, they held you back. Wow. That *does* seem unfair." Jack rolled his eyes.

"Well, are we going to the movies tonight or what?" Ollie asked through clenched teeth.

"I'll go," said Jack.

"Me, too," said Lip.

Jack checked the movie theater app on his iPhone. "It says the movie starts at ten. So, let's meet there around nine thirty. I heard they got a new racing game in the arcade. That should give me enough time to whup Ollie's ass in a few races."

Ollie laughed. "In your dreams."

"Does that work for you guys?"

Both Lip and Ollie **concurred (#17)**.

Jack looked at his phone again. "Hey, I have to go, guys. My parents are having some people over for dinner, and my mom wants me home early to clean my room."

Ollie looked at his watch. "What time are they coming over?"

"Six thirty, I think."

Ollie laughed. "Jack, there's no way you can clean that pig sty by then."

***

Jack entered his house through the back door to find his mother putting the final touches on the night's meal. He sniffed the air when he walked into the kitchen. "What's for dinner?"

Knowing what she was going to say, Jack mouthed the words as she gave her usual reply. "Escargot, pheasant under glass, and crepe suzettes for dessert."

"And what does that translate to today?"

"Chicken Marsala, mashed potatoes, mixed vegetable, and a salad." His mother smiled. "I also made two pies. Mr. Hendrix at the bakery was nice enough to give me two boxes to store them."

Jack countered his mother's **facetious (#18)** comment with, "Oh, I can't wait for dessert. You bake the best pies."

"Honey, how'd your exams go today?"

"The Algebra exam was hard. Mr. North said to have Dad give him a call. He knows several military schools he can recommend."

His mom chuckled. "I don't think you'll have to worry about that. Listen, the Andersons will be here around six thirty. Make sure your room's clean."

"I will."

"I'm serious this time, Jack. I have been asking you for several weeks, and you haven't done it. So, stop **procrastinating (#19)**. Go up there and get to work." His mother gave him a stern look. "And don't just throw your dirty clothes under the bed or in your closet."

"Mother, you know I'd never do that," Jack said **sarcastically (#20)**.

His mother rolled her eyes and shook her head. "Grab your dry cleaning from the back porch before you go upstairs."

Jack grabbed a bottle of water from the refrigerator, got his clothes, and then headed to his room.

"I'll be up shortly to check on you!" his mom yelled from the kitchen.

"Can't wait," Jack mumbled as he shut his bedroom door. On the way to his closet, he stepped over a laundry basket full of clothes. He could not remember if they were clean or dirty. After a month of being **negligent (#21)** in his responsibilities, he was left with a room that looked like a bomb had exploded inside. *Where do I begin?* He looked around the room, and then he stretched, yawned, and fell face-first onto his bed.

By six thirty, Jack was sitting with his father in the living room while his mother finished some last-minute details before the dinner party. His dad glanced up from his magazine. "What did you do today?"

"Took two exams. Oh, by the way, you might want to start looking for military schools. I went to lunch with Lip and Ollie. Talked to Courtney on the phone for a while. Stuff like that."

The sun reflecting off a silver Porsche sports car pulling into the driveway caught Jack's attention, and he jumped to his feet. "They're here, Dad." Jack stood by the living room window and watched their guests get out of their car. "Wow, you should see this guy's car. You should buy one."

Mr. Graystone stood and looked out the window with his son. "Love to. Let's see. I could use your college fund to pay for it. You don't really want to go to college, do you?"

Jack patted his father on the back. "Maybe you should keep driving your Buick." His father chuckled. "Dad, what does this guy do?"

"He owns a bunch of car dealerships. One's a Porsche dealership."

"Cool."

"Be nice to him. He might have a summer job for you."

"How'd you meet him?"

"My law firm closed the sale of his house."

"Where's his house?"

"Oceanside Drive."

"Really? What'd that cost?"

"Twelve million."

"Must be nice," Jack mumbled to himself.

"Liz, the Andersons are here," Mr. Graystone yelled on his way to the front door.

The Anderson family consisted of Robert, Christina, and their only child, fourteen-year-old Ian. They had only lived in town for a few weeks, having moved from an apartment on Manhattan's Upper East Side. They wanted to escape the **cosmopolitan (#22)** lifestyle of New York City and thought Worthington would be a great place to raise their son.

"Hello, Robert," Mr. Graystone said, extending his hand.

"Thomas, this is my wife, Christina, and my son, Ian."

"It's nice to finally meet you. This is Elizabeth and my son, Jack."

Everyone shook hands and talked in the foyer for a moment before Mr. Graystone said, "Jack, why don't you take Ian up to your room?

Show him your yearbook and tell him about the school. You two will be schoolmates next year."

"Okay, follow me." Jack waved Ian over to the staircase, and the two disappeared upstairs.

"Why don't you grab the desk chair," Jack said when they entered the room. "Just step over all that stuff." Jack grabbed the school pants that he had draped over the back of the chair and tossed them on the floor. He then reached for the yearbook on the shelf above his desk. It was under a stack of car magazines, several of which fell to the ground as he placed it in front of Ian.

"Here," Jack opened the yearbook, "look at this." Jack flipped through the pages and pointed out the different buildings on the campus. He told Ian which teachers he liked and disliked and explained which sports and activities were the most fun.

Ian said little at first, answering questions with just "yes" or "no." His eyes never left the pages of the yearbook. Jack made every attempt to be a **convivial (#23)** host, but he could tell by the **brevity (#24)** of Ian's answers, he was shy. It wasn't until Jack asked, "Do you play video games?" that he came out of his shell.

He looked up at Jack with wide-open eyes. "Yeah. *Assassin's Creed's* my favorite. What about you?"

"*Forza Motorsport*, but I play a lot of *Call of Duty* with my best friend, Ollie."

"I love that game. Here's my online name." Ian grabbed a pen and a scrap piece of paper and wrote Reilly1234. "Let me know when you're playing. I'm online all the time."

For the next several minutes, the one-sided conversation was entirely about video games. Ian wouldn't shut up. "I'm getting really good at *Assassin's Creed*. I almost beat the guy that runs the video game store over on Main Street. Uh, what's it called?"

"GameSpot. Ollie says he's the best player around. I guess if your job is to sell video games, you should know how to play them."

"Boys," Mr. Graystone yelled up the stairwell. "Seven o'clock. Time for dinner."

"It's about time," Jack said. "I'm starving."

"Me too," Ian replied before they bolted out of the bedroom. The sound of their footsteps filled the house as they ran down the stairs.

When the boys entered the dining room, Mr. Graystone directed everyone to their seats. Jack and Ian were on one side of the table, and Mr. and Mrs. Anderson were on the other. Jack's parents were at either end. Mr. Graystone gave a quick blessing and then conversations began.

"Jack, I understand you're looking for a summer job," Mr. Anderson said with genuine interest.

"Yeah. They're hard to find around here. Most of the local college students get them before the high school kids finish school."

"Well, I talked to Burt Chambers, the general manager of my Porsche dealership. He has an opening to clean cars and do odd jobs around the dealership. It's part-time. You would get about thirty hours a week. You interested?"

"Yeah, that'd be great."

"I'll talk to him again on Monday. He'll want to interview you. But I have to warn you; he's not very friendly. So, be prepared."

Not knowing what to think or say, Jack replied, "Okay, I will. But, Mr. Anderson, if he's not very friendly, why does he work for you?"

Mr. Anderson shook his head. "Well, he's really good at what he does. So, I put up with him."

The conversations continued for almost two hours. Since Jack had plans to meet his friends, he was eager to leave. Since Ian wanted to walk his dog, he was eager to get home. So, after what turned out to be a big production, the adults agreed to let Jack drive Ian home while they continued to talk.

Jack and Ian jumped up from the table. "See you later, Mom and Dad. Nice meeting you, Mr. and Mrs. Anderson." The two scurried out of the room. "Wait here," Jack said when they entered the foyer. "I have to go get my keys. I'll be right down." Jack dialed Ollie's number on the way to his bedroom. The call went to voicemail, so he left a message saying he was on his way.

Jack returned moments later with his keys and met Ian at the bottom of the staircase. "You ready to go?" Ian replied with a nod. After a quick wave to their parents, the two boys bolted out of the house. The screen door closed with a loud crash behind them.

Ten minutes later, they arrived at Ian's house. Jack stared at the wrought iron gate and ivy-covered stone wall that protected the property. *Wow, this is impressive.* He glanced toward Ian. "How'd we get in?"

"Pull up to that keypad." Ian pointed toward the left side of the driveway. "Punch in two, nine, eight, six, seven, open." Jack punched in the numbers, and the gate's electric motors began to hum. "Head over there."

Jack eased along the crushed stone driveway toward the house. The stones crackled beneath the Explorer's tires. "Wow. What a big house," he said when he caught his first glimpse of the two-story limestone mansion.

"Yeah, it's big. It's a lot bigger than our apartment in Manhattan. Want to see my room?"

Jack glanced at his iPhone. *Nine o'clock. I really need to go. Ah, screw it.* "Yeah. I have to make it quick though."

The Explorer's doors closed with a thunk. Ian bolted toward the house. Jack followed, leaping up the front steps to a massive double door. After reaching into his pocket, Ian removed a keychain containing three identical keys. They jingled as he inserted each one into the lock. "I never know which one it is," he said with a glance toward Jack. Ian shook his head. "It's always the last one."

Ian ran inside to silence the alarm. Before he disappeared into the darkness, he tossed his keys and phone onto a table in the foyer. The phone landed on the table, but the keys slid across, falling to the floor with a clank. Jack followed, taking two steps inside. The light spilling in through the open front door cast a dim glow over the two-story foyer. It was bright enough, though, that Jack could make out white marble floors and a double staircase. Ian flipped several light switches on his way back into the room. Jack looked around. *This house looks like a museum.* Before he could say anything, he heard what sounded like someone running in the hallway upstairs.

"Reilly!" Ian yelled to a dog barreling toward them at full speed. The medium-sized tan dog's paws hit every other step on the way down. In a matter of seconds, he was jumping on Ian with his tail wagging so quickly his entire body shook.

"Jack, this is Reilly."

"What kind of dog is he?"

"A soft-coated wheaten terrier."

Jack ran his hand over Reilly's coat. "Yeah, he sure is soft."

Ian grabbed his keys from the floor before the two boys, followed by the dog, headed to his bedroom. Their footsteps resonated through the silent house as they hurried up the staircase, past the landing, down a wide hallway, and then through a set of double doors. They entered a room furnished with a couch, a couple of chairs, a table, many bookshelves, and a large-screen television.

"Cool room."

"My dad calls it my 'boy cave.'"

Jack walked over to a bookshelf and inspected Ian's video game collection. "You need to meet my friend Ollie. You two like the same games."

"That'd be great. My bedroom's through here. Follow me."

They walked through another door into a large bedroom that looked like something from a magazine. The walls were dark blue and covered with pictures depicting English hunting scenes or men playing polo. Centered in the room was a perfectly made bed—its linens matched the drapes. Above its headboard were two polo mallets hung in an X. There was nothing out of place.

Jack glanced around and thought, *let me live in this room for a few days. It won't look like this for very long.* "Where do those doors lead?"

"I'll show you. This one goes into my bathroom." Jack followed Ian into a massive bathroom. "And this door leads to my closet." He then followed Ian into a large closet. It was so large, Ian's clothes filled only a small portion. When Jack's eyes scanned the room, he noticed something on the sleeves of Ian's shirts. They were monogrammed with a large *A*, flanked by a small *I* and *C*.

"Ian, are all your shirts monogrammed?"

"Most of them. My mom had them done before I went to boarding school last year. This way I knew which ones were mine."

"What does the *C* stand for?"

Ian frowned and shook his head. "Uh, Claybourne."

"Claybourne? Is that a family name?"

"No, it's kind of embarrassing. It's the name of my dad's first dog."

Jack laughed as the two walked back into the bedroom. "My middle name is Furthur."

"Furthur?"

Jack glanced at Ian and also frowned. "My mother's maiden name."

Jack looked at his phone and realized he was running late. "Ian, it was nice meeting you. I'll give you a call tomorrow. Maybe we can go hit some tennis balls."

"Cool. I'll look for my racquet tonight. I'm sure it's around here somewhere."

Ian and Reilly followed Jack out of the house. Ian started to lock the front door behind him but stopped. He glanced at Jack. "Oh, crap. I forgot something. I'll see you tomorrow. Okay?" He then looked at Reilly and shook his finger at him. "You stay here." Ian gave Jack a quick wave before he disappeared into the house.

Jack jumped into the Explorer, started the engine, and then reached for his phone. He called Ollie to tell him his tank was on empty and he had to stop to get gas. The conversation lasted only a minute or two before Jack put the Explorer into gear and set off for the movies. In his rearview mirror, he could see Ian leaving for Reilly's walk.

CHAPTER TWO

Nighttime in the small town of Worthington was typically quiet. This chilly June night was no exception. With a window slightly opened, the only sounds were that of an occasional truck driving down Main Street a few blocks away, and two of the neighbor's cats having their nightly quarrel.

Jack arrived home before his midnight curfew having only a few minutes to spare. After saying goodnight to his parents, he went straight to bed. With everyone peacefully sleeping, all was content in the Graystone household.

A single ring from the doorbell and several loud knocks caused Jack to jump out of bed. He glanced at his phone. *Who's knocking on the door at five in the morning?* He opened his bedroom door and met his father in the hallway.

"Stay in your room," Mr. Graystone said before he disappeared down the dark staircase.

Jack closed his door and retreated to his bed where he sat and stared at the floor. This lasted only a few seconds. He then began to pace—his heart pounding in his chest. *I wonder who this could be? I hope nothing's happened to grandma.* The views from his bedroom windows were of no help. One overlooked the backyard, and the other overlooked the carport. With no clue as to the stranger's identity, his mind raced while he waited for his father to return.

Mr. Graystone turned on the porch light and looked through the peephole. Through the fish-eyed lens, he saw two men. They stood like statues, their hands at their sides and no expressions on their faces. The man closest to the door was a uniformed police officer. The other, dressed in plain clothes, had a badge and holstered gun strapped to his belt. Mr. Graystone unlocked the deadbolt and slowly opened the door. Its creak echoed through the silent house.

"Are you Thomas Graystone?" the police officer asked.

"Yes, I am. What's the problem?"

"Is your son Jack at home?" asked the detective.

"Yes, he is. What's this about, Detective…" Mr. Graystone glanced at the man's badge, "Faulkner?"

"Officer Cummings and I would like to ask him a few questions. May we enter the residence?"

"After you tell me what this is about."

"Ian Anderson is missing. According to his parents, when they arrived home tonight, he wasn't there. His dog was sitting at the front gate with his leash still attached, but Ian was nowhere to be found. Since Jack was the last known person to see Ian, Chief McKinney wanted us to ask him some questions."

After a few seconds, Mr. Graystone said, "Come in." When the men entered the foyer, he stopped them. "Wait here. I'll go wake him."

Mr. Graystone hurried upstairs to Jack's room and opened his door. "Jack, when was the last time you saw Ian Anderson?"

"When I dropped him off. Why?"

"Did he say where he was going?"

"Yeah, to walk his dog."

"Anywhere else?"

"No. Why are you asking? What's going on?"

"There are two policemen downstairs who want to ask you some questions. Apparently, Ian is missing. And you're sure you don't know where he is?"

"Yeah, I'm sure."

Mr. Graystone glanced around Jack's bedroom. "Your mother **explicitly (#25)** told you to clean this place."

"I forgot."

Mr. Graystone closed his eyes and shook his head before he walked to the edge of the stairs and motioned for the men.

When they entered the room, the detective said, "Jack, I'm Detective Faulkner. This is Officer Cummings. We're looking for Ian Anderson.

Do you have any idea where he is?"

"No. I just dropped him off at his house. Then I went to the movies. He and Reilly were going for a walk when I left."

"So, there's nothing you need to tell us?"

Jack shook his head. "No."

The detective glanced at Mr. Graystone. "You don't mind if we take a look at the clothes he wore last night, do you?"

Before his dad could answer, Jack pointed to the ground. "They're right here on the floor." He started to pick them up, but the detective stopped him.

"I'll get those." The detective bent over and examined each piece of clothing.

Jack's eyes darted toward his father. "Dad, I'm not getting arrested, am I?" Jack's mind raced with the thoughts of the detective handcuffing him and throwing him into the back seat of a police car.

Mr. Graystone put his hand on his son's shoulder. "No, Jack. The policemen are just doing their job. Don't worry. We'll figure all this out."

After the detective finished examining the clothes, he opened a small black notepad, flipped through a few pages, and then studied his notes. When he finished, he looked at Mr. Graystone. "The chief of police is at the Anderson house. Sir, would you mind taking your son over there to talk to him. He'll need everyone's help to find this boy."

"Yes, we can do that."

"Also, can we look in Jack's truck?"

Mr. Graystone glanced at his son before he said, "That'll be fine."

As the police officers exited the room, Mr. Graystone tapped Jack on the shoulder with the back of his hand. "This is why you should keep your room clean. Get dressed. I'll meet you downstairs."

Jack and his father followed the police car to the Anderson residence. The police officer did not turn on his flashing blue lights for the trip. However, he did drive above the speed limit and rolled through every stop sign. While Mr. Graystone followed, Jack explained the events of the evening. He started from the time he took Ian home and ended when he went to sleep. The trip to the house took about ten minutes. The last half was in complete silence and seemed to take an hour.

CHAPTER THREE

The gravel crackling underneath the car's tires let Jack know they had arrived at the Anderson mansion. This time, when he saw the massive house, every light was on and it appeared to be glowing. Jack slowly climbed out of the car and then stopped to stare at the house. The onset of a morning fog, which caused halos to form around the exterior lights, gave the place an eerie appearance.

Jack's legs weakened on his walk to the front door. *I really don't want to be here.* He looked around and counted eight police cars and at least that many uniformed police officers and detectives inspecting the property. *I hope the Andersons don't think I did anything to him. Or worse, the police. What if they do and they throw me in jail?*

Jack was the last to enter the house. When he poked his head inside, he saw Callam McKinney, the chief of police. Jack knew him well. He had been dating his daughter for over a year. Chief McKinney, a man of **irreproachable (#26)** character, was standing next to Mr. Anderson. Mrs. Anderson sat next to them on a couch, hunched over, quietly crying.

"Hey, guys, glad you're here." Chief McKinney walked over to the Graystone men and shook their hands. The chief's calm tone relaxed Jack. Mr. Anderson followed and also shook their hands. Mrs. Anderson, who remained on the couch, looked up and acknowledged their presence with a half-hearted smile.

"Thomas, can I talk to you outside for a minute?" asked Chief McKinney.

"Sure."

The chief put his hand on Mr. Graystone's shoulder as they

disappeared through the doorway. "Thomas, my gut tells me that Jack had nothing to do with Ian's disappearance. But, if this boy doesn't show up soon, this is going to be a high-profile case. I can't afford to make any mistakes. I need to ask Jack questions regarding the events of the past evening. Do you have a problem with that?"

Thomas Graystone, the attorney, not Thomas Graystone, the father replied, "No, not at this time. But I reserve the right to stop this interview."

The chief nodded. "Okay, I understand. Let me ask you one more thing. The Andersons will both be under suspicion until their stories check out. I need to know if they are dressed the same as they were at your house. Are they wearing the same clothes?"

Mr. Graystone walked into the foyer and glanced at the couple. "Yes, they appear to be."

While the two men went outside, Jack stood at the entrance to the living room, hands in his pockets, looking at the ground. The cool night air seeping through the open front door sent a shiver up his spine.

"Would you like a seat?" Mr. Anderson asked, pointing to a chair. His voice sounded different. It was softer and slower than the previous evening.

Jack nodded and then sat down in a large wingback chair across from the couple. He didn't know what to say. He stared at an oriental rug and tried not to make eye contact. The house was quiet. The faint voices of two men several rooms away and the ticking of a grandfather clock were the only sounds he heard. Mrs. Anderson never looked up from her lap. She continued to cry, occasionally wiping tears from her eyes. *What should I say?* Jack slowly raised his head and looked at Mr. Anderson. After an awkward moment of silence, Mr. Anderson asked only one question. "Jack, do you have any idea where my son is?"

Jack shook his head. "No. I have no idea. I dropped him off around nine, then went to the movies." The chief and Mr. Graystone reentered the living room just as Jack finished his sentence.

"As you are aware, Ian is missing," explained the chief. "We need to begin gathering leads. We're hoping he's just upset over the move to Worthington and has temporarily run away. Nevertheless, we can't take any chances." The chief removed a notepad and pen from his pocket and glanced at Jack. "Let's start piecing together everything we know. I talked briefly to Mr. and Mrs. Anderson, but since you were the last person to see him, Jack, we'll start with you. Tell us what you know, starting with the first time you met Ian."

Jack sat upright in his chair. He could feel the stares from the Andersons. "Well, the Andersons came over around six thirty. After everyone met, my father suggested I take Ian upstairs to my room and show him my Worthington Prep yearbook. So, we went upstairs to look at it."

"What did you talk about?" asked the chief.

"We talked about school for a little bit. I asked him if he played sports. Then we talked about sports for a while. We both like tennis and talked about playing sometime."

"Did he seem upset or depressed?"

"No, he was quiet at first, but he didn't appear to be depressed. He did say he misses his friends from the city."

"Did he say what he's been doing for fun since he moved to Worthington?"

"Ian said he plays a lot of video games. We like the same games, so we planned to play each other online. He gave me his online name and said to give it to anybody who wanted to play with him. I have it here in my wallet." Jack stood and removed the wallet from his back pocket. "His online name is Reilly1234."

"Reilly1234?" asked the chief.

"Reilly is his dog," Mr. Anderson said. "The two are inseparable."

"Yeah, that's what he told me. He said Reilly is his best friend and he takes him everywhere he can. He wanted to bring him to our house last night, but his mother wouldn't let him. Ian told me that every night right around nine o'clock Reilly wants to go for a walk. He said you could set a watch by him. That's why I took Ian home. So he could walk Reilly."

"Did you talk about girls?"

"Not really. I told him I had a girlfriend during one of our conversations, but that was it. He didn't say whether he had one or not."

"Did you talk about anything else?"

"Not that I can remember. Around seven o'clock, my dad called upstairs and told us it was time for dinner. So, we both went down and ate."

"What did you talk about at dinner?"

"I told Mr. and Mrs. Anderson about Worthington Prep. Then Mr. Anderson said he might have a summer job for me at his Porsche dealership. That's pretty much it."

"So, after you finished dinner, you left with Ian. What time was it?"

"Let me look at my phone. I called Ollie right before we left."

While Jack looked at his cell phone, the chief asked, "Who's Ollie?"

"Ollie is one of my friends I was meeting. His full name is Oliver Hamilton Culver IV."

"Oh yes, I'm acquainted with his parents."

"I was meeting him and Phillip Simpson at the movies. Here it is. I called Ollie at 8:46 on my way up to my bedroom to get my keys. That was a minute or two before we left."

"Where did you go then?"

"I took him straight home. There was hardly any traffic, so it took only about ten minutes."

"What did you talk about in the car?"

"We discussed his dog, Reilly. He told me again that every night at nine o'clock Reilly wants to go for a walk. And every night, you can set your watch by him. We both thought it was cool that a dog could be so smart."

"What happened when you got to his house?"

"Well, he asked if I wanted to come in to meet Reilly and see his boy cave."

"What's a boy cave?"

"It's what his dad calls his TV room. It's a kid's version of a man cave."

"Okay, then what?"

"So, we both got out of the Explorer and went into the house. He showed me around. Then I left."

"Did you see anyone or did anything look out of place?"

"No, I didn't see anyone. I have never been to their house before. So, I couldn't tell if anything was out of place."

"What happened next?"

"We both walked out the front door. But when Ian went to lock it, he said he forgot something and went back inside. I got in my truck and called Ollie again to let him know I was going to be late."

"What time was that?"

Again, Jack looked at the call log on his cell phone. "I made the call at 9:14."

"Did he say what he forgot?"

"No, he didn't say. I saw him leaving the house in my rearview mirror on my way down of the driveway. But there were bushes in the way, and I didn't have a clear view of him."

"So, then exactly what time did you leave?"

"It had to be 9:15 or 9:16."

"Okay, as far as we now know, 9:16 was the last time anyone had contact with Ian," said Chief McKinney. Everyone looked at each other and nodded. "Then where'd you go?"

"I went to the movies, but I stopped to get gas on the way."

"Where'd you get your gas?"

"The Shell station on Main Street."

"When did you get to the theater?"

Jack thumbed through his wallet and pulled out his ticket stub. After he examined it, he said, "It says I bought the ticket at 9:38."

"Who'd you meet there?"

"Two friends from school. Ollie and Lip."

"I'm going to need their full names and addresses before you leave." Jack nodded in agreement. "So, what time did you leave?"

"I looked at the clock on my phone before I left. It was a few minutes before midnight. I raced home." Jack glanced at his father. "I mean I drove straight home and got there at midnight."

"Actually, it was 12:04 in the morning when he said goodnight," Mr. Graystone remarked. "I know that for a fact. I have trouble falling asleep until he gets home."

Chief McKinney looked at his notepad and recited the facts. "So, the last time anyone saw him was 9:16. And, Mr. and Mrs. Anderson, you left the Graystones' house just after eleven. You got home shortly after and entered the house at 11:18 based on the first call to Ian's cell. Did you see anyone or anything out of the ordinary?"

"No," said Mr. Anderson. "Everything looked fine and there was no one around."

"What did you do when you got home?"

"Well," Mr. Anderson closed his eyes and rubbed his forehead, "when we pulled up to the gate and found Reilly, we immediately knew something was wrong." He glanced at his wife. She had stopped crying. "Christina jumped out of the car and called for Ian, but he didn't answer. So, she grabbed Reilly and put him in the car. I tried calling Ian's cell as we drove to the house, but the call went to voicemail. When I stopped, Christina ran to the front door and went inside. I could hear her calling Ian's name as she ran upstairs. Reilly and I got in the house just as Christina came running down the stairs saying, 'He's not here. He's not here.' I tried calling him again. This time, I heard his phone ringing in the house. He apparently forgot it because I found it on the table in the foyer." Mr. Anderson shook his head. "That's not like Ian. He always has his phone."

"Jack, did he have his phone when he left the house?"

"I don't remember him picking it up when we left. But I do remember it on the table."

"Why's that?"

"Because, when we came in the house, the alarm was beeping. When Ian ran to turn it off, he tossed his keys and phone on the table. The phone landed on the table, but the keys slid across and fell to the floor. When he came back into the room, he picked up the keys and stuck them in his pocket. That I know, but I don't remember him grabbing the phone on our way out."

The chief glanced at Mr. Anderson. "Was the alarm on when you got home?"

"After Christina came downstairs, I asked her if Ian had set the alarm. She said no. Which upset me because the security cameras are only activated if the alarm is set."

"Does he usually set the alarm?" asked the chief.

"Sometimes. But not every time."

"So, then what happened?"

"I told Christina to look throughout the house while I took Reilly to the Ocean Walk. I kept calling Ian's name as I jogged along his usual route." Mr. Anderson glanced toward the ground. "But he never responded. When I got home, we decided to call the police."

The chief flipped through his notes. "That call came in at 11:52 p.m. according to the 911 operator. Mr. or Mrs. Anderson, do you have any enemies or anyone who's angry with you? Maybe a business relation or family member?"

They both looked at each other. "Nobody we can think of," they said.

"Well, I am a car dealer," remarked Mr. Anderson. "I'm sure there are many people who don't like me."

The chief nodded. "Any weird events or a stranger you encountered in the last several weeks?"

Mr. and Mrs. Anderson looked at each other. Mrs. Anderson shook her head, but Mr. Anderson spoke up.

"Well, there is something that happened last…let me think…Saturday," replied Mr. Anderson. "I didn't tell Christina, because I didn't want to upset her. I have a son from my first wife who lives in Middlebury. His name is Robert Anderson, Jr., but everyone calls him Bobby. I haven't seen him much over the past years. We kind of grew apart. Anyway, he called me last Saturday evening wanting money."

"How much and for what?"

"He said he needed $5,000 for bills. He claimed he ran up a credit card, was behind on his rent, and stuff like that. He wanted me to wire him the money." Mr. Anderson paused and shook his head. "Something didn't seem right. He was acting really weird. I asked him if he was in trouble. He claimed he wasn't, but I didn't believe him. I told him to bring me the bills, and I'd pay them directly. I was in Manhattan when he called. So, I told him to meet me on Monday morning at my office."

"Where's your office?"

"At my Porsche dealership. It's about a two-hour drive for him."

"Did he show up?"

"No. I tried calling his cell several times, but it kept saying it was no longer in service. I called his mother, but she never answered or returned my calls. So, I just gave up." Mr. Anderson held out both palms of his hands and shook his head. "I didn't know what else I could do. He knows where I am if he needs me."

"Does he have any reason to or is he capable of harming Ian?"

"No, I don't think he's capable, and I don't know why he would."

"Could he be capable of kidnapping him? He did say he needed money."

"I honestly don't believe he's that clever. Now, who he's hanging out with is another story. Maybe he owes someone money, and they did it."

"Well, we'll investigate him just to be safe. I'll talk to the Middlebury Police Department today. Okay then, anyone or anything else suspicious?"

"Ian did mention the guy at the video game store a couple of times," Mrs. Anderson said in a soft voice.

Before the chief could ask his next question, Jack interrupted. "Yeah, I forgot about that. He mentioned him to me, too."

The chief looked at Mrs. Anderson. "Which video game store?"

"I can't remember the name. I think it's…"

"GameSpot," Jack said.

"What did he say about this guy?"

Mrs. Anderson cleared her throat. "Ian rides his bike there to get different games. He said the guy who worked there was nice. Sometimes, they'd play video games together online. I thought it was strange that a guy in his early twenties was still playing video games."

"Mrs. Anderson, I have grown men on my force who still play them."

"I thought it was safe since they weren't in the same room."

"Well, they can still talk to each other over the internet. We'll research his call log to determine if the two have called each other. We'll also send a unit over to this guy's house right away. Jack, do you know this guy's name?"

"No, but my friend Ollie does. He's always buying video games there. Want me to call him?"

"Yes. If he doesn't answer, I'll send a unit over to his house to wake him up."

Jack could feel everyone's eyes on him as he made the call. After five rings, Ollie answered. "Ollie, it's Jack…I know it's almost six in the morning…I don't care who you were dreaming about. Listen to me, this is important. I'm here with the entire Worthington Police Department, and I need to ask you something…Ollie, stop kidding around. This is serious. We need to know the full name of the guy who manages the GameSpot…Don't worry why. I'll tell you later…Brian what? Concentrate. It's important…" Jack looked at the chief. "Brian Carter. Do you know where he lives?…" Jack nodded. "In a garage apartment somewhere on Oak Street, he thinks. What type of car does he drive?… A white Toyota Corolla with ugly-ass rims. Anything else?… He's a youth pastor at a church. Thanks, Ollie. I have to go. I can't talk now. I'll call you later. Bye."

"Good job, Jack," said the chief. "Is there anything else anyone can think of?" Everyone shook their heads. "Okay. My men have a lot of work ahead of them. Let me get out there and start delegating. Jack and Thomas, you can go. Just let me know immediately if you think of anything, no matter how **inconsequential (#27)** you might think it may be. The same goes for you, Mr. and Mrs. Anderson. I want you two to stay by your phones in case he calls. I'll be just outside, so let me know immediately."

An uncomfortable silence fell over the room. Jack leaned forward. He rested his elbows on his knees with his hands clasped between them. The ticking of the grandfather clock seemed to be getting louder. Mrs. Anderson went back to staring at her lap, crying softly. Mr. Anderson sat restlessly on the couch, his right knee bouncing up and down. Jack did not know what to say, and judging by the look on his father's face, neither did he. Jack gave his father a wide-eyed glance, hoping he would say something. But his dad just stared at the ground, biting the end of his reading glasses.

Mr. Anderson eventually mumbled something, then jumped to his feet and began to pace. His breathing was shallow, and he kept rubbing his forehead with his right hand. "Where is he?" or "Where can he be?" he said, or something along those lines.

Mr. Graystone countered by saying things like, "I'm sure he'll be home soon," and, "There's got to be a perfectly good explanation for why he's not home yet." These words, however, did nothing to **foster (#28)** any comfort. Mr. Anderson continued to pace, stopping only to place his forehead against a living room window to look outside. Jack remained seated, not knowing what else to do.

After twenty minutes of strained conversation, the Graystone men could do no more. They said goodbye, and just as Jack walked through the front door, he turned and gave the Andersons one last look. Mr. Anderson was back on the couch, sitting next to his wife, holding her in his arms. Jack could see tears flowing from their eyes.

CHAPTER FOUR

While the sun was rising, the search continued. The sounds of the day grew louder with every passing minute. Birds began to chirp, and traffic along Oceanside Drive began to roar. Several police officers combed the Anderson residence and grounds. Slowly, silently, they examined each crack and crevice for any clue. Roscoe, the police dog followed. He wedged his nose into every plant on the property. Occasionally, he sat to indicate he had found something. Hours passed. Nothing and no one turned up.

By sunrise, several news trucks had formed a line along Oceanside Drive. They parked in front of the Andersons' ivy-covered wall and hoisted their large antennas. One by one, the local reporters stood at the iron gates and spouted their robotic messages for the morning news. Their monotone voices told the story of a missing boy.

The Andersons walked around like zombies. They refused to eat or sleep despite the pleas of close friends who came from Manhattan that morning. Mr. Anderson insisted on helping in the search. But, as Chief McKinney explained, he would not be any help in his condition. His time was better spent at home trying to remember any possible clues.

The preliminary investigation of Bobby Anderson had not provided any leads. The Middlebury Police Department went to question him at his last known address. It was his mother Julia's house, but nobody was home. Following a lead from Mr. Anderson, they went to the surf shop where Bobby worked. Nobody had seen him all week. The store manager said Julia called on Monday to inform them that Bobby would not be able to work for a while. She gave no reason why.

By noon an all-out search was underway for Julia Anderson and her son. Three pairs of Middlebury detectives knocked on their neighbor's doors and asked a series of questions.

"When was the last time you saw her or her son?"

"Have you noticed anything unusual lately?"

"Is there anything you can remember about the past few days that stand out?"

They finished by showing a picture of Ian, but the investigation turned up no clues. The only information they gained was where Julia worked. She owned a catering business that she ran from a warehouse in an industrial park. At three o'clock that afternoon, a fleet of police cars converged on the building.

With all exits covered, four detectives entered through the front door. The **subtle (#29)** smell of garlic lingered in the air. They found Julia sitting behind a desk. She was chewing the end of a pen while sorting through a stack of bills. Her eyes widened when two of the detectives walked into her office. The other two detectives remained in the reception area, just in case.

Julia was an **acrimonious (#30)** woman. When she heard the name of her ex-husband, she threatened to call her lawyer. But after several minutes of diplomacy by one detective, her **impudent (#31)** attitude changed. She calmed down and answered his questions. It did not take long to solve the mystery of the missing Bobby Anderson. He was in a drug rehabilitation facility near Boston. On the previous Monday, Julia had him committed. She said she saw no other choices. As far as she knew, he was still there. A call to the facility confirmed this. For verification, however, two detectives went to question the young man.

The investigation of Brian Carter was a different story. Earlier that morning, Chief McKinney reviewed Ian's call log. What he found was disturbing. There were several calls between Ian and Brian. One particular call, on the previous Wednesday, occurred at 1:04 a.m.

"Something's not right here," said Detective Faulkner. "Why is a twenty-three-year-old man talking to a fourteen-year-old boy at that hour of the morning?"

The chief nodded. "I agree. Grab a few men and go over to Oak Street. There can't be many garage apartments on that street. Look for his car. It's a white Toyota Corolla with ugly-ass rims."

Detective Faulkner's forehead wrinkled. "What do 'ugly-ass rims' look like?"

"I don't know. I guess you'll see when you find it."

Just before seven o'clock in the morning, three detectives and one police officer, each in a separate vehicle, headed to Oak Street. Oak Street was in the heart of Worthington. It was a short, one-way road having only a couple dozen houses. All the houses were over a century old and crammed onto small lots. Most did not have driveways, so the residents parked on both sides of the street. This left little room for passing cars to maneuver.

Detective Faulkner led the way, driving slowly down the crowded street. He made one pass and saw only two garage apartments. Detectives Frantz and Riches each picked an apartment and pulled into its driveway to investigate.

"I think I found it," Detective Frantz reported over his police radio. "I'm looking at a white Corolla with gold rims. And they are ugly."

"Wait until I get there," replied Detective Faulkner.

The four men converged on the house. With room for only two cars in the driveway, two cars remained in the road, blocking traffic. At this time of the morning, it was not much of a problem.

The garage apartment was just that, an apartment over a garage. It had two single garage stalls separated by a door, which opened onto a set of stairs that led to the apartment. It was behind a two-story house and covered most of the backyard. What little space remained was a gravel parking area.

The police officer knocked several times on the door with the end of his flashlight. The four men waited for a minute before knocking several more times. They stood silently, but they never heard a sound. Another minute or two passed before the back door of the house opened, and a gray-haired man wearing a bathrobe and slippers walked outside. "Can I help you guys?"

"We're looking for Brian Carter. Is this his apartment?"

"Yeah, but he's not here."

"Do you know where he is?" asked Detective Faulkner.

"At a church youth weekend retreat."

"Are you the landlord?"

The man nodded. "Yes, I am."

"Do you know if he was home last night?"

"I didn't see him. He should've been at the retreat."

Detective Faulkner closed his eyes and rubbed his forehead. "The search warrant from Judge Skinner should be here soon. When we get it, we're going in. I want to make sure Ian's not hiding in there. Or worse?" He paused. "Sir, do you have a key?"

The man nodded. "Let me go inside to get it." He then shuffled across the gravel driveway and disappeared through the door. Moments later he returned with a keychain jingling in his hands.

"We can't go in just yet." Detective Faulkner dialed his phone. "Let me see where the warrant is." He stared at the ground while he waited for someone to answer. "Turner, do you have it?" The detective nodded at the landlord. "Good. Bring it straight here. We're behind the house." The detective placed his phone in his pocket." Sir, he'll be here in a minute. You can unlock the door now." The landlord searched through the keys and opened the door on the first attempt. "You three go inside and look for the boy. If you don't find him, look for any signs that he was in there. I'll stay outside and ask this gentleman a few questions."

The two detectives and the police officer climbed the stairs in a single file line. When Detective Frantz entered the dark apartment, he sniffed the air. He then turned toward the others with a look of disgust. "This place smells like a high school locker room." He moved his hand along the wall until he felt a light switch. After he turned it on, all three men stopped and stood silently for a moment. "Damn, this place is a mess," Frantz said, glancing around the tiny apartment. "Ian Anderson, this is Detective Frantz with the Worthington Police Department. Are you in this apartment? You're not in trouble. We just need to speak to you." They all waited for a response, but one never came. "Start looking around. Make sure he's not hiding anywhere. And keep an eye out for anything that looks suspicious."

The center staircase separated the apartment into two rooms. The room on the right was a bedroom with a bathroom. The room on the left was a living area with a small kitchenette. Detective Frantz walked into the living area and shook his head. "Does this guy know how to clean?" he said to the police officer who followed. "Look, there must be a dozen empty pizza boxes over there." The detective walked over to the overflowing trash can. He closed his eyes and fanned his nose. "When's the last time this guy took out the garbage?"

"Look in the sink," barked the police officer. "These dishes haven't been washed in weeks. Some even have mold growing on them."

Detective Frantz's eyes scanned the room. "There must be a dozen unfinished sodas in here."

The furnishings in Brian Carter's apartment were **spartan (#32)**. The living area contained only a well-worn couch, a coffee table stained with water rings, and a small dinette set with one broken leg patched up with a scrap piece of wood. Mounted to the wall, however, was a high-tech, flat-screen television connected to every video game system currently available. The detective reached into his pocket for a pair of rubber gloves. He looked around the room while he inserted his hands. "I don't know where to begin."

"I'll start in this corner," said the police officer.

"I'll start over here," replied Detective Frantz.

Both men rummaged through the piles of stuff scattered around the room. But, after several minutes of searching, they found nothing suspicious.

Detective Frantz walked into the bedroom. "Find anything?"

"No, just a lot of dirty clothes scattered on the floor. Nothing under the bed."

While the men were inside the apartment, Detective Faulkner questioned the landlord. He started by showing him a picture of Ian. "Have you seen this boy around here in the last two weeks?"

The man grabbed the photo and stared at it for a moment. "No," he said, shaking his head. "Never seen him."

"Seen any other kids hanging around here?"

"I have seen some young people come and go. But I wouldn't call them kids. They all drove cars."

"Girls and guys?"

"Mostly guys."

"Hmm." Detective Faulkner paused and looked at the ground.

"Brian Carter's a good kid," said the landlord. "I have known him and his parents for years. I don't know what you think he's guilty of. I just can't believe he's done anything wrong."

"I hope you're right." Detective Faulkner excused himself and went into the apartment. "Anything?" he asked the three men standing in Brian's bedroom. "Damn, this place is a mess."

Detective Frantz shook his head. "Nothing. We looked everywhere and saw no signs of Ian or anything suspicious. What do we do now?"

"Let's head back to the Andersons'. I need to talk to the chief. You three can help with the search."

Several neighbors had congregated across the street; however, none of the officers stopped to explain the situation. They each jumped into their car and headed to the Anderson residence. The roar from their engines echoed off the houses as they sped down Oak Street.

After the unsuccessful search of the apartment, the chief contacted the minister of the church. The minister **corroborated (#33)** Brian's presence at the retreat. Although Brian appeared to have an alibi, the Worthington Police Department was not ready to exclude him as a suspect. Chief McKinney sent Detective Faulkner to verify his whereabouts during the previous night.

The day continued with constant searching and questioning. Several police officers went door-to-door asking the neighbors if they had seen anything suspicious, while two police dogs followed the **presumptive (#34)** path of the missing boy. Around noon, a fleet of police and Coast Guard boats began to **scour (#35)** the rocky coastline. Occasionally, a diver plunged into the water for further exploration. By the end of the day, however, the searchers had made no further progress.

Detective Faulkner arrived at the church retreat around noon. The kids were just starting to eat lunch. Minister Palmer arranged for him to question Brian in an unused office. The office was small. It had only a desk, two wooden chairs, and a bookcase filled with bibles.

Detective Faulkner was sitting behind the desk—a pad of paper and two pens placed in front of him—when Brian entered the room. The blood had drained from Brian's face, and his wide-open eyes darted around the room. Detective Faulkner stood and extended his hand. "Brian, I'm Detective Faulkner. I want to ask you a few questions about where you were last night. Please, take a seat." The detective pointed to a chair.

Wrinkles formed on Brian's forehead as he shook the detective's hand. "I was here all last night. Why do you need to know that?" He slowly took his seat in the chair. His body appeared stiff, and his movements were almost robotic.

Detective Faulkner paused to observe his subject. "You were here the whole night. You have people who can verify this?"

Brian nodded. "Yeah, a bunch of them."

"Tell me the events from the time you arrived yesterday until now."

"Uh..." Brian glanced around the room with a puzzled look. "I arrived around six o'clock yesterday evening. I had a meeting with Minister Palmer and the other counselors. The kids started showing up just before seven. At seven thirty, we broke into groups and did different activities...Why do you need to know this?"

"Just answer the question, please."

Brian shook his head while his eyes looked toward the ceiling. "Around nine o'clock, the pizzas we ordered arrived. We all sat in the fellowship hall while we ate pizza and watched *Ghostbusters*. A little after eleven, we separated the boys and girls, and they went to sleep. The other counselors and I stayed up and talked 'til just after midnight. Then we went to sleep."

"Where did you sleep?"

"In the room with the boys. Why do you need to know this?"

"When was the last time you talked to Ian Anderson?"

"Ian who?"

"You're telling me you don't know Ian Anderson?"

Brian stared at the ground. His forehead wrinkled before he looked up at the detective. "You mean, Ian, the kid who just moved here from New York?" Detective Faulkner nodded. "I don't know. Maybe a couple of days ago. Why?"

"He's missing."

"What do you mean he's missing?"

"No one has seen him since nine o'clock last night."

"I, I'm sorry to hear that. But what does this have to do with me?"

"Well, I'll tell you what it has to do with you." Detective Faulkner's demeanor turned aggressive. "You were the only person he knew in Worthington. We know you've been talking to him. We have his cell phone."

"I play video games with him online. He's called me a couple of times to see if I wanted to play."

"Do you give your phone number out to a lot of kids?"

"No." Brian sighed and then shook his head. "I called him one time to tell him a game he wanted came in. I used my phone and not the store's phone. I guess he kept the number because he called me a couple of times after that."

"When you talked to him, did he mention any other friends he's made around here?"

"No."

"When he was in your store, was he ever with anyone?" Brian shook his head. "Did you see anyone talking to him or paying unusual attention to him?"

"No."

Detective Faulkner stopped talking and started writing. Brian sat uncomfortably in the wooden chair listening to the sound of the ballpoint pen scratching against the paper. Each time Brian moved, the old chair squeaked. As time passed, the squeaks grew more frequent. When the detective finished his notes, he looked up at Brian. "You can go. We know how to get in touch with you if we need you." He then looked down and flipped the notepad to a clean page. Brian walked out of the room without saying a word. "Shut the door," yelled the detective. Brian, however, kept walking. Halfway down the hall and out of the detective's line of sight, he raised his right hand and extended his middle finger.

Detective Faulkner sat motionless for a moment while he analyzed Brian's statement. It appeared that Brian's work at the retreat would **preclude (#36)** his involvement in Ian's disappearance. "I need to call the chief," he mumbled. The detective leaned back in his chair with his phone against his ear. He stared at the ceiling while he waited for the chief to answer. "Chief, I don't think he's our guy."

"Why's that?"

"He seems to have a solid alibi that would prevent him from having any opportunity to commit a crime."

"Well, just to be safe, talk to the other counselors. Make sure he's telling the truth."

"Okay. I'll head back to the station when I'm done."

Detective Faulkner met separately with each of the four remaining counselors. Three of the four said they saw nothing out of the ordinary. The best they could remember, Brian was around the church all night. However, one counselor named Karen told a different story.

"I saw Brian and Conner leave during the movie."

Detective Faulkner quickly looked up from his notepad and tilted his head. "For how long?"

Karen closed her eyes. "Let me think. It had to be about forty-five minutes."

Detective Faulkner flipped through the pages of his notepad. "Uh, who's this Conner person? I haven't talked to anyone by that name."

"He's one of the counselors."

"Where is he?"

"He left the retreat last night. After he and Brian came back inside, he said he wasn't feeling well and went home. Now that I think of it, he was acting kind of strange."

"Oh, shit," mumbled the detective, "maybe our hunch was right."

"Are you sure he was gone for forty-five minutes? It's important that you're sure about this."

Karen stared at the floor for a moment and then looked up. "Yeah, I'm sure."

"Do you know where they went?"

"I was sitting on the window sill in the fellowship hall during the movie. I saw them walk outside into the courtyard. After a few minutes, they went around the front of the building, and I lost sight of them."

"Karen, don't repeat this to any of the other counselors, especially Brian. I need to find out where they went before I start jumping to any conclusions." Detective Faulkner escorted her out of the office, shut the door, and then reached for his phone. "Chief, our hunch might have been right." He paced around the room while he explained his recent discovery. "Something's not right here. I think leaving the retreat for forty-five minutes is worth mentioning."

"I agree. These two have to be hiding something."

"So, what do we do next?"

"Talk to the minister and get Conner's address. Text it to me, then come back to the station. I'll send an officer over to pick up Brian and another one to pick up Conner. We need to talk to these two young men."

***

The chief stood next to Detective Faulkner in the Worthington police station's conference room. They were looking at a map of Worthington and analyzing the **proximity (#37)** of the church to Ian's house. "The church is here," said the chief, pointing to the map, "and the Anderson house is here. That's only three-and-a-half miles. Forty-five minutes is plenty of time to pick up Ian, take him somewhere, then get back to the church."

"Yeah, plenty of time."

"What do we know about Conner?"

"He's nineteen-years-old. His mother said he just got back in town two days ago from his first year away at college. As far as we can tell, he has not talked to Ian on his cell phone. We're not even sure if they know each other."

The chief scratched his head. "They could've played video games together online."

"Yeah, you're right. I'll look into that."

"Okay. Here's the plan. I'm going to talk to Brian first, then Conner. Watch through the window and tell me what you think."

Brian sat motionless on the far side of a metal table placed in the middle of the small interrogation room. The air conditioning, which whistled through a vent in the ceiling, ran the entire twenty minutes he waited. Brian's breaths were slow and deep. His eyes rarely blinked as he stared into his lap with his arms crossed. Occasionally, he rubbed his hands against his goose-bumped arms. The sound seemed to echo off the concrete block walls.

The squeak from the opening door made Brian look up. The whites of his eyes were visible from the other side of the room. The door slammed shut before the chief took his seat. The sound made Brian flinch. The chief dropped his notepad on the table and sat directly across from Brian. He removed a pen from his shirt pocket, wrote something, and then looked across the table. "Brian, I'm Chief McKinney, the Chief of Police for the Town of Worthington. Do you know why you're here?"

"Not really. The other detective said something about Ian Anderson being missing. But I don't know what that has to do with me."

The chief paused to observe his subject. Brian sat upright. He was stiff as a board. His glassy eyes darted around the room, rarely making eye contact with the chief.

"I know you already told Detective Faulkner, but could you please tell me the events of last night, starting with when you got to the church."

Brian retold the same series of events. Again, leaving out the fact that he had left the church.

"At any time did you leave the retreat?"

"No," he said shaking his head.

"So, you didn't walk outside during the movie?"

Brian's forehead wrinkled. "Uh, yeah. But only for a short time."

"And why didn't you tell us this earlier?"

"I didn't think it was important."

"What did you do outside?"

"I talked with Conner. He just got home from school a few days ago, and this was our first chance to catch up."

"How long were you outside?"

"We were only outside…maybe fifteen minutes."

"Where did you go?"

"We went to talk by Conner's car."

"Really? That's strange."

"Why's that strange?"

"Because Karen said you were gone for at least forty-five minutes."

Brian shook his head. "We couldn't have been gone for more than thirty minutes."

"Well, which was it, fifteen or thirty?"

"Uh. Uh. I don't know. I can't remember." Brian looked into his lap. Small droplets of sweat began to form above his eyebrows and upper lip.

"So, when was the last time you saw or spoke to Ian Anderson?"

"I don't know. A couple of days ago."

The chief flipped through the notepad and removed a few sheets of paper inserted between the pages. The papers rustled in his hands while his eyes scanned the document. "Can you tell me why a twenty-three-year-old man is talking to a fourteen-year-old boy at one in the morning?"

Brian **nonchalantly (#38)** said, "We were playing *Call of Duty* online, and his game console kept messing up. He called to ask me how to fix it. That's it."

The chief flipped through the printed pages of Ian's call log. "Well, what else did you two talk about on your seventeen phone calls?"

Brian squinted his eyes and shook his head. "Video games. All we talked about were video games. If you look at your list, you'll see Ian called me most of the time. The few times I called him were to return his calls."

Chief McKinney had observed that the majority of the calls originated from Ian. But he continued his interrogation by asking, "Well, do you think it's appropriate for a man of your age to be talking to a boy?"

Brian looked at the chief as if he were an idiot. "I talk to kids all day long. I work at a video game store. Also, I'm a youth pastor. I believe it's my calling to be their friend." Brian paused for a few seconds. "I felt sorry for Ian. He just moved into Worthington and hadn't made any friends. I was the only person, other than his parents, he had to talk to."

The chief shook his head. "I'll be back." He met Detective Faulkner in the hallway. "What do you think?"

The detective frowned. "I don't know. Something doesn't seem right. But he does have a convincing answer every time you **impugn (#39)** his statements. I want to hear what Conner says before I jump to any conclusions."

"Yeah, I agree. Let's wait 'til we hear what he has to say."

The chief entered Conner's interrogation room and found him pacing back and forth.

"Why am I here?" Conner asked as soon as the chief walked through the door.

"Take a seat, young man." The chief dropped his notepad on the table and looked down to grab the back of his chair.

"No. Tell me why I'm here."

The chief stopped and looked up at the **recalcitrant (#40)** young man. "I suggest you take a seat."

Conner defiantly shrugged his shoulders before walking to the table. He grabbed the chair and pulled it toward him. It screeched against the floor. Conner sat, leaving the chair a couple of feet away from the table, and then leaned forward with both elbows on his knees and his hands clasped together in his lap. He stared at the chief with a blank face.

"Conner, I'm Chief McKinney, the…"

"I know who you are. What do you want from me?"

The chief leaned back in his chair and stared at Conner for a moment. Both men locked eyes. Neither of them blinked. "I want you to tell me what you did from yesterday evening to this morning."

"Why do you need to know that?"

The chief was not an **irascible (#41)** man, but he had grown tired of Conner's **insolence (#42)**. He slammed both hands on the table. The noise made Conner jump in his seat. He then leaned forward and aimed his squinted eyes at Conner. "BECAUSE I ASKED. THAT'S WHY."

Conner leaned back in his chair and glanced toward his lap. "I was at a youth retreat at my church yesterday evening."

The chief sighed in **exasperation (#43)**. "What time did you get there?"

"Got there around six thirty, kids showed up around seven thirty, we did some activities, watched a movie, then I left because I wasn't feeling well. Can I go now?"

The chief's frustration grew as Conner continued to **equivocate (#44)** his answers. "What time did you leave?"

"Uh. Around eleven."

"At any time while you were at the retreat did you leave the church?"

"No."

The chief stopped writing and looked up from his notepad. The veins in his temples started to bulge. "You never left the church?"

"No."

The chief leaned back in his chair. "According to two people, you went outside with Brian."

"Yes, I went outside with Brian."

"Well, what is it. You did, or you didn't leave the church?"

"I went outside, but I never left the church grounds."

The chief sighed. No matter what question he asked, the **incorrigible (#45)** young man gave a defiant answer. "How long were you outside?"

"I don't know." Conner shook his head. "Maybe fifteen, twenty minutes."

"When was the last time you talked to Ian?" The chief never looked up while he scribbled his notes.

"What?"

"When was the last time you talked to Ian?"

Conner's forehead wrinkled. "Who's Ian?"

The chief looked up and made eye contact with Conner. "You don't know Ian Anderson?"

"No. I don't know anyone named Ian Anderson. Who is he?"

"Ian Anderson is a fourteen-year-old boy who went missing last night."

"Why in the hell would you think I had anything to do with that?"

"We have our reasons."

"So, that's what all this is about. You think I did something to some kid." Conner clenched his teeth and shook his head. "That's it. I want an attorney."

The chief leaned back in his chair and stared at Conner. Conner sat silently, not making eye contact.

The chief left the room without saying anything. He met Detective Faulkner in the hallway. "Come to my office."

The chief sat at his desk with his eyes closed and rubbed his forehead with the fingertips of both hands. "What do you think?"

"They're not telling us something," said Detective Faulkner.

"Yeah, I agree. Conner seemed overly anxious."

"According to Detective Frantz, Conner's parents said he got home just after midnight. Conner claims he left the retreat around eleven. So, either his time is off, or there's almost an hour where he's unaccountable.'

"That's not good."

"What are we going to do?"

The chief leaned back in his chair and stared at the ceiling. "Well, the evidence against them is **tenuous (#46),** and we have nothing to hold them on. So, we can't keep them in jail. We'll hold them until we get a warrant to search Conner's car and bedroom. After the search, we'll let them go. But, from the second they walk out of this police station, I want them followed, and all of their phone calls monitored."

"Do we have the manpower to do that?"

"It will only be for a day. I talked to an agent from the FBI earlier. He said if we don't find Ian by tomorrow morning, they're going to take over the case."

CHAPTER FIVE

When Monday morning arrived, Jack was wide-awake by seven o'clock. His body still in school mode. He stared at the rotating ceiling fan while thinking about the past weekend. *What a way to start my vacation.*

Jack wiped the sleep from his eyes while he descended the stairs and headed for the kitchen. The **aroma (#47)** of bacon grew stronger with each step. When he entered the room, his parents were sitting at the breakfast table.

"What are you doing up so early on your first day off school?" Mr. Graystone asked, his head barely above the top of the newspaper.

"I woke up and couldn't fall back to sleep. My body doesn't realize it's on vacation yet." Jack shook his head. "I hope it finds out soon. I don't want to get up this early every morning if I don't have to."

"Do you want me to make you some scrambled eggs?" asked his mother. "I have plenty of time. I don't have to be at the clinic until nine."

"Yeah, that'd be great."

"Jack, what are your plans for today?" his father asked, his head now entirely hidden behind the newspaper.

"I was going to look for a summer job. With Ian missing, I'm sure Mr. Anderson has other things on his mind and has forgotten about me working at the dealership."

"Well, I have plenty of work for you at the clinic. I can keep you busy all summer."

"I know. But the pay isn't that great." Actually, the job didn't pay at all. Jack's mother was one of two dentists who ran a not-for-profit dental clinic that provided free or almost-free dental care to people of lesser means. The clinic relied on grants, volunteers, and donations. Since Jack had no money to donate, he could only provide his labor. And although he spent many hours scrubbing floors and cleaning toilets, his volunteering was not purely motivated by **altruism (#48)**. It was primarily motivated by his parents making him work.

"Mr. Collins gave me a list of things to do before the big party. Ollie and I will be over there today and tomorrow to work on them."

Mr. Collins was the head volunteer at the clinic. A retired policeman with little sense of humor, he demanded a lot from his workers. All the staff and board members (people who didn't have to work for him) thought the world of Mr. Collins. Jack, however, often wondered if it was worth keeping him around. He ran off most of the volunteers. But Jack did not have the option of leaving. Mr. Collins knew this and always gave him the work no one else would do. Most of the time Jack brought Ollie along to help. But for some reason, Mr. Collins liked Ollie, and he would let him get away with doing next to nothing.

"What does he want you to do?" his mother asked.

"He wants me to mow and clean up the site for the new clinic and a bunch of other stuff."

"Make sure you do a good job. A lot is riding on this fundraiser."

For the past year, the clinic's board of directors were trying to raise $2 million for a new building, equipment, and supplies. They already had the building site. A wealthy real estate developer had donated it a couple of years back. So far, though, they had raised only $310,000. Next Saturday's fundraiser would be their best chance to raise a big chunk of the money.

Jack's mom slid a plate of bacon and eggs in front of her son. "Has anyone heard anything about the missing Anderson boy?"

"The chief told Courtney that they still don't have any solid leads."

"That's what I heard too," replied Mr. Graystone. "It's like Ian just vanished off the face of the earth."

"I feel so bad for Robert and Christina. I can only imagine the pain they must be feeling." Jack could sense the **empathy (#49)** in his mother's voice.

Mr. Graystone glanced at his watch. "I have a meeting in fifteen minutes. I'll see both of you tonight." He kissed his wife on the cheek before he grabbed the brown paper bag that contained his lunch and headed for the back door. Jack's dad was a **frugal (#50)** man. He always brought his lunch to work. He did not believe in wasting time or money on going out to eat.

"Dad, you might not see me. If it's okay with both of you, I was going to spend the night at Ollie's."

Mr. Graystone gave him a hard look. "Are his parents going to be home?"

"Yes."

"It's okay with me if it's okay with your mother."

Jack turned toward his mother and stared.

"It's okay with me. Just be safe."

"Thanks, Mom." He gave her a hug before he bolted out of the kitchen and ran to his room.

Jack was heading to Ollie's house just after ten o'clock. The plan was to pick up Ollie, and on the way to the clinic, look for anyone hiring.

Ollie lived in a large, old house on Oceanside Drive that his grandfather owned. From what Jack had overheard, Ollie's grandfather did not trust his son with money or any other responsibility. The house had been in the family for generations, and Grandpa Culver was not about to **abdicate (#51)** its control to his irresponsible son.

Jack wheeled the Explorer into Ollie's driveway and drove up the winding pavement toward the house. He parked by the front entrance, and as he walked to the door, Mr. Culver was leaving.

"Hey, Jack. How you doing?"

"Great. Glad to be outta school. Off to work, Mr. Culver?"

"Yes, I have a busy day. Lots of appointments. If you're looking for Ollie, he's in his shed."

Jack smiled. "Okay. Have a nice day." *Busy? Lots of appointments? You don't even have a real job. And it's almost ten thirty. Who leaves for the office at ten thirty in the morning?* Several times Jack had asked Ollie what his father did for a living. Each time, Ollie replied, "He works for my grandfather." There was, however, one major problem with that statement. Ollie's grandfather was retired and didn't work.

The two had an office with a secretary. But every time Jack was there, Grandpa Culver was reading the newspaper, and Ollie's dad was nowhere to be found. And judging by the appearance of his father's office, he was never there. His desk was always clear of any papers or files, and the office was spotless.

Ollie's house sat on a large piece of property that faced the ocean. The area toward Oceanside Drive was heavily wooded and shielded the house from the view of passersby. Within these trees, down a stone pathway, was an old building that the Culvers referred to as Ollie's shed. The building was originally constructed in the late 1800s as a barn. Over the years, it was converted to a servants' quarters and then to a gardener's shed. Last summer, Ollie commandeered it after several small wars with his younger brother and sister over the use of the game room in the basement of the main house.

Ollie's shed consisted of two rooms. One room resembled a garage and the other a small apartment with a bathroom and a kitchenette. The inside looked like a paint store that had exploded. Ollie had used the leftover cans of paint from several of his mother's decorating projects and painted the walls tan, dark blue, cranberry, and lime green. He furnished the apartment with an old gold couch and two powder blue reclining chairs he had acquired from his grandfather's friend, Mr. Smithton. He furnished the garage with an old red, white and blue pool table he bought off Craigslist.

Jack entered the shed to find Ollie in the middle of a fierce video game battle. He never made eye contact with Jack. All he did was nod his head and kept on playing. When the game was over, he put the controller down and then stood and stretched.

Ollie looked worn out. "How long have you been playing?"

"Since six o'clock this morning. I couldn't sleep, so I came out here."

"I was up by seven. I couldn't sleep either." Jack walked to the refrigerator and grabbed a bottle of water. "I told your buddy, Mr. Collins, we'd be there at noon. I thought we'd leave a little earlier, so I could look for a job."

"Cool. Let me go take a shower, and then we'll leave."

After Ollie left, Jack picked up the controller and started fighting his own battle. He played until Ollie returned, and then the two decided to play one game before they left. One game turned into five, and when Jack glanced at his phone, it was fifteen minutes before noon.

Jack jumped up and tossed the controller on the chair. "Ollie, we've gotta go. We're gonna be late."

Both kids bolted out of the shed and ran to the Explorer. They arrived at the clinic by noon to find Mr. Collins waiting in his truck with his mower in the back. He glanced at his watch. "Follow me. Jack, you can start cutting. Ollie and I have some work to do in the clinic."

Great. Ollie gets to sit in the air conditioning while I bust my ass outside in the heat.

The site for the new clinic was down the street. Jack followed, and after he and Mr. Collins removed the mower, went to work in the **torrid (#52)** midday sun cutting an acre of ankle-high grass. The tall grass was difficult to cut, especially with a push mower. It took three hours to complete the **onerous (#53)** task. And by the time he finished, he had become **disaffected (#54)** with Mr. Collins and his volunteer work. It took another thirty minutes for Mr. Collins to pick up his mower. The longer Jack waited, the angrier he became. *That's it. I'm telling Mom and Mr. Collins that I'm not doing any more volunteer work,* were his last thoughts as Mr. Collins pulled up.

When Mr. Collins stopped his truck, Jack saw him and Ollie laughing. Jack pushed the mower behind the tailgate and waited for help. He waited for several minutes while the two continued to talk and laugh. Finally, Jack had enough. He smacked the truck's fender with his open hand. The sound startled the two. They stopped talking and glared at Jack through the rear window. Ollie apparently got the hint because he quickly jumped out of the passenger seat. "See you tomorrow, Mr. Collins."

By now, Jack was so angry that he could barely speak. He knew it would be for the best not to say anything he would regret, so he chose not to confront Mr. Collins.

"Ollie, get over here and help me lift this mower."

Ollie stopped and looked at Jack. "What's wrong with you?"

"I've been out here in the heat while you've been having fun with your friend in the air conditioning."

"Hey, I worked hard today."

Jack glared at Ollie through squinted eyes. "Just grab the mower and help me lift it."

Ollie bent over and grabbed the front of the mower. He had a look of disgust as he lifted it into the back of the truck.

After Jack shut the tailgate, Mr. Collins lowered his window. "See you two tomorrow at noon." He then quickly drove away.

Jack turned his glare toward the departing truck. "You could at least say thank you." He let out a huff and then looked back at Ollie. "Come on. I don't have all day."

Jack headed to the Explorer at a quick pace. Ollie, who followed closely behind, wiped his hands on the back of Jack's shirt. Jack flinched. "What are you doing?"

"Your shirt was already dirty." Ollie laughed. "See, I got my hands dirty at work today, too."

Jack sighed and shook his head. "You're an idiot."

Ollie laughed. "Let's go through the drive-thru at McDonald's. I'm hungry."

"Me, too. I need some **sustenance (#55)** before I pass out."

Ollie gave Jack a quizzical look as he buckled his seatbelt. "You need what?"

"Sustenance. You know, like food, water, the things you need to stay alive."

"What's up with the big words?"

"I'm trying to **augment (#56)** my vocabulary."

Ollie rolled his eyes.

They finished their meals before they arrived at the shed. When the Explorer came to a stop, Ollie reached for the empty fast food bag. "Give me your empty sustenance wrappers, and I'll throw them away."

Jack shook his head. "That's not the proper way to use the word."

"Well, excuse me for being so dumb. You ready to get your butt whupped in *Call of Duty*?"

"Bring it on," Jack said with a nudge to Ollie's shoulder.

The competition between the two started with a coin toss. They were flipping to see who got the better of the two powder blue reclining chairs. Mr. Smithton, a short, skinny man, must have had a fat wife because one chair's springs were shot. When you sat in it, your left side sank about six inches. The standing rule was whoever won the toss would remain in the good seat until they lost in whatever game they were playing.

With Ollie winning the coin toss, the games began. They played until seven thirty, changing seats many times. They did not stop until Ollie's phone rang. He had a brief conversation and then hung up. "That was my mom. She said the sustenance is ready. Is *that* better?"

"Close enough."

The two entered the Culvers' house to the smell of garlic bread baking in the oven.

"Mom, what did you make for dinner tonight?"

"Lasagna, salad, and garlic bread."

Ollie tapped Jack on the shoulder with the back of his hand. "My mom makes the best lasagna."

Jack laughed to himself. When Mrs. Culver said she had made lasagna, she actually meant she turned on the oven and inserted the pan of food that the housekeeper made earlier in the day.

Dinner at the Culvers' was always a crapshoot. You never knew when Mr. and Mrs. Culver would be in the middle of World War III. This night, however, everyone was happy and the meal was enjoyable.

"What did you two do on your first day off of school?" Mr. Culver asked as he handed Jack a plate of lasagna.

Before Jack could speak, Ollie said, "We went to Jack's mother's dental clinic and did some volunteer work."

"What did you do?"

Jack was in the middle of taking a sip when Ollie replied, "Well, we mowed some grass and made a seating chart for the big fundraiser. Stuff like that."

When Jack heard Ollie say, "We mowed some grass," he almost spit his drink all over the table. *We mowed some grass? All you did was help lift the mower into the truck.*

"Dad, you're not going to believe this, but I even got my hands dirty."

Jack shook his head. *I bet he really thinks he was partly responsible for cutting that grass.*

"Ollie, you need to keep track of all your volunteer work. It'll look good on your college applications," said Mrs. Culver.

The two were back at the shed right after dinner. Shortly after that, Lip and another kid from school showed up. The kid's name was Edward Sumpter, not Ed Sumpter or Eddie Sumpter. If you called him anything but Edward, he ignored you, which he did most of the time anyway. Edward Sumpter was the one person in this world that Jack truly disliked. He was a **pretentious (#57)** jerk who thought highly of himself. And when Edward talked, he was very **condescending (#58)**. He talked down to you if he even talked to you at all. Some days he would just give you a smug look and act as if you were not there. And never did he ask you anything about yourself. It was always about him.

Jack was shocked to see him with Lip. Even though Edward and Lip were the same age and in the same grade, Edward always hung around older kids, mostly seniors. Jack figured that after Edward's friends graduated, they didn't want to be seen with a high school kid. Jack sighed. *Oh great. Does this mean he's going to be around all summer?*

Jack's **disdain (#59)** for Edward had grown over many years. It culminated a year ago after Edward had made several **aspersions (#60)** about Jack being a grade behind. He had implied that Jack was a slow learner. After about the fourth **disparaging (#61)** remark, Jack yelled at him in Russian. He called him every cuss word he knew and made several mean comments about his mother. When he finished his **tirade (#62)**, he said, "I told you I'm behind because I lived in Russia for a year. If you were smart enough to speak Russian, you would've known what I said."

Edward shook his head. "I think you're just making up words that sound like Russian." He then turned and walked away, never giving Jack a chance to respond to his **pejorative (#63)** remark.

From that day on, Jack wanted nothing to do with Edward. But unfortunately, their paths always crossed. This summer, it appeared, they were going to cross even more.

When Lip walked into the shed with Edward behind him, Jack never made eye contact. *Oh great. He's here.* Jack was not in the mood for Edward and his **mercurial (#64)** personality. *I wonder which Edward is here tonight?*

"What's going on?" asked Lip.

"Jack and I are in the middle of a battle." The two watched in silence until the game was over a few minutes later.

Ollie stood and stretched. "What are you two up to tonight?"

"Nothing," Lip replied. "We stopped by to see what you guys are up to."

Before Jack could do or say anything, Edward jumped in Ollie's seat and grabbed his controller. "Come on, Graystone. Let me show you how a pro plays this game." Jack never had a chance to get away.

The game ended with Edward winning. Edward tried to **impute (#65)** his success on his gaming skills, but that was not the case. Jack hated every second he was around Edward, and he could not concentrate.

"Who wants their ass whupped next?"

"Not me, that's for damn sure," Jack mumbled under his breath before he stood and walked away.

"Ollie, what about you?"

Ollie gave his usual reply to any bet or contest. He threw his hands in the air as he said, "Game on, challenge accepted!"

While the two fought their battle, Lip and Jack went into the other room to play a game of pool. Lip broke and made the two ball. He was solids. "What are you doing hanging out with that asshole?" asked Jack before Lip made his next shot.

"Six-ball, corner pocket. He called and said he had nothing to do." Lip eyed his shot. Click! The ball went straight into the pocket.

"Where are all his friends?"

"Four-ball, back left pocket. He told me some of them went off to college already. I don't know where the other ones are." Lip stoked the cue stick. Click! The ball just missed and bounced off the bumper.

Jack leaned over the table. "Ten in the side pocket. Where's Kate? Why isn't he with her?" He tapped the side pocket with the end of the cue to indicate which one. Click! His shot missed. "Damn."

"They broke up."

"Wow, that's a shocker."

Lip lined up his shot but stopped because he started to laugh. "Her friend Maria told me that Kate broke up with him because he thought she was gaining too much weight. He wanted her to weigh herself in front of him every day."

"Are you serious? That sounds like something that jerk would do."

"Yeah, he is a jerk, but he's really not that bad once you get to know him."

"He's being nice tonight because he has no other choice. Just wait until you see him around his other friends. Then you'll change your mind."

The four alternated playing pool and video games for the next three hours. Jack was in misery listening to Edward brag about his new car. His parents had bought him a four-year-old BMW. The car cost a fraction of what Ollie's BMW cost, but in Edward's mind, they were equal. Lip was not very impressed with the car, though. He thought the ride was too rough and the seats were too hard.

Edward and Lip left at eleven thirty. By this time, Jack was worn out. He was tired from work, tired of listening to Lip complain, and tired of Edward's **haughty (#66)** attitude. He looked at his best friend and shook his head. "I sure hope Edward doesn't come around here all summer. I'm sick of hearing him tells us how great he is and how dumb we are."

Ollie laughed. "If he does start coming around, I'll close the entry gate at night. I won't give him the code, and we can ignore his calls. That should keep him away."

CHAPTER SIX

Since Ian's disappearance, despite the efforts of several agencies, no one had found any solid clues. Further questioning of both Jack and the Andersons revealed no more information. Neither did their lie detector tests nor the forensic analysis of their clothing. The surveillance cameras from the gas station also **substantiated (#67)** Jack's alibi. Therefore, based on the facts, timeline, and overall appearance of these three, it was apparent to everyone involved in the investigation they were not responsible for Ian's disappearance.

The FBI had assumed the surveillance of both Brian and Conner on the previous Sunday. Their search of Conner's car produced no fingerprints or DNA from Ian. They did, however, find a receipt from a local liquor store at 9:28 p.m. on the night Ian went missing. The location of the store was between the church and the Anderson house. When they interviewed the store's clerk, he confirmed Brian had purchased a bottle of vodka.

Brian and Conner's **fallacious (#68)** alibis were beginning to fall apart. Not only did they lie about meeting in the courtyard, but they also lied about leaving the church grounds. With every passing day, their suspicion of guilt grew greater.

***

Wednesday morning arrived with no further clues on Ian's disappearance. Exhausted from an all-night James Bond movie marathon, Jack slept until ten thirty and then lay in bed trying to muster enough energy to take a shower. With his bed sheet covering most of his body, he stared at the rotating ceiling fan while every so often a

zephyr (#69) from the open windows swept across his feet. The light breeze brought with it the subtle scent of gardenias from his mother's garden.

This morning was unusually quiet. The only sounds that filled the air were the repetitive clicking of the next-door neighbor's sprinkler and the **mellifluous (#70)** songs from birds chirping and singing outside Jack's bedroom window. Eventually, the faint buzz of Mr. Wallace's lawnmower joined in. The sound grew louder as Mr. Wallace worked his way throughout his front yard.

As Jack lay in bed, he could not stop thinking about Ian Anderson. He wondered what could have happened to him or what he could be going through. He also had a nagging feeling that people might believe he had something to do with Ian's disappearance. He knew this feeling would never go away until someone found Ian or the case was solved.

Jack's thoughts changed to what to do for lunch when his stomach started to growl. His choices were to eat at home or spend some of his remaining birthday money on McDonald's. These thoughts, however, were interrupted when his phone, which was somewhere on his bed, began to ring. He rooted through the covers until he located it. He answered by the fourth ring.

"Hello."

"Is this Jack Graystone?" a raspy voice asked.

"Yes, it is."

"This is Burt Chambers of Anderson Porsche. Bob Anderson said he talked to you about a summer job."

"Yes, he mentioned it at dinner the other night." Jack hoped the casual mention of their meeting would give him a better chance at the job.

"Can you come in today around four for an interview?"

"Yes, I can."

"Okay, see you then." Click.

***

Jack's stomach churned as he pushed open the large glass door to the Porsche dealership's showroom. He was in awe of the machinery placed upon the glistening marble floors. The fluorescent lights, which shone down from the two-story ceiling, made the cars so shiny they appeared wet. Jack surveyed the room and spotted a large, curved, granite-topped counter. Behind it was a young, well-dressed woman wearing a headset and sitting in a chrome and leather chair. Positioned in front of her were a computer and an elaborate phone system. Assuming she was the receptionist, he cautiously approached.

"I'm here to see," Jack began, just before the receptionist raised her index finger as if to say, *Hold on, I need to take this call.*

"Anderson Porsche, how may I direct your call? Hold please." After pressing several buttons, she looked at Jack and raised her eyebrows to indicate it was time for him to speak.

"I have a four o'clock appointment with . . ." were his only words before the index finger greeted him again.

"Anderson Porsche, how may I direct your call? Hold please," was followed by another set of raised eyebrows.

This time "I'm here" were the only words spoken before the finger rose. Jack shrugged in frustration, but the **pert (#71)** receptionist snickered.

"I'm joking," she said with a smile. "Who were you here to see?"

"Mr. Chambers. I have a four o'clock appointment," Jack replied in a **tremulous (#72)** voice.

"Okay, let me call him."

Jack's legs weakened waiting for her response. He grabbed the counter for fear he would lose his balance. After a brief phone conversation, she gave Jack another smile. "It'll be a few minutes. I'll let you know when he is ready."

"Thank you," replied Jack, his stomach still churning. To calm his nerves, he walked into the showroom and inspected the cars on display. One car, in particular, caught his eye. It was a new, silver Porsche Carrera 4S with black interior. *I wonder if I can touch it. I don't see why not.* He cautiously approached, opened the door, and inserted his head. The smell of the leather was overpowering. In his **peripheral (#73)** vision, he caught sight of someone walking toward him. *Oh, crap. Maybe I'm not supposed to be touching it.* He quickly closed the door and took two steps backward.

"You can sit in it if you'd like," said a well-dressed man who emerged from a glass-walled office.

"Really? You don't mind?"

"Not at all. Go ahead."

Jack reopened the door and slid into the driver's seat.

The salesman extended his hand. "I'm Bill Russo."

Jack shook the man's hand. "Graystone, Jack Graystone. Wow, this is really nice."

"Yes, it is. It's one of the most expensive Carreras we have. It has a bunch of options."

Jack was unable to read the window sticker from his seated position. "I'm afraid to ask, but how much is it?"

Bill Russo walked to the other side of the car and looked at the price. "$146,800."

Jack shook his head while he gripped the steering wheel with both hands. *Damn, this is nice. Maybe I can sell a body part to pay for it. I wonder what a kidney's worth.* "I hate to waste your time, but I'm here to apply for a summer job washing cars. You never know, though. If I get the job, maybe we can make a deal. I'll come to see you with my first paycheck."

Bill Russo chuckled. "I'll see what I can do." He handed Jack a business card. "Come see me when you get older. I'll make you a great deal."

Jack continued his tour of the showroom moving around quietly. The occasional squeak from his rubber-soled shoes was the only sound he made. He inspected each car and looked at its window sticker. He then considered if he had the money would he buy it. He wanted each one.

Between the soft music playing in the background and the distraction of the cars, his nerves began to settle. That was until the receptionist said, "Mr. Chambers is ready to see you." Instantly, his body filled with fear. He gave the receptionist a wide-eyed glance. "He's down the hall, second door on the left."

Jack nodded and turned toward the hallway. After a long exhale, he took two steps and then stopped. Not only had his stomach started to churn and his legs weaken, but now he was also lightheaded.

"Are you all right?" asked the receptionist.

"My first job interview."

"Oh," she said before looking down at her desk. "Well, good luck."

Good luck? That doesn't sound very good. Jack lowered his head, and with a deep breath, headed toward the office. His steps were uneasy, and when he got to the door, he paused. After a few seconds, he built up the courage to knock.

"Come in. Have a seat. I'll be with you in a minute," said the raspy-voiced man who was shuffling through a stack of papers.

Jack tensed his muscles, then entered the office and sat in front of Mr. Chamber's desk. He gripped the arms of the chair with both hands while he silently repeated to himself, *Don't throw up.*

"So, you want a summer job?"

"Yes, I do."

"How's your driving record?"

"Perfect, never had a ticket." Jack hoped he would not have to reveal that he had his driver's license for only three months.

"Can you drive a car with a manual transmission?"

"Yes, I can."

"Are you on drugs?"

The question caught Jack off guard. He hesitated and then replied, "No."

Mr. Chambers cracked a small smile. Jack assumed this was his attempt at humor.

"Mr. Anderson went over the hours with you? Monday, Thursday, Friday, eight to five. Saturday, eight to twelve."

"Yes, he did."

"Start tomorrow?"

"Yes."

"Here's the paperwork. The conference room is around the corner. Start filling it out. Someone'll be in shortly. Questions?"

"No."

Mr. Chambers rose to his feet and extended his hand. "See you tomorrow."

Jack stood, shook his hand, and then walked to the conference room. By the time he entered, his body was back to normal—although the armpits of his shirt were soaked from sweat. He paused for a moment and thought, *Man, I can't believe how easy that was.* He then flopped into one of the leather chairs that surrounded a large conference table and let out a long sigh.

Jack thumbed through the stack of forms in front of him. Only two required completion. They consisted of an application and an Internal Revenue Service information form. The other pages were each marked with a large red *X*. There were at least ten of them, which consisted of forms for retirement funds, health insurance, and other things that did not apply to him. After he read a few of them, he thought, *I'm sure glad I'm still a kid. It would suck to fill out all this junk.*

It only took a few minutes to finish the paperwork. Jack completed most of the information but left a few blanks on the IRS information form. He was unsure of what to put for the number of dependents he could claim. *I know Courtney depends on me, and definitely Ollie. But I'm pretty sure that's not what they mean.*

Jack's mind wandered as he stared at the framed posters of Porsches hanging on the conference room's walls. For the next several minutes, while he sat at the table waiting for whoever was coming to see him, he thought about the missing Anderson boy. Finally, the conference room door opened. To his surprise, it was Mr. Anderson.

"Hi, Jack." Mr. Anderson said upon entering the room.

This was the first time Jack had seen Mr. Anderson since his son's disappearance. When he caught a glimpse of the man's face, he saw it was pale and withdrawn. The black circles under his eyes were so dark that he resembled a raccoon. *I wasn't expecting to see Mr. Anderson. What do I say to him?* "Uh, hi, Mr. Anderson. How are you and Mrs. Anderson doing?"

"Not well. Neither of us can eat nor sleep. I keep playing different scenarios in my head of what could've happened to Ian. With every passing day, they say the chances of finding him grow slimmer. We're coming up on a week now, and there isn't even one clue." Mr. Anderson paused and closed his eyes. "I know he wouldn't run away. He wouldn't know where to go or what to do. Besides, he's a happy kid. My gut keeps telling me someone's kidnapped him," he shook his head, "but nobody has called and asked for a ransom."

Mr. Anderson stopped talking and the room went silent. Jack wanted to say something, but he did not know what to say. By the expression on Mr. Anderson's face, Jack could tell his mind was racing with thoughts of his son.

Jack finally stopped the silence by asking, "Whatever happened with Ian's half-brother or the video store guy?"

"The FBI investigator told me they ruled out both of them as suspects. They both **purportedly (#74)** had solid alibis although they wouldn't tell me what they were." Mr. Anderson sighed and shook his head. "The FBI said they had a few loose ends to tie up before they released any information. I tried again to get in touch with my son, but his evil mother said, 'At this time he is indisposed and cannot talk to you,' whatever that means." Mr. Anderson stopped talking and stared at the wall. After the brief pause, he looked at Jack. "Could you do my wife and me a favor?"

"Sure, anything."

"Reilly is having a hard time, too. He just mopes around the house. Every time he hears a noise outside, he thinks it's Ian coming home and runs to the front door. My wife and I don't have the energy or the mental strength to walk him right now. I'll pay you if you can come over in the evenings and walk him. He likes to go around nine, but I know you have things to do with your friends. So, anytime during the day would be fine. Is that possible?"

"Sure. But you don't need to pay me. I'll do it for free."

"That's nice of you to offer, but I'd feel better if I paid you. Have you finished the paperwork?"

"Almost. I have a question on this form." Jack pointed to the IRS information form. "I don't know what *number of dependents* means."

"It means how many children you have or people you support." Mr. Anderson cracked a small smile. "As far as I know. You're not a baby-daddy, are you?"

Jack let out a quick laugh. "No, I'm not."

"Put a zero in the blank. Your father claims you on his taxes."

Even though Jack had no idea what Mr. Anderson was talking about, he put the zero in the space. *I still think I should put one to claim Ollie.*

"Is that it?"

"Yeah, I think that's it." Jack took a final look at the forms and then nodded his head.

"Okay, follow me. I'll introduce you to the head of the service department."

Mr. Anderson introduced Jack to Dwayne Barrini, the service manager. Mr. Barrini was a nice man. He showed Jack around the building and explained his duties. The meeting lasted for only fifteen minutes. Jack was on his way home shortly after that.

One of the problems with being an only child in the Graystone residence is that there were no other siblings to tell mom and dad about their day. Therefore, dinnertime for Jack was like a police interrogation. His **solicitous (#75)** parents wanted to hear about every minute of their only child's life. They were concerned he was making the right decisions, and the barrage of questions started even before they sat down to eat. "What are you going to do at the dealership? Who are you working with?" These were among the many questions that continued even after dinner while the family watched television.

By eight forty-five, Jack was exhausted and could not think of anything else to say. "I have to go get Reilly. I'll see you later." He sprung from his chair and headed for the door. *How many more questions can they possibly think of?*

Jack arrived at the Andersons' house and pressed the intercom button at the front gate. A static-filled, "Can I help you?" blasted out of the tiny speaker in the box.

"It's Jack Graystone. I'm here to walk Reilly."

After a few **indiscernible (#76)** words, the electric gate motors began to hum. Jack drove to the house and nervously approached. When he stepped onto the porch, the door opened and Mr. Anderson appeared. He looked worse than earlier in the day.

"Thanks for doing this," Mr. Anderson said in a slow, soft voice. "Reilly will be happy to get out of the house." His gaze never left the ground.

"No problem."

Jack walked into the foyer, which seemed abnormally quiet. Although the light was dim, he could see Reilly lying at the top of the stairs.

Mr. Anderson gave a quick whistle and slapped his knee. "Come on, Reilly. Jack is here to take you for a walk."

Reilly lifted his head, looked at the two, and then lumbered down the stairs. The **docile (#77)** dog entered the foyer with his tail gently wagging. A lick on Jack's arm was all the greeting he gave before he walked to the table that stored his leash. He sat until he heard the click of the leash on his collar and then went to the front door where he waited to go for his walk.

Mr. Anderson explained how Ian would walk Reilly along the Ocean Walk—a pathway that followed the edge of the ocean along most of Worthington's coastline. They would leave through the backyard and walk around the peninsula. The pathway eventually ended at Oceanside Drive, a quarter mile from the front entrance to their house. They would then walk along the sidewalk the rest of the way home.

With this in mind, Jack and Reilly left for their first walk. The night sky grew darker with every step along the path. Eventually, the light faded and it became difficult to see. With a flick of a switch, Jack's flashlight lit their expedition. Reilly led the way, walking briskly, but stopped every so often to mark his territory. He zigzagged along the path, constantly sniffing the ground. Jack had the feeling Reilly was searching for any trace of Ian.

When the two reached the tip of the peninsula, Jack stopped. He stared across the ocean and into the barely visible horizon. He could not stop thinking about the missing boy. After a few minutes, a faint roar in the distance interrupted his thoughts. He turned toward the sound. It grew louder by the second. Gazing into the night sky, he spotted the lights from an oncoming plane. It was heading directly toward the middle of the cove. He froze. The plane was about to crash, and he did not know what to do.

CHAPTER SEVEN

Jack closed his eyes and reached into his pocket for his phone. *I hope no one gets killed*, he thought while he waited for the devastation to occur. He heard a splash, but when he opened his eyes, he saw the plane skimming across the water. This was a seaplane landing, not an airplane crashing. He let out a sigh as the seaplane floated to a stop a half mile from shore.

While the seaplane bounced back and forth in the ocean, he watched and wondered what it was doing out there. After a minute or two, a small boat appeared out of nowhere and rafted next to it. A few more minutes passed before the boat sped off into the darkness, and the seaplane took off.

When the excitement was over, Jack and Reilly continued their walk. It wasn't long before Reilly began to tire, and his pace slowed considerably. He lumbered along the pathway, only to occasionally deviate when something caught his attention. They eventually arrived at Oceanside Drive and then followed the sidewalk back to the Andersons' house.

Jack knocked on the Andersons' front door. Soon after, the door slowly opened, and the pale-faced Mr. Anderson greeted them. He looked at his gold watch. "Forty-five minutes, not too bad."

"We would've been here a little sooner, but we stopped to watch a seaplane land."

Mr. Anderson bent over and scratched Reilly's head. "Was he a good boy?"

"Yeah, he was a very good boy."

"I appreciate you doing this for us. It's too difficult for my wife and me right now. Any night you can walk him would be greatly appreciated." Mr. Anderson reached into his wallet and handed Jack a twenty-dollar bill.

Jack was stunned by the more than **equitable (#78)** gesture. "That's too much. I can't take this, Mr. Anderson."

"You're doing me a big favor. I insist."

After shaking hands, Jack half-whispered, "You really don't have to do this. I'd walk him for free."

***

With a jolt, Jack woke to the sound of Guns N' Roses blasting from his iPhone's alarm. Instantly, he rolled out of bed and staggered across the room toward his dresser. By the time he pressed the button to put a stop to the song, he was mostly awake. He glanced back at his bed. *Don't do it,* he repeated to himself. *This is your first day of work at a real job, and you don't want to screw it up by being late.* Over the past couple of years, Jack had worked at his mom's dental clinic and dad's law office. But those didn't count as real jobs. Everyone knew he was the boss's son and gave him special treatment. Until today, this would be Jack's first real job—a job where none of his coworkers knew his parents.

Jack arrived at the dealership early, hoping to make a good impression. He found Mr. Barrini who said, "You'll be helping Buddy wash cars today. He has a routine, so I'll let him explain it. Wait in the shop. He should be here soon."

Jack sat impatiently in the quiet room. The only noise being the ticking clock hanging on the wall, which he constantly checked. At one minute to eight, Buddy arrived. The twenty-one-year-old was a small, wiry person. When he spoke, Jack noticed he had a few teeth missing and several showing signs of decay.

For the next eight hours, the two washed and vacuumed. Cars came in dull and dirty and then departed shiny and clean. The entire time, the local radio station played in the background. It seemed to repeat the same dozen songs. Jack found this almost as irritating as Buddy's attempt to sing along.

When Buddy wasn't singing, he was talking. Most of what he said was mindless babble. During these **fatuous (#79)** conversations, he told Jack about his personal life. He said he came from a dysfunctional family. His mother was nowhere to be found, and his father had died several years earlier. He lived with his older sister who refused to work and his younger brother who refused to go to school. Buddy's life was not easy. This was partly due to misfortune, but mostly due to poor decisions. Despite this **adversity (#80)**, he seemed to be happy.

With his first day of work behind him, Jack headed home, exhausted. He arrived at the same time as his father and followed his Buick into the driveway. After he parked, Jack jumped out of the Explorer and ran to the back door.

"I'm the winner," repeated Jack while he did a victory dance on the back porch. He looked like a pro football player scoring a touchdown.

His father shook his head and laughed. "I didn't know we were in a race." He grabbed his briefcase from the backseat and walked to the door.

"Dad, you must have a lot of work to do tonight."

"Yes, I do. How'd you know that?"

"Your right shoulder is lower than usual. So, I assumed you must have more files in your briefcase today."

Mr. Graystone patted his son on the back. "Very observant, Sherlock."

They entered the house through the kitchen to find Jack's mother preparing dinner.

"Hello, honey," Mr. Graystone said to his wife who was standing in front of the sink washing vegetables. He then walked up behind her, put his arms around her, and kissed her repeatedly on the neck.

Jack shook his head and rolled his eyes. He then opened his mouth and inserted his index finger.

His mother grabbed a dish towel and dried her hands. "So, how was your first day, Jack?"

"It was good. I washed a lot of cool cars."

"Did you work by yourself or with someone?" asked his father.

"I worked with Buddy, the guy who runs the detail shop."

"Is he nice?"

"He seems okay, but he cusses a lot. Mom, he uses cuss words in every sentence." Jack glanced at his father. "Dad, I'm learning a whole new vocabulary." His father laughed. His mother rolled her eyes.

After dinner and another thousand questions, Jack grabbed his phone and went upstairs. For almost an hour, he lay on his bed talking to Courtney. She was in the middle of final exam week and needed a break. According to her, her head was about to explode.

A glance at his clock reminded Jack it was time for Reilly's walk. After their usual long-winded goodbye, he hung up and then drove to the Andersons' house. He grabbed Reilly and followed the usual routine. The walk was uneventful. There was no seaplane to distract him, and they were back within a half-hour.

***

The plans for Friday night were to celebrate Courtney's last day of school by going to dinner and an early movie. After the movie, they would pick up Reilly and take him for his walk. The plans went like clockwork, and the two arrived at the Anderson residence a few minutes before nine. Jack and Courtney entered through the back door to find Mr. Anderson in the kitchen. His eyes were red as if he had been crying.

Jack tried to act upbeat in an attempt to **ameliorate (#81)** the situation. "Mr. Anderson, this is my girlfriend, Courtney McKinney. She's Chief McKinney's daughter. She's going to walk with me tonight."

Mr. Anderson gave a strained smile and said hello. After a brief conversation, Jack, Courtney, and Reilly were about to leave when Mr. Anderson said, "Jack, here's a key and the alarm code to the back door. I might not be here every night. So, come anytime. I'll put a stack of twenty-dollar bills in the drawer here. When you return Reilly, take one. Tell me when they run out. I'm going to bed."

"Okay, Mr. Anderson."

"Oh, and, Jack, make sure the door is locked when you leave."

"Got it," he replied and then closed the door behind him.

The three began their stroll along the Ocean Walk with Reilly leading the way, followed by Jack and Courtney. They were walking arm in arm. After they rounded the point, the two sat on top of a large rock that projected into the ocean. With their legs dangling over the side, they looked out over the cove. Small waves splashed against the rocks below, and a fine mist filled the air. Occasionally, a larger wave hit, spraying the legs of their jeans. With one arm around his girlfriend, Jack pointed toward the cove and told her the story of the seaplane. He explained how cool it was to watch. At no time, however, did he admit to his fear of the plane crashing. When he finished his story, he heard the faint roar of the seaplane's engine.

"Courtney, I think it's going to land again."

Sure enough, the seaplane landed and followed the same routine. It had its **transitory (#82)** meeting with the small powerboat and then took off into the night sky. Jack and Courtney remained on the rocks during the plane's entire routine. Neither spoke. After it was over, the couple continued their walk. The landing of the seaplane dominated their conversation.

Jack gave Reilly one last pat on the head. "See you tomorrow," he said and then locked the back door behind him.

Jack was silent on the walk to the Explorer. He had a blank look on his face and stared straight ahead. "What's the matter?" Courtney asked.

Jack shook his head and frowned. "This is the third time I've been here, and I still haven't seen Mrs. Anderson. I asked where she was once. Mr. Anderson said she was sleeping. I hope she's okay."

"I bet she's really depressed with her son missing and all."

"I hope she doesn't hurt herself."

Courtney placed her hand on Jack's shoulder and gently rubbed it. "Honey, I'm sure she'll be okay."

Jack looked into Courtney's eyes and smiled. "You sound like my mother."

***

The next day, Jack worked until noon. He stopped by the tuxedo rental shop on his way home and pulled into his driveway at half-past one. He entered the house to find his mother talking frantically on the phone. From what he gathered from her conversation, there was a problem with the flowers. Jack scribbled, *If I'm not up by four, please wake me!* on a notepad, handed it to her, and then went upstairs to rest before the big party.

Jack was in his tuxedo and ready to go by five. He knew Mrs. McKinney would want to take pictures, so he headed to the McKinney's house a little early. As anticipated, Courtney was not ready when he arrived. So, for the next fifteen minutes, Jack entertained himself in the living room by looking at Snapchat on his phone.

Courtney looked like a model when she descended the staircase wearing a blue dress **complemented (#83)** by a pair of blue shoes. Her mother could not stop talking about how beautiful she was. Jack concurred. While they both stared at Courtney in her finest **raiment (#84)**, Jack put his hand around Mrs. McKinney's shoulder and said, "She takes after her mother." Mrs. McKinney laughed at the **compliment (#85).** Then, just as expected, Jack and Courtney had to pose by the fireplace before they could leave.

The clinic's board of directors was holding the fundraiser at a mansion owned by the local historical society. It was anticipated to be one of Worthington's biggest social events of the year. Everyone of importance would be there. Jack and Courtney arrived to find Ollie talking to his buddy, Mr. Collins. Mr. Collins wasted no time putting the three to work. Jack and Courtney were to help the party planner set the table decorations. It wasn't a difficult job, but it did require making several trips back and forth to the florist's van. Ollie and Mr. Collins were to place the name cards in front of each dinner plate. Jack watched the two work and thought, *does it really take two people to do that?*

Jack, Ollie, and Courtney's final job of the evening was to escort the attendees to their assigned tables after the board members greeted them. The guests began arriving at seven thirty. By eight o'clock the party was in full swing. Dinner was served at eight thirty, followed by a presentation that lasted until ten o'clock. Most people stayed for another hour before leaving. The last guests to go were Mr. and Mrs. Culver. Toward the end of the evening, Jack overheard Mr. Culver say with a lack of **decorum (#86)**, "My car's too drunk to drive," while he and his wife waited for Ollie to give them a ride home.

At the end of the evening, Jack stood with his parents and several of the board members on the fronts steps to the mansion and listened to their conversations. According to the chairman of the board, the fundraiser was an **unequivocal (#87)** success. They had raised $735,000—much more than expected. "This leaves less than a million dollars to go," the chairman said. "We should have enough now to at least start the building."

Jack had never seen his mother this happy. She beamed while she walked arm-in-arm with her husband to their car.

CHAPTER EIGHT

The skies were dark and gloomy on the following Sunday. A constant drizzle filled most of the day. Jack spent the morning in church with his parents and then spent the rest of the afternoon at home. He vegged on the couch while he tried to find ways to get out of cleaning his bedroom. This proved difficult since none of his friends were around. Courtney was visiting her grandmother in Connecticut, and both Ollie and Lip were on vacation with their families.

Just after three o'clock, his mother apparently had enough. Tired of asking her **torpid (#88)** son to get his lazy butt off the couch and clean his room, she took it upon herself to do it. It did not take long for Jack's **apathy (#89)** toward cleaning his room to change. The sound of his mother opening and closing drawers made him jump off the couch. *I hope she's not going through my desk.* Jack leaped up the stairs. "What are you doing?" he asked, standing in the doorway to his bedroom.

"If you're not going to clean this place, then I will." She went around the room and gathered his dirty clothes. "What's in this closet?"

"Stuff."

"What kind of stuff?" His mother opened the door and gasped. "Oh, my god! When was the last time you cleaned it?" She took two steps backward and fanned her nose to **diffuse (#90)** the **noisome (#91)** smell.

"I don't know."

"Start pulling this stuff out. Put your **grimy (#92)** gym clothes in a separate pile and take your cleats to the mudroom. I'll start on your desk."

"No! I'll clean it." Jack's body blocked her from getting too close.

For the next two hours, they cleaned. In between battles over what stayed and what went, they dusted, vacuumed, and polished furniture. When they finished, Dr. Graystone glared at her son. "From now on, the cleaning ladies are coming in here whether you like it or not."

"Whatever," Jack mumbled as he shut the door behind her.

Jack glanced around his bedroom and marveled at how nice it looked. *I should really try to keep it this way. Oh, don't kid yourself. It's going to look like a tornado came through here in a few days.*

Jack flopped onto his perfectly made bed. He laughed to himself and thought, *I can't remember the last time it was made.* He then texted his friends. Courtney was at her grandmother's, bored out of her mind. Lip was somewhere on Interstate 95 fighting with his sister in the back seat of his parent's car. And Ollie had just won a croquet tournament in Upstate New York. Lip, Courtney, and Jack informed Ollie he should probably keep that a secret. At six o'clock, he sent his last group text. It read:

Off to see Comrade Kraskoff. Call me when you get home.

Jack was leaping down the stairs shortly after that.

"Mom, I'm off to Comrade Kraskoff's," he yelled on his way out of the back door. "I'll be home after Reilly's walk."

"Jack, did you forget something?"

Think! What did you forget? "Maybe," he said slowly.

"You forgot Svetlana's present."

"Oh! I knew I was forgetting something." He ran back inside and grabbed a box wrapped in pink and white paper.

Svetlana Romanovna Kraskoff was Jack's Russian tutor. She had begun tutoring him when he was seven, just after he and his family returned from Russia. His parents had hired her so he could continue learning the Russian language. They did not want his year in the Moscow kindergarten to go to waste. Over time, Svetlana became part of the family, almost like an aunt. She even ate most holiday dinners with them.

For almost every Sunday over the last nine years, Jack had spent two hours with Svetlana perfecting his Russian language skills. Now, at sixteen years old, he could speak, read, and write Russian fluently.

During the summer break, however, he would see her only twice a month. He looked forward to seeing her during the summer because there was no pressure to learn anything new. She would cook dinner, and the two would talk in Russian for a couple of hours. Most of the time, Svetlana did the talking. She would tell Jack fascinating stories about living in Communist Russia.

Two knocks on Svetlana's front door and the squeak of its hinges let her know that he had arrived. "Svetlana, I'm here."

Svetlana's house was interesting, to say the least. The rooms were small and jam-packed with an **eclectic (#93)** assortment of furniture and art. The living room was the best example. Almost every square inch of the walls was covered with a picture, painting, or some form of art from all around the world. The furniture was a combination of antiques mixed with modern pieces. Some of these modern pieces looked like they can from outer space.

"I'm in the kitchen."

"Happy birthday. We got you something." Jack placed the gift on the kitchen table and gave her a hug. "Something smells good."

"It's your favorite, beef stroganoff."

Jack grabbed a bottle of water from the fridge before he took a seat at the kitchen table. "So, you're turning forty. How does it feel?"

Svetlana laughed. "I'll be fifty-eight on Tuesday."

Svetlana said few words while she finished cooking the meal. Jack could tell her mind was elsewhere. "Something wrong?"

Steam fogged her glasses when she emptied the pot of boiling noodles into a colander in the sink. "I just got word one of my brothers died."

"I'm sorry. Which brother was it?"

"Yuri."

"Are you going back to Russia for the funeral?"

Svetlana shook her head. "I'll never go back there."

"Never?"

"Never. I told my family when I left that I was never coming back."

"Really, why?"

Svetlana did not answer. "Get the plates and the silverware," she eventually said.

For all the years Jack knew her, Svetlana was very guarded with regards to her personal life. All he gathered was she had been a college professor and had six brothers and four sisters.

As usual, the time with Svetlana flew by. With it approaching nine o'clock, Jack had to leave for Reilly's walk. He collected his furry friend and then started down the path. Like clockwork, the seaplane arrived, did its routine with the powerboat, and then left. The novelty of the seaplane was wearing off. This time, when Jack walked past, he did not stop. He continued along the path while he texted Courtney.

The final stretch of the Ocean Walk was well worn. The gravel had long since washed away, leaving an uneven dirt path scattered with protruding rocks. When Jack neared the sidewalk on Oceanside Drive, he tripped over one of these rocks and lost his balance. As he fell, he let go of Reilly's leash. Reilly, who would never run away, bolted down the path. He jumped over a low hedge and landed in the yard of a large mansion. He then began to bark, and bark, and bark.

"Reilly, get back here," Jack repeated several times while he rose to his feet and wiped the dirt from his hands on his pant legs. Reilly did not respond. *What do I do now?* Jack jogged over to the hedge. He looked to his right and then to his left. *Dammit, I have to go in there and get him.* Climbing over the hedge was not an option. It was more than Jack could scale. His only way into the yard was through an old metal gate. He pressed his face against the cool wrought iron pickets and surveyed the surroundings. The half-moon cast just enough light to see Reilly off in the distance. "Here goes nothing," he whispered before he grabbed the handle and pushed open the gate. The rusty gate hinges let out a loud screech. The sound was so piercing he assumed he had awakened half of the neighborhood. Jack's eyes scanned the large old house while he trespassed into the well-manicured yard. The house was dark, so he assumed no one was home. He turned off his flashlight just in case he was wrong and then continued toward Reilly.

Halfway through the yard, Jack stopped, slapped his knee, and whispered, "Reilly, come here." Reilly did not budge. He was in a frenzy. He bounced back and forth with his tail wagging a mile a minute. By the time Jack reached him, Reilly had stopped barking and now began a high-pitched whine. Jack grabbed his collar. "Calm down, boy," he said several times. He petted the dog's back in an attempt to **quell (#94)** his excitement.

Reilly, however, was not calming down. Jack pointed the flashlight into the shrubbery to inspect the cause of Reilly's excitement. As he looked around, he caught a glimpse of a black object wedged between the branches of a holly bush. *What's that?* Jack leaned forward, but he still did not know. He took one cautious step into the shrubbery and then another. Dried twigs snapped beneath his shoes. When he was three feet away, a pair of binoculars came into view. *I wonder how they got here. They look too expensive for someone to leave outside.* He stopped for a moment—hunched over like an old man—to analyze the situation. *I'd better grab them. I'll return them tomorrow.* He took another step closer. The tips of a holly bush poked through his pants and pricked his right leg. With his left hand holding the flashlight, he crouched down and reached for the binoculars. But just before he grabbed hold, he noticed something that stopped him. Etched into the side of the binoculars was the word, *Anderson.* Jack sprung to his feet and staggered backward, almost tripping over Reilly. He stood motionless while he stared at the binoculars. *These have to be Ian's. I bet that's what he went back inside to get. I need to call the chief.*

Jack reached his trembling hand into his pocket and removed his cell phone. It took three attempts to enter the correct passcode, and then several more to find the chief's number. Finally, he dialed. After a few rings, Chief McKinney answered.

"Chief McKinney, this is Jack. I, I found something you need to see right now."

The chief cleared his throat. "What is it?"

"I was walking Reilly, and he found a pair of binoculars in a bush with the word *Anderson* etched on its side. I think they're Ian's binoculars. I think that's what he went back to get the night he went missing."

"Have you touched them?"

"No."

"Don't! I'll be right over. Where are you?"

"I'm at the end of the Ocean Walk where the path meets Oceanside

Drive. I'm in the yard of the big house that always looks empty. On the opposite side of the hedge along Oceanside Drive. You know where I mean?"

"Yeah. Don't move. I'll be right there."

Jack knelt on one knee next to Reilly. The dew from the grass quickly soaked his pant leg. With his stare fixated on the holly bush that held the binoculars, he stroked Reilly's back and whispered, "Good boy, good boy."

It was quiet. At this time of night, no one was around. There wasn't even a car traveling along Oceanside Drive. Jack's body was tense and his senses heightened. Every sound, from the waves slapping against the rocky shoreline of the cove, to the puffs of wind rustling the leaves of the surrounding trees, resonated in his head. After several minutes of petting, Reilly finally settled down. Jack continued to stare, his mind racing with thoughts of how the binoculars became lodged in the branches of the shrub. *I hope there are clues here, maybe fingerprints or something.* Suddenly, a noise grabbed his attention. From the side of the house came a faint cry. "AHHHH . . . AHHHH," repeated several times. *It sounds like someone moaning in pain. Could it be Ian?*

Although Chief McKinney told him not to move, Jack decided to tie Reilly to a small tree and investigate. He crept to the side of the house, keeping a constant lookout for anything suspicious. When he was a few steps away, a metal cellar bulkhead door came into view. The moans, which came from inside, grew louder. "AHHH . . . AHHH." Now it sounded like someone crying in pain or being tortured. Jack's body trembled. *Do I open it or not?* He leaned forward to reach for the handle but stopped. *I'd better wait for the chief.* Jack stood and was about to head back to Reilly when he heard a sound that made him freeze. *Click, click.* It was the cocking of a gun. Now he felt the cold metal of the barrel pressing against the back of his neck. Jack was in a daze and thought he was going to die.

CHAPTER NINE

"Give me one good reason why I shouldn't kill you right now?" asked an unknown man.

Jack was delirious. Instantly, so many thoughts raced through his typical sixteen-year-old mind: from his parents, to his girlfriend, to all the things he wanted to do in life. And having never been in this situation, he said the first thing that came to him. In a whisper, Jack replied, "Because I haven't done it yet."

After a brief pause, the gunman let out a quick, soft laugh and removed the gun from Jack's neck. "Turn around."

Jack slowly turned, only to be blinded by a powerful flashlight.

"Son, what are you doing? Why are you trying to break into my house?"

Jack was unsure of how much time he had left in this world. So, as quickly as possible, while trying to make sense, he said, "My friend went missing, and his dog found his binoculars in your bushes. Then I heard someone being tortured in your basement. So, I was going to see if it was Ian. I've called the cops, and they'll be here in just a few seconds. So, if you kill me, they'll know. They'll know if Ian's in the basement. So, this is your only chance to get away."

The gunman's forehead wrinkled. "Son, what in the hell are you talking about?"

Before Jack answered, a police officer came around the corner of the house and shone his flashlight on the two. "Both of you, freeze," he yelled. "This is the Worthington Police Department. You with the gun, place it on the ground and take two steps backward."

Without incident, the gunman placed the gun on the ground and backed away. The police officer cautiously approached and grabbed his gun. At this time, a **comely (#95)** woman came around the corner of the house holding a cell phone in her hand. In a **congenial (#96)** voice, she said, "Excuse me, officer. The man with the gun is the homeowner. We're the ones who called you about the burglar. I have the 911 operator on the phone here."

"Miss, stop and don't move." With his eyes darting back and forth between the three individuals, the young police officer reached for his radio. "Base, this is Officer Turner requesting backup." His eyes continued to dart back and forth while the police dispatcher's response blasted out of the radio. "Everyone stay where you are until backup arrives."

The chief was the first to arrive moments later. He entered the driveway with his blue lights flashing. His tires chirped as he came to a stop. He rounded the corner of the house at a jog and asked, "Officer Turner, what's the situation here?" before he came to a stop.

"Well, Chief, as far as I can tell, this young man," pointing the flashlight at Jack, "was trying to break into this house. And this man, who owns the place," now pointing the flashlight at the gunman, "came out to stop him while his wife called 911."

After a short pause, Chief McKinney said, "Jack, come over here."

Jack scurried over to the chief and stood partially behind him—as if the chief was protecting him.

"Chief, you know this young man?" asked Officer Turner.

"Yes, he just called me. He found a pair of binoculars in the bushes that might belong to the missing Anderson boy. I'm here to investigate."

"Oh yeah, I recognize him from the Andersons' house the night the boy went missing."

As soon as Officer Turner stopped talking, more cries came from behind the basement bulkhead door.

"What's that?" asked the chief.

"It sounds like someone in pain," said Officer Turner.

"Chief McKinney, I'm sure they have Ian tied up in the basement."

"Turner, cuff this man and woman while we figure out what's going on here."

As Officer Turner handcuffed the couple, the gunman, who appeared to be in his mid-forties, became **irate (#97)**. "What in the hell are you doing? You're putting us in cuffs, while the little virgin over there was the one trying to break into my house! You should put him in cuffs."

By now, everyone had confused looks on their faces. That is, everyone except Jack. He was **discomfited (#98)** by the gunman's statement. It embarrassed him to the point his face turned beet red.

"Sir, we have probable cause to go into your basement. Are you going to make it easy and give us the keys, or do we have to cut off the lock?"

"The keys are on the table in the foyer. Go get them. We have nothing to hide. We were in Zurich for the last month and just got home a half-hour ago."

By the time Officer Turner returned with the keys, three more police officers were at the house.

"Let me see them," said the gunman. Officer Turner tossed him the keys, forgetting the man's hands were in cuffs. They bounced off his right arm and landed by his feet.

Officer Turner's face turned white. He glanced at the chief before he said, "I'm sorry. I, I forgot…"

"That's okay," said the gunman. He bent over, grabbed the keys, and then rattled through them until he found the right one. "Here. It's this one."

Officer Turner leaned forward and unlocked the bulkhead doors. He opened the left one and then the right one. It was dark inside, and a musty smell permeated the air. Everyone grew anxious while he waved his flashlight into the opening. Then, without warning, another loud moan echoed from within, which was immediately followed by an object catapulting from the basement and into the yard. Everyone gasped and jumped backward.

It took Jack a few seconds to process what had just happened. Then he let out a quick laugh as a gray Persian cat stagger across the yard and into the bushes.

"Well, I believe we found the source of the cries," said the shackled man. "Can you take the cuffs off now?"

"Not just yet," replied the chief. "Turner and Fleming, go in and look around."

The two descended into the dark basement. Moments later, Turner flipped a switch that lit the room. The spectators outside stood motionless—their eyes glued to the bulkhead doors. Nobody said a word. Minutes passed before the duo reappeared. "Chief, there's nothing suspicious down here," said Officer Turner.

"Okay, uncuff these two. I'm sorry to put you through this, but one of your neighbor's kid is missing. This may be our first lead. I'll need to get you and your wife's statement, Mister..."

"Poulter."

"Also, we're going to rope off your entire property as a potential crime scene, so please stay out of the yard for now. And just to be thorough, do you mind if we go through the house?"

"Not at all," said Mr. Poulter. "Do whatever you need."

"Jack, show me where you found the binoculars."

"Follow me."

On the walk to the binoculars, Jack remembered he had tied Reilly to a tree. When they saw him, he was lying in the grass chewing on a stick. Jack pointed to the bush, which Chief McKinney cautiously approached and investigated. He moved the beam from his flashlight throughout the shrubbery and then slowly backed out without touching anything.

"I need to call Mr. Anderson to find out if they're Ian's. If they are, this area is most likely the scene of the crime. Something must have happened on the other side of the hedge, and the binoculars were tossed over here." Before he made the call, he gave his men directions on which areas to barricade. Not only did they barricade the Poulter's property but also the adjacent street and sidewalk.

Chief McKinney walked away to make the phone call. Jack and Reilly did not follow. Instead, they walked back to Officer Turner who was talking to the Poulters.

"Sorry about all this," Jack said to the couple.

"No problem." Mr. Poulter smiled. "Sorry I almost killed you before you got a chance to...you know."

Officer Turner looked back and forth between the two but did not say anything. Jack let out a quick laugh and then looked at the ground. He hoped nobody continued the conversation.

"We were in Europe for the past month and have no idea what's happened around here. What's all this about a missing boy?"

"He just vanished," said Officer Turner.

"I dropped him off at his house around nine o'clock. He was taking Reilly for a walk when I left him. That was the last time anyone saw him. When his parents got home, they found Reilly sitting at the front gate with his leash still attached, but Ian was nowhere to be found."

"Hmm," replied Mr. Poulter with his forehead wrinkled. He was about to ask a question when the chief approached.

"They are Ian's binoculars. Bob Anderson checked the case in Ian's room, and it was empty. I have called the FBI agents assigned to this case, and they're on the way. Mr. Poulter, please don't disturb anything in the yard for right now. It shouldn't take more than a day, and we'll be gone."

"No problem."

"Excuse me, Chief McKinney," said one of the police officers who had inspected the inside of the house.

The chief turned to the man who was walking toward him. "Yes?"

"The house looks clean. I don't see the need to investigate any further."

"Okay. Officer Turner, could you take Mr. and Mrs. Poulter's statements. I need to go and wait for Mr. Anderson."

While Officer Turner took the Poulters' statements, Jack and Reilly stood in the background and watched the activity. A few minutes passed before Jack saw Mr. Anderson's Porsche approach. It came to a stop at the front of the barricade. Chief McKinney hurried over and opened his door. Mr. Anderson did not move. He looked up at the chief, and they had a brief conversation. Jack tried to read their lips but could not tell what they were saying. He knew, however, based on Mr. Anderson's expression, he was upset.

Mr. Anderson shook his head a few times before he slowly got out of the car. The chief grabbed his left arm and helped him to his feet. He kept hold of it on their walk through the yard to the binoculars. With every exterior light on the Poulters' house now illuminated, Jack could see Mr. Anderson nodding as he peered into the shrubs. Before they walked away, Mr. Anderson put his head in his hands for a moment and then wiped his face. The chief continued to hold Mr. Anderson's arm on their walk back to the Porsche. After the chief helped the grieving man back into his car, they had another brief conversation before Mr. Anderson slowly drove away.

Jack looked at the clock on his phone. It read 10:22 p.m. He walked over to Chief McKinney. "Do you mind if I take Reilly home? I'll be right back."

"No, Jack, I don't mind. Actually, we're through with you here. So, you can go home."

"Well, if you don't mind, I'd like to come back and watch what's going on."

"Okay, but stay out of everyone's way and make sure your parents know where you are."

Jack made a quick call to his father to explain the situation before he and Reilly jogged the last quarter mile to the Andersons' house. When they approached the back door, a strange feeling overcame him. He did not know what to say if he encountered Mr. Anderson. He hoped he had gone to bed. But, as he inserted the key into the lock, Mr. Anderson walked into the kitchen and opened the refrigerator. Jack finished opening the door and entered with Reilly at his side.

"Hi, Mr. Anderson."

Mr. Anderson tried to smile. "Well, hopefully, we can start making some progress now. Chief McKinney told me the whole story. Thanks for being on the ball, Jack. And you too, Reilly." He bent over and petted Reilly on the head.

"You're welcome," was all Jack could reply.

"If you need to take tomorrow off, it's okay. Call Chambers in the morning and tell him I said it's all right. I'll see you later, Jack."

"Good night."

Mr. Anderson looked at Reilly and slapped his knee. "Come on, boy." Reilly lumbered over to his master, and then they disappeared up the back staircase.

On the drive back to the crime scene, Jack was overwhelmed with sorrow. He could not erase the image of Mr. Anderson standing in the kitchen, staring blankly into the fridge.

By the time he returned, the two FBI agents had arrived. They were not hard to miss. They wore dark blue jackets with FBI in large, yellow print on the back. Jack recognized the men. They had come to his house to question him a few days after Ian's disappearance. The two men had taken over control of the situation. No one challenged their **ascendancy (#99)** while they spouted orders to the chief's men.

Jack approached Officer Turner who was standing by himself. "Found any clues?"

"Not yet. The crime scene unit is on their way. They should be here soon. Hopefully, they'll find something when they process the area."

From across the yard, one of the FBI agents hollered for Officer Turner. "Oh, great. I wonder what he wants," mumbled Officer Turner before he left.

Jack stood alone for a moment and observed the activity. On the other side of the yard, he saw the Poulters standing by themselves. He decided to walk over and introduce himself.

As Jack approached, Mr. Poulter extended his hand. "We haven't officially met. I'm Chris Poulter, and this is my assistant Allison Martin."

Jack shook both of their hands. "Graystone, Jack Graystone. Nice to meet you."

Chris heard a ding from his cell phone. He looked at the text message, laughed, and then showed it to Allison. "I wondered how long it will take."

Not knowing what they were talking about, Jack smiled and did not say a word.

The three stood silently for a moment and watched several police officers scurrying about the property. They were unrolling yards of yellow plastic tape with the words, 'POLICE LINE DO NOT CROSS,' printed in black. Chris eventually broke the silence when he turned to Jack and asked, "When did you say this boy went missing?"

"Two Fridays ago."

"You said you saw him leave for his walk?"

"Yeah."

"And the dog was waiting at a gate when his parents came home?"

Jack nodded. "What kind of gate was this?"

"The gate for their driveway. They live just around the corner. It's the house with the ivy-covered wall and big metal gate."

Chris smiled. "That describes half the houses around here." Jack laughed. "When you were leaving, did you close the gate?" Jack nodded. "You're a hundred percent sure?"

"Yeah."

"Where does this boy walk his dog?"

"Ian would leave out of his backyard and walk along the Ocean Walk until he got here. Then they would walk the rest of the way home on the sidewalk along Oceanside Drive."

"Ian, that's his name?" Jack nodded. "So, we know something happened to Ian on his walk, most likely on the other side of that hedge." Chris pointed toward the shrubbery that contained the binoculars. He paused and stared at the ground for a moment before he turned to Allison. "He clearly was abducted, but why?"

"That's the million-dollar question," she said, nodding her head.

Chris glanced at Jack. "When was the last time you saw him?"

"Around nine fifteen."

"Where did you go?"

"To the movies."

"Do you have people who can confirm this?" Chris gave Jack a suspicious stare.

"Yeah, lots of them." Chris kept his eyes locked on Jack's. Jack glanced at Allison and then back toward Chris. He did not know what to say.

"How well do you know Ian?"

"Not very. I just met him earlier that evening. He's new in town."

"Hmm. So, you probably don't know much about his personal life?" Jack shook his head. "No, I don't."

Chris went silent and stared at the ground with his forehead wrinkled. This lasted about a minute, and then the questions continued with each one getting more in-depth.

Man, how many questions can he think of? It sounds like he's a detective.

The questions stopped when the two FBI agents approached Chris.

They each extended their hand. "Mr. Poulter, we're big fans of your work. If you can offer any insight, we'd greatly appreciate it. Here are our cards. If you think of anything, please call us."

Chris shook both men's hand. "Thanks. Jack has been filling me in with all the information he has. If you have any other information, I'd like to know it."

"Unfortunately, we have nothing else," replied the other agent. "Jack knows as much as we do. We're hoping we find something tonight. We'll let you know if we find any clues." The two men excused themselves and went back to work.

"What was that all about?" asked Jack.

"Well, I'm good friends with the head of the FBI. Normally, I wouldn't have said anything. But these two guys looked like jerks running around here firing orders at everyone. I wanted to bring them down a few notches."

Jack and Allison laughed.

"Is that who you were texting?"

"Yep."

"What do you do, Mr. Poulter?"

"Jack, you can call me Chris. I hate being called Mr. Poulter."

"Okay, then. What do you do, Chris?"

"Well, I have several careers. Mostly I'm an author of spy and mystery novels, but I also do some consulting detective work."

Jack glanced at the house and then at the new Aston Martin parked in the garage. *Wow. Who'd of thought you could make this much money from writing books.* "Sounds cool. It must pay well." Jack nodded toward the house.

Chris smiled. "It pays the bills."

Jack looked at his cell phone and saw his curfew was in five minutes. "It was nice meeting both of you. I have to get home before midnight, or I'll get in trouble."

"Nice meeting you, too," Chris replied.

Allison smiled. "Yes, it was nice meeting you, too."

Jack turned to walk away, but Chris stopped him. "Hey, Jack, this case intrigues me. I might have more questions for you. Do you think you can stop by tomorrow sometime?"

"Sure. I work until five. I can stop by before I walk Reilly. Is that okay?"

"That'll be perfect. See you then."

CHAPTER TEN

The next day, Jack followed his typical routine. He arrived home from work and entered through the back door. He found his parents in the kitchen. His father was leaning against the refrigerator drinking a beer. His mother was standing over the stove stirring a pot of spaghetti sauce. They were in the middle of a conversation, which stopped when Jack entered the room. Since he had not seen either of them in the morning, they were full of questions and the interrogation began.

"Jack, what happened last night?" asked his father.

Jack spent the next few minutes explaining the events of the previous night. When he finished, he said, "Chris said he's a detective. He asked me to stop by tonight to go over the case. He's going to try to solve it."

"Really? He's a detective and lives in that huge house?"

"Well, he said he also writes books."

"Did he tell you his full name?"

"Yeah. He said it was Chris Poulter. He must be important because he knows the head of the FBI. He texted him last night."

Mr. Graystone's forehead wrinkled. "He didn't say his name was Christian Poulter, did he?"

"Nope, just Chris Poulter."

"Come with me."

Jack followed his father into his study. The room contained a desk, two chairs, and walls lined with bookshelves. Jack's dad was an **erudite (#100)** man who read constantly and had a well-rounded knowledge of the world. He walked over to the far wall and removed a book. It came from a group all written by a man named Christian

Poulter. Mr. Graystone turned to the back cover and pointed to a picture of a man sitting next to two golden retrievers. "Is this the man you talked to last night?"

Jack looked at the picture, and sure enough, it was Chris. "Yeah, it is."

"And he wants you to come over this evening to go over the case?"

"Yeah, is that okay?"

"Sure. You do realize he's one of the **preeminent (#101)** authors of our time?"

"I could tell he must've been important since the FBI guys were kissing his butt."

***

That night, around seven thirty, Jack went to Chris's house. He drove his Explorer up the cobblestone driveway, parked near the detached garage, and then walked to the massive Victorian mansion. Nervously, he climbed the steps to the large front porch. After he rang the doorbell, he caught a glimpse of Allison approaching through the leaded glass doors. She greeted Jack with a big smile. "Hello, Jack. Come in. Chris is in his study. He's been expecting you."

"Hi," was Jack's only response before she escorted him to the study.

They entered the study through a set of double doors. The large room consisted of dark wood-paneled walls with several built-in bookcases. An oversized wooden desk, along with two maroon leather chairs, occupied the center of the room. Off to one side was a large dry-erase board, covered with writing. Chris stood and approached. "Hey, Jack. Thanks for coming."

Jack extended his hand. "Hello, Chris." While Jack shook his hand, something caught his eye. From behind the desk emerged a perfectly groomed golden retriever wagging his tail.

"Jack, this is Sherlock."

"Wow, that's a beautiful dog."

When he finished, Jack caught a glimpse of another golden retriever entering the study. This dog's tale was also wagging, and he appeared to be smiling.

"Jack, this is Sherlock's brother. Of course, you know what his name must be."

Jack was dumbfounded. *How could I know the dog's name?* "Uh," Jack shrugged his shoulders. "I have no idea."

"It's easy. His name is Mycroft."

And how was I supposed to know that?

"Surely, with that knowledge, you can guess the cat's name."

Jack squinted his eyes and shook his head.

"Jack, this will be your first detective assignment. Tomorrow, I want you to tell me the name of my cat. And don't ask Allison."

"Okay, I'll work on that."

"Come over here to the board. I have started making a few charts. First, I made a timeline of events. Second, a list of all the facts. Third, a list of potential suspects. And fourth, possible motives."

Jack examined the board. When he viewed the list of suspects, he saw his name. The other names included Mr. and Mrs. Anderson, the first Mrs. Anderson, Brian Carter, Bobby Anderson, and Unknown Suspect #1.

"Wait, do you think I did it?"

"No, I don't believe there's a snowball's chance in hell you did it. But until you're one hundred percent cleared, you'll remain on the board. Based on the timeline, you had about twenty minutes to commit a crime and get to the movies. That seems almost impossible. Besides, you don't act like a guilty person." Chris pointed to the board. "Let's examine the timeline. Does everything appear to be correct?"

"Some of the times are off. Do you want me to change them?"

"Sure, that'd be helpful."

Jack grabbed the eraser. "We arrived at his house at nine o'clock, not eight forty-five. That's what time we left my house." The marker squeaked as he changed the numbers. "And his parents got home at eleven fifteen, not eleven o'clock."

Chris nodded and then walked to the window. He stood motionless, hands in his pants pockets, looking outside. "Two hours," he mumbled and then returned to the board. "Okay. So, this is what we know. He disappeared between nine fifteen and eleven fifteen. And our only clue is the binoculars in the bushes." He glanced at Jack. "Let's analyze this clue. How could they have ended up in the bushes?"

"He tossed them there."

"Okay. But why there and not somewhere else?"

"Because someone attacked him on the other side of the hedge."

Chris tilted his head. "Yeah, that's a strong possibility. But what if he ran into my yard trying to hide or get away from someone. And that's where they caught him."

Jack nodded. "Yeah. If the attacker knew you weren't home, they could've done anything to him, and nobody would know."

Chris tapped Jack's shoulder with the back of his hand. "That's a good point."

"Did the crime scene unit find anything in your yard?"

"I talked to one of the investigators, and he said they found nothing suspicious." Chris grabbed a marker and made several notes on the board. "So, he could have been taken from my backyard or the sidewalk on the other side of the hedge. Those are the two most likely possibilities." Chris walked back to the window. "The location of the binoculars interests me, though. If someone knew Ian's routine, they would know he passes my house around nine thirty. So, if they wanted to abduct him, they could park at the end of the Ocean Walk and grab him as he stepped onto the sidewalk. They could easily throw him in a car and drive off."

"Or, if they knew you weren't home, they could have grabbed him when he walked by your gate." The room went silent. "Chris," Jack said softly, looking at the ground, "do you think he's dead?"

Chris sighed. "Honestly, there's a good chance he is."

"Why's that?"

"Because no one has called for a ransom." Chris glanced at Jack. "They would have called by now."

"Well, what if he ran away?"

"Do you know if he's ever run away before?"

"His dad said he hasn't."

"I think that's unlikely. Ian seems to have a pretty good life. And, as far as we know, he's never been in trouble."

"What if his parents abuse him and he finally had enough?"

"Again, I think that's highly unlikely. There would've been signs."

Chris shook his head. "But you never know what goes on behind closed doors."

"What if he fell into the water and drowned?"

Chris paused and rubbed his chin. "Then, how would the binoculars get in the bushes?"

"Oh, yeah. You're right." They both stood silently staring at the board for a moment before Jack said, "Mr. Anderson told me that the FBI ruled out Brian Carter and Bobby Anderson as suspects."

"Really? Do you know why?"

Jack shook his head. "They wouldn't tell him."

Chris quickly glanced at Jack. "They wouldn't tell him. That doesn't sound good."

"They said they had to tie up some loose ends before they gave out any information."

"That's interesting. If they were positively ruled out, there would be no reason not to tell him why. They must be holding something back."

"My gut tells me Brian's involved."

Chris nodded. "Mine, too."

Jack looked at the clock on his phone. "Chris, I have to go and walk Reilly."

"Okay. There's a lot to digest here."

"If you want, I can stop by tomorrow. Remember, I need to tell you your cat's name."

"That's right, you do," Chris said with a smile. "I'll try to get in touch with my contact at the FBI tomorrow to find out more about Brian Carter and Bobby Anderson. Although," he paused to think, "I believe he's on vacation this week. Either way, we can still discuss the case."

CHAPTER ELEVEN

The next morning, Jack was off work and slept until ten. He grabbed two Pop Tarts on his way out the back door and headed to Courtney's house. They planned to spend the day at the Worthington Bath and Tennis Club, a private beach club of which both families were members.

The day was perfect. There were few clouds in the sky, and a slight breeze blowing off the Atlantic Ocean made the sun's heat bearable. The two spent the rest of the morning lying next to each other on oversized beach towels. While they constantly flipped from their stomachs onto their backs in an effort to even their tans, Jack enlightened Courtney on the events of the past two days. The story amazed her. "That beats all the excitement I had. I watched my grandmother knit for two days while she told me stories about when she was young. She told me about all her boyfriends. I know I shouldn't say this because she's my grandma and all, but it sounds like she kind of slept around."

Jack laughed and then flipped onto his back.

Ollie and Lip, whose families were also members, arrived around noon. This was Ollie's first time back to the beach club since the previous summer. Toward the end of last season, Ollie had an altercation with a lifeguard. The lifeguard asked him several times to stop using **indecorous (#102)** language while playing beach volleyball. When the lifeguard told him to leave the premises, Ollie, acting very immaturely, flipped him off and mooned him. These **puerile (#103)** actions **contravened (#104)** the club's policies and resulted in Ollie's permanent expulsion. Since he had nothing to do during this summer except stay at home and irritate his parents, his father convinced, or probably bribed, the club manager to lift his son's expulsion.

"So, Ollie, do you think you can keep your suit on this year?" asked Jack.

While Jack, Courtney, and Lip laughed, Ollie jumped up, turned, and started to pull down his boardshorts. "I came prepared this year. I'm wearing a Speedo underneath." He finished dropping his suit to reveal a fluorescent green Speedo. The three laughed. And before he lay back down, he raised his hands. "Look. I even taped my middle and forefingers together, so I can't flip anyone off."

Jack shook his head. "Ollie, you're an idiot."

The four hung out at the beach for the rest of the afternoon. When they weren't playing beach volleyball or swimming in the club's pool, Jack and Ollie alternated using the stand-up paddleboard Ollie received as a Christmas present. Neither of them had tried paddleboarding before. But with every turn, the **neophytes (#105)** became more proficient and went a little farther into the ocean. One time, when Ollie was well offshore, Jack and Courtney noticed he had taken off his boardshorts. He wore only the green Speedo. You could see him from a mile away.

Lip refused to try the paddleboard. Actually, he was **phobic (#106)** about going into the ocean. Lip would never admit it, but he was afraid a shark would eat him. So, he stayed on land, occasionally launching a model rocket, which either Jack or Ollie would paddle into the ocean to retrieve. They found about half of them.

Since Courtney had to be at her hostess job at Scully's Seafood Restaurant by five o'clock, the couple gathered their belongings just after three. They said goodbye to friends, and after Jack lugged two beach bags to the Explorer, they headed to Courtney's house.

Throughout the day, when Jack wasn't swimming, playing beach volleyball, or paddleboarding, he thought about the Anderson case. He analyzed what little information they had and tried to think of new lines of investigation. But he came up with nothing. His thoughts kept returning to Chris's comment that the FBI must be holding something back.

Courtney had her eyes fixed on Jack who was staring straight ahead.

He had not said a word the entire time they drove along Oceanside Drive. Finally, she tapped his shoulder. "What's the matter?"

"I keep thinking of a comment Chris made about the Anderson case."

"What'd he say?"

"Mr. Anderson said the FBI ruled out his son and the video store manager as suspects, but they wouldn't tell him why. Chris said that sounds suspicious. He thinks the FBI is keeping something from Mr. Anderson." Jack shook his head. "I'd sure like to see the files on those two guys."

"I bet my dad has a copy in his office."

Jack's eyes widened. He looked at Courtney with a grin. "I bet he does." He touched her hand. "I want to see them."

"How do you plan on doing that?"

Jack rubbed his forehead. "Why don't we stop by his office? Then you can distract him while I look at the files."

Courtney glanced at Jack. "How am I going to do that?"

Jack's mind went a mile a minute while he tried to think of a **surreptitious (#107)** plan. With the police station swarming with people, he knew they had to be very quiet, extremely cautious, and maintain the utmost secrecy. If anyone found out what they were doing, they would be in big trouble. "I know what we'll do. Tell him one of your favorite customers wants to buy two of the Police Youth Athletic League fundraiser shirts. When he goes to the storage room to get them, you can stand guard at the door while I look for the files. How does that sound?"

"Sounds great, but it won't work."

"Why's that?"

"Because my father would never leave the files out in the open. If he's not using them or he leaves his office, they get locked up."

"Oh, crap." *How am I going to see those files?*

"But," Courtney paused.

"But what?"

"I think he has a key to his filing cabinet hidden in his office."

"Where?"

"In a coffee cup full of change on the bookshelf behind his desk."

"How'd you know that?"

"About a year ago we stopped by after we went out for dinner. He wanted to grab a file to take home with him, but he forgot his keys. I watched him dig through the change and remove a key that unlocked it."

"Do you think it's still there?"

Courtney smiled. "We won't know unless we look."

Jack steered the Explorer toward the police station. After he pulled into a parking space at the far end of the lot, he looked into Courtney's eyes. "Are you sure you want to do this? If you don't, I'll understand."

Courtney smiled and nodded. "Yeah. I want to do it." She leaned over and kissed his cheek. "I feel like Nancy Drew."

Jack laughed, and then he handed her thirty dollars to pay for the shirts.

Jack and Courtney were holding hands when they entered the police station. They were greeted by Mrs. White, the police station's longtime receptionist. Mrs. White, an **amiable (#108)** woman in her late fifties, welcomed the two with her usual smile. "What are you two kids up to today?"

"We just left the beach. Now we need to buy a couple of shirts for one of my customers at the restaurant. Is my dad in his office?"

"Yes, dear. I'll tell him you're heading back."

"Thanks, Mrs. White," said Jack and Courtney in unison.

While the two made their way to the chief's office, Jack glanced at Courtney and smiled. "Courtney, your flip-flops sound like a dying duck quacking."

Chief McKinney was at his desk flipping through a stack of papers when the two appeared in his doorway. Courtney gave a quick knock to get his attention. "Daddy, is this a bad time to see you?"

"Princess, there's never a bad time for you." Courtney shuffled over and hugged her father. "To what do I owe the pleasure of your company this afternoon?"

"Daddy, one of my favorite customers from the restaurant wants to buy two shirts for the Police Youth Athletic League fundraiser." Could you get me a medium and an extra-large?" She handed him the thirty dollars and gave him a smile.

"What color do you want?"

"Dark blue."

"Okay, I'll be right back." The chief left the room and headed for the storage closet that contained the shirts. With the closet on the opposite side of the station, Jack estimated he had only four or five minutes to get his information.

Courtney stood with her back against the door jamb, half inside, half outside of the room. After her father disappeared around the corner, she glanced at Jack and mouthed, "Go."

Jack grabbed the coffee cup from the bookshelf and placed it on the chief's desk. The metal coins clinked against the porcelain as his fingers searched for the key. "Got it."

"Try the top drawer first. That's where he keeps the most current cases."

Jack nodded. He took a deep breath to settle his nerves before he inserted the key and unlocked the drawer. When he pulled on the handle, the drawer let out a loud screech that filled the quiet room. He glanced at Courtney. She put her index finger to her lips.

The drawer contained several brown accordion files. Each file had a label on the top right corner indicating the corresponding case. Jack scanned them until he found the one labeled, *'Anderson Case.'* He removed the file, placed it on the chief's desk, and then thumbed through the contents until he found a folder labeled, *'Suspects.'* Inside this folder were the written statements, interview transcripts, and other pertinent information for each suspect. He shuffled through the pages until he found Bobby Anderson's information. Jack set his iPhone to the camera mode and snapped several pictures. Next, he looked for Brian Carter's information. Again, he shuffled through the pages. But after looking through them twice, he found nothing. *Dammit, where the hell can it be?* His heart pounded faster while time quickly ticked away.

Courtney coughed to get Jack's attention. "My father's coming," she whispered, trying not to move her lips.

"Stall him. I'm almost done."

Courtney left the doorway and took several squeaky steps down the hallway to intercept the chief. Jack could barely hear their conversation but knew they were standing still. Courtney's flip-flops would let him know when they were getting close.

Since Brian Carter's information was not in the suspect folder, Jack knew he had to look elsewhere. *Where can it be? It has to be in one of the other folders.* He found a folder labeled, '*Working Leads.*' *I bet it's in here.* He looked inside and saw a file with Brian Carter's name on it. *Great! I found it.* He grabbed his iPhone, but when he opened the file to photograph the contents, his heart sank in his chest. The file was empty.

Jack heard the squeak from Courtney's flip-flops and knew he was out of time. He quickly put the folders back into the brown accordion file and replaced it in the filing cabinet. After he pushed the key into the coffee cup, which he replaced on the bookshelf, he scurried away from the desk. By the time the chief entered the office, Jack was sitting in a chair reading a magazine. "You ready to go?" he said casually, trying not to give any indication as to the **furtiveness (#109)** of their visit. "You don't want to be late for work."

"Yeah, I'm ready." She hugged her father. "Thank you, Daddy. I'll see you tonight after work."

It was not until the two exited the police station that Courtney grabbed Jack's arm and asked, "What did you find?"

"Well, I found information on Bobby Anderson's in the '*Suspects*' folder. But there was nothing on Brian Carter."

"Really?"

"Yeah. So, I looked in a folder labeled, 'Working Leads,' and I found a file with Brian's name on it. But when I opened it up, it was empty."

"That doesn't sound good."

"The FBI must know something."

Courtney nodded. "Yeah, but what?"

"I don't know. I think we need to do our own investigation. Let's talk to Ollie. He knows Brian Carter. Maybe we can find out something through him."

***

That evening, around seven o'clock, Jack went to his computer to determine the name of Chris's cat. He typed in Sherlock and Mycroft. Several hits popped up that talked about Sherlock Holmes and his brother Mycroft Holmes. That made sense since Chris wrote mystery novels. He read several articles and concluded the cat's name was most likely Dr. Watson, Sherlock's assistant. But, after a few more articles, he realized the cat's name must be Professor Moriarty. Professor Moriarty was Sherlock Holmes's nemesis in several of the mysteries. Since cats and dogs usually do not get along, it would make sense for Chris to call his cat Professor Moriarty. Armed with this knowledge, he drove to Chris's house.

Jack leaped up the porch stairs and rang the doorbell. Within seconds, Sherlock and Mycroft were at the door barking. Their tails were wagging a mile a minute. Chris held the dogs by their collar while he signaled for Jack to enter. "Hey, Jack, did you do your homework?" Chris released the dogs. They immediately converged on Jack looking for any form of attention.

"Yup. I even did some extra credit." Both dogs rubbed against Jack's legs as he walked into the study.

"Go lay down." Chris snapped his fingers and pointed at two dog beds in the corner of the room. Sherlock and Mycroft quickly obeyed. "Have a seat, Jack." Chris patted the back of one of the two leather chairs as he walked to his desk. Jack sat. Sherlock and Mycroft were at his back. Their tails continued to wag. He could hear them smacking against the wood-paneled walls.

The leather chair Jack sat on had a slippery texture. Coupled with the slick nylon material of his boardshorts, and he had trouble sitting still. His butt wanted to slide toward the end of the seat. He did not want to appear uncomfortable, so he placed both hands on the wooden arms and held himself in place. It did not take long for the muscles in his arms to tire.

"Well, what do you think his name is?"

Jack explained the process he went through on his internet search and explained how he deduced his conclusion. When he finished, he said, "So, I think the cat's name is Professor Moriarty."

Chris laughed. "You're absolutely correct. Good job. I see you got the relationship between Sherlock and Moriarty to that of cats and dogs.

We call him 'Mory' for short. So, you mentioned you did some extra credit?"

"Yes. Open your email."

Jack removed his iPhone from his pocket, and as his butt slid toward the end of the leather chair, made several keystrokes that forwarded eight pictures to Chris.

Chris looked at his inbox to find an email from Jack.

"Open it up."

When it opened, Chris could see the pictures of Bobby Anderson's statement. He read them and then glanced at Jack with a questioning face. "Where'd you get this?"

"My girlfriend, Courtney, is Chief McKinney's daughter. When we stopped by his office this afternoon, Courtney distracted him while I looked through the case file."

Chris finished reading the notes and then looked at Jack. "As an adult, I must tell you what you've done is illegal and don't do it again. But as a fellow sleuth, I'll tell you good job. Did you read through this?"

"Yeah, I did."

"So, Bobby Anderson was in a drug rehab facility. Most likely, it'd be impossible for him to leave and come back. They probably aren't telling Mr. Anderson for privacy reasons."

"Yeah, that makes sense."

"Where's Brian Carter's information?"

"Well, here's the strange thing," Jack said, scratching his head. "I found Bobby Anderson's information in a folder labeled, *'Suspects.'* I looked through that folder twice, but I never found any information on Brian Carter. So, I looked through the other folders and found one labeled, *'Working Leads.'* Inside this folder was a file with Brian's name on it. But when I opened the file, it was empty."

"Really?"

"Yeah. There was nothing in it."

"Hmm...That's interesting. I bet the FBI knows something that they're not even telling Chief McKinney."

"That's what I think. But what could it be?"

Chris shook his head. "It could be anything."

The two continued to talk about the case for another hour. Several times during their conversation, Jack walked to the dry erase board and either pointed to something or wrote a note. Every time he moved or made eye contact with Sherlock and Mycroft, they sat up with their tails wagging. Mycroft always had a tennis ball in his mouth.

Since Jack's arms had gone numb from propping himself up, he stood most of the time. He did not have the heart to tell Chris that his leather chairs, which looked expensive, were extremely uncomfortable. Eventually, there was a lull in the conversation, and Jack looked at his iPhone. "Chris, it's almost nine o'clock. I have to go and walk Reilly. Call me if anything comes up."

"Jack, you always check your phone for the time. Don't you own a watch?"

"I did, but I broke it several months ago. I'm going to buy a new one as soon as I save enough money."

"Stop by tomorrow. I have a few of old watches lying around. I'll give you one."

"Wow, that'd be great. Thanks, Chris. I'll see you tomorrow."

CHAPTER TWELVE

The next evening, Jack arrived at Chris's house around eight. After the usual greeting by Sherlock and Mycroft, he and Chris went into the study to discuss the case. Several minutes into their discussion, Chris changed the subject. "Jack, there's something I want to show you. Can you keep a secret?"

That's a strange question. "Yeah, I can." His forehead wrinkled. "Why do you ask?"

Chris smiled. "Oh, it's nothing illegal. I just want to keep it a secret."

"What are you talking about?" Jack asked cautiously.

"Come over here." Chris walked over to one of the built-in bookcases. Jack followed. Chris reached to the top left corner, placed his hand behind the molding, and then released a hidden latch. He knelt and released another latch at the bottom. "This is what I wanted to show you." He then stood and pulled the bookcase toward him. Behind the bookcase was a steel vault door with a built-in combination lock.

"What's this?"

"It's my spy room," Chris said while he entered the combination. "When I write books, many of my characters use different types of gadgets for their espionage activities." Chris opened the door and flipped a switch on the wall. Several fluorescent lights hummed and flickered a few times before they lit a room six feet in depth that ran the length of the study. The room had shelves extending along each side filled with all types of equipment. "Many of these items were given to me by the manufacturers who try to get free advertising in my books. I test each of them in order to understand how they work. This makes my writing more accurate and my books more **plausible (#110)**."

Jack gazed throughout the room and saw several shelves with labels for such items as: listening devices, cameras, binoculars, video surveillance equipment, tracking devices, and more.

"This is incredible. It looks like you have everything you need for spying."

"Yeah, there aren't many gadgets I don't have, or at least, that I haven't tried."

The two walked through the room and inspected the gadgets. When they arrived at the video surveillance section, Jack browsed through the assortment of cameras. They ranged in size, and several resembled items such as radios and clocks. Jack smiled and glanced at Chris. "Don't let my friend Ollie see these. Who knows where he'd want to hide them?"

Chris laughed. They continued to look throughout the shelves until Chris stopped in front of a section labeled *'Miscellaneous.'* "This is what I wanted to show you." He reached above his head, grabbed what appeared to be a brown leather jewelry box, and placed it on the shelf in front of him. The top of the box had a glass insert that revealed several watches. The bottom portion of the box had two drawers.

Chris pulled opened the bottom drawer. "I have several of my old watches here. They're mostly Breitlings. Since the main characters in my books always wear their watches, they send me free samples. I get two or three a year. I have so many watches that I end up giving some of them away." Chris pointed to six watches in the bottom drawer. "Do you like any of these?"

Jack glanced over the watches, and one, in particular, caught his eye. "I like this one," he said, pointing to a watch with a silver metal band and an orange face.

Chris removed the watch from the drawer and gave it a quick examination. "Actually, I can give you any of these watches, except this one."

"Okay, I like this one, too." Jack pointed to a similar watch with a black face.

"That's a good one." Chris handed Jack the watch.

"Chris, can I ask what's so special about the watch with the orange face? They both look about the same to me."

"It's one of the original Breitling Emergency watches. It has a built-in personal locator beacon."

"That's cool. How does it work?"

Chris pointed at the watch. "You unscrew this knob and pull out the antennae. This activates a beacon, which sends a signal from the watch into the sky. Planes flying overhead can detect the signal and then alert the authorities. Satellites used to monitor this frequency for these distress signals, but they stopped several years ago. So, it's not as helpful anymore. However, it's better than nothing."

"Well, if it's better than nothing, why don't you still wear it?"

"They came out with a new Emergency watch. It sends a signal on two different frequencies that are monitored by satellites."

"Do you have one of those?"

Chris nodded. "I have two." He pointed at two watches under the glass case. "The one with the blue face and the one with the black face."

Jack leaned forward to get a better look. "Someday I'm going to have a watch like that."

Chris sighed. "I'd give you my old one, but I don't know if I can."

'Why's that?"

"It's a long story. But basically, it's currently registered in Switzerland. And to use it now, it has to be reregistered in the states with the FAA."

"Why's that a problem?"

Chris shrugged his shoulders. "Actually, I don't know if it is." He picked up the watch and examined it again. "I have two other Emergency watches. I'm never going to use it. I guess I can give it to you. But listen. This is a serious piece of equipment. If it's activated by accident, there is an enormous fine." He handed the watch to Jack.

Jack examined it from all angles. "I don't know. This looks really expensive. I wouldn't feel right taking it."

"Well, they're not cheap. But I'm never going to use it again. So, it's up to you. It's yours if you want it."

"Okay, I guess I'll take it if you really don't need it."

"I should have its original box around here somewhere." Chris knelt in front of the shelves and dug through an assortment of boxes. "Here it is." He placed the Breitling in the box and then handed it to Jack.

"Listen," he said while they walked to the front door. "Before you use this watch, you need to visit Mr. Overton at Overton Jewelers. He needs to register it. Since the watch came straight from the factory and it's registered in Switzerland, there are special registration instructions. He knows me and knows what to do. Ask him to adjust the band for you. If there's any cost, tell him to send me the bill. I'll call him tomorrow and tell him you'll be stopping by. Got it?"

"Got it. I'll stop by after work." Jack headed toward the Explorer with a huge smile on his face. After he opened the driver's door, he turned to his friend. "Thanks again," he said with a wave.

CHAPTER THIRTEEN

Thursdays were typically slow at Anderson Porsche and today was no exception. By four o'clock, Jack had finished washing the last car. He handed Mr. Barrini the key and then asked if he could leave an hour early. Mr. Barrini was agreeable to his request. So, Jack jumped into the Explorer and headed home.

Jack showered, put on a pair of khakis and a button-down shirt, and then headed over to Overton Jewelers. Mr. Overton was the **purveyor (#111)** of the most exclusive jewelry in town. He sold high-end watches and gold and diamond jewelry.

With his watch in a brown paper bag, Jack entered the store. The place was impressive. The floors were marble, and several crystal chandeliers hung from the ceiling. Aside from one clerk, he was the only other person in the building. Jack approached the well-dressed man who was thumbing through a stack of receipts. He stood silently on the opposite side of a glass display case. After a moment, the clerk looked up and asked, "May I help you?" with a **supercilious (#112)** tone.

"Yes, I need to speak with Mr. Overton. Is he available?"

"What's it pertaining to?"

"I need to get my watch registered and the band adjusted. Mr. Overton is expecting me."

"Mr. Overton isn't here right now. I'm the manager and do all the registrations of watches. Mr. Overton is a very busy man."

"When will he be here?"

The clerk tilted his head. "He doesn't keep a set schedule. I don't know when he'll be here. Kid, I have work to do. Do you want your watchband adjusted? Whether or not you talk to him, I'll be the one doing the work."

Jack was unsure of what to do. What the clerk said made sense. After he thought about it for a few seconds, he decided to let him register the watch and make the necessary adjustments. The brown paper bag crackled as Jack reached in and removed the Breitling box. He placed the box on the glass case and then slid it toward the clerk. The man's eyes opened wide in surprise. He looked at the watch and then at Jack. The **juxtaposition (#113)** of a teenager with a Breitling caused wrinkles to form on his forehead. "Uh, where did you get this watch?"

Jack wanted to say; it's none of your business where I got it you meddling jerk. But he kept his cool and calmly replied, "A friend gave it to me."

The **officious (#114)** clerk glanced at Jack and frowned. "A friend gave it to you. This is an expensive watch. And he just gave it to you?"

"Yeah, he has several of them. He gets them for free."

The clerk, still frowning, removed the watch, examined it, and then went to his computer. After typing what appeared to be the serial number, he said, "I need to get some paperwork from my office. I'll be back momentarily." He excused himself and then left for several minutes.

"It'll only be a few more minutes. I have to finish filling out these forms. Then I can adjust the band."

While the clerk completed the forms, Jack caught a glimpse of a police car stopping in front of the store. He ignored the distraction and continued to gaze at his new Breitling watch. Upon hearing the front door open, the clerk stepped back from the counter and exclaimed, "That's him, officer!"

Jack's eyes were the size of golf balls. "What's happening? Why are you pointing at me?" When he turned toward the police officer, he recognized the man. It was Officer Turner.

Officer Turner shook his head. "Jack, what've you gotten into this time?"

Before Jack answered, the clerk asked, "You know this kid?"

"Yeah, he dates the chief of police's daughter. I hardly think he's a criminal."

The clerk tilted his head, squinted his eyes, and pointed to the computer. "Well, he's trying to register a stolen watch."

"Stolen? Christian Poulter gave it to me!"

The clerk shook his head. "Christian Poulter, the famous author gave you a six-thousand-dollar watch. Yeah, and J. K. Rowling gave me a Rolex."

Jack took **umbrage (#115)** to the clerk's accusations. While anger filled his body, he quickly explained to Officer Turner how he had acquired the watch. "I don't think a man as rich and famous as Christian Poulter would steal watches."

Still pointing at the computer, the clerk said, "Well, when I registered the serial number, it said to contact Breitling. It only says that when a watch is stolen or it's counterfeit."

Jack grew more frustrated by the second and finally lost his cool. "Chris said there are special instructions for his watches. That's why Mr. Overton needed to register it, you idiot!"

The clerk backed away from the counter. "Don't call me names."

Jack's anger was quite apparent. Officer Turner quickly grabbed the **pugnacious (#116)** young man's arm and directed him to the other side of the store.

"I think you need to call Mr. Overton," said Officer Turner to the clerk in a **conciliatory (#117)** manner. "I'll call Mr. Poulter. Between the two of them, I'm sure we can figure out what's going on."

Officer Turner and the clerk made their phone calls. Both Chris and Mr. Overton confirmed Jack's story, and after giving the registration instructions to the clerk, Mr. Overton apologized to Officer Turner for the misunderstanding.

"Well, I guess the kid was right," replied the clerk, staring at the ground. "It'll only take a few minutes to finish the paperwork."

While Officer Turner proceeded to **mollify (#118)** Jack by explaining what had happened, Jack received a text message from Chris. It read;

This is why I told you to speak only to Mr. Overton

Jack replied by simply texting,

Oops

Jack approached the clerk. "I'm sorry for calling you an idiot." The clerk returned the apology and the two shook hands.

"I have to go to my car and do some paperwork." Officer Turner gave Jack a stern look and then cracked a smile. "Is it safe for me to leave you with this man?"

Jack let out a quick laugh. "Yeah, I think so."

While the clerk adjusted the band and demonstrated the watch's features, Jack watched and listened in amazement. He could not believe he was the owner of such a fine watch.

"Let me know if you have any other questions," the clerk said when he finished. "Here's my business card." Jack grabbed the card, thanked the man, and then started for the door. He was reaching for the door handle when he heard the clerk say, "And Jack..." Jack stopped and looked at the man, "remember, don't set off the distress beacon unless it's a matter of life or death. You understand?"

"Yes, I understand."

Jack strutted out of Overton Jewelers with the Breitling on his wrist and a grin on his face. He passed Officer Turner who was sitting in his police car with the windows down. "Can I see it, Jack?"

Jack extended his arm through the open window. "Pretty cool, don't you think?"

"Yeah, it sure is." Officer Turner grabbed Jack's wrist and took a closer look. "Oh, look at that. It's time for my dinner break. What are you doing right now?

"Going home to eat."

"I'll buy your dinner if you want to come along."

"Sure. Let me call my mom and tell her I won't be eating with them. Where are we going? The donut shop?"

Officer Turner smiled and shook his head. "No, we'll go to the Worthington Diner."

"Oh, cool. My dad will be happy," Jack said with a smirk.

"Really, why?"

"He says that's the safest place to eat in Worthington."

Officer Turner squinted his eyes. "Why's that?"

"There's always a cop in there. No matter what time of day you go. My dad says it'd be impossible to rob the place."

Officer Turner chuckled and shook his head. "Want to ride with me or follow?"

"I'll follow. If my friends see me in your car, they might think you're arresting me."

When the two arrived at the diner, the waitress seated them in a booth toward the front of the restaurant. "See? They put you right up front to scare the robbers away."

Officer Turner smiled. "Come to think of it, Jack. They do always sit me up front. I guess your father is right."

The Anderson case was the main topic of discussion throughout the meal. "If he was kidnapped, I think somebody would have called for a ransom by now," said Officer Turner. He then glanced down at the table. "That's not a good sign."

"That's what Chris said. He thinks there's a good chance he's dead." The table went silent for a moment. "My gut tells me the guy who runs the video game store is involved."

"Who's he and why do you think that?"

"He's a guy named Brian who works at GameSpot. You know the store by McDonald's. Mrs. Anderson said he was the only person Ian knew in Worthington. They played video games together online almost every day."

"That doesn't sound too suspicious."

Jack was not about to tell Officer Turner that he broke into the chief's filing cabinet and found Brian's file in a section labeled, '*Working Leads*.' "I know, but something's not right." Jack took a few bites of his hamburger. "Have you ever seen a case like this before?"

"No. I studied similar cases in college. But I just graduated and have only been on the force for two weeks."

"Shot anyone yet?"

"No. I have only drawn my gun once. That was when I thought you were breaking into Mr. Poulter's house." He smiled. "I hate to admit it, but I was probably more scared than you and Mr. Poulter.

Jack shook his head and laughed. "I don't know. I almost pissed my pants when I felt Chris's gun against my neck."

Several times during their conversations, the two heard a group of young women laughing in the background. During one of their outbursts, Jack thought he recognized one of their voices. When he turned to look, he saw his English teacher, Pam Baxley. The twenty-four-year-old was the most popular teacher at Worthington Prep.

"Officer Turner, the short, dark-haired woman over there is my English teacher."

Officer Turner leaned to get a better look. "She's pretty."

"Want me to introduce you?"

"Sure. Why not?"

Jack approached the women's table with Officer Turner at his side. "Hello, Miss Baxley. How are you doing?"

Miss Baxley looked up toward Jack. "Hi, Jack. How's your summer vacation?"

"Great. I'm working at a Porsche dealership washing cars. How's yours?"

"Busy. I just returned from Italy. And, in four weeks, the three of us are going to Las Vegas."

"Miss Baxley, this is my friend Officer Turner."

"Nice to meet you, Officer Turner."

Officer Turner extended his hand. "Kevin Turner. Nice to meet you, too."

"I'm Pam Baxley." She shook his hand. "These are my friends Mary Connerton and Jeanie Desrosiers. How do you two know each other, Kevin?"

Before Officer Turner could answer, Jack said, "He's almost arrested me twice so far this summer."

Officer Turner smiled. "Well, that and he dates my boss's daughter."

While they were talking, Jack caught a glimpse of someone waving their arms outside of the restaurant. He turned to see a desperate-looking Ollie making the **obtrusive (#119)** gesture to get his attention. Jack excused himself and hurried outside. "Ollie, what's the matter?"

Ollie had a bewildered look on his face. He held out both palms and slowly shook his head. "What are you doing? Why are you talking to the enemy?"

"What in the hell are you talking about?"

"Not only are you talking to a cop, but you're also talking to a teacher. What are you, a narc?"

Jack sighed and shook his head. "Ollie, you're an idiot."

"Well, when you're done kissing butts, call me. I'm not doing anything tonight. Let's hang out."

"I don't know if I can. I'll call you later."

When Jack returned to the table, the conversation stopped and everyone looked at him. His forehead wrinkled. "What? Why are you all looking at me?"

"No reason," Miss Baxley said with a smile.

Officer Turner glanced at his watch. "Well, I have to get back on duty. It was nice meeting all of you."

"Nice meeting you too," said Miss Baxley. "We were also about to leave."

Jack thanked Officer Turner, said goodbye to everyone, and then jumped in his Explorer. When he drove away, he saw Officer Turner opening Miss Baxley's car door.

Jack went straight home to show his parents his new watch. He found them in the dining room finishing dinner. They were sitting next to each other drinking wine by candlelight. Jack entered the room and stopped. "I'm not interrupting anything, am I?"

"No, son," replied his father. "Believe it or not, even us old farts can be romantic sometimes."

Jack sat next to his father, removed his watch, and held it out for his parents to see. He was proud of his new acquisition and explained all its features.

His mother held the watch and analyzed it from all angles. "Jack, this looks very expensive. Maybe you should give it back to Mr. Poulter."

"Mom, they send him like three a year. He can't wear them all, so he gives them away. If I don't take it, someone else will."

"How much does a watch like this cost?" she asked.

"It's only like five or six."

"Five or six hundred dollars? I don't think a boy your age should wear such an expensive watch."

Jack said nothing and glanced toward his father. Mr. Graystone shook his head and rolled his eyes. Jack imagined his father knew how much a Breitling watch costs.

"Mom, if I give it back, he'll probably just throw it away."

His father chuckled. "Jack, you can keep the watch. Just take care of it. And don't wear it to work or when you play sports." His father held the watch and examined it carefully. He slid it onto his wrist, but his wrist was too large. It was impossible for him to wear. "Jack, I hope you saved the extra links."

"I did. They're in the box. Why?"

"Because if you get in trouble or get poor grades, I'm going to take it away from you and start wearing it myself."

As his parents laughed, Jack countered with an exaggerated smile. "Yeah, you know that'll never happen since I am the perfect child, and I'd never do anything to upset you." His father rolled his eyes when he heard the **mawkish (#120)** statement.

CHAPTER FOURTEEN

It was a picture-perfect Saturday, and the beach club was in full swing. Having left work at noon, Jack arrived just before one o'clock to find parking impossible. He circled the lot three times, but due to the **dearth (#121)** of parking spaces, he gave up and parked along Oceanside Drive. With the backpack containing his swimsuit dangling from his shoulder, he zigzagged between the parked cars as he headed for the club. The sounds of kids screaming and whistles blowing grew louder with each step. By the time he entered the locker room, it was almost deafening.

After changing, Jack sat on a wooden bench in the musty locker room and dialed his friends' numbers. No one answered. *Where the hell are they?* He swatted at the metal locker door, which closed with a clank. *I'll go outside and look around the pool first.*

The bright sun reflecting off the pool deck stung his eyes. He stood at the pool's edge with his hand on his forehead, as if he was saluting, and scanned the crowd. He saw Edward off to his left with a bunch of older kids. The two made eye contact, but Edward quickly turned away. He found Ollie and Courtney on the far side of the pool. They were staring into the water while they walked along the side. Jack worked his way through a swarm of screaming kids and saw that the two were watching Lip swim underwater. He was trying to break his record of eight laps. Ollie and Courtney were there to cheer him on.

"How many has he done?" Jack asked while giving Courtney a hug.

"The most he's done today is seven and a half."

Lip popped his head out of the water. "Darn." He took several deep breaths. "I was so close that time."

Ollie nodded. "Yeah, you're really not doing very well today. You need to hold your breath longer."

"You think you can do better?"

"Sure can."

Lip, who knew he was a better athlete, stared at Ollie. "I bet I can stay underwater longer than you can."

Ollie's eyes lit up. "You know I can hold my breath a long time."

"So can I."

"Well, what's the bet?"

"I'll bet you ten bucks I can sit at the bottom of the pool longer than you."

"That's it? I just have to sit at the bottom of the pool? And the last one sitting wins?"

"Yeah, that's it."

Ollie looked at Jack and Courtney. He smiled and then threw his hands in the air. "Game on. Challenge accepted!"

Jack shook his head. He knew Lip had the **disposition (#122)** to be **impetuous (#123)**. Lip often acted impulsively and did not stop to consider the situation. "Don't do it, Lip. You know you can never beat Ollie in a bet."

"Well, Jack, not this time. My superior brain and athletic ability will win."

"Don't do it, Lip."

Courtney shook her head. "Lip, I agree with Jack. I wouldn't do it if I were you."

"Let's go, Ollie. Jump in."

"Where's your money?"

"In my bag over there. Jack, go get ten bucks out of my wallet."

Jack grabbed Lip's wallet and removed a five and five ones. This left Lip in the **penurious (#124)** position of having only one dollar. If he did not win the bet, there would be no more trips to the snack bar for him.

Ollie handed Jack his money. "Lip, get out of the water and we'll both jump in at the same time."

Lip glared at Ollie. "Okay, but when we get underwater, I don't want you to look at me. I know you're going to try to make me laugh or do something to make me quit."

Jack smiled. *Make you laugh? That's about impossible.*

Ollie nodded. "That's fine. We'll sit at the bottom with our backs to each other."

Lip jumped out of the pool, stood next to Ollie, and then looked at Courtney. "On three. Courtney, you count."

Jack glanced at Ollie from head to toe. He wore a baggy pair of boardshorts, a loose-fitting T-shirt, and a pair of swimming goggles. Jack couldn't exactly tell, but it looked as if he had a bottle of soda in his pocket.

"Are you going to take off your shirt?" asked Lip.

Ollie shook his head and then looked at Courtney.

"One, two, three." Both boys jumped into the pool, sank to the bottom, and then sat with their backs to each other.

Jack set the stopwatch on his iPhone. At thirty-five seconds, Ollie exhaled. Jack tapped Courtney on the shoulder. "That's not good. I think Lip's going to win this time." Just then, Ollie reached into his pocket and removed the bottle. It wasn't a bottle of soda. It was a small scuba tank. He inserted the mouthpiece and began to breathe. He looked up at Jack and Courtney and waved.

Courtney glanced at Jack. "Lip never said he had to hold his breath. The bet was who could sit at the bottom the longest."

Jack smiled. "That's right."

When Lip poked his head above water, he had an angry face. "He's cheating. I know he's cheating."

Jack shook his head. "The bet was who could sit at the bottom the longest. Ollie is there and you're not. So, Ollie's the winner."

Lip swam toward the middle of the pool and looked at Ollie. "I told you he's cheating. He has a scuba tank in his mouth."

"Lip," said Courtney, "the bet was whoever could sit at the bottom the longest. Those were your exact words. And Ollie is still there, so he wins."

Ollie remained in the pool doing what appeared to be a victory dance. He was raising the roof while he bounced around on his butt.

By the time Ollie jumped out of the pool, Lip was fuming. "Ollie, you cheated. I'm sick and tired of you always trying to **bilk (#125)** me out of money."

Ollie didn't say a word. He just smiled and looked at Jack and Courtney.

"I'm giving this one to Ollie," said Jack. "The bet was who could stay at the bottom the longest and that was Ollie." Jack handed Ollie the twenty bucks.

"Thank you, Lip. Anytime you want to use your superior brain and athletic ability to make another bet, just let me know."

Lip was so angry that he could barely speak. Teeth clenched, he grunted, and then said, "As my mother would say, you're a **charlatan (#126)**." He pushed Ollie aside as he walked away. The push was not that hard, but Ollie over-exaggerated the nudge by staggering backward and falling into the pool. Lip kept walking.

When Ollie's head popped out of the water, he yelled, "You don't have to be a sore loser."

With Lip gone, the three found a couple of empty lounge chairs and formed a huddle. While Jack inspected the scuba tank, Ollie explained that it was called Spare Air and told him how it worked.

"Ollie, why in the world do you need a small scuba tank?" asked Jack.

Ollie smiled. "You never know when you're going to need one."

Jack rolled his eyes and shook his head. "Listen, Ollie. Courtney and I need to talk to you about something."

"What is it? You know you can talk to me about anything."

"Yes, we know we can talk to you. The problem is you talking to everyone else." Jack leaned forward, looked to his right, then to his left, and even though the roar of screaming kids masked his words, he whispered, "Listen, you have to keep what we discuss only among the three of us. What do you know about that Brian Carter guy?"

"You mean the guy who runs the GameSpot?" Jack and Courtney nodded. "Not much, other than he's a youth pastor at a church. He seems like a nice guy, though. He invited me to his apartment once to play video games with a couple of his friends." Jack and Courtney looked at each other. "I didn't go. I had other things to do. Why'd you ask?"

"Jack and I think he might be involved in Ian Anderson's

disappearance."

"Really?"

"Yeah, really," replied Jack.

"What does your father say about him?"

Courtney glanced at Jack and then at Ollie. "My father doesn't discuss his cases with me. But Jack and I came across something, or should I say we *didn't* come across something that makes us think he's involved."

"What was it?"

"I really can't say. But trust me, there's something not right here."

"How late does the store stay open on Saturdays?" asked Jack.

"Nine o'clock. But he usually doesn't stay that late."

Jack stared off into the distance for a moment. "When we leave here, I'll drop Courtney at her house and then go to the store. Meet me there at five o'clock. If Brian's there, try to get him to invite us back to his apartment. I want to do my own investigation."

"Cool. We'll be like Sherlock Holmes and Doctor Watson."

Jack looked at Courtney. "I was thinking more like Andy Griffith and Barney Fife. You know, from that old TV show."

Courtney laughed. "That's funny, Andy."

Ollie looked back and forth between the two of them. "What? I don't want to be Barney. Why can't Jack be Barney?"

Courtney shook her head and smiled. "Too late. I already called him Andy."

***

By five minutes before five, Jack was parked in front of the video game store. Brian's Toyota Corolla was three cars away, but Ollie was nowhere to be found. *Come on, Ollie, hurry up.* Jack fidgeted in his seat. *Screw it. I'll go in and wait for him.*

Besides another kid, Jack was the only other customer in the store. While the pimpled-faced clerk helped the other customer, Jack walked through the aisles of the **multifarious (#127)** game store and inspected the merchandise. The store was large compared to other game stores in the area. It had every game you could think of for sale or rent. It even had games for old outdated systems.

Brian, who stood behind the checkout counter, looked up and made eye contact. "Need any help?"

Jack shook his head. "Just looking."

Brian went back to shuffling through a stack of papers but stopped when his phone rang. After glancing at the screen, he answered the call. Jack stood only feet away with his back toward him. He grabbed a video game and pretended to read the case. Jack could barely hear Brian say with a strange tone to his voice, "Did you get the stuff?... You got the heavy-duty garbage bags, right?... What about the cleaning supplies? I hope you got a lot of bleach... I'll be outside in two minutes. We'll go straight there, clean up the mess, then head over to Steve's. If you talk to him, tell him we should be there by nine... Cool. See you in a minute."

"I'm leaving you in charge," Brian said to the clerk on his way out the door. "Don't forget to set the alarm." Pimples nodded in agreement.

Jack waited until Brian was out of the store before he followed. He saw Brian get into a red Honda Civic. Jack scanned the parking lot for Ollie, but he could not find him anywhere. *Great. The one time I need him to be here, and he's late. I have to follow them.*

Jack opened his driver's door and was about get in when he saw Ollie pulled into the parking lot. Jack glared at him while he parked. "Get in here, now." Ollie said nothing and jumped into the Explorer. Jack started the truck, put it in gear, and then gunned the engine before either of them had a chance to buckle their seatbelts.

"What's going on?"

"I think we might've found Ian's kidnappers."

"What? How do you know that?"

Jack told him about the conversation he had overheard.

"We should call Chief McKinney."

"Not yet. We don't have time to explain everything to him. We need to see where they're going. Then we'll call."

They followed Brian to a house on the outskirts of town. The small house was set far back on its lot and was barely visible through the trees. "That looks like a perfect place to commit a crime," said Jack while they slowly drove past.

"Yeah, sure does."

"Ollie, here's the plan. I'm going to turn around, and then we'll switch seats. You'll drive, and when we get in front of the neighbor's house, slow down and I'll jump out. Grab your phone." Jack reached into the center console, removed his Bluetooth earphone, and stuck it in his ear. "I'm going to call you. We'll stay on the phone, and I'll tell you what's happening. I'm going to try to get a closer look. If I see anything suspicious or I get in trouble, I'll say 'Barney, call the police.' When you hear those words, and only those words, hang up and dial 911. What's the name of this street?"

"Alexandria Avenue."

"After you drop me off, look at the mailbox and get the number. I want you to turn around and then wait a couple of houses down the street. Got it?"

"Yeah. Got it."

The two switched seats, and with Ollie behind the wheel, headed toward the house. Neither of them said a word. They both had their eyes fixed on the gravel driveway in which the Civic disappeared.

"I'll get out by that mailbox." Ollie nodded and then slowed to almost a stop. The two glanced at each other as Jack opened the door. "Wish me luck." Again, Ollie nodded.

Jack jumped onto the side of the road and landed on loose gravel. He slid momentarily, but he never lost his balance. He used his momentum to hop across a small ditch and then forged into the overgrown yard. The waist-high plants scraped against his legs. *I wish I were wearing jeans.* Within a few yards, he had disappeared into the trees.

Slowly, methodically, Jack crept toward the house, hiding behind trees along the way. The dried vegetation crackled beneath his shoes despite his efforts to strategically place each step. He hoped the constant buzzing from this summer's batch of locusts masked the sound.

Jack stopped behind a tree a few yards from the front of the house, grabbed the bottom of his untucked T-shirt, and wiped his face. The evening sun, which had begun to drop behind the house, was blinding. Through the glare, however, he could see the front porch.

"Ollie, I can see the front of the house. I'm going to wait here for a few minutes to make sure they got everything out of the car."

"Okay. Let me know when you move."

After a few minutes, Jack whispered, "I'm going in," then ran to the side of the house. He ducked behind several trees along the way and stopped with his back against the old wooden clapboards. The flaking white paint poked through his shirt. The first window he approached had its shade drawn, making it impossible to see inside the room. Standing on the tips of his feet, he placed his ear to it and listened. He heard only two garbled voices; Brian's and who he assumed was the other young man. He listened until the pain in his feet was unbearable, hoping to hear Ian's voice. No such luck.

Jack took two steps toward the back of the house but stopped when he heard a noise coming from a partially opened basement window. It sounded like someone dragging a heavy object across the floor. *This can't be good.* He dropped to his knees, crawled to the basement window, and looked inside. The basement was dark and he saw nothing.

"What's happening now?" asked Ollie.

"Shhh," was Jack's only reply. He continued around to the back of the house. There, he found two more windows. He attempted to look in each one. But similar to the others, their shades were drawn.

"What's happening now?"

"Ollie, shut up."

Jack paused to let his heart rate settle. After taking a deep breath, he poked his head around the last corner of the house. He saw no one, so he approached the only window and placed his ear against it.

"What's happening now?"

Jack did not reply. He stood on the tips of his feet and listened. But he heard nothing. There were no voices or sounds of any kind. Just silence. *Now, what do I do?* His thoughts, however, were interrupted by an unfamiliar voice asking, "Hey, what are you doing?"

In his earpiece, Jack could hear Ollie asking, "Do you want me to call the police now?"

"Not yet."

A guy who looked a few years younger than Brian ran up to Jack with a crowbar in his hand. "I said, what are you doing?"

Out of the corner of his eye, Jack saw Brian running toward him from the other direction.

Brian stared at Jack momentarily. "Didn't I just see you at the store? What are you doing snooping around here?"

Jack's mind raced. He was unsure of what to say. "Uh, if you think you can get away with Ian's murder or killing me, you're wrong. I have five friends waiting at the end of the driveway. When I tell them to, they'll be here in ten seconds."

Brian looked at his friend and then tilted his head. "Ian? Do you mean Ian Anderson? We didn't kill Ian Anderson. What makes you think that?"

"You are the only person he knew in Worthington."

Brian shook his head. "That doesn't make me a killer. I don't know why you and the FBI are hell-bent on framing me for his disappearance."

Jack's eyes darted back and forth between Brian and his friend while Ollie repeatedly asked, "Do you want me to call now?" Jack finally answered by saying, "No. Not yet." Brian gave him a strange look. "Well, why do you need all those cleaning supplies? I bet you're in there cleaning up the crime scene."

"Crime scene? You think this is a crime scene? This is my grandmother's house. She died six months ago. We're cleaning it so we can sell it."

"I don't believe you."

"What? Do you want to go inside and look around? Would that make you happy?"

Jack wanted to say yes, but he did not trust these **dubious (#128)** characters and worried it could be a trap. "I'll go inside, but you two have to stay outside."

"Why do we have to stay outside?"

"I don't trust you."

Brian's face grew angry. "Okay." He threw his arms up in the air. "Go in and look around. Conner and I will stay outside. We have nothing to hide."

Jack walked to the front door. He glanced at the two standing in the front yard before he entered. "Ollie, I'm going in. If they try anything, drive to the end of the driveway. I'm sure I can outrun these two."

"Do you want me to come up there now?"

"No. Brian doesn't need to know you're involved. Just stay where you are for right now."

Jack stood in the living room and looked around. The room was a mess. There were boxes stacked to the ceiling, magazines piled everywhere, and old furniture scattered throughout the room.

"What do you see?" asked Ollie.

"It's a mess in here. There's junk everywhere." He walked further into the room and stopped. "It smells in here."

"Does it smell like a dead person?"

"I don't know. I've never smelled a dead person before."

"Neither have I."

Jack walked into the dining room and scanned it from floor to ceiling. In the far corner was an empty china cabinet. Its contents were stacked on a dining table covered with a white tablecloth. *Nothing out of place in here.* He turned to leave. *Maybe I should check under the table.* He raised the tablecloth and stuck his head underneath. "Nothing here," he mumbled before he removed his head. Jack's head had not yet cleared the table when he saw a mouse dart across the floor. He gasped, and as he sprung to his feet, his head hit the bottom of the table. The dishes rattled like there was a small earthquake.

"Jack, what was that? Did they attack you? That's it. I'm calling the police."

"No, Ollie. I just hit my head on the table."

With his heart pounding, Jack headed for the kitchen. "The smell's getting stronger."

"You want me to call the police now?"

"No, not yet." He reached for the refrigerator door and opened it. Between the sight and the smell, he took two steps backward and gagged. "Oh gross," he repeated several times.

"What's the matter? Jack, is everything all right? Did you find Ian? Do you want me to call now?"

"No, don't call. I didn't find Ian, but I found where the smell was coming from. The fridge is turned off, and there's a bunch of rotting food in it." After he regained his composure, he walked down a short hallway and looked into each of the three bedrooms and the bathroom. "Ollie, I see nothing strange in the house. It's a pigsty, but I see no signs of Ian."

"Are you coming out now? Don't stay in there longer than you have to. I don't trust these guys."

"I just have to look in the basement, and then I'm coming out." Jack went into the living room and glanced outside. The two were still standing next to the red car. He hurried to the basement door. It opened with a squeak. A flick of a switch on the wall provided little light. He looked inside the darkened stairwell and mumbled, "Here goes nothing." The old wooden staircase creaked with every step. When he got to the bottom, he stopped and scanned the room. It was dark and musty. The only light came from two single light bulbs hanging from the ceiling. He made a quick trip around the room, looking behind or under anything that was suspicious. He saw nothing odd. "I'm coming out now," he said as he leaped up the stairs. *I hope they don't attack me when I come through the door.* He busted into the living room ready for anything. Thankfully, Brian and Conner were not there. "I'm going out the front door. I'll meet you at the end of the driveway."

Jack jumped down from the front porch. "I didn't see anything in there."

Brian shook his head. "I told you. Now, will you leave me alone? Next time you bother me, I'm calling the cops."

"Whatever. I'll be keeping my eye on you two," Jack yelled as he jogged down the gravel driveway.

Ollie had the Explorer at the end of the driveway and had moved to the passenger seat. Jack jumped behind the wheel and gunned the engine.

"Were you scared?" Ollie asked, staring at Jack with wide eyes.

"No, not at all."

"Bull. I bet you were about to piss your pants."

Jack glanced at him and smiled. "I was really scared, especially when I went into the basement."

Ollie laughed. "I was scared too. And I was just sitting in the car. So, do you still think these guys had anything to do with Ian's disappearance?"

Jack was not ready to **dispel (#129)** their involvement. There were too many factors pointing to their guilt. "I don't know. For some reason, my gut tells me they're involved somehow. But if they are, I don't think that was the crime scene."

Jack put on his blinker before he came to a stop. He looked both ways, and seeing no cars, turned left. He was heading toward Worthington Boulevard when a white car pulled out in front of him from a side street. Jack slammed on the brakes. "What's this idiot doing?" He couldn't see the driver through the dark tinted window. "You pull out in front of me, and now you drive ten miles an hour." After he finished his rant, the car came to an abrupt stop. "Are you serious?" By the time Jack stopped, he was too close to maneuver around the car. He glanced in the rearview mirror before he put the Explorer in reverse. He was about to change gears when he saw a black SUV speeding toward them. "Hang on, Ollie, we're about to get rear-ended!"

CHAPTER FIFTEEN

Jack closed his eyes, and with a death grip on the steering wheel, waited for the impact. A few seconds passed, but none occurred. When he opened his eyes and looked in the rearview mirror, he saw two men dressed in black standing behind the open doors of their SUV. Each man had a handgun pointed at the Explorer. "Ollie!" was all he could say before a voice came over a loudspeaker.

"Driver and passenger, step out of the vehicle with your hands in the air and place them on the hood."

"What's going on?" Ollie yelled in a panic.

"I don't know," Jack hit the button that unlocked the doors, "but I think we need to do what they say."

Jack slowly opened his door and stepped outside. Ollie followed.

"Keep your hands where we can see them."

Jack raised his hands, walked to the front of the Explorer, and then placed them on the hot hood. His body slightly trembled as he gave Ollie a frightened stare. Ollie looked like he was in shock.

Within seconds, the two men converged on Jack and Ollie. Jack could feel the man's breathe against his neck. "Put your hands behind your head and spread your legs." Jack complied and the man proceeded to frisk him. He ran his hands over Jack's chest, back, and around his waistband. "Is there anything in your pockets that can stick or poke me?"

"No, Sir," Jack said with a squeak in his voice.

The man inserted his hands in Jack's pockets and then ran them down the inside and outside of Jack's shorts. When he finished, he grabbed Jack's right arm, then his left arm, and pulled them behind his back. Click, click. Jack felt the metal handcuffs squeeze against his wrists.

"Why are you cuffing me?"

The man said nothing.

Out of the corner of his eye, Jack saw a white van come to a halt behind him. He heard its sliding door open, and then the man pushed him inside onto the van's floor. Before the sliding door closed, Jack saw Ollie being escorted to the black SUV.

"What's going on? Who are you?" The door slid shut and the van took off. Jack was laying with his back against the warm metal floor. He saw two men staring at him. Neither of them said a word. "Where are you taking me?" Jack glanced around the van. It was not your typical van. There was electronic equipment stacked from the floor to the ceiling.

Finally, one man spoke. "Jack Graystone, what were you doing in that house?"

"Who are you? How do you know my name?"

"I know everything about you, Jacob Furthur Graystone," said the poker-faced man whose eyes pierced through Jack. "I know that you are sixteen years old and were born on March 7th. You live at 217 Maple Avenue, and your parents are Thomas and Elizabeth Graystone."

"What do you want from me?"

"What were you doing in that house?"

"I followed the manager of the GameSpot there. I overheard him saying that they were going to clean up the mess. I thought he killed Ian Anderson. So, I went to stop him before he destroyed the evidence."

"What did you see in there?"

"Nothing. It was full of old junk. Brian said it was his grandmother's house who just died. They were cleaning it so they can sell it."

"Did you go into each room?"

"Yeah. And the basement."

"What about the attic?"

"No. I didn't think to go into the attic."

The man closed his eyes and rubbed his forehead. "Jack Graystone. I want you to know that you're interfering with an FBI investigation.

You could've just ruined our only lead."

"I didn't know you were following them. I planned on calling Chief McKinney if I saw anything suspicious."

The man looked at his partner. "We'll wait until they leave. Then I want that house inspected with a fine-tooth comb. That might not be the crime scene, but I want to know if Ian Anderson was ever there." He turned to Jack. "Jack Graystone, don't discuss this incident with anyone. If I find out you have, you'll be arrested. Understand?"

"Yes, I understand."

The man looked at the driver. "Stop here."

The van came to a stop, and the sliding door flew open. The same man who had thrown Jack into the van grabbed him by his handcuffed hands and pulled him out onto the street. He quickly uncuffed him and then returned to the black SUV. Within seconds, all three vehicles sped away, leaving Jack and Ollie on the side of the road standing next to the Explorer.

They stared at each other for a moment before Ollie asked, "What just happened?"

"I think we interrupted an FBI investigation."

CHAPTER SIXTEEN

Another week had passed without any new information on Ian or his whereabouts. It was now Friday, and this particular Friday was busier than usual at Anderson Porsche. Although Jack cleaned as fast as possible, the line of dirty vehicles never decreased. When one went away, at least one more appeared. After a while, Jack was in the zone, and before he knew it, it was lunchtime.

Since Buddy had gone to cash his check, Jack was left to eat alone. He retrieved his lunch from the refrigerator, went over to the tray that stored his phone, and checked for messages. When he looked at the screen, he saw ten missed calls and a text message, all from Courtney. He became worried and read the text message first.

There's been a break in the Anderson case. CALL ME!

Jack did not listen to the messages. Instead, he dialed Courtney's number. He paced back and forth while the phone rang. Finally, on the fifth ring, she answered.

"Courtney, what's going on?"

"I'm not sure. My dad got a call from the station this morning. Someone who lives on the Ocean Walk has a security camera with video from the night Ian went missing."

"And they're just getting this to the police now?"

"I heard my dad say that the people have been out of the country for a long time. They just now learned Ian was missing."

"What does the video show?"

"I don't know. This is the only information I have. I'll try to find out more tonight after work."

"Okay, keep me posted. I'll call Chris. Maybe he can get more information." After several attempts, Chris finally answered. "Chris, there's been a break in the Anderson case."

"Really, what kind of a break?"

"Someone on the Ocean Walk has video from the night Ian went missing. They've been out of the country and are just now getting it to the police. What are the chances of your FBI connections sending you a copy of the video?"

"Let me see what I can do."

"Send me a text if you get any information. I'm at work until five. I'll call you then."

"Okay, talk to you later."

Jack grew more anxious as the afternoon progressed, and he constantly checked his phone. It wasn't until four o'clock that he received a text from Chris that read,

FBI emailing a copy of video soon. Stop by after work.

The Friday night traffic into Worthington was horrendous. Even with taking every shortcut he knew, it took forever to get to Chris's house. Jack arrived just before six o'clock, jumped out of the Explorer, ran to the front door, and rang the bell three times in his excitement. Sherlock and Mycroft were the first to arrive. Chris was not far behind. He waved Jack into the house from the opposite side of the leaded glass doors. "Well, Jack, you're 100 percent cleared now," Chris shouted over the barking dogs.

"Why? What does the video show?" Jack asked while they walked to the study.

"Well, not much so far. You can see Ian running frantically toward Oceanside Drive at 9:47, based on the time-stamp on the video. But no one is chasing him. They have video of you at the gas station around that time, plus witnesses at the movie theater. So, you're no longer a suspect."

"Can I see the footage?"

"Sure."

Jack stood silently and watched the video of Ian running past the camera. After it finished, he continued to stare at the blank screen for a moment. Then he flopped into Chris's desk chair, closed his eyes, leaned forward, and buried his face in his hands.

Chris glanced at Allison who had just walked into the room. "Jack, what's the matter?"

Jack said nothing.

"Are you all right?" asked Allison.

He answered with a shake of the head.

Allison stood next to Jack and placed her hand on his shoulder while Chris sat on the edge of the desk. They didn't say anything. They waited for Jack to speak.

After a minute, Jack leaned back in the chair. "Since Ian went missing, I think of him constantly. I think about what could've happened to him or what he could be going through. Seeing that scared look on his face really upset me." Jack glanced toward the ground and shook his head. "But there's something else."

"What's that?" asked Allison.

"Ever since Ian went missing, I've had this nagging feeling that people might think I was involved in his disappearance. Like you said, Chris, 'until you are totally cleared, you're still on the list.' Now that I'm cleared, I don't feel any better. For some reason, I feel bad that I'm happy I'm off the list."

Chris paused. "Jack, you had nothing to do with Ian's disappearance, so you shouldn't feel guilty." Chris looked at Allison. "Maybe I shouldn't have shown him the video."

Jack jumped up from the chair. "No, I'm glad I saw it. I now know that I have to find Ian. If it takes the rest of my life, I'll find him. Let me see the video again."

Chris patted Jack on the back. "Now you're talking like a detective."

The three watched the video several more times. They analyzed the camera angle and determined that it pointed westerly over a backyard and across the cove.

"It looks like he still has the binoculars in his hands, doesn't it?" asked Jack.

"Yeah, I believe that's what he's carrying," said Chris.

"Look at Reilly," remarked Allison. "He doesn't appear to be overly excited. But look at Ian. He looks scared."

"How much video did they send you?"

"About an hour. I fast-forwarded through the whole thing but saw no one else. My contact at the FBI said they viewed twenty-four hours before and after, but they found nothing out of the ordinary."

"Chris, if Ian left for Reilly's walk at nine fifteen, he should've passed this camera around nine thirty. So, there are seventeen minutes in which something could've happened."

"Yes, that'd be correct."

Jack's forehead wrinkled. "Can I watch the video without fast-forwarding?"

"Sure, that's what I planned to do."

"Before we start, does anyone want something to drink?" asked Allison.

"I'd like a vodka martini, shaken, not stirred," Jack replied with a smile.

Chris laughed. "Oh, I see you've been watching James Bond."

"If that's too much trouble, I'll have a Coke instead."

"I'll also have a Coke," said Chris.

"Okay, two Cokes it is. I'll order a couple of pizzas in case we get hungry."

As soon as Allison returned with the drinks, Chris started the video. The three stared at the screen in silence. At 9:31, Jack noticed something flash across the top of the screen. It lasted only a second or two. Since the object was small, it was barely visible during the fast-forward playback. "Chris, can we go back to nine thirty and play it in slow motion?"

Chris nodded and then reversed the video.

"When I tell you to, press Pause." The three sat in silence waiting for the command. "Now," said Jack. "Look at the top of the screen. Do you see that object crossing from right to left?"

"It looks like interference in the video to me," said Chris.

"I don't think it is. Ian went missing on a Friday night, right?"

Both Chris and Allison concurred.

"I've been walking Reilly for three weeks. Every Sunday,

Wednesday, and Friday night around nine thirty, a seaplane lands in the cove. It stops offshore, and a small powerboat rafts up next to it. They stay for a few minutes, then both the plane and the boat leave. I think the object at the top of the screen is the bottom of one of the plane's pontoons."

"Interesting." Chris walked to the window and stared outside. After a minute, he turned to Jack and asked, "Okay, if it is the pontoon, what does it prove?"

"I don't know." Jack scratched his head. "Maybe the people on the plane could've seen something."

Chris quickly **debunked (#130)** this idea. "Don't you think they would've said something by now?"

"Maybe Ian saw something with the binoculars while the plane rafted next to the boat."

"Possibly, but how far out does the plane meet the boat?"

"About a half-mile."

"That's awfully far away to see something clearly with those binoculars. You need to remember the boat and plane would be bouncing around in the ocean."

"Well, what if they were closer?"

"Okay, let's say they were closer. And let's say Ian saw something on the plane or the boat. How does he end up missing? Whatever happened to him most likely happened outside my house. How could the people get from the boat to Oceanside Drive that quickly?"

"Actually," Jack said, looking at the ground, "we would've seen the boat coming to shore on the video."

"That's right."

"So, you don't like any of my theories?"

"No, quite the contrary. You're doing what a good detective would do. Analyze all the possibilities and think outside the box."

Jack was about to say something when the doorbell rang. Sherlock and Mycroft sprung from their beds and began to bark. "I bet that's the food," Chris said. "Allison, put the dogs in the backyard."

Chris returned carrying two pizza boxes. Jack and Allison followed him into the kitchen, where Chris grabbed three plates and served the food. They were discussing the possible connections between the plane and Ian's disappearance when Jack's face went blank. He dropped his slice onto his plate and sat in silence for a moment. Then he walked back to the computer, set the video to 9:31, and pressed play. Jack appeared to be in a trance when Chris and Allison entered the study. They didn't say a word. They just watched.

Jack increased the playing speed and stared at the screen. He rewound and fast-forwarded the video several times. Then, without saying a word, he walked out of the study, through the house, and toward the back door. Before exiting, he grabbed a pair of binoculars lying on a coffee table. He proceeded through the backyard—Sherlock and Mycroft by his side—toward the squeaky gate. Chris and Allison followed. Jack opened the gate, which let out a loud squeal. Without looking at Chris, he said, "You need to oil this," then kept walking. He walked only a short distance along the Ocean Walk before he stopped and placed the binoculars to his eyes. Standing as still as a mannequin, he stared out toward the horizon for over a minute.

Jack lowered the binoculars and walked back to the computer in complete silence. Again, he rewound and fast-forwarded the video several times. Finally, he spoke. "There," he said, pointing at the computer screen. "That proves the plane was close to shore. Very close, actually. Do you see it?"

Chris and Allison looked at each other. "No," they both replied.

"Look at the pattern of the waves. They change. The video shows it was very windy that night, with the wind blowing northeasterly toward shore. Look at these waves. They change as if something was blocking them. When I went outside, I looked to see if any submerged rocks could have caused the change. But there doesn't appear to be any rocks in the area. I **construe (#131)** that the wind blowing the boat and plane toward the shore caused the changes in the waves. It would've been too rough to raft together out in the ocean, so they probably came in closer that night."

"Son, that's a brilliant deduction," Chris remarked in total astonishment. "Now I see exactly what you're talking about." Chris paused for a moment. "Something's not right here. There has got to be a connection somehow."

"Yeah, but what?"

"I don't know, Jack. We'll have to work on that. We need to investigate this boat and plane further."

The three went back into the kitchen. There was little conversation while they ate their pizza. It wasn't until they finished that Chris asked, "What days did you say the plane arrives?"

"Sunday, Wednesday, and Friday."

"So, it's coming in tonight?"

"Yeah, in about two hours."

"Jack, do you want to go for a boat ride?"

CHAPTER SEVENTEEN

Worthington was your typical New England tourist town, and Friday nights during the summer season were out of control. The population **burgeoned (#132)**, which made parking difficult to obtain. With this in mind, Chris arranged for Allison to drop him and Jack at the local marina. The marina, located at the end of a wharf in the middle of town, was where Chris docked his new twenty-five-foot Chris Craft Corsair speedboat.

While Allison retrieved her Range Rover, Chris and Jack entered the spy room to gather several pieces of equipment. Chris removed a duffle bag from a shelf that he filled with two pairs of high-powered binoculars, a digital camera with a large telephoto lens, night vision goggles, and a black plastic case.

Jack reached into the duffle bag and grabbed the case. "What's in here?"

Chris opened it and revealed a handgun and several clips of ammunition. "Always be prepared."

"You mean like a boy scout?"

Chris smiled. "Yeah, like a boy scout with a gun."

Chris finished packing the items and grabbed two jackets before they hurried out the front door. Allison was already waiting and they jumped in—Chris up front and Jack in the back. As soon as she heard the doors shut, she gunned the engine and headed downtown. As expected, traffic was horrible.

"This is going to take forever," said Chris, fidgeting in his seat while stopped in the middle of a traffic jam. "Jack, let's get out here. It's only a few blocks. It'll be much quicker if we jog the rest of the way."

"You think you're in good enough shape. I don't want to have to do CPR."

Chris chuckled. "I think I can make it. Let's go."

Chris jumped out first and took off. Jack followed. Jack's comment must have struck a nerve because Chris kept a quick pace as they weaved between cars, jumped over medians, and power-walked down the **pedestrian (#133)** crowded sidewalks. By the time they arrived at the marina, they were both out of breath.

When they approached the slip, they found the dock master had lowered the boat into the water and started the engine. Chris thanked the man, handed him a twenty-dollar bill, and then the two jumped aboard the rumbling vessel. After inspecting the gauges and pressing a few buttons, Chris backed from the slip. The boat transferred from reverse gear to forward gear with a loud clunk. Chris eased the throttle forward and idled out of the marina. He constantly scanned the area while he maneuvered between the moored boats. The night air was still, and the waters of the harbor were **placid (#134)**. The sleek lines of the Chris Craft barely made a wave.

They remained at idle speed until they passed the last '*No Wake*' marker. "Hang on," Chris said just before the engine roared, and he brought the boat up to full speed. The city lights shimmering off the harbor quickly faded as the boat disappeared into the dark horizon.

It approached nine o'clock as the two men sped through the calm ocean waters along the rocky Worthington coast. Occasionally, they hit a wave, which covered their faces with a fine saltwater mist. Chris constantly looked at his GPS and followed the shoreline to the cove. As they closed in on their destination, he turned off the boat's running lights and then settled a mile offshore. Without saying a word, he removed the binoculars from the duffle bag and handed a pair to Jack. The two stood in silence, gently swaying back and forth. They looked like statues while they scoured the coastline for any boat traffic.

Jack found it peaceful out on the ocean. There was no roaring traffic, no annoying conversations, and especially no interrogating parents. The only sounds came from a slight breeze that rustled the American flag mounted to the back of the boat and the small waves lapping against its hull.

Since the episode with the FBI, Jack had mentioned nothing of it to Chris. He agonized over whether he should. But the FBI agent's words, "Don't discuss this incident with anyone. If I find out you have, you'll be arrested," kept repeating in his head. After much thought, Jack felt like he had to say something and this would be his best opportunity to do so. "Uh, Chris," he said in a hesitant voice.

"Yes."

"Something happened the other night that I'm not allowed to talk about. I want to tell you, but if I do, I can go to jail. So, what should I do?"

"What do you think you should do?"

"Anyone else I wouldn't tell. But I think I should tell you since we're both working on this case."

"Well, there's no need to tell me you interrupted an FBI investigation last Saturday at Brian Carter's grandmother's house."

"You know?"

Chris lowered his binoculars and looked at Jack. "I know everything, Jacob Furthur Graystone." He then raised the binoculars and continued scouring the coastline.

"Do you know if they found anything?"

"Nothing so far. They're still waiting for some results. I'll let you know when I hear something."

After a few more silent minutes, they spied a boat that came to rest at the opening of the cove.

"I believe these are our guys," Chris remarked. He switched from the binoculars to the camera. "Did you see where they came from?"

"No, I didn't."

Within a couple of minutes, the seaplane landed and rafted next to the boat. Through their high-powered lenses, Jack and Chris watched the pilot exchange two aluminum suitcases from the plane with two larger aluminum suitcases from the boat. After they completed the exchange, a well-dressed man climbed out of the plane and boarded the boat. Within seconds, the boat sped away, and the plane prepared for takeoff. During the entire transaction, Jack could hear the constant snapping of the camera's shutters.

"Did you see that?"

"Sure did."

The two followed the boat to a small cove west of the rendezvous point. After snapping several more pictures, Chris said, "Hang on, we're heading out to sea." He placed the camera in the duffle bag and then engaged all of the boat's 420 horsepower. The engine roared and the bow pointed toward the sky. The force pinned Jack in his seat. The Chris Craft got up to speed quickly, and they never slowed down until the plane was out of sight. Chris eased back on the throttle, made a sweeping right turn, and then set a trajectory toward shore.

"I wanted to make sure the plane didn't see us," Chris yelled over the loud engine.

"Good idea."

Chris turned on the running lights before backtracking on their previous course. They motored by the inlet in which the powerboat retreated and set a waypoint on the GPS.

"We'll drive by on the way home tonight. Maybe we can tell which house they went to."

"Sounds good."

"You want to drive?"

"Yeah, I'd love to."

Chris **relinquished (#135)** command, and the two headed back to the marina. The rhythmic movement of the boat's bow going up and down over the calm ocean waters hypnotized the two men. They both stared straight ahead and did not say a word until they reached the no-wake zone.

"That seems very suspicious," said Chris. "Why would one person have so much luggage? And why would they put suitcases back on the plane?"

"I don't know. Do you think it could be drugs?"

"Possibly. We need to find out who owns that boat."

Chris regained control of the Chris Craft on the approach to the slip. "Give Allison a call. Tell her we're ready to be picked up."

Jack made the call. "She said she should be here in fifteen minutes. That is, if the traffic has calmed down."

Chris killed the engines, flipped several buttons, and then looked at his shirt. It was soaked from the ocean spray. "Want a dry shirt?"

"Sure, if you have one."

Chris stepped into the small cabin and pulled out two white polo shirts embroidered with the boat's name. "This one should fit you," he said, tossing it to Jack. They both removed their wet shirts, but before Chris could put his on, Jack noticed a scar on his right shoulder.

"Is that a bullet wound?"

Chris glanced down at the scar and rubbed it a few times. "Yeah, it sure is."

"How'd you get that?"

Chris did not say anything at first. He just looked off into the distance. Finally, he spoke. "Gang initiation."

"What?"

"When I was younger, I joined a gang. The initiation was you had to shoot yourself somewhere other than the foot. I chose the shoulder. The bullet went in and out and didn't do much damage."

Jack was speechless. "Really?"

Chris looked at him and smiled. "No, I've never been in a gang."

Jack laughed. "Well, how'd it happen?"

Chris paused again. "It's a long story."

Jack glanced at his watch. "We have a few minutes before Allison gets here."

Chris smiled. "Let's just say that I was in the wrong place at the wrong time."

"Were you mugged?"

Chris squinted his eyes. "Well…not exactly."

Not exactly. What the hell does that mean? "I don't understand."

Chris closed his eyes for a few seconds. "They say if you're being held at gunpoint, do whatever the person wants. If he wants your money, give it to him. Your life isn't worth the contents of your wallet. In most cases, the person with the gun is just as nervous as you are. So, you should stay calm and talk to the person. Tell them your name or something about you. Humanizing yourself makes it harder for them to shoot. If you attempt to wrestle the gun out of their hands, there's a very good chance you're going to get shot. In my particular case, I knew if I didn't get the gun, I'd definitely be killed. So, I played the odds." He glanced at Jack. "And that's all you need to know."

Jack didn't want to push the subject. He knew, for some reason, Chris didn't want to talk about the incident. "Could you at least tell me how you got the gun away?"

Chris nodded. "He had the gun in my back and forced me to walk ahead of him. When he had to step over something that was in his way, he looked down. That's when I made my move. I jumped on him and wrestled him to the ground. I had my left hand on his wrist and my right hand on the barrel of the gun. I know you should never attempt to take a gun away from someone more **robust (#136)** than you, and this guy was much bigger and stronger than me. But, like I said, I had no choice. When I had a chance, I kneed him in the stomach. It knocked the wind out of him, and he loosened his grip on the gun. I stuck my finger into the trigger guard, then pulled the trigger twice. The first bullet hit him and the second bullet hit me."

"Where did the first bullet hit?"

Chris frowned and shook his head. "Let's go. Allison should be here soon." Chris started walking toward the end of the wharf. Jack followed. Chris said nothing more of the incident.

They drove the long way home along Oceanside Drive. While Chris debriefed Allison on the recent events, he stared at his GPS looking for the waypoint he had set earlier. When it was directly south of them, he tapped Allison on the shoulder. "Slow down. We're getting close. It has to be one of these houses."

Within this section of Oceanside Drive, they found three separate gated entrances. But due to the vegetation that flourished on the side of the road, their corresponding houses were barely visible.

Between the second and third driveways was a small bridge that provided a glimpse into a cove. "Stop here," Chris said. "I'll be right back." He hopped out, ran to the guardrail, and placed the binoculars to his eyes. A few seconds later, he was back in the Range Rover. "I think I see the boat. It's over there. It belongs to the house in the middle. Turn around. I want to get the address."

After obtaining the address, they continued to Chris's house. The tires screeched as Allison came to a stop in the driveway. Jack and Chris were running for the computer before she killed the engine. While Jack tried to calm Sherlock and Mycroft, who acted as if they had not seen them in years, Chris pecked at the keyboard. It did not take long to find a **plethora (#137)** of information. The owner was Hunter Edward Harrison. According to the county records, he had owned the house for five years. Further investigation revealed he owned a successful investment company in New York City called Harrison International Investments. On the company's webpage, his bio painted a picture of a man whose business **acumen (#138)** was the equivalent of a financial genius.

With his eyes fixed on the computer, Chris began thinking aloud. "So, he commutes from Manhattan." After a short pause, he raised his eyebrows and nodded. "A seaplane would be the quickest commute." Chris paused again, "But why so much luggage? And why would he put luggage back on the plane? Rich people with two houses tend to have two sets of everything. He wouldn't need to bring clothes home for the weekend."

"Are you speaking from experience?" Jack mumbled.

Chris, still fixated on the computer, snapped out of his trance when he heard Jack's comment. He smiled. "Yes, I am."

It was getting late, and the three decided to call it a night.

"I have a friend in New York who works on Wall Street. I'll give him a call tomorrow and find out what he knows about our boy Hunter Harrison. Allison and I have obligations in California and won't get home until late on Tuesday. If I find out anything important, I'll call you. If not, I'll see you on Wednesday."

"Cool. See you then."

Chris, along with the dogs, followed Jack out of the house. Jack opened the Explorer's door, but Chris stopped him before he got in. "I don't believe we should tell anyone about this just yet. Let's do a bit more research before we start jumping to any conclusions. And besides, if we're right and he is involved, he might get spooked if some cops come around asking a bunch of questions."

"You're right. I'll keep quiet. See you next Wednesday."

CHAPTER EIGHTEEN

Since it was Saturday, Jack left work at noon and went straight to the beach club. The gray, overcast sky did little to deter the members, and the place was packed.

The first friend Jack found was Ollie. He was at the pool, standing in front of three college girls doing a magic trick. Jack watched from a distance. The girls seemed generally impressed.

Ollie had a theory that all girls like puppies and magic tricks. Since he could not carry a dog with him everywhere he went, he used magic to meet girls. And it actually worked. Ollie was not **bashful (#139)**. He would go up to any girl and do a simple trick to break the ice.

Jack approached and tapped Ollie on the shoulder. "Excuse me, Oliver the Magnificent. Have you seen Courtney?"

Ollie flinched. "Oh, hey Jack. Yeah. She's at the far end of the beach with Lip and some other kids from school." Ollie put his hand on Jack's shoulder and pushed him closer to the girls. "This is Jack. Jack this is Mary, Heather, and Annabelle."

"Hey," Jack said with an upward nod of the head. The girls returned the greeting. "Ollie, I need to talk to you when you're done."

"I'll be there in a minute."

Jack trudged along the sandy beach, weaving through the mass of people. He saw Edward up ahead in a group trying to **emulate (#140)** his older friends. About eight of them were standing around having an **inane (#141)** conversation while seeing who could be the biggest jackass. Jack assumed Edward was winning. They made brief eye contact when he passed, but Edward quickly looked away. Jack mumbled, "Asshole," and kept on walking.

When he found Courtney, Jack spread out his towel and lay on his back looking up at the cloudy sky. "Any new info on the case?" he asked while wiggling the imprint of his body into the sand.

"I heard my dad say they hadn't gained anything from the video yet. The FBI is still analyzing it. Hopefully, they can find something."

"Yeah, hopefully." Although Jack wanted to tell her about the previous night's adventure, he kept his word and said nothing.

"Courtney, you're up," yelled Lip from the volleyball court.

"Be right there." Courtney stood and dusted the sand from her legs. "Are you going to watch me kick his butt?"

"Not this time. I'm going out on the paddleboard." After she walked away, Jack scanned the crowd for Ollie. He saw him approaching with a big smile on his face. "What are you so happy about?"

"I think Annabelle likes me."

"Ollie, you're a junior in high school, and she's in college. What makes you think she'll go out with you?"

For some unknown reason, Ollie preferred older women. "Age means nothing when two people like each other."

Jack rolled his eyes. He found Ollie's **predilection (#142)** for older women ridiculous. "Did you bring the stuff I asked for?"

"Sure did. Come over here." Ollie dug through his beach bag and removed a GoPro waterproof video camera with a headband mount and a wide-brim fishing hat.

"Thanks. Where's the paddleboard?"

Ollie pointed toward the surf. "Over there. Why'd you need all this stuff?"

Jack's idea was to paddle through the cove in which the speedboat retreated. The entire time he would video Hunter Harrison's house and grounds. He was not about to tell loudmouth Ollie of his plans. Instead, he made up a **convoluted (#143)** story. "I was riding my bike along Oceanside Drive the other day and got tired. So, I stopped at the little bridge next to the cove. You know where I'm talking about?"

"Yeah, the one by old man Simmons's pond. Why didn't you call me?"

"I just wanted to be alone. Anyway, I saw this old man in a rowboat. He was fishing in the cove. Every time he cast his line, he caught a fish.

I watched him reel in about a dozen fish."

"What kind of fish were they?"

Think. What kind of fish were they? "Flounder. I think they were flounder."

"No way! I love flounder. I'll go get my fishing poles and meet you there."

"Let me check it out first. Then we'll make a plan."

"It will only take me a few minutes to get my poles."

"Ollie, just let me check it out first. I don't know how long it's going to take to get there. Hell, I don't even know if I'll make it. I'll see you in a little while, okay?"

"Okay," Ollie replied, looking down at the sand like a sulking eight-year-old.

Jack gave Ollie a fist bump before he headed toward the paddleboard. "Why did I even say anything?" he mumbled to himself. On the way, he saw Edward carrying a tackle box and a fishing pole. Jack made eye contact. "Hey, Edward. Going surf fishing?"

Edward gave him a condescending stare for a moment. "No. I'm going to play tennis." He shook his head and kept on walking.

This **gratuitous (#144)** comment infuriated Jack. *What an asshole. Why do I even try to be nice to him?*

Jack was still fuming when he walked up to the paddleboard. He took several deep breaths before he placed the GoPro video recorder on his head. After he adjusted the headband, he put on Ollie's fishing hat. The hat had a three-inch brim that went around the entire circumference. The large, floppy brim made the camera less obvious.

A chill shot through Jack's body when he stepped into the water. Several small waves crashed against the paddleboard as he headed out into the ocean. By the time he was underway, he was soaked from head to toe.

After a half-hour of paddling, Jack approached the entrance to the cove. Before entering between two large rock formations, he turned on the GoPro camera and adjusted his hat. When he paddled into the cove, he saw Hunter Harrison's house straight ahead. The massive two-story house sat upon a rocky peninsula, atop a bluff of about twenty feet.

Jack followed the shoreline to the left and paddled around the peninsula. The entire time he looked at the Harrison estate in hopes of recording every square inch. When he was almost finished, the speedboat came into view. The docked boat was barely visible through the surrounding vegetation. *I need to get a closer look.* He started paddling toward it, but as he approached, a man exited the house and marched toward him.

"What are you doing here? This is private property," barked the man.

"I'm paddle boarding. What does it look like?"

"This is private property. You need to leave."

Anger filled Jack's body, and he let his emotions get the better of him. "I'm in public waters. I don't have to leave."

"These aren't public waters. You better leave before I call the law, or worse."

Jack spotted the outline of a handgun underneath the man's loose-fitting shirt. *I better not press my luck.* "I'm leaving," he yelled and then paddled toward the open ocean.

The more Jack paddled, the angrier he became. *This cove isn't private property. Why do I have to leave? He can't tell me to leave.* Jack glanced back at the man before he exited through the two large rocks. The man stood at the edge of the rocky bluff. He never let Jack out of his sight. *That seems strange. Why is he so protective of his property? I wonder what he's hiding?*

Jack arrived back at the beach club in just over an hour. He scanned the crowd looking for Ollie but could not find him. "Courtney, where's Ollie?"

"He left a few minutes ago. He looked kind of upset."

"I wonder why?"

"He said something about 'if he only had a puppy,' then grabbed his bag and walked away."

Throughout the afternoon, the **capricious (#145)** ocean breeze brought with it more clouds. The darkening sky was a **portent (#146)** of an approaching storm, and people started to leave. By four o'clock, a brief thunderstorm ran off almost everyone except the staff. Jack was one of the last to leave. He went straight home and downloaded the video. His mind raced the entire time. Deep inside, he started to believe

Hunter Harrison was up to no good. He had the **inchoate (#147)** feeling that somehow he was involved in Ian's disappearance. But how to prove it, he did not know.

Jack began his analysis of the Harrison estate that night after Reilly's walk. He reviewed the video and printed still shots that covered most of the property. He used Google Earth to print aerial photographs of not only the Harrison estate but also the surrounding properties. Since several video cameras covered the grounds, he marked the location of each one and made a note of the area it covered. By the time he finished, which was three in the morning, he had everything he needed to formulate a plan to infiltrate the property.

Sunday morning started with church at ten o'clock. Jack, still half asleep, sat on the hard, wooden pew next to his father. Between the monotone voice of the minister and the cool air blowing from the vent above, he had a hard time staying awake. Occasionally, his eyes closed and his head dropped. Each time it was met by a nudge from his father's left elbow.

Jack had no idea what the minister was saying. When he could concentrate, his mind was too busy analyzing the events of the last few days. From the information gained in the video, the suspicious aluminum suitcases in the plane, and the heavily guarded estate, he **espoused (#148)** the belief that Hunter Harrison probably had something to do with Ian's disappearance. By the end of the service, he had made up his mind. He was going that night to get a closer look at the Harrison estate.

Jack spent Sunday afternoon alone in his bedroom planning his mission. There were maps and photos scattered everywhere. They covered his bed, his desk, and part of the floor. He moved throughout the room like a robot examining each sheet of paper. Occasionally, he would walk to the window and stare outside. His mind raced with ideas.

His plan came to fruition during the analysis of an aerial photo. The aerial was of the property to the east, on the opposite side of the cove. *If I can sneak onto this property and hide in the bushes, I can watch the boat come and go. I might even get an idea of what's in the suitcases. You never know, maybe I'll see signs of Ian.* He stared out the window for a moment and thought how great it would be to find his friend.

Images of Chief McKinney escorting Ian, wrapped in a blanket, toward his father with dozens of police cars in the background—their flashing lights illuminating the night sky—filled his head. After he snapped back to reality, he sat at his desk for over an hour plotting a course across the terrain. His final plan had him hiding in the neighbor's yard around nine o'clock to watch the boat leave and return. If needed, he had an additional route that would take him directly to Harrison's front door.

"Mom, I'm going to Ollie's," Jack yelled up the staircase. He heard her muffled voice, which he assumed was her usual **trite (#149)** response, "Drive carefully, honey." *Why does she always say that? Like I'm going to drive like a maniac on purpose.* Jack gave his usual sarcastic reply of, "I wouldn't think of doing anything but," and then bolted out the back door.

"Drive carefully, honey," repeated in Jack's head while he drove along Oceanside Drive. It stopped, however, on his approach to the Culver's house. For what he saw almost made him turn around and go home. Parked in front of the path that led to Ollie's shed was Edward Sumpter's BMW. *What the hell is that asshole doing here?*

Jack reluctantly headed down the path to the shed. He let out a series of sighs along the way. When he opened the door, he found the two sitting in front of the television playing *Call of Duty*. Ollie had the better of the two powder blue chairs.

Edward and Ollie both glanced at Jack but did not say a word. They kept on fighting. Apparently, there was a lot at stake. The game ended with Edward jumping to his feet. As usual, he was full of **hubris (#150)**. For almost a minute, he bragged about his gaming skills while Ollie kept saying, "But I beat you in eight out of ten games."

When the argument ended, Edward turned to Jack. "Hey, haven't seen you in a while. How have you been doing?" He walked over and shook Jack's hand. Ollie followed.

You just saw me yesterday you dumbass. "Uh, okay I guess."

"You want to play? You can have the good seat."

"No, Edward. I can't stay. I just stopped by to drop off some of Ollie's things." Edward's **duplicity (#151)** drew great concern from Jack. *He sure is being awfully nice. He must have taken his medication* *today. Either that or he wants something. I don't trust the two-faced jerk.* "Ollie, here's your GoPro. You don't mind if I borrow your camera and your night vision goggles, do you?"

"Not at all. Why do you need them?"

Think. Why do you need them? "Uh, I'm going bird-watching tomorrow."

"In the dark?"

Oh, crap. He's right. You don't bird watch in the dark. "Uh, I'm leaving really early and have to walk deep into the woods before daybreak."

"Why don't you take a flashlight?"

"It will scare the birds."

"I thought you worked on Mondays?"

Damn. How many more questions can he think of? "I, I meant I'm going on Tuesday. Ollie, I'm kind of in a hurry."

"Okay. Follow me. They're in the closet in the other room. Edward, I'll be right back."

"What's he doing here?" Jack whispered while Ollie unlocked the door.

Ollie removed the camera and goggles and then handed them to Jack. "He just showed up."

Jack shook his head. "You're much nicer than me. I would have told him to leave."

"He's not that bad."

Jack frowned and turned toward the door. "I'll see you later. I have a few things to do before I take Reilly on his walk." Jack was reaching for the doorknob when he saw Ollie's fishing pole and tackle box. Since they usually stayed in the closet, he knew what was about to happen. *Oh crap. Now he's going to ask me fifty questions about a fishing hole that doesn't exist.*

Sure enough, the next words out of Ollie's mouth were, "What did you find out about the fishing spot?"

Jack drew a blank. The hours spent formulating his plan had fried his brain. Couple that with a lack of sleep, and he was speechless. He could think of only one way to get out of the conversation. He paused and acted as if he heard something. "Ollie, I think your phone's ringing." Ollie's eyes widened, and then he bolted to the other room. "I'll see you guys later," Jack yelled on his way out the door. He didn't wait for a response. *He'll fall for that every time.*

The last part of his preparations required a stop at Wal-Mart to purchase a pair of black sweatpants, a black sweatshirt, a cheap pair of black sneakers, and a black stocking cap. When the check-out clerk scanned the last item, she looked at Jack with a wrinkled forehead. "Looks like you're going to rob a house."

The comment caught Jack off guard. "Well, my friends and I are going to have a paintball war tonight."

"Yeah, right. I believe you," she said with a smile and then handed Jack his change.

For the past several nights, no one was home at the Andersons' house. This night, however, Jack found Mr. Anderson sitting alone in the kitchen. He was eating a sandwich while staring at the wall with solemn eyes.

"Mr. Anderson, are you all right?"

"Well, no. My wife is so depressed that she stopped eating. I had to commit her to a hospital the other day."

Jack sat silently while Mr. Anderson talked about his wife and his son. He didn't know what to do or say. He quickly realized that Mr. Anderson just wanted to talk. No matter who sat in front of him, he would likely say the same thing.

Images of the heartbroken Mr. Anderson raced through Jack's head while he and Reilly performed their evening ritual. When he wasn't thinking about the man whose life was falling apart and his wife who had reached her **nadir (#152)**, he was analyzing his upcoming mission. By the time he returned with his furry friend, he had become more **resolute (#153)** than ever in his quest to find Ian.

The house was dark and quiet when the two returned from their walk. Jack hung Reilly's leash on a hook near the door and then reached down and gently grabbed Reilly's little head. Reilly sat and
stared at Jack. "I'll find him for you little buddy. Even if it takes the rest of my life." Jack scratched Reilly between the ears for a moment before he headed home.

CHAPTER NINETEEN

The state park located a half-mile west of the Harrison estate would be the staging point for Jack's mission. Its parking lot ran parallel to Oceanside Drive and overlooked the ocean. At this time of night, the poorly lit lot was sparsely populated. The only people there were those who watched the sunset and had not yet left, or teenagers hanging out.

Jack parked the Explorer near the entrance to the park. He sat in silence, hands still gripping the steering wheel, while he contemplated what he was about to do. *What if I get caught? I guess that depends on who catches me. If it's the neighbor, I'll probably just get in trouble for trespassing. If it's Harrison's security guard, I might go missing, like Ian.* His mind raced. "I'll take that chance. I'm going to do it," he mumbled.

Jack scanned the area while he walked to the back of the Explorer. As far as he could tell, no one saw him remove his bike. "Here goes nothing," he whispered. He slipped his backpack over his shoulders and began his journey along Oceanside Drive. A stiff breeze that blew in from the ocean made it difficult to peddle.

The half-mile trek started with a shiver running up Jack's spine. His choice of clothing—boardshorts and a short-sleeve T-shirt—did little to protect him from the cool night air. By the time he approached the observation area, however, beads of sweat had run down the sides of his face.

Jack turned off his bicycle light and inspected the surroundings while he slowly peddled past. Seeing no oncoming cars, he doubled back, stashed his bike in a small clearing along the side of the road, and then put on the black sweatpants, sweatshirt, and stocking cap. He slipped the backpack over his shoulders, placed the night vision goggles on his head, and then took one last look for any oncoming cars.

Tree limbs and sticker bushes scraped against his body as he maneuvered through the vegetation. With every poke and scratch, he let out a series of cuss words, but only at a whisper. Thanks to Buddy, he had a few new ones to add to the mix. Several painful minutes later, he reached a gravel driveway. He paused for a moment to analyze the surroundings and then ran along this driveway to the bottom of a small hill. At this point, the natural vegetation ended and the manicured yard began. He crawled along the edge of the yard until he reached the rocky shoreline of the cove. There, he found a small clearing with just enough room to sit. While his eyes darted in every direction, he removed the camera from his backpack and installed the telephoto lens. A glance at his watch indicated it was eight forty-five.

The trek through the vegetation was more work than Jack had anticipated. An occasional breeze did little to lower his body temperature. He wiped his face with the bottom of his sweatshirt. *I should have brought a towel.*

Surrounded by sticker bushes and large clumps of seagrass, he waited for something to happen. The ground seemed to be getting harder by the minute. He constantly shifted his weight from one butt cheek to the other in an attempt to get comfortable. He wasn't having much luck.

A small separation in the foliage provided enough room to aim the telephoto lens across the cove. The night's full moon cast just enough light on the east side of Harrison's property to make most of it visible. Jack could see the front door, the docked boat, and a large portion of the driveway. He surveyed the estate but saw no activity.

The estate remained quiet until shortly after nine o'clock when a vehicle entered Harrison's driveway. Jack reached into his backpack and removed his iPhone. After a couple of taps on the screen, he had it set to voice memo mode. He looked through the camera lens and began to take notes.

"9:01, black Mercedes SUV enters the driveway. Dark-haired man, looks to be about thirty-years-old, removes two large aluminum suitcases from the back of the vehicle." *They look like the ones the men unloaded from the seaplane. Hmm. Looks like he's having a hard time carrying them.* "Suitcases are similar to those on the seaplane and appear to be heavy." Jack leaned forward and knelt close to the small opening. He extended the camera lens and adjusted its angle in an attempt to see the back end of the SUV. *Damn, I can't see the license plate. Maybe I can get it when he leaves.*

"9:04, driver walks to the front door and enters the house." *That's strange. He doesn't knock or ring the doorbell, he just walks in.*

"9:08, driver returns to Mercedes with two smaller aluminum suitcases and places them in the backseat." *Now, what's he doing? Looks like he's opening one of the suitcases. I need to see what's inside.* Jack leaned as far forward as possible and adjusted the angle of the camera lens in every direction. But no matter how he positioned it, he could not get a clear shot. *Damn, he's in the way.* Moments later, the man shut the case and returned to the driver's seat. *Looks like he's carrying a stack of papers.*

Jack kept his lens fixed on the driver and the SUV. After a minute, a light illuminated the interior of the vehicle. "9:10, driver appears to have opened a laptop." *Now, what's he doing? Is that a sheet of paper in his hand?* "Driver appears to be entering something into the computer."

Jack's knees started to ache, so he returned to his seated position. With his body temperature dropping and the breeze increasing, he could feel the chill in the air. At this point, however, it was tolerable. He went back to shifting his weight between butt cheeks while he stared through the camera lens.

"9:15, two men exit the residence through the front door." *That looks like the asshole that told me to leave the cove yesterday. The other guy must be Harrison. Yeah, he looks like the picture on the website.* "Harrison and the security guard head to the boat." *That's strange, they didn't wave or even look at the man in the Mercedes.* "9:18, boat leaves the cove."

Except for the man in the Mercedes SUV, who continued to work on his laptop, there was no other activity around the Harrison estate. Jack lowered the camera and rested it on his lap. *Now the waiting begins.* He pulled the sleeves of his sweatshirt over his hands as a shiver ran up his spine. Occasionally, he raised the camera to his eye and scanned the property. But all he ever saw was the man in the Mercedes.

Jack found it peaceful sitting amongst nature. When he wasn't looking through the camera lens, he was staring up at the clear sky. For some reason, the stars appeared brighter this night. He had settled into his surroundings, and the ground did not seem as hard as before—probably because his butt had gone numb.

After several minutes with no new activity, his eyelids became heavy. The **concomitant (#154)** of the water lapping against the rocky shoreline, the **serene (#155)** surroundings, and the breeze whistling through the trees made it hard to stay awake. *Don't fall asleep, Graystone,* he repeated several times. An occasional slap to the face assured he did not.

The sound of a boat motor got Jack's attention. He glanced at his watch. "9:47, boat enters the cove with only the security guard onboard." The guard quickly tied the boat to the dock and then headed for the house carrying two smaller aluminum suitcases. He walked directly to the front door, opened it, and went inside. A few seconds later, the front porch light turned off. *That's strange. He just walked by the man in the Mercedes. He didn't wave or say anything to him.*

The man in the Mercedes remained in the driver's seat making his entries into the laptop. Five minutes passed. Then ten minutes. *Hurry up, you asshole, I'm freezing out here.* Jack was now back to his kneeling position hoping to get a shot of the license plate. The camera was lying on the ground in front of him. His hands were underneath the sweatshirt.

"Finally," Jack muttered when he heard the Mercedes' engine start. He leaned forward with the camera next to his eye and his finger on the button. The white reverse lights lit a large area behind the SUV; however, he still had no direct line of sight on the license plate. *Back toward me, you asshole.* The Mercedes started down the driveway, moving parallel to Jack. At some point, it would have to turn around and change directions. If the vehicle turned to the right, he would not be able to get his picture. If the vehicle turned left, he should have a clear view of the tag. *Turn left. Turn left. If you don't turn left, I don't think I can get to the road before you drive by, you asshole.* Jack, still kneeling, was ready to snap a picture at any second. *Thank you, you asshole.* The Mercedes turned toward the left. Click, click, click. "Got it," he mumbled and then reached his iPhone. "10:02, Mercedes leaves the Harrison estate."

Jack moved back into the small clearing and grabbed his backpack. When he returned the camera to its case, he glanced at the counter. It indicated he snapped one hundred and thirty-six pictures. *Hopefully, I can get some information from these pictures.* He placed the camera case in the backpack and slid it over his shoulders. *That's enough. I'm freezing my balls off out here.* "10:05, only a few lights on in the house and I see no more activity."

Jack exited his vantage point the same way he had entered—night vision goggles on his head and cuss words flowing from his mouth. At his bike, he removed the black clothes (except for the sweatshirt), replaced all his gear into his backpack, and then began his trek back to the Explorer. While he peddled along Oceanside Drive, his mind raced. His **intuition (#156)** told him that Hunter Harrison was doing something illegal. The more he thought about it, the more questions he had. But of all the theories he purposed, none were without holes.

By the time he arrived at the Explorer, Jack had beads of sweat running down his cheeks. He leaned with his back against the truck while he caught his breath. "I bet I catch a cold," he mumbled before he opened the rear hatch and inserted his bike. He was just about to close the hatch when he heard the roar of an engine. He looked to his right and saw a car speeding toward him. Its high beams blinded him. Jack covered his eyes and jumped toward the side of the Explorer. *Dammit, I'm caught. Who could have seen me? I hope this isn't the man in the Mercedes. If it is, I'm running.* His body started to tremble.

The car was only a few feet away when blue lights on top started to flash. It was one of Worthington's finest. The police cruiser stopped behind the Explorer, blocking Jack in the parking space.

"You behind the car. Place your hands in the air!" directed a man with an unusually deep voice over the loudspeaker.

Jack closed his eyes and mumbled, "Oh, shit."

CHAPTER TWENTY

Jack complied and followed the police officer's orders. *The neighbor must have seen me. How am I going to talk my way out of this one?*

"Now, turn around and walk backward toward the police car."

Again, Jack was **compliant (#157)** with the officer's demands.

"Stop." The police officer did not speak for several uncomfortable seconds. Then Jack heard a familiar voice. "Now do ten jumping jacks."

Confused by the command at first, Jack quickly realized it was Officer Turner. He let out a long sight before he walked over to the driver side window. "Very funny." When he looked inside the police car, he noticed Officer Turner had a passenger. "Hi, Miss Baxley. Did you get in trouble tonight?"

She chuckled. "No, I'm just riding along."

"Jack. What are you doing out here at this time of night?" asked Officer Turner.

That's a good question. What am I doing? Uh…I'm trying to get in shape for football, so I went for a long bike ride. I lost track of time, and it got dark before I could get back here. Luckily I have a light on my bike."

Officer Turner pointed toward Jack's feet. "What happened to your legs?"

Jack looked down and saw several dried blood trails on both legs. *Oh crap. I didn't think I got that scratched up. Hmm. How could this have happened?* "I was playing with Courtney's cat earlier today, and it scratched me. I guess pedaling my bike made the scabs open." *That sounds reasonable. I hope he buys it.*

"You should have put some Band-Aids on them."

He bought it. "I'll do that when I get home."

"Be careful tonight." Officer Turner gave a quick wave before he gunned the engine and drove away.

Jack watched the police car disappear down the road and wondered if Officer Turner's and Miss Baxley's relationship was merely a **dalliance (#158)** or the start of something serious.

***

The following two days seemed to pass slowly. Jack, who analyzed the case constantly, was anxious to meet with Chris. When Wednesday finally arrived, he skipped going to the beach with his friends and went straight to his house. He arrived around noon to find Chris waiting in the study.

"Hi, Chris. How was the trip?"

"Let's just say it was very rewarding."

Jack sat upright in one of the slippery leather chairs with his eyes focused on Chris. "Did you get a chance to talk to your Wall Street friend?" he asked while his butt slowly slid toward the end of the seat.

"Yes, I did. He told me Hunter Harrison runs a very successful hedge fund called Harrison International Investments or HII for short.

"What's a hedge fund?"

"It's a company that invests people's money into different types of investment in hopes of making massive profits. The hedge fund receives its payment from these profits. So, the more money the investors make, the more money the hedge fund owner receives.

"Okay. HII is a hedge fund and Hunter Harrison is the owner?"

"Correct. My friend said the company is so successful that the Securities and Exchange Commission and FBI have been examining it for years. But their books are flawless, and they can't find any illegal activities. The joke among the Wall Street crowd is that he must be laundering drug money."

"Well, they might not be too far off."

"Why's that?"

"I did some of my own detective work while you were gone. Look at this." Jack played the video of the Harrison estate and showed Chris the pictures from the stakeout. He then went on to explain how the man made him leave the cove and described the events that occurred during the exchanging of the aluminum suitcases from both the boat and the black Mercedes. Throughout the conversation, Jack continued to proclaim his belief that Hunter Harrison was responsible for Ian's disappearance.

"Jack, you never cease to amaze me. This is great detective work. There's only one problem. What does it prove? Harrison is into all kinds of businesses. The aluminum suitcases might have a perfectly good explanation. As for Ian's disappearance, we still can't explain how they could've abducted him."

"So, you think this was all a waste of time?"

"Absolutely not. I agree with you. I think Harrison could very well be involved in Ian's disappearance. But this theory is one among many. We shouldn't put all our eggs in one basket."

Jack looked at the floor and rubbed his chin. "Well, what should we do next?"

"When I was in California, I asked my Wall Street friend to set up a meeting with Harrison. He thinks I want to invest with him. My meeting is tomorrow at his office in Manhattan. Allison and I are taking the train in the morning. We'll be back tomorrow evening. Stop by then, and we'll go over whatever I find out. We can decide at that time whether to get the FBI involved. Does that sound like a good plan?"

"Yeah, sounds good." Jack was about to leave but stopped. "Chris, do you have a lock-picking set I could borrow?"

"Yes, but why do you need it?"

"I want to learn how to pick locks."

"I don't know. Lockpicking can get you in trouble."

"Well, don't you think if I'm going to be a good detective, I should know how to do it?"

Chris looked at Jack and tilted his head. "Yeah, I guess so."

"And as my mentor, don't you think it's your obligation to show me?"

Chris laughed. "No, I don't think it's my obligation to show you." He then patted Jack on the back. "It's nice to know that you think of me as a mentor." Chris started to walk out of the study. When he got to the door, he looked at Jack and shook his head. "Against my better judgment, I'll give you a quick lesson. But if I find out you used this skill for any reason other than detective work, you'll be in big trouble."

The two went into the spy room where Chris retrieved one of his lock-picking sets. For the next half-hour, Chris, an **adept (#159)** lock-picker, demonstrated the process on several locks throughout the house.

"It's not as easy as it looks," said Jack.

"It takes practice. Take this set home with you. I'm sure after a while you'll get the **knack (#160)** of it."

"Thanks, Chris. I'll talk to you tomorrow." Jack leaped down the steps to the front porch with a smile on his face. His **sophistry (#161)** had worked. He now had a special skill that could come in handy when he snooped around Harrison's house.

CHAPTER TWENTY-ONE

By quitting time on Thursday, the smell of automobile fumes had taken its toll on Jack. Exhausted from cleaning a record number of cars, he folded his arms over the steering wheel and rested his head. He sat in silence, absorbing the cool air from the Explorer's vents while he mentally prepared for the dreaded commute home. After a quick slap to the face by both hands, he put the Explorer in drive, turned on the radio, and then started his trek.

It was the usual ten-minute interrogation, which started the second Jack walked through the door. After several attempts to get away from his parents, he finally escaped and went to his bathroom to take a shower. Steam had begun to fill the room when his phone buzzed and almost vibrated off the vanity. He identified the caller as Chris on FaceTime.

"Hey, Chris."

"Hey, Jack. Allison and I got a late start." Chris pointed his phone toward Allison. She waved and said hello. "We just got on the train and won't be home until after midnight. I wanted to call and tell you about my meeting with our boy Hunter Harrison before it got too late."

"How'd it go?"

"It was very interesting. We met in his office for over two hours. He gave me a **prospectus (#162)** that explains where his company has invested and what they plan to do in the future."

"Did you tell him that you also live in Worthington?"

"Yeah, I mentioned it, and he volunteered that he commutes by seaplane from the city. I asked him if he commutes daily because I see the plane during the week. He explained to me that he has invested in a natural gas exploration company that has a new drilling process. It's supposed to 'make billions' according to him. Since the process requires **copious (#163)** amounts of water, the Environmental Protection Agency makes them take water samples to check for ground contamination. He told me the plane also picks up the samples and delivers them to his house before being sent for processing."

"So, do you think that's the reason for the suitcases?"

"That's the **ostensible (#164)** reason. It could be water samples. It could be drugs. Or, who knows what else. I went ahead and called my contact at the FBI. I explained everything we uncovered so far. He said he was going to check up on old HH."

"Did you tell him about the seaplane being close to shore right before Ian ran past the camera?"

"Yeah, I told him everything in great detail. He said to give him a couple of days to look into this."

"So, what do we do next?"

Chris frowned and shook his head. He knew the **paucity (#165)** of clues left few leads and he was becoming **disillusioned (#166)** with the investigation. "Well, that's a good question. I'd say start following our other leads, but we don't really have any other than Brian Carter. I guess we wait to hear from my FBI contact. Meanwhile, we keep looking for clues. Stop by tomorrow. We can regroup and make a new plan of attack."

"Okay, I'll see you tomorrow."

After his shower, Jack sat at his desk and stared out the window. With his gaze was fixed on two squirrels chasing each other up and down a tree, he analyzed the few clues to Ian's disappearance. The longer he analyzed these clues, the more convinced he became that Hunter Harrison was involved. But exactly how, he did not know.

Jack changed his attention to the photos, maps, and plans he had gathered and studied their every detail. Earlier in the week, he had obtained a copy of the Harrison estate's architectural drawings from the Building Department at city hall. These plans showed the exact layout of the residence. One at a time, he memorized each of the residence's three floors. He also analyzed the topography of the site, in addition to the location of each video camera. He ate dinner alone in his room, and by the time he was ready to leave for Reilly's walk, he had formulated his mission to infiltrate the Harrison estate.

After Reilly's walk, Jack stopped by Wal-Mart and purchased the remaining items needed for his mission. These included: two black towels, a vacuum-sealable plastic clothes storage bag, a black backpack, camouflage face paint, two voice-activated digital recorders, and a waterproof case for his iPhone. He then stopped by Ollie's house on the way home to borrow his short wetsuit, surfing booties, scuba mask, and the Spare Air scuba tank.

Ollie pointed at the Spare Air as Jack walked out of the shed. "See, I told you it might come in handy someday."

Jack laughed. "I should've never doubted you. See you tomorrow."

When Jack arrived home, his parents were already in bed. He stopped by to say goodnight and then went to his room to assemble the gear for his mission. He filled the plastic storage bag with a set of black sweats, a pair of black sneakers, a black stocking cap, Ollie's night vision goggles, and a black towel. The storage bag served two purposes. First, it would condense and secure the items. And second, it would provide a watertight method of transporting. For the bag to work, however, he had to attach it to a vacuum and remove all the air. Jack knew this would be a noisy operation that would most likely wake his parents. So, he went to the basement to finish the job.

After returning to his bedroom, he placed the two digital recorders, several pairs of latex gloves, and the lock-picking set into a separate Ziploc bag. He put this Ziplock bag, along with the other gear, inside the black backpack. The last items he backed were the Spare Air, his surfing booties, the diving mask, and the face paint. He finished around midnight and then jumped into bed.

Jack went over his plan one more time while he tried to fall asleep. Everything hinged on one main event. While on his **reconnaissance (#167)** mission last Sunday, he had discovered a critical flaw in the Harrison estate's protection. The security guard did not lock the front door before he departed in the boat. If he did not lock the door, he most likely did not set the alarm. Jack assumed the person waiting in the Mercedes was responsible for guarding the property. But from this man's vantage point, he could not see the front door. With this **astute**

(#168) observation in mind, the southerly side of the house would be penetrable through the cove. As long as the door continued to remain unlocked, his plan should work.

Jack's plan required him to ride his bike to the hiding place he had found on his previous mission while wearing a short wetsuit underneath a long-sleeve T-shirt and boardshorts. He would hide the bike and then enter the cove wearing only the wetsuit, booties, and the backpack that contained his gear. After the boat left, he would swim underwater to the far end of the property where he would take off the wetsuit, dry off, put on his sweats, and then enter the house. While inside, he would search for any signs of Ian and hide the voice-activated recorders. He would place one of them in the kitchen/family room area and the other in Hunter Harrison's office. Finally, he would exit the way he entered and be back at his bike before the boat returned. The following Sunday, he would perform the same mission. But this time, he would extract the recorders.

Based on his calculations, Jack determined he had thirty minutes to get in and out. In his mind, he **allocated (#169)** specific amounts of time for each task. He knew if he fell behind it would be difficult to get off the property.

***

The anticipation of the mission had weighed on Jack all the following day. The big question, should I, or shouldn't I, dominated his thoughts. He tried to analyze the pros and the cons, but all he could think about were the cons. At least a dozen times throughout the day, he decided to abort the mission. But every time, the image of Ian running along the Ocean Walk with that terrified look on his face made him change his mind.

That evening, Jack skipped dinner and went to Chris's house before Reilly's walk. It wasn't that he didn't have time to eat, he was just too nervous and had no appetite. By the time he flopped into one of Chris's slippery leather chairs, he still did not know what he was going to do.

"So, did your FBI friend look into Harrison?"

"I just got off the phone with him before you got here. We talked for over an hour. He said 'at this time they don't think it's very likely Harrison is involved.' After analyzing everything I told him, they just don't have enough to go on."

The words "they just don't have enough to go on" resonated in Jack's head. He leaned forward, placed his elbows on his knees, and stared at the ground. *That's it. I'm going. I know Harrison is involved somehow.* Jack was **adamant (#170)** in his beliefs that Harrison was up to no good, and he was not about to give up. *If they want proof, I'll get it.*

"Jack, something wrong?"

Jack gave no **intimation (#171)** of what he was about to do. If he did, he knew Chris would stop him. "No. I just have a lot on my mind. Now, what do we do?"

"I have no idea. They have Brian and Conner under surveillance. So, there's not much we can do there." Chris stood and looked out the window. "This can't be a random abduction. Someone had to know Ian would be walking along Oceanside Drive at that time of night." Chris walked over to the dry erase board. "His father isn't telling us something," he said tapping the board with the end of a marker. He uncapped it and circled Mr. Anderson's name.

"Why do you say that? I see Mr. Anderson almost every day. He's devastated. I can't see him being involved."

Chris shook his head. "So many times, people try to handle these situations themselves. As soon as the kidnappers say they're going to kill their victim if the police get involved, people do crazy things. I have a guy who can look into Mr. Anderson's affairs starting on Monday." Chris glanced at Jack. "We may need to borrow your key to his house."

"He works late on Mondays. You can go in while I walk Reilly." Jack glanced at his watch. *Seven thirty. If I walk Reilly now, I can be home just after eight and at Harrison's house before nine.* "I have to go. I'll get with you tomorrow to make a plan."

"You might have to wait until Monday. Allison and I will be gone most of the weekend."

"Okay, I'll stop by after work."

***

Jack returned home from Reilly's walk by eight fifteen. Ten minutes later, he grabbed his backpack and started his mission. While he peddled along Oceanside Drive, his nervousness turned into an adrenaline rush. He tried not to think about what he was about to do. He knew if he overanalyzed it, he would turn around.

It took two passes to find the hiding place he used on the previous mission. Just as before, sticker bushes scraped against his arms and legs when he pushed his bike into the small clearing. From the time he left home to until this point, he had never stopped peddling, and his legs now felt the burn. He leaned against a tree while he waited for the tingling to subside.

A glance at his watch indicated it was 8:53 p.m. By this time of day, the hot summer sun gave way to a crisp, moonlit New England night. This cool air had little, if any, effect on his body. Between the peddling and the adrenaline, sweat rolled down both cheeks. He used the bottom of his shirt to dry his face. Then he reached into his pocket, removed the can of camouflage paint, and smeared it all over.

After he removed his outer layer of clothing—T-shirt, boardshorts, and sneakers—Jack went over the details of his mission one last time. While wearing only the short wetsuit, he leaned back against the tree, closed his eyes, and visualized the house's floor plan. *Okay, you're going to check the rooms on the main level first. It's mostly open, so you shouldn't have any trouble. Hide one recorder in the family room and the other in Harrison's study. I bet the study is locked. That's okay. You have your picks. Then, go upstairs to the second floor. There's four bedrooms and three bathrooms to check. Finally, go to the basement. If Ian's there, that's most likely where he'll be. Remember to look at your watch. You want to be crawling out of the house with ten minutes to spare. That should be plenty of time to get back to safety.*

The doubts started to race through his head again. *Stop it. You know what you have to do.* His hands had a slight tremor as he removed the surfing booties and scuba mask from his backpack. The booties went on his feet. The mask stayed in the clutch of his hand.

Jack was about to climb out of the thicket when the sound of an oncoming car made him duck for cover. He could hear the engine before he saw headlights. After it passed, he adjusted the iPhone strapped to his left arm, and although he had checked three times that he had turned it off, he checked once more to be sure. He was paranoid that it would ring at an inopportune moment.

The safest route into the cove was to run along Oceanside Drive for about a hundred yards to a small bridge that connected the cove to Old Man Simmons's pond. Jack poked his head out of the thicket and looked both ways. He listened for the sound of a car's engine, but all he heard were the **intermittent (#172)** breezes that rustled the surrounding foliage and the faint roar of the ocean off in the distance. His heart started to pound. "Game on," he whispered before he stepped onto the road and began to run. The booties provided little protection from the pebbles scattered along the roadside. With each step, they poked his feet. His running motion looked more like someone walking on hot coals, rather than a sprinter in a race.

When he reached the bridge, he descended the rocky embankment into the pond. Cautiously, he walked under the bridge and then stopped to catch his breath. With only his feet in the water, he continuously scanned the area while he removed the Spare Air from his backpack and placed it in his mouth. His heart continued to pound, but not from exhaustion or fear. Fear had left his body. It was from adrenaline. His head was clear, and he had all his senses focused on his mission. He had memorized what to do and thought of nothing else. If his mind started to wander, he concentrated on the image of Ian running along the Ocean Walk with that frightened look on his face.

With the backpack securely attached and the scuba mask now covering his face, he slowly immersed himself into the cold water. The water was shallow at this point, and he could walk far enough into the cove to see that the boat had not left. He waited behind a large rock with only his head above water while he analyzed how far he needed to swim.

As anticipated, the Mercedes entered the driveway, and the man went to exchange his suitcases. Shortly after, two men exited the house. One was the driver who carried two smaller aluminum suitcases that he placed in the rear of the Mercedes. The other was the security guard who walked to the boat carrying two larger aluminum suitcases.

Jack glanced at his watch. It was 9:21 p.m. He remained hidden behind the rock while the boat motored out of the cove and disappeared into the darkness of the open ocean. *Okay, Graystone. Here is the moment of truth. Do you really want to do this? Once you enter that house, there's no turning back. And you don't know what you're going to find. It could be good, or it could be bad.* Jack closed his eyes. *Or you could get caught. And if that's the case, your dad and the chief won't be able to get you out of this one.*

Jack took a moment to process his thoughts. "I have to find Ian. I'm going in," he mumbled. Without making a ripple, he sank underwater and swam toward the far end of the cove. When he thought he was close, he surfaced to check his location. With fifty feet to go, he submerged and swam until he felt the rocky shore. He then eased his head out of the water and glanced around. Ahead of him was Harrison's mansion sitting on its rocky perch.

The shoreline was narrow, having only five or six feet of level ground before the jagged rock shot twenty feet up out of the water. At its base were several large boulders that would provide protection while he made his preparations. Jack crawled onto the shore and then scurried behind one of these boulders. He then removed his backpack and placed it on the ground in front of him. Slowly, he unzipped it, trying not to make a sound. It did not matter, though. The roar of the ocean and the gentle waves lapping against the shore concealed any noise he made.

His eyes darted in every direction while he emptied the contents of the plastic storage bag. He grabbed the black sweats, sneakers, and towel, and after he peeled off his wetsuit, he quickly dried off and dressed. Next, he grabbed the night vision goggles and stocking cap, both of which he placed on his head. Since he had no pockets, he put one end of the Ziploc bag containing his tools in his mouth and held it with his teeth. With one last look around, he was ready to go.

The small cliff situated between him and the house seemed much larger when he stood in front of it. "Here we go," he whispered before he reached into the air and grabbed hold. Slowly, cautiously, he scaled the rocks being careful of where he placed his hands and feet. His main concern was that a large portion of rock would break loose and fall to the ground below. If that happened, he was sure the noise would get the attention of the man in the Mercedes. His only option at that point would be to abort the mission.

Only a few pebbles broke loose while he made the **arduous (#173)** climb. They looked like pinballs bouncing to the ground. At the summit, he paused to catch his breath. Slowly, he peeked over the edge and analyzed the surroundings. Harrison's house was about one hundred feet directly north of him. It was a large stone structure surrounded by an elaborate planting of trees and shrubs. The front door was located on the east side, within a covered porch that was elevated three feet. On either side of this porch was a large, perfectly manicured holly bush.

From what he could see, the safest route to the front door was to crawl behind the shrubbery that paralleled the stone foundation. If he stayed close to the house, he would be out of the line of sight from the man in the Mercedes. With this in mind, he took one last scan of the area and then crawled on his hands and knees toward the corner of the house.

Jack kept a constant lookout for any signs of activity while he maneuvered through the bushes. He passed two basement windows set in wells that were about two feet deep. Both windows were dark, similar to most of the windows in the house. When he arrived at the porch, he stopped. He remained on his hands and knees and stared at the ground. His heart continued to race. But now, it wasn't from adrenaline. Now, it was from fear. Not only the fear of breaking and entering. But also, the fear of what he might find. He knew that once he opened the door, there was no turning back. *Stay focused, Graystone. You know what you have to do.* He cleared these thoughts by visualizing his frightened friend running along the Ocean Walk.

From where the man parked the Mercedes, he did not have a direct view of the front door. Jack could hop on the porch undetected; however, there was one problem. His body would create shadows from the front porch lights. These shadows, the man could see. Jack knew he had to stay close to the building, but there was barely enough room to squeeze behind the holly bush that flanked the left side of the porch. "Here goes nothin," he mumbled before he shimmied toward the porch.

He whispered a series of cuss words as his back scraped against the rough stone wall and holly bush poked his stomach and face.

Before Jack climbed onto the porch and approached the door, he opened the Ziploc bag and put on a pair of latex gloves. He then took several deep breaths. He knew this was a decisive moment. *Will the door be unlocked? Will the alarm not be set?* He hopped onto the porch, extended his trembling hand toward the doorknob, grabbed hold, and then gave it a twist. The internal latch clicked just before the door opened with a soft squeak. He paused for a moment to listen for any alarms. It was quiet. So, with a flick of a switch, he turned on his night vision goggles and stepped inside.

With the floor plan memorized, Jack began his assault on the house. It looked like a well-choreographed dance as he went room by room looking for Ian. The first floor contained the main living areas and was mostly open. Unfortunately, he found no signs of his friend. When he entered the family room, he scanned the furnishings for the best place to hide the first voice-activated recorder. On a shelf near the breakfast table was a decorative vase. Jack turned on the recorder, dropped it inside, and then proceeded to Harrison's study. As anticipated, Harrison had locked the door. *What do I do?* He scratched his head. *I'll come back to this room after I check upstairs.*

Without hesitation, he went upstairs and inspected each bedroom and bathroom. He looked in every closet and under every bed—he even checked the showers—but found nothing to indicate Ian was ever there. Jack glanced at his watch. It was 9:32 p.m. He had nineteen minutes to plant the last recorder, check out the basement, and get back to safety.

Jack decided to deviate from the plan by checking the basement first, followed by planting the recorder in the study on his way out. He headed to the basement knowing there were two bedrooms separated by a bathroom and one large open room. He entered the open room first. It was furnished with a pool table, several couches, and in one corner, a large bar. Jack looked around but saw no signs of Ian. He then ran to the first bedroom door and found that it was made of steel. He grabbed the handle and turned, but the door was locked. He then went to the second bedroom door. Similar to the first door, it was made of steel and also locked. He knocked on both doors, called Ian's name, and then listened for a response. But one never came.

Jack checked his watch and determined he had thirteen minutes to finish the mission. He ran back at the study's door, removed the lock-picking set, and then went to work. He had practiced at home and had become quite the **deft (#174)** lock picker. After three minutes, which felt like a lifetime, the door finally opened. Jack gazed throughout the room for a hiding place. He spotted a fake plant on a shelf next to a large desk that dominated the room. After placing the recorder under the decorative moss in the pot, he scanned the room for clues. Finding nothing, he left, locking the door behind him.

Jack glanced at his watch while he prepared to exit the house. He had eight minutes remaining. With one last scan to survey the area, he opened the door, crawled off the porch, squeezed by the holly, and then crept through the bushes along the side of the house. After a short pause to catch his breath, he continued his crawl to the edge of the property. This was where Jack was most **vulnerable (#175)**. If the boat returned while he was scaling the rock face, he would have nowhere to hide. His body became tense, and he struggled to find footholds as he backed down the small cliff. It was much easier ascending than descending.

The descent was taking much longer than anticipated. Jack knew the boat could return at any moment. Due to these **exigent (#176)** circumstances, he decided to jump the last five feet. He looked down, and with all his energy, pushed away from the jagged cliff. He lost his balance when he landed on the slippery rocks below. While he fell backward, he held out a hand to break his fall. When his hand hit the ground, his wrist bent at such an angle that an intense pain shot up his arm. He jumped up and shook his arm. He hoped this would **palliate (#177)** the pain; however, it did not. His wrist continued to throb.

With no other choice, Jack painfully opened the storage bag and inserted his gear. He removed his clothes and shoes, finished packing the bag and backpack, put on his wetsuit, and then slid into the water. Before submerging, he listened one last time for the motorboat. Not hearing a sound, he turned on the Spare Air, submerged, and then swam toward the bridge.

It did not take long for Jack to realize there was air in the storage bag, which made the backpack more **buoyant (#178)**. Consequently, this made the swim considerably more difficult. With his wrist hurting and his muscles aching, he persevered. He had counted 110 strokes on the swim out of the cove. He was at eighty-five strokes on the swim into the cove when his body began to give out. His legs started to cramp, and his lack of energy **exacerbated (#179)** his ability to stay submerged. He wanted to stop, but he could hear the engine from the motorboat echoing through the water. He continued to swim, and when he got to 110 stokes, he painfully added ten more for security.

When Jack popped his head out of the water, he was not far from the bridge. He staggered the remainder of the way and then rested under the concrete structure until the Mercedes left the Harrison estate. When it was safe to leave, he jogged back to his bike, wiped the camouflage paint from his face, dressed, and then peddled back home.

CHAPTER TWENTY-TWO

Washing cars the next morning proved to be a difficult task. Although his **resilient (#180)** muscles had recuperated from the swim, Jack's wrist continued to ache. He muddled through until noon, and then he and his throbbing wrist went directly home.

Other than the fact that he could not stop thinking about the recorders hidden in Harrison's house; the rest of the day was a typical Saturday. He went to dinner and a movie with Courtney, followed by the couple walking Reilly, and then finished the evening by hanging out at Ollie's shed. Luckily, by the end of the night, the pain in his wrist had subsided.

The anticipation of retrieving the recorders continued to weigh on Jack the following day. By that evening, it was almost unbearable. He walked Reilly earlier than usual and arrived at his hiding place around nine o'clock. He was in the cold water waiting for the boat to leave shortly after that.

Jack was considerably less nervous on this mission. He thought it should be simple. *All I have to do is get in and retrieve the recorders. I should be in and out within six or seven minutes.*

Like clockwork, the Mercedes entered the driveway, and the men made their usual exchanges of suitcases. Jack glanced at his watch when the boat motored out of the cove. After one last inspection of his surroundings, he took a deep breath and began his underwater swim. He surfaced when his hand hit the rocky shoreline, and then he followed the same routine as on the previous mission.

Jack was ready to scale the small cliff within a couple of minutes. In an effort to make his descent easier and less painful, he made a mental note of the best footholds on his climb. When he reached the top, he slowly poked his head over the edge to survey the area. Seeing no one, he crept across the lawn to the corner of the house. Similar to last time, he crawled between the house and the shrubbery to the front door. His only hope was that the door remained unlocked. Carefully, he turned the doorknob, and sure enough, the door opened.

With a flick of a switch, Jack activated the night vision goggles and began retrieving the recorders. He acquired the one in the breakfast room, first, and then made his way to the study. Just as before, he picked the lock and was in the room within three minutes. He dug through the moss to obtain the second recorder and then headed for the front door. His heart started to pound. The anticipation of listening to the recordings and finding out what was on them was almost more than he could bear. *Stay focused,* he repeated to himself. At the rate he was going, it would not be too much longer until he knew.

Jack hopped off the porch, squeezed by the holly bush, and then started his crawl toward the cliff. He was looking straight ahead when he saw a grasshopper heading for his face. Before it hit, he turned his head to the right, toward the house. He was now staring at one of the two basement windows, and what he saw made him freeze in astonishment. The hairs on his arms stuck straight up and a rush of adrenaline pierced through his body. This **fortuitous (#181)** glance would change the course of the investigation. From the illumination of the porch light, he could make out three small letters smeared in the dust and dirt on the lower left-hand corner of the window. These letters were a small, backward *C*, a large *A*, and a small *I*. If seen from the inside of the room, they would be I. A. C., the same monogram embroidered on almost every article of Ian's clothing.

Jack crawled toward the basement window and placed his night vision goggles against his face. When he peered inside, he noticed metal security bars on the inside of the window. Through a small separation in the curtains, he could barely make out a sparsely furnished room consisting of a single bed, a television, and a chair. Unfortunately, there was no Ian. He crawled to the other basement window, but it was impossible to see through the blacked-out glass.

Based on his quick calculations, he had eighteen minutes to get back to the bridge. *Okay. I can get back to the bridge in eight minutes if I* push it. *That leaves me with no more than ten minutes to make this **digression (#182)** and go back inside. But will that be enough time? Or, should I stick to the original plan and get back to the bridge now? I could then go straight to the chief. But if I get the police involved, will they be able to get him out safely if he's in there? Or, if he's not in there and the cops start asking a lot of questions, will they remove any evidence that he was?* Several seconds ticked away before he mumbled, "Screw it. I can't take any chances. I'm going in."

His heart continued to pound while he crawled back to the front door and reentered the building. With the precision of a ninja, he made his way to the basement where he opened the lock-picking set and went to work on the locked bedroom door. The lock proved challenging to open. With a constant eye on his watch, he jiggled the slim metal picks in the keyhole. After what seemed like an eternity, the door finally opened.

Jack entered the room with his heart pounding in his chest. "Ian, are you in here?" He waited a few seconds before he said, "Ian, it's me, Jack Graystone. Can you hear me?" Again, he waited, but to his **chagrin (#183)**, he heard no response.

With little time to spare, he went over to the window. He needed to take a picture, but worried the flash from the camera on his iPhone would get the attention of the man in the Mercedes. Not knowing how the picture would turn out, he turned off the flash, placed the phone a foot away from the initials, and then snapped the photo.

Next, he went to the other door in the bedroom. He knew this door opened into a bathroom that separated the two bedrooms. But what he did not know was who could be on the other side. Slowly, he opened the door and poked his head inside. He listened for a moment but heard nothing.

The bathroom appeared as if no one had recently used it. There were no bottles of shampoo in the shower or bath towels hanging on the towel bar. The only items were a dirty hand towel lying next to the sink and a toothbrush and tube of toothpaste sticking out of a plastic cup in the medicine cabinet. On the opposite side of this bathroom was another door that opened into the other bedroom.

Jack placed his ear to the door. Again, he heard nothing. Carefully, he opened it but stopped before he entered the room. He was amazed at the sight before him. Inside this room were two large tables. One contained a money-counting machine and stacks of cash. The table was **rife (#184)** with bundles of twenties, fifties, and hundred-dollar bills. There was enough **currency (#185)** to fill the trunk of an average-sized car. A variety of items sat on the other table: several digital scales, a chemical testing kit, an assortment of plastic bags, and, as Jack assumed, bricks of cocaine.

Jack looked at his watch. He had only one minute remaining before he had to leave the house. *What should I do? I know, get proof.* He grabbed two ten-thousand-dollar stacks of hundred-dollar bills and several small Ziploc bags containing the white powder. He then put his iPhone on video mode and recorded the entire room. *That should be enough proof. I need to get out of here.* He started to leave but stopped in the bathroom. *I wonder if that's Ian toothbrush.* He snatched the toothbrush and then bolted out of the bedroom, locking the door behind him.

With only a hundred-foot crawl, a three-hundred-foot swim, and a fifteen-minute bike ride between him and solving the case, Jack became light-headed. His entire body tingled with excitement as he started up the basement stairs. But halfway up, just as the front door came into view, his worst fear became a reality. Through the side windows that flanked the door, he saw the figure of a man approaching. There was no time to retreat. His only option was to drop to the ground and hope this person did not look down the stairwell. The tingling in his body turned to a tremble, and his heart was pounding so hard, he could feel it in his throat. The sound of the doorknob turning and the creak of the opening door rang through his ears. All his senses were hyperactive. With his chin resting on a stair and his eyes fixed on the entrance to the foyer above, he waited, holding his breath. *If he sees me, I'm going to catch him off guard and tackle him. Then, I'm going to kick him in the balls and run as fast as I can. That should give me enough time to get away and hide in the bushes. The cops should get here before he finds me.*

Jack could not see this person. He did not know whether it was the man in the Mercedes or the security guard. The front door shut, and then he heard footsteps. *Don't come down here. Don't come down here.* Seconds that seemed like minutes passed. Luckily, the footsteps continued toward the kitchen. Jack exhaled. With his eyes still looking upward, he crawled down the stairs and ducked behind a wall in the basement. *Shit! I only have seven minutes. I hope this is the man from the Mercedes. But what if it's the security guard? He couldn't have gotten back this quick. Oh no. What if it's the man in the Mercedes and he doesn't plan on leaving right away. I could be trapped in here all night.*

Jack listened to the person walk into the kitchen and open the refrigerator. He then heard the click from the opening of a metal can, followed by footsteps leading toward the front door. Jack breathed a sigh of relief, but this was **ephemeral (#186)**. The person came to an abrupt stop and changed directions. He was now walking toward the basement stairs.

Jack scanned the basement and found several pool cues hanging on the wall. He quietly removed one and waited. If necessary, he planned to hit the person in the head, and then run away as fast as possible. But before he got the chance, the man began using the bathroom above. When he finished, Jack heard the man walk out of the house and shut the front door.

That must have been the man in the Mercedes. Jack glanced at his watch again. *Okay. I have four minutes to do what typically takes ten. You know what you have to do.*

In his days of preparation, Jack had formulated a contingency plan for this situation. He went back upstairs and looked through the kitchen window to verify that the man was in the Mercedes. Seeing that he was, he then opened the front door and crawled to the corner of the house where he waited for the boat to return.

A few minutes later, the boat entered the cove. As soon as it docked, Jack crawled to the cliff where he started his descent. Just before his head dropped below the cliff's edge, he saw the security guard heading toward the house. He stopped and listened for the front door to close. Time ticked by slowly. Almost a minute passed, and he never heard the sound. He had the feeling if he looked up, he would see the man standing over him with a gun. He remained motionless, dangling from the cliff. It did not take long before his hands began to cramp from his **tenacious (#187)** grip on the jagged rocks. Finally, the door closed and the porch light went dark. He breathed a sigh of relief before he continued downward, reversing the moves he used climbing up the jagged face.

When he reached the bottom, he changed clothes and packed his gear. Jack knew from his previous mission that the backpack would be more buoyant, making the swim to shore more difficult. To **attenuate (#188)** this buoyancy, he placed a rock of about ten pounds in the bag for **ballast (#189)**.

After one last scan of the area, Jack eased into the water and swam toward the bridge. With every stroke, his nervousness turned to excitement. He now had the **empirical (#190)** evidence he needed. It was no longer a theory that Hunter Harrison was involved in Ian's disappearance. And although he was upset that he did not find his friend, he knew the investigators would start getting answers to their questions.

Jack reached his destination in a record ninety-eight strokes. He poked his head above water just as the Mercedes passed over the bridge. Within a matter of seconds, he was at his bike. He stopped to catch his breath before he slipped his T-shirt and boardshorts over his wetsuit, slung the backpack over his shoulder, and then pushed his bike out of the thicket. His excitement was so great that he could feel no pain while he peddled his bike along Oceanside Drive.

With one last hill to climb, he would be at Chris's house. He shifted the bike into second gear and used his remaining energy to conquer the hill. He coasted the rest of the way to the house, but when he arrived at the front gates, they were not open. Jack dropped his bike and then staggered to the gate on the Ocean Walk.

The house was dark. He didn't know whether Chris and Allison were sleeping or had not returned from their weekend trip. Hoping the screeching gate would get their attention, he turned the handle and pushed. Much to his surprise, the gate opened without a sound. *Hmm. Chris listened to me the other day.*

Jack staggered through the yard, and by the time he got to the front door, he was exhausted. He rang the doorbell several times. He could hear Sherlock and Mycroft barking upstairs but saw no signs of Chris. With no energy left, he sunk to his knees, fell forward, placed his hands on the ground, and then began to pant.

Moments later, Chris opened the door to find Jack face down on his hands and knees, soaking wet. "Jack, are you all right? What's happened?" Chris helped him to his feet.

Jack stood and took off the wet backpack. Still breathless, he said, "Harsntokan."

While Chris helped remove the backpack, he caught his first glimpse of Jack's face. Jack had forgotten to remove the camouflage paint. Chris's forehead wrinkled. He was unable to decipher Jack's **incoherent (#191)** statement. "What did you say?"

Still out of breath and unable to **articulate (#192)** his words, he said again, "Harsntokan."

"I have no idea what you're saying. And what's on your face?"

Chris helped Jack into the house and guided him to the kitchen. "Catch your breath," Chris said as he placed him in a chair. By the way Jack was panting, Chris knew he must be **parched (#193)**. So, he poured him a glass of ice water and placed it in front of him.

It took a moment before Jack could **elucidate (#194)** what happened. After he caught his breath and took a big gulp of water, he explained, "Hunter Harrison took Ian!"

"What? How do you know that?"

Jack unzipped the backpack and removed his gear. "When I was crawling out of his house, I saw this."

While Jack opened the picture of Ian's initials on his iPhone's screen, Chris asked, with great concern, "You broke into Harrison's house?"

Jack nodded and held up two fingers.

Chris grabbed the edge of the counter. "Twice? You broke into his house twice?" he asked with a face full of astonishment.

Jack handed Chris the phone. "Yes. Look at this."

Chris grabbed the phone. "What is it?"

"Look closely. You can see Ian's initials smeared into the dirt on the window. See the large *A*, flanked by a small *I* and *C*? All of Ian's shirts have this monogram. He had to be in this room."

"Wow!"

"And look at this." Jack reached into the bag and pulled out the twenty thousand in cash, the bags of white powder, and the toothbrush. "I found this toothbrush in the bathroom. This may be **incontrovertible (#195)** proof that Ian was there."

Chris stared at Jack in amazement for a moment before he grabbed the money and the bags. "Is this what I think it is?"

"Yeah, I think it's cocaine."

Chris held one of the bags up toward the light above the kitchen table. "Sure looks like cocaine." He looked at Jack and shook his head in disbelief. After a few seconds, he walked over to the table, pulled out a chair, and then sat. "Now tell me everything, starting from the beginning."

Jack explained everything in detail. He started from when he first decided to go on his mission to when he knocked on Chris's front door. When he finished, he glanced at his watch. It was 10:56 p.m. "We need to call Chief McKinney right away."

"Yes, we do."

"Let's have him meet us at my house. I need to download the pictures and video from my phone onto my computer. I also have the docking stations for the digital recorders set up and ready to go."

Chris stood. "Let me get my keys. I'll drive. Why don't you call the chief?" Chris bolted out of the room and went upstairs.

Jack fumbled with his phone as he dialed Chief McKinney's home number. Mrs. McKinney, who sounded as if she were sleeping, answered the call.

"Mrs. McKinney, this is Jack. I need to speak to Chief McKinney. It's very important."

"Jack, do you know what time it is?"

Jack looked at his watch. "I know it's late. It's about Ian Anderson."

After a short pause, the chief got on the phone. "Jack, what's going on?"

"I know who took Ian Anderson, and I have proof."

"What?"

"I know who took Ian Anderson. I have pictures, money, a bunch of cocaine, and maybe even Ian's toothbrush to prove it. Christian Poulter and I are on the way to my house with the evidence. I'll explain everything there. Can you meet us?"

"Yes, most definitely. I'm on my way."

Jack and Chris arrived at the same time as Chief McKinney. After a quick hello, they all entered the house and scampered up the stairs. When they reached the top step, Mr. Graystone walked into the hallway in a pair of boxers and an undershirt. He appeared shocked to see the chief of police and a famous author with his son.

"Jack, what's going on here?"

Before Jack could say anything, Chris said, "You're not going to believe this. You need to come in here and listen."

"Let me get my pants. I'll be right back."

Jack had changed his clothes and was downloading the pictures and video when his father entered the room. Once again, Jack told the whole story to his new listeners.

His father sat and listened in amazement to every word. Occasionally, he shook his head and mumbled, "Jack, you could've been killed."

When Jack got to the part where he had found the money, the cocaine, and the toothbrush, he pulled out the evidence from his backpack and placed it on his desk.

His father picked up the money and fanned through it. "Oh my God, this is ten thousand dollars."

At the same time, the chief grabbed one of the bags of white powder. "I need to go to my car and test this. I'll be right back."

Chris walked over to the desk and grabbed the toothbrush. "Chief, don't forget to take this. We need to test it for Ian's DNA."

"I'll send it off to the lab first thing in the morning."

While the chief was away, Jack, Chris, and Mr. Graystone looked at the picture and watched the video several more times.

Minutes later, the chief returned. "Yep, it's cocaine. And, judging by the test results, it appears to be very high-quality stuff." The chief placed the items into individual evidence bags. "I wonder what's on the recorders?"

Jack glanced at his computer. "According to the file information, the study's recorder captured an hour and twenty-six minutes of sound. And the family room's recorder captured eighteen hours and twelve minutes." He started to play the recording from the family room;

however, it quickly became evident that most of the recording was from the television playing in the background. They switched to the study's recording and found that it was all talking.

"We need to have these transcribed. It'd be much easier to read these conversations than to listen to them," said Chris.

"I use one of these recorders at my office," said Mr. Graystone. "Chief, do you want my secretary to transcribe them?"

The chief paused to think. "That might be best since any of the evidence we've obtained would most likely be inadmissible."

Mr. Graystone stood. "Let me call my secretary. I'll ask her to come in early to transcribe them." He left the room and returned moments later "She's on her way to the office now. Jack, can you send the files to this email address?"

Jack looked at the address, and with a few strokes of the keyboard, he had sent the digital files.

The chief closed his eyes and rubbed his forehead. "We can't tell anyone about these recordings. They'll never hold up in court. It'd be best if you keep this data on your computer. If anyone finds out I have them, it could blow the prosecution's case."

"What do we do next?" asked Jack.

"Well, I need to go outside and call the FBI," said the chief.

Mr. Graystone stood. "Let's all go downstairs. We'll be more comfortable in the living room."

Jack opened his bedroom door and followed the men into the hallway. When Mr. Graystone passed, Jack tapped his father's shoulder with the back of his hand and said, "This is why I like to keep a clean room." His father shook his head and rolled his eyes.

It was just after one in the morning when Chief McKinney stepped outside to phone the two agents assigned to the case. During their brief conversation, they agreed to meet at nine o'clock that morning. The meeting place would be at the Worthington Police Station.

Chief McKinney reentered the house to find Chris, Mr. Graystone, and Jack sitting in the living room discussing the case. The four men continued to talk until two in the morning, by which time they were exhausted. With only seven hours before the meeting, the group disbanded to get some much-needed rest.

CHAPTER TWENTY-THREE

With one hand on his son's shoulder, Mr. Graystone opened the door to the Worthington Police Station. On their walk to the reception desk, Jack noticed an unusually high amount of activity. Both well-dressed people and uniformed police officers were scurrying throughout the building. The ordinarily quiet lobby had a low roar, which echoed off the recently polished floors.

Mrs. White looked up from her computer and smiled. "Hi, Jack. The chief said you'd be coming in today. He's waiting for you in the conference room."

Jack returned the smile. "Hello, Mrs. White. How are you today?"

Mrs. White leaned back in her chair, placed both hands on her cheeks, and let out a sigh. "Busy, very busy. It's been crazy all morning. In thirty-six years, I have never seen this place so busy."

Jack shook his head. "I think it's about to get even crazier." After a quick introduction of his father, they continued to the conference room. Along the way, Jack encountered Officer Turner. "What's up, Jack?" he asked, giving him a high five in passing.

"Just trying to solve crimes."

Before they entered the conference room, Mr. Graystone tapped his son on the shoulder. "How do you know all these people?"

"Well, Officer Turner almost arrested me, twice. And I know Mrs. White from coming in here with Courtney to visit her father."

Mr. Graystone chuckled. "Son, you'll make a good politician someday."

Jack entered the conference room to the stares from many unfamiliar faces. Their conversations stopped as he approached Chief McKinney.

With a quick scan of the large conference table, he recognized Chief McKinney, Chris, and one other man sitting next to Chris. He could never forget this man. He was the FBI agent who interrogated him in the van.

Chief McKinney stood when the Graystones entered the room. "Hey, guys. Glad you could make it." He pointed to two empty chairs. "Take a seat over there."

While Jack and his father took their seats, the chief introduced everyone. There were too many names to remember, so Jack nodded and smiled at each person. The attendees consisted of FBI agents, attorneys from the State Attorney's Office, Drug Enforcement Administration agents, and state police officers. Based on their professional titles, he realized he was sitting among many important people.

Jack settled in his chair positioned directly across from the chief. He felt uncomfortable from the emotionless stares of the other attendees. When he glanced around the room, he saw the maps, pictures, and diagrams he had created for his missions exhibited on the walls. Toward one end of the room was a dry erase board, covered in writing.

With his elbows on the table, the chief leaned forward. "Jack, I realize you told your story several times today, but I need you to tell it once more."

"Where do you want me to begin?"

"Start with your observations on the video from the house on the Ocean Walk."

For the third time that day, Jack **rehashed (#196)** the whole story. Well, almost the whole story. His fear of public speaking subsided with every word. Occasionally, he would stand, point to something on one of his maps, and then return to his seat. During his **oration (#197)**, several people asked questions. Jack confidently answered each one.

After Jack finished, Chief McKinney turned control of the meeting over to one of the state attorneys. The man, who was around his father's age, had an **egotistical (#198)** air about him. He stood at the front of the table in his knock-off designer suit and made notes on the dry erase board. For the next half hour, everyone in the room discussed the case. The representatives from the different agencies weighed in with their knowledge and expertise. With each person believing they knew more than the other, conclusions were hard to obtain.

Since the analysis had begun, no one had asked Jack any additional questions. In fact, most of them did not even acknowledge his presence. Jack sat in his chair and listened to the overconfident men and women attempt to outdo one another. He tried not to laugh as he tapped his father on the shoulder and whispered, "Dad, I feel like I'm at the lunch table at school listening to all these people bickering." His father smiled and nodded in agreement.

After the intense discussion, the group began to formulate their final **hypothesis (#199)** for Ian's disappearance. Not once during this time did they ask Jack for his opinion. Chris, it appeared, sensed Jack's frustration, because midway through the discussion, he interjected, "I think we need to get the analysis and opinion of the man who knows the most about this case. Jack, tell us what you think."

Caught by surprise, Jack looked at the man in charge for approval to speak. The man nodded, and then Jack **promulgated (#200)** his theory to his audience. "I believe Ian saw something, either on the boat or on the plane, that he wasn't supposed to see. Since the wind blew the boat and plane close to shore, I assume it was the cocaine transfer. When the men on the boat saw Ian running away, they called the man in the Mercedes SUV. This man drove from Harrison's house and waited for Ian at the end of the Ocean Walk. Before I came here this morning, I timed myself running from the tip of the peninsula to where I found the binoculars. It took two minutes and forty-eight seconds. I also timed myself driving from Hunter Harrison's house to where I found the binoculars. That took two minutes and twelve seconds. So, the man in the Mercedes grabbed Ian, threw him in the SUV, then took him back to Harrison's house." Jack paused and then leaned forward and bowed his head. "From here on, I can only imagine what happened to Ian."

Mr. Graystone placed his hand on his son's shoulder while Jack's **advocate (#201)**, Chris, continued the conversation. "That seems the most **trenchant (#202)** explanation to me. Does anyone disagree?"

Although Jack's explanation was full of keen observation and was thoughtful and to the point, the **deliberations (#203)** continued for another fifteen minutes. When the group finished arguing, those who had **dissented (#204)** had changed their minds and were in **concordance (#205)** with Jack.

"Okay," said the chief. "Now that we have an idea what happened to Ian, what do we do next?"

The man in charge looked at the FBI agent sitting next to Chris. "This is where the FBI takes over. Agent Stadler, would you like to tell us the plan?"

Agent Stadler was a middle-aged man who appeared to be in perfect physical condition. With a confident demeanor, he stood and said, "We currently have Harrison's house and both his apartment and office in New York under surveillance. We are also monitoring his phone calls and credit card transactions. But, as of yet, we have not been able to locate him.

"We're walking on a slippery slope here. As the state attorney's office has informed us, there are legal issues with how we've obtained some of our information. We have to be very careful how we proceed. Harrison will have the best legal defense. If we make any **erroneous (#206)** moves, they'll crucify us in court. With that said, our priority continues to be the safe return of Ian Anderson.

"Jack has informed us that the plane will be here on Wednesday. He and Mr. Poulter have provided pictures of this plane from which we obtained the tail numbers. We, in turn, have located it at an airfield in the town of Northport. It's currently under constant surveillance. Our agents are working with the Federal Aviation Administration to follow the plane by radar and reconnaissance plane as soon as it leaves the airport.

"We're also sharing information with the DEA in respect to the drug-trafficking aspect of this case. Depending on when we locate Mr. Harrison, we'll set up a joint operation to arrest him and everyone involved. In the meantime, our agents are covertly looking for any sign of Ian at Harrison's other properties.

"So, to answer the question, what's the plan? As of now, there isn't one. There are almost three days before the plane arrives. We'll all have to **collaborate (#207)** and figure the best course of action. If we work together, we can find this boy."

It was almost eleven o'clock when the meeting adjourned. On their way out of the conference room, Chief McKinney pulled Jack, Chris, and Mr. Graystone aside. "I talked to Mr. Anderson this morning. I told him we were working a lead. I was **ambiguous (#208)** and didn't tell him everything. I also didn't mention that the three of you were involved. So, please don't say anything to him, not just yet. I'm not trying to be **callous (#209)**, but I don't want to get his hopes up. Or worse, have him do something crazy."

The three concurred, and after a few minutes of small talk, the Graystones headed for their car. When they walked through the police station's crowded lobby, they found most of the meeting's attendees huddled in groups having a variety of discussions. Through the **cacophony (#210)**, Jack caught bits of these conversations, which ranged from drug trafficking to where to go to lunch. He was almost at the door when he heard a raised voice say, "Jack Graystone, I would like to speak to you. Alone." Jack turned and saw Agent Stadler approaching.

"Come over here," he said with a stern tone.

Jack glanced at his father. Mr. Graystone gave him a nod as if to say, "it's okay."

Oh, crap. What does he want? Jack's stomach instantly tied in knots. He approached the man, and when he got close, Stadler put his hand on Jack's shoulder. With a firm grip, he directed him away from the crowd.

The two stood at the entrance of a hallway facing each other. The roar from the lobby, which was not quite as loud, was at Jack's back. Stadler, standing only two feet away, had a stare that pierced through Jack. "Jack Graystone, I don't share the chief's enthusiasm for what you have done. You can't keep being a **maverick (#211)** and taking matters into your own hands. What you did was not only illegal but extremely dangerous."

"Well, I…"

"Don't speak. This is a one-way conversation. As soon as you saw those initials on the window, you should have called the chief." Stadler closed his eyes and rubbed his forehead. "Not only that, but you shouldn't have taken that toothbrush out of the house. If it turns out to be Ian's, we can't use it in court. There's no proof that it came from the house. Jack, there's a whole host of other legal issues with what you have done." Stadler sighed and shook his head. "I understand you want to help. But you have to realize that you do not have the **qualifications (#212)** to do this type of work. Next time you do something like this, I'm going to arrest you." After Agent Stadler finished **admonishing (#213)** Jack for his conduct, he gave him a stern look. "Understand?"

"Yes, sir," Jack mumbled as the agent walked away. Agent Stadler's **pellucid (#214)** statement was clear and to the point. Do it again and go to jail. Jack looked at the ground and thought, *I don't think this guy likes me.*

Mr. Graystone held the door for his son when they walked out of the station. "What was that all about?"

"Agent Stadler said he didn't share the chief's enthusiasm for what I did."

"Well, Jack, I agree with him. A lot could have gone wrong."

***

When Jack and his dad arrived home, Jack went straight to his room and turned on his computer. In his email, he found the transcript from the study's recorder. He sent the document to the printer, and after fifty-eight pages printed, he began to read. The conversations were mostly about investments and water samples. Occasionally, there was a call from a woman named Maria. From what Jack gathered, she was married and having a torrid love affair with Harrison. Some of their conversations were so explicit that they made Jack uncomfortable. He could only imagine what his father's secretary thought while she typed them.

Toward the end of his **perusal (#215)** of the transcript, Jack came across a conversation that provided a clue. He read aloud from the transcript.

"Hello."
"No, I'll be at the mountain house for two weeks."
"Yeah, deliver it there."
"I need everything on that list."
"That's correct."

"No, the first one."
"Yeah, you'll see the old man in the rocking chair."
"Second driveway on the right, past the old bison barn."
"Yes."
"Right."
"About four point six."
"See you then."

Jack read the remaining conversations. They were mostly about business and provided no clues. When he finished, he sat at his desk and stared out the window. He recalled that the FBI had Harrison's house and both the office and apartment in New York under surveillance. He did not remember, though, the agent mentioning anything about a mountain house. With this in mind, he called Chris.

"Did you get the email from my father's secretary?"

"Yeah. I'm about halfway through the transcript from the study."

"If you read toward the end, Harrison says he's going to be at his mountain house for two weeks. Do you remember the FBI agent saying anything about a mountain house?"

Chris paused, "No. Let me see what you're talking about." He paused again. "Okay. I see it here. This doesn't give us much information. Let me call Agent Stadler."

"Uh, Chris, if he doesn't know we have these recordings, how are you going to tell him about the mountain house?"

"Hmm. That's a good question."

"I don't think Agent Stadler likes me."

"Why'd you say that?"

"He chewed my ass out when I was leaving the station today."

"Really? What did he say?"

"He said that I what I did was dangerous and I shouldn't be snooping around places I don't belong. He also said there are a bunch of legal issues with how I obtained the evidence."

"He's right. That was a **foolhardy (#216)** thing to do. If I would've known you were going to break into his house, I would've stopped you. But, what's done is done. Let me handle Stadler. I have known him for a long time. I'll discreetly tell him that Harrison said he would be at his mountain house this week. If he has one, I'm sure the FBI can find it."

***

Using the Worthington Police Station as a command center, the agencies conceived a plan to take down Harrison's empire by Wednesday morning. Operation 'Hunted Harrison' would start that evening. As soon as the seaplane took off, several agencies would follow it to its final destination. The pilot and its cargo would stay under constant surveillance until the next flight on Friday night. Several unmarked units would also follow the Mercedes when it left Harrison's house. Similar to the seaplane, its occupant and contents would stay under surveillance over the next two days.

From this investigation, the agencies hoped not only to determine how the drugs came into the country and how they were distributed, but they also hoped to get a lead on the whereabouts of Harrison and Ian. They would gather as much information as possible over these two days. Finally, at dawn on Saturday, the agencies would raid all of Harrison's properties simultaneously.

CHAPTER TWENTY-FOUR

Dressed like airplane mechanics, two FBI agents peered into the engine compartment of a small private plane. Occasionally, they inserted a tool and pretended to perform routine maintenance. Next to them sat Hunter Harrison's seaplane, awaiting its pilot.

It was just after four in the afternoon when a silver Chevrolet Suburban with dark tinted windows drove into the airport and parked on the far side of the neighboring plane. The agents discreetly watched two men load two large aluminum suitcases into the passenger compartment. Within a matter of minutes, the Suburban drove away and the pilot prepared for takeoff. As soon as the Suburban departed the airport, three unmarked cars began their tail. And, by four thirty on Wednesday afternoon, Operation Hunted Harrison was underway.

The seaplane rumbled down the runway, achieved lift, and then headed toward the setting sun. The FAA immediately began their radar coverage, relaying the information back to a large video screen in the command center. Shortly after, a high-tech DEA reconnaissance plane took off and monitored the seaplane's every move.

Over the next two hours, the task force followed the seaplane to New York City. It landed and docked at a port on Manhattan's Lower East Side. The agents observed the occupant make another exchange. They recorded the discreet transfer of two aluminum suitcases by a man wearing a baseball cap and sunglasses. Hoping the concealed man was Harrison, several strategically placed operatives, unfortunately, confirmed it was not. When the bagman left, the FBI and DEA task force shadowed his every move.

Shortly after the exchange, the seaplane taxied to the middle of the river, took off, and then made a course toward Worthington. The estimated flight time was approximately two hours, during which it would remain under constant surveillance.

After ninety minutes in the air, the seaplane suddenly disappeared from the radar screen. Frantically, the air traffic controller called the pursuit plane. "Alpha, Delta, Five, Niner, Niner, we lost radar coverage of the plane at latitude 40°49'34" north and longitude 72°01'50" west. Can you relay information on its current condition?"

"Affirmative. We'll fly over them in approximately three minutes," replied the plane's pilot.

With everyone at the command center on the edge of their seats, the three minutes felt like an hour. Finally, they received the video footage.

Agent Stadler stared at the large video screen hanging on the command center's wall. "It appears the plane has landed. But I don't see any other boats."

Chief McKinney jumped to his feet, hurried to the screen, and pointed to something in the upper left-hand corner. "What this?"

Several people approached the screen and inspected the object as it moved closer to the floating seaplane.

Agent Stadler smacked his hand on the table and jumped to his feet. "It's a submarine. That's how they're getting the drugs into the country."

"Where do you think it came from?" asked Chief McKinney.

Agent Stadler crossed his arms. "I'm not sure. But it probably gets the drugs from a passing freighter. Agent Phillips, contact the Coast Guard and inform them of our situation."

The video footage stopped before they witnessed the exchange. The DEA plane did not make another pass. They feared of the seaplane would discover their surveillance. Instead, they circled and spectated from afar.

With the exchange taking twenty minutes, the seaplane returned to the sky. It continued its course toward Worthington, where it followed the same routine. The seaplane landed in the cove, made its exchange with the boat, and then returned to Northport.

The silver Suburban was waiting when the seaplane came to rest. The pilot removed one aluminum suitcase, which he placed it in the back of the SUV and then jumped into the passenger seat. The two men had a brief conversation before they speed away.

For the next two days, a massive undercover operation was underway. The task force had everyone involved under surveillance. They also performed stakeouts at almost every property owned by Hunter Harrison. The one exception being the mountain house, which they had not located.

CHAPTER TWENTY-FIVE

Since his meeting at the chief's office, the task force had kept Jack out of the loop. The minimal information he received came from Chris, through Agent Stadler. Jack knew his hard work had provided the agents with most of their evidence. And, after stewing over it for a day, he began to get irritated. Finally, he made up his mind. After work on Thursday, he planned to march into Chief McKinney's office and demand more information.

Several FBI agents continued their attempt to locate Harrison's mountain house. But, as of Thursday morning, they'd had no luck. Hunter Harrison was smart. He rarely used credit cards, and his purchases with cash left no paper trail. To make things more difficult, the few calls he made were always from burner cell phones. Therefore, locating Harrison was next to impossible.

Around ten o'clock Thursday morning, an FBI agent reviewing Harrison's driving record noticed that two months earlier he had received a speeding ticket in the rural mountain town of Lexington. The agent contacted the local authorities and talked to the patrol officer who had issued the ticket. The officer remembered Harrison because he drove a new, orange Lamborghini Aventador. Although he remembered the **exotic (#217)** car, he had no additional information. On a hunch, the agent contacted the surrounding police departments to check if anyone had seen this rare car. By four o'clock that afternoon, he received a call from a sheriff who confirmed a sighting. One of his men saw the car twice in the little town of Highlands. With this in mind, the agent reviewed the county records for property titled under the name of Hunter Harrison or one of his companies. After an exhaustive search, however, he found nothing that matched.

Agent Stadler sat behind a borrowed desk in a back office of the Worthington police station. Two knocks on the door made him look up.

"Excuse me, do you have a minute?" asked a young field agent.

"Yeah, come in. What's up?"

"I can't find anything on the mountain house. I have checked all the counties in the entire state, and I don't see anything titled under Harrison's name or any of his companies. I thought maybe he's renting a place, so I checked his bank records for any transactions that might give us a clue. But I found nothing."

Agent Stadler leaned back in his chair and stared at the ceiling. He didn't say anything for almost a minute. Finally, he leaned forward and placed his elbows on the desk. "You said someone saw his Lamborghini twice in the same town?"

"Yeah, in Highlands."

"Start there. Look online for real estate firms in the area. Call the one that looks like they sell the most properties. Find out who is the most prominent realtor and talk to them. Email pictures of Harrison and see if they have seen him. If he were buying a place that he wanted to keep secret, he would most likely use an alias."

"Or, he would have somebody else buy it for him."

Agent Stadler nodded. "Yeah, that's a good possibility. Either way, a good realtor knows their market and would be familiar with all the transactions in the area. Harrison has lots of money. I'm sure if he purchased a house, or even rented a house, it would be expensive. People remember those kinds of sales."

An internet search for realtors in Highlands revealed one who was the most prominent. Her name was Pricilla Osborne. Agent Stadler's hunch was right. Mrs. Osborne knew of a transaction a few months prior involving a man who fit Hunter Harrison's description. Although he used another name, she was sure it was Harrison. One look at Harrison's picture confirmed it. By five o'clock that evening, the FBI was confident they had found the mountain house.

***

On the drive home from work, Jack's mind raced with thoughts of what he was going to say to the chief. By the time he entered the house, the anticipation of his meeting had made him lose his appetite. He skipped dinner, changed clothes, and then went directly to Chief McKinney's office.

Jack entered the station to find Mrs. White was not at the reception desk. Instead, a young man, whom Jack did not recognize, sat in her chair. When he approached the desk, the man looked up but did not say a word.

"I'm Jack Graystone, and I'd like to see Chief McKinney."

The man tilted his head slightly. "Do you have an appointment?"

"No, I don't."

The man lowered his head and began shuffling through a stack of papers. "He's very busy and doesn't want to be disturbed. Come back later."

With his blood pressure rising, Jack responded, "Oh, really?"

In front of the man, Jack dialed the chief's cell number. When the chief answered, Jack said in a louder-than-usual voice, "Chief McKinney, this is Jack. I'm in the lobby. Can I speak to you in your office for a minute?" After a short pause, Jack replied, "Thanks."

The man glanced up from the paperwork and gave Jack a dirty look.

Moments later, Chief McKinney appeared in the hallway. "Jack, come on back." When Jack passed the new receptionist, he returned the look.

Jack entered the office with the chief closing the door behind him. "What can I do for you?" The chief pointed to a chair in front of his desk. Jack gave the chief a hard look as he sat. The man seemed different. He showed no emotion.

"Chief, I know I'm only a kid, but I was the one who discovered the connection between Harrison and Ian. Ever since the meeting on Monday, you've told me nothing. I think that with everything I have done, I deserve to know what's happening."

The chief leaned backward in his chair and rubbed his chin. "I understand your frustration, but this is a very serious investigation. There's information I cannot tell you or anyone outside of this department." The chief's **dispassionate (#218)** demeanor took Jack by surprise. He seemed unaffected by Jack's concerns. "Mostly, Jack, it's for your safety."

Jack sighed in frustration. "So, there's nothing you can tell me?"

The chief closed his eyes for a moment and then looked at Jack. "Against my better judgment, I'll tell you this. That was Ian's toothbrush."

"Are you sure?"

"Yes. We tested it against DNA from several objects we took on our initial investigation, and it is **irrefutably (#219)** his."

"I knew it would be." Jack leaned forward in his chair. "What about the mountain house? Have you found it yet?"

The chief paused. "Again, I shouldn't be telling you this, but we're almost positive we found it."

Jack's eyes lit up. "Really? Where is it? Do you think Ian's there?"

"It's about four hours north of here. We found it about two hours ago, so we haven't had time to investigate. We're hoping that both Harrison and Ian are there."

"When will you know something?"

"Well, the FBI is flying a team there now. The plan is to stake out the house and try to find any signs of Ian. If they make positive contact, they'll go in right away. If not, and this is not to leave this room, they'll raid the house on Saturday morning. Jack, I'm serious. You cannot tell anyone about this."

"I won't. But if they don't find him today, I want to be there on Saturday when they do find him."

"Jack, I can't let you go to the raid on the mountain house."

"I don't want to go on the raid. I'll drive up early Saturday morning, and I'll stay out of the way until after the raid. Seriously, you won't even know I'm there. Please, Chief, let me go."

"Why are you so insistent on being there?"

"Because Ian will need to see a familiar face when you find him."

The chief paused and then calmly said, "It's good that you have a positive attitude, but you have to realize the chances of finding Ian alive are very slim."

"I know, but my gut tells me he's still alive. I have put a lot of time and effort into finding him, and I want to follow this through to the end.

No matter what that is."

"Well, let me talk to Agent Stadler. If he says it's okay and they don't find him by tomorrow, I'll talk to your dad." The chief paused. "I guess you could drive up early Saturday morning. I'll tell you where to wait, then call you when the raid is over."

"Thanks, Chief. Can I call you tomorrow after work?"

The chief stood. "That'll be fine," he said before they walked out of his office.

That evening, Jack explained the situation to his father and told him that he might be getting a call from Chief McKinney. Although his father was reluctant at first, he eventually agreed to let Jack make the four-hour drive north. There was, however, one stipulation. He had to follow the chief's instructions. After confirming that he would, Jack left for Reilly's walk.

Jack arrived at the Anderson's house a few minutes before nine. While he stopped to enter the gate code, he noticed a newly installed *'For Sale'* sign. Shocked by the sight, he continued to the house. He entered through the kitchen, grabbed the leash, and then called for Reilly. Usually, Reilly would be there almost instantly. But today he never appeared. Jack called for Reilly again, this time a bit louder.

"We're in the living room," replied Mr. Anderson.

Jack walked into the room and found Mr. Anderson sitting alone in the dark with Reilly at his feet. From the light in the foyer, he could see that Mr. Anderson eyes were puffy and bloodshot. Reilly glanced at Jack but never left his master's feet.

"Are you all right, Mr. Anderson?"

Mr. Anderson shook his head. The **vicissitude (#220)** of having a missing child was taking its toll on the man. "Not really. This is the worst chapter of my life." He wiped a tear from his eye. "I give up. I'm emotionally, mentally, and physically whipped."

"Is that why you're selling the house?"

"That's one reason. But mainly it's because my wife refuses to come back here. She says it'd be too hard for her."

"Where are you going to move?"

Mr. Anderson wiped a few more tears from his eyes. "We're moving back to our apartment in Manhattan."

"Is there anything I can do for you?"

"I appreciate you asking. For now, just keep walking Reilly."

On the walk that evening, Jack thought about Mr. Anderson's situation. Seeing the man in such an **enervated (#221)** state really upset him. He wanted to tell Mr. Anderson everything he knew to **assuage (#222)** the pain of the grieving man. But, since he gave his word to the chief, he remained silent.

By the time Jack returned, Mr. Anderson had gone to sleep. Jack sat alone in the kitchen for a moment and watched Reilly drink from his water dish. The sound from his metal leash clanking against the metal bowl filled the quiet house. Jack's mind raced with thoughts of what might happen in the upcoming days. And for the first time, he considered the worst. When Reilly finished drinking, he walked over and sat in front of Jack. Jack knelt and unclasped his leash. Before he stood, he grabbed Reilly's head and looked into his brown eyes. "It won't be long until we know what happened to him, little buddy." He gave Reilly one last pet before he walked out the door.

***

Jack heard from neither the chief nor Chris all day and assumed Ian remained undiscovered. In anticipation of heading north in the morning, he asked Mr. Barrini for permission to take off work on Saturday. Mr. Barrini concurred.

Before his drive home, Jack sat in his Explorer and made the call to Chief McKinney. After several rings, he finally answered. "Chief McKinney, did you find Ian?"

"No, Jack. We're sure it's Harrison's house. But it's so heavily guarded, we can't get close enough without someone seeing us. We know there are at least two people in there. So, we're raiding it in the morning."

"Chief McKinney, did you talk to Agent Stadler and my dad?"

"Yes, I did."

"What did Stadler say?"

"Believe it or not, he thought it was a good idea for you to be there."

"Really?"

"It was your father who said you couldn't go."

Jack let out a sigh. "He said I could last night."

"Apparently, the more he thought about it, the more his **apprehension (#223)** grew. I told him it was his decision, and I wouldn't question his judgment."

"So, I can't go?"

"Well, I told your father what you told me. How you were the one who'd found the connection between Harrison and Ian. And how you wanted Ian to see a familiar face after they rescued him. I also said that Agent Stadler thought it was a good idea and that it's an easy drive up the interstate."

"Then what did he say?"

"He said you could go."

"Oh, thank you."

"But listen," the chief said in a stern voice, "there are going to be several rules you must follow."

"Yes sir, I'll do whatever I'm told."

The chief explained that the raid would take place anywhere from six to eight o'clock on Saturday morning. Jack was to leave his house around 4:00 a.m. and drive to the town of Highlands. Once there, he was to wait at a truck stop located by the interstate interchange. After completion of the raid and everything was under control, the chief would then call and give him the final directions to the house.

CHAPTER TWENTY-SIX

Jack hit the road by four o'clock Saturday morning with Homer Simpson as his iPhone navigation system leading the way. After twenty minutes and ten traffic lights, most of which were red, he made it to the interstate. From there, it was a straight shot north to Highlands.

With very few cars on the road, the drive seemed to pass quickly. It was ten minutes to eight when Jack arrived at the Highlands exit. Once he exited the interstate, he looked for the truck stop where he was told to wait. There was no problem finding it. It was the only building around.

Jack parked in a space toward the back of the lot, then placed his phone on the dashboard and adjusted it for the strongest signal. *Now the waiting begins.* He was relatively **sedate (#224)** all morning, but sitting in the truck with nothing to hold his attention, his mind was full of questions. *I wonder if Ian is in that house? If he is, can they get him out without hurting him? What if he's not there? Does this mean they did something bad to him? I guess we won't know until they talk to Harrison.* The anticipation of the phone call began to grate on his nerves. He found himself continually looking at his watch.

***

Unknown to Jack, the simultaneous raids started at precisely seven o'clock. The four main properties raided were: Harrison's Worthington house, both his apartment and office in Manhattan, and the mountain house. Several smaller raids were performed on the pilot's house and a few other buildings used as drug distribution centers.

For the raid at the mountain house, the FBI commandeered a

neighboring property to use for a staging area. Agent Stadler was in charge of coordinating the raid. Chief McKinney remained in the background and assisted only when asked. He sat quietly in the corner and spectated as twelve heavily armed men dressed in camouflaged fatigues discussed their mission. It was organized chaos as a multitude of people scurried about in preparation for the raid.

Hunter Harrison's mountain house was a three-story wood and stone structure perched on the side of a mountain. The front of the house faced north, up a heavily wooded slope. The rear of the house, which had several wooden decks, looked out over what appeared to be half of the country. Off in the distance, another roadway and a lake were barely visible through the trees.

The only access to the house was by a single-lane gravel driveway that wound down the mountainside for about a thousand feet. This driveway, along with the house, was covered with security cameras. They were everywhere. There were two at the entrance gate, at least three along the driveway, and one on every corner of the house.

With clipboard in hand, Agent Stadler had one last debriefing before the raid. "Okay. Let's go over this one more time. You seven," he said pointing to a group of men huddled together, "will be dropped off on the north side of the house, east of the driveway. You will descend the mountain and cover the north, east, and southerly half of the perimeter." He then glanced at another group of men. "You five will be dropped off west of the driveway and cover the west and the remaining southerly half of the perimeter. Once in place, you will wait for my signal. When you're told, Gifford, Sanchez, Barker, and Sutton will enter through the rear of the house on the first floor. Ralston, Elliot, Greene, and Brockman, you will enter through the front door. The remaining four will stay outside and cover each corner of the residence.

"Once inside, our primary objective is to find the boy. If he's located, do whatever it takes to provide for his safety. Our second objective is to locate Harrison. If engaged, do not shoot to kill. We need him alive.

"Chief McKinney, once the agents have entered the building, you will drive to the end of the driveway and stand guard. Do not let anyone in or out. Agents Keymer and Wilson will be situated a half mile east and west of the driveway to stop any oncoming traffic."

Agent Stadler pointed toward two paramedics. "Once the raid begins, I'd like you to follow me and park behind my van. I'll be situated around two hundred feet from the end of the driveway. I hope we will not need you or the Life Flight helicopter waiting in the nearby field.

"You all have worked with each other for a long time and know the drill. Just remember to keep in constant contact amongst yourselves and be safe. Any questions?" After a few minor questions, the men had a moment of silence before they loaded into the vans and left for the raid.

At six thirty, three vans departed the staging area and made their way toward Harrison's mountain house. As the first van slowed, seven agents exited and scattered into the woods. Shortly after that, the second van released its five agents. Fifteen minutes later, each of the twelve agents had forged their way down the heavily wooded slope and obtained their positions.

Thermal imaging from the previous day indicated two or three active individuals in the residence. With this in mind, and having memorized the floor plan, the agents hid behind trees and brush within different areas of the property. They were ready to spring into action at a moment's notice.

At precisely seven o'clock, Agent Stadler gave the signal to begin. Simultaneously, the convergence on all properties was underway.

At the mountain house, the southerly four agents climbed to the rear ground-floor entrance within less than a minute. The northerly four had it easier. They waited close to the driveway and had a straight shot to the front door. While corresponding through their headsets, both teams arrived at their entry points simultaneously. With a signal from Agent Brockman, they blew both doors open with small explosives. Before the dust settled, the heavily armed men entered in a single file and swept through the house with military precision.

Agent Stadler sat in his surveillance van and studied multiple video screens. He could see and hear all the action relayed by the assault team's head-mounted cameras. From one of these cameras, he watched Agent Ralston bust into a bedroom and encounter a groggy, half-naked man staggering out of bed. Before the man could grab his gun, Ralston yelled, "Freeze! FBI!" Seeing a high-powered rifle pointed at him, the man quickly complied.

Throughout the radio chatter, agents yelled the "all-clear" signal after they swept each room. While the men in the basement conducted their search, Agent Sanchez encountered a locked door. He gave it a strong kick, but it did not fully open. A piece of furniture blocked its path. Agent Sanchez gave the door another kick. This time, however, the room's occupant responded with machine gun fire. Bullets sprayed through the walls.

From inside the van, Stadler yelled, "Hold your fire! Hold your fire! Sutton, have you been hit?"

"The bullets bounced off my body armor. I'm fine."

"Before you shoot, make sure he's not using the boy as a hostage," explained Agent Stadler.

Through the partially opened door, Agent Sanchez spotted no activity. "FBI. Come out with your hands up!" he yelled to the gunman. It was silent for about twenty seconds. Then, without warning, another burst of bullets sprayed randomly through the wall. Agents Sanchez and Sutton, who hid behind a couch, waited for their break.

"Brockman and Gifford, get outside to the basement window," ordered Agent Stadler. But, before they could respond, the outside agent covering the southeast corner yelled, "He's exiting through the window. We have a runner."

The shirtless man headed directly toward the agent, carrying a machine gun. "Stop! FBI!" yelled the agent from behind a tree.

The man raised his gun in an attempt to fire. But before he had a chance, the agent shot him in the upper left arm. The force of the bullet pushed the man's shoulder backward. He screamed, then dropped his gun and fell to the ground. He attempted to crawl to his gun, but another bullet pierced his leg. Now moaning in pain, the man lay motionless on the ground.

The outside agents had orders to remain at their posts until Agent Stadler gave the "all-clear" signal. They stood guard until the search of the last room was completed at seven fifteen. Agent Stadler performed a quick roll call and then gave the signal.

Agent Stadler's van came to a screeching halt at the front door. He jumped out and directed the paramedics to the injured man in the backyard before he entered the house. "Any sign of the boy or Harrison?"

"None," said several of the agents.

"Let's go through this house one more time before the crime scene investigators get here. I want every room, closet, attic, and basement completely searched."

As the men started their sweep, Chief McKinney walked into the house. "Any sign of the boy?"

"None," Agent Staler said. "No sign of Harrison, either. We're going to interrogate the man downstairs. Hopefully, he can tell us something."

The chief assisted in the sweep, but after an hour of searching the house, they had found no signs of the boy. At eight fifteen, Chief McKinney reached into his back pocket for his cell phone and dialed Jack's number. Jack answered after the first ring.

"Hey, Chief. Did you find him?"

After a short pause, the chief let out a sigh. "No, Jack, I'm afraid not. There was no sign of him or Harrison. We arrested two men in the house, but neither of them claimed to know anything about Ian. Head over this way and I'll tell you everything."

Jack sat in his car for a few minutes before leaving. He contemplated the events of the past couple of weeks and tried to **envision (#225)** possible scenarios of how Ian might still be alive. With few coming to mind, his morale plummeted. From all the information obtained, he believed this was their last chance to find Ian. Jack remembered Mr. Anderson's comment that the longer it takes to find someone, the greater the chance that person is not alive. And, for the first time since Ian had gone missing, he became **bereft (#226)** of hope.

Jack arrived at the house, parked the Explorer at the end of the driveway, and then walked toward the front door. There was a chill in the air, so he went back to the Explorer to grab his sweatshirt that had *Property of Worthington Preparatory School Football Department* printed on the front. Both Agent Stadler and the chief greeted him upon entering the house. After a few minutes of small talk, they debriefed Jack on the events of the morning.

With his usual serious demeanor, Agent Stadler said, "Jack, walk through the house and look for any signs of Ian. Make sure you disturb as little as possible. The crime scene investigators haven't had a chance to dust for fingerprints."

Chief McKinney followed Jack while he walked throughout the house. They started in the basement and worked toward the top floor. When they reached the second floor, they encountered three agents escorting the captured man out of the house. Jack stepped aside to let them pass. He made brief eye contact with the man whose piercing gaze made a chill run up his spine.

Room by room, floor by floor, Jack and the chief continued their sweep. For almost thirty minutes, they hardly said a word. Halfway through the residence, they stopped for a break and began a conversation with two agents cleaning their guns.

"That looks like a powerful weapon," said Jack, staring at the black rifle.

"Here, hold it." The agent handed Jack the rifle. "Look through the scope. It's accurate to over a thousand feet."

Jack pointed the gun out a window and focused the crosshairs on a tree three hundred feet in the distance. He could see the laser's red dot shining on the bark. "That's cool." He returned the gun to the agent. "I hope I never see one of these red dots pointed at me."

The agent laughed. "Yeah, you're screwed if you do."

"Thanks," Jack glanced at the man's nametag, "Agent Ralston."

"Anytime," he replied. Jack shook the agent's hand before he and the chief went back to work.

With two rooms to go, Agent Stadler called for the chief. The tone of his voice seemed different. It was filled with despair. "McKinney, could you come down here? I need to talk to you."

Before leaving, the chief gave Jack a glassy-eyed glance. "This can't be good."

Jack followed the chief downstairs. When they entered the two-story living room, Agent Stadler said, "McKinney, I need to speak to you outside."

Knowing he was not invited, Jack remained in the living room and watched their conversation through the large picture windows. The two men stood on the deck facing each other. Agent Stadler, who appeared overly serious, was doing all the talking. Moments later, the one-sided conversation stopped, then Agent Stadler's shoulders sank, and his stare turned toward the ground. Instantly, the blank-faced chief lost his balance and reached for the railing. Without hesitation, Jack ran to the chief's side.

***

Meanwhile, the raids on the apartment and office in Manhattan provided no significant information. The house in Worthington, on the other hand, did.

The Worthington raid also started at seven. With agents assaulting from the water and land, they gained control of the premises without incident. They encountered only one person. After taking him into custody, a team of crime scene investigators searched the house. Knowing what to expect from Jack's investigation, they confiscated twenty-two pounds of cocaine and almost $12 million in cash.

The man in custody claimed he was only the caretaker of the property and knew nothing. But after confronting him with video evidence of his involvement in several illegal activities, he stopped talking and asked for his lawyer. When the agents explained they had knowledge of Ian's imprisonment in Harrison's basement, his attitude changed completely. He sat anxiously, handcuffed to a chair in one of the Worthington Police Station's interrogation rooms. The man, who appeared to be in his late forties, showed signs of panic. "I want a deal," he kept repeating.

While several state attorneys and agents from several departments gazed through the one-way glass, an FBI interrogator pounded his fist on the table and asked, "Why should we give you a deal? We have you and Harrison nailed. And unless you can tell us right now where Ian is, you're done."

The man stared directly into the interrogator's eyes, never blinking. He said nothing for almost a minute. Then, with no expression, he said, "I can tell you everything you want to know and everything you don't want to know. But I have to have a deal."

"What kind of a deal?"

With panic in his voice, the man said, "Total immunity and the witness protection program."

The interrogator leaned back in his chair and laughed. "No way. We have you, Harrison, and a bunch of other people nailed. They'll be open-and-shut cases. All of you will spend the rest of your lives in jail. And if we can't find the boy, you and Harrison will get the death penalty."

The man slowly shook his head and said in an uncomfortably low voice, "You don't understand. We're already marked for death. None of us will last a week in jail before an inmate or a guard will kill us."

Intrigued (#227) by the comment, the interrogator leaned forward, placed both elbows on the table, and rested his chin in the palm of his right hand. "What are you talking about?"

"La Mangosta."

"What?"

With his eyes piercing through the interrogator, the man repeated, "La Mangosta. The Mongoose. Hunter Harrison is a peon compared to him." The man stopped talking but continued to stare.

"Go on. You got my attention," said the interrogator in hopes of extracting more information.

Now clenching his teeth, the man said in a louder voice, "No, I have said too much already. Call my attorney and get the deal. If you don't, you'll have nothing. Because everyone involved will be dead shortly."

While the man continued to stare at his interrogator, someone began tapping on the privacy glass. This was the signal for the agent to leave the room. He entered the hallway to find it buzzing with conversations. The two DEA agents were both pale-faced and frantically talking on their phones.

One of the DEA agents removed the phone from his ear and said with a look of desperation, "I have the head of the DEA on the line, and he said to make him any deal he wants."

"What's going on?" asked the interrogator.

"We thought La Mangosta was only a legend. Recently, we acquired intel indicating he might truly exist. We need this man's information. It's worth whatever he wants."

Over the next hour, the lawyers hammered out a deal. With the signed papers in hand, the interrogator went back into the interrogation room, dropped his notepad and pen on the table, and then handed the documents to the man. "Here you go. Tell us what we want to know, and after you testify in court, you'll disappear forever."

After looking over the papers, the man began to tell his story. "Between divorcing my wife and sending two kids to college, I had no money. I couldn't make ends meet on my high school gym teacher's salary. So, several years ago, I started selling a little bit of pot and cocaine to some of my friends and a few other people. About a year ago, my supplier got caught and went to jail. I looked for another source, and within a week, I was introduced to a man who could supply me with whatever I needed. I consistently bought small quantities. But after a few months, they began to pressure me into selling more. So, I did, and I doubled my sales. I didn't cause any trouble, and I always paid them on time. This made the supplier very happy. Well, one day he made me a proposition I couldn't refuse. He said he knew a man who could use some help in the upper end of the network. If the man felt that he could trust me and I checked out, I'd be paid twenty thousand dollars a month. I realized I could make in two months what I made in a year. So, I agreed to do it. About a week later, I met the man in a hotel room in Manhattan. I didn't know his name at the time, but it was Hunter Harrison. I worked for about five months before seeing him again. This time, he moved me into his house here in Worthington. A man named Bo Pritchard and I were in charge of swapping the drugs and the money from the plane three times a week. During the week, we'd bust up the bricks of cocaine into smaller packages and count money. Millions of dollars in drugs and hard currency flowed through that house weekly.

"I did my job and kept my mouth shut. This pleased Harrison. Over the next five or six months, I learned more and more about the operation, mostly from Harrison's drunken babbling when he was at the house on weekends. If he were drunk, he'd tell me anything and not remember it the next morning.

"This is what I found out. The cocaine was grown and processed somewhere in the middle of Colombia. They'd drive it to the coast, then take it out to sea in a homemade semi-submersible submarine. When out in the ocean, a freighter carrying coffee beans to the U.S. would pick up the drugs. Somewhere off the East Coast, I think around Virginia, they'd drop off the drugs, and a small submarine would retrieve them. The submarine would travel back to a large boat disguised as a research vessel. This vessel would pick up the sub, then go somewhere off the coast of Connecticut. There, they'd deploy the sub to meet the seaplane for the exchange. The seaplane would drop off the drugs here, under the guise of transporting Harrison back and forth to Manhattan and shipping water samples for testing. Once we had the drugs, we'd package them, then give it to our runner, Julio."

The interrogator listened in amazement. "Is that the man in the black Mercedes SUV?"

"Yes. He delivers the drugs and picks up money from five places throughout the Northeast. From these places, the drugs are distributed to all the low-level dealers."

"Well, who's this La Mangosta character? And where's the kid?"

"I'm getting to that. Just wait. About two months after I started working for him, Harrison began to change. He started drinking more and more. I could tell he was worried about something. One night, in a drunken stupor, he told me about the man in charge of the drug trafficking. Even Harrison didn't know his real name. They just called him La Mangosta, meaning 'the mongoose.' The story goes that La Mangosta was the youngest of four boys whose father was one of the biggest Colombian drug lords. One Sunday afternoon, at a family dinner, La Mangosta, who was only twenty-three years old and had just graduated from one of the Ivy League colleges, was complaining that he didn't have enough responsibility and wasn't making enough money. Believing that the family didn't respect him, he left the room, and shortly after, returned with a machine gun. He killed everyone. This included his parents, brothers, their wives, and their kids. From that day on, he took over the family business and **amassed (#228)** a great deal of wealth and power. They say a mongoose is ferocious and hard to kill. Even snake venom won't hurt them. They say the same about La Mangosta. And that's how he got his name."

"How did Harrison and The Mongoose get together?"

"Harrison met La Mangosta through his hedge fund, Harrison International Investments. They had an arrangement where HII would launder some of the dirty drug money. At first, La Mangosta gave Harrison a big cut of the profits. But after a while, Harrison got in too deep and the rules changed. La Mangosta knew he had Harrison by the balls and **coerced (#229)** him into laundering even more money. Eventually, he forced him into trafficking the drugs and money through the house here in Worthington."

"Well, if no one knows who this Mongoose guy is, why are you so scared of him?"

"I'll tell you why. We had a couple of low-level dealers steal drugs from one of our distribution places. Within two days, everybody involved was killed. No one knows how he did it. But, as I said, everyone was dead. This included one man's wife. We also had five or six small-time dealers get caught by the police. Within a few days in jail, someone killed all of them, so that they couldn't testify. I heard one rumor that La Mangosta kidnapped a prison guard's eleven-year-old daughter. He threatened to kill her if the guard didn't arrange the execution of one of the dealers." The man sighed and shook his head. "Any **perfidious (#230)** activity that could hurt his drug cartel was handled by death. At first, I didn't believe all of this and thought they were rumors. But after I met him, I believed every word."

"You met him?"

"Yeah, one time for about twenty minutes. And, in that amount of time, I watched him kill one person and order another one dead."

"What happened?"

"One Friday night, Bo and I got a call from Harrison who told us that there'd be another passenger on board the seaplane. We weren't supposed to look at him or talk to him. Just do our regular job. So, that night, we got in the boat and went out for the rendezvous. It was very windy, and the waves were too large to exchange in the ocean. So, we came into the cove. We rafted next to the plane, but the wind kept blowing us closer to shore. The water was still choppy, and it was hard to maintain your balance. When Harrison handed Bo one of the suitcases, Bo dropped it in the water. This infuriated the passenger, who I later found out was La Mangosta. He started yelling at Bo. He told him to jump into the water and retrieved the case. So, Bo jumped in and got it. He then swam back to the boat, and I helped him aboard. While Bo regained his balance, La Mangosta said something in Spanish, then shot Bo between the eyes. Harrison and I were both shocked. We could not believe his **flagrant (#231)** disregard for life."

"Did you get a good look at La Mangosta?"

"No. La Mangosta was smart. He wore a hat and had a bandana around his face. So, I have no idea what he looks like. I think only Harrison and Julio have seen him." The man paused to take a sip of water. "I do remember the smell of his cologne. I don't think I'll ever forget that smell."

"What happened next?"

"Well, then it got worse. We noticed we were drifting too close to shore. And when we looked over our shoulders, there was a boy watching us through his binoculars."

"I assume that boy was Ian Anderson."

"Yeah, it was. La Mangosta called Julio and told him to drive over and get the boy before he got away. Julio raced over and snagged the boy as he ran home. When we got back to Harrison's house in the boat, Julio had just pulled into the driveway. La Mangosta ordered Harrison to kill the boy, then get rid of both bodies."

"What did you do next?"

"Harrison took the boy in the house and locked him in the basement bedroom. Then, I drove the boat far out into the ocean and dumped Bo's body. When I got back, I told Harrison this was not what I signed up for. I'd sell drugs, but I wouldn't kill anybody. To my surprise, Harrison agreed. Well, at least I thought he did. We sat up all night and tried to figure out what to do. But every way we looked at it, the kid, and most likely both of us, were going to die. If we let the kid go or he escaped, La Mangosta would find him and kill him. If we all went to the police, he'd somehow arrange to have us killed. By the end of the night, Harrison decided that the boy was our best insurance policy. He said if the authorities caught us, we could exchange the boy for our freedom."

The man leaned forward and stared into the interrogator's eyes. "Listen to me," he said. "I guarantee La Mangosta will find out who's involved in this operation. He'll come after you, your wife, your kids, or your girlfriend to get to me and everyone you arrested today. So, you and everybody watching through that window better make some calls because everyone you love is in great danger."

"Okay. We will. But what happened to the boy?"

"We couldn't figure out what to do. So, we kept Ian locked in the basement for about three weeks. The boy panicked at first. He cried for two days and pleaded, 'I just want to go home.' Harrison tried to explain to him that if he let him go or he escaped, La Mangosta would come after him and his family. The boy calmed down a little when Harrison told him he was getting out of the business soon and would let him go at that time. He also told Ian that he had written a long letter explaining everything. Harrison wanted Ian to give the letter to the FBI after he was released. The boy believed everything. So, he stayed locked in the room and didn't cause any trouble. Harrison bought him a bunch of video games. The kid played them all day long. I guess the games helped keep his mind off being kidnapped because he didn't cry as much.

"After three weeks, we still didn't know what to do. Then, one day, Julio unexpectedly came into the house to take a piss and heard the boy in his room. The next day, Harrison got a call from La Mangosta. He told Harrison that if the boy was still there in two days, Julio had orders to kill him. So, that night, Harrison told Ian he was taking him fishing. They left around midnight." The man glanced down at the table, "Only Harrison came back the next afternoon." The interrogator gasped. "I met Harrison at the boat and saw that he was drunk. When I looked inside the boat, there was blood everywhere. He wouldn't tell me what he did to him. But when I cleaned the boat, I found Harrison's camera. There were two pictures of the boy lying on his back, across the stern of the boat. It looked like Harrison had shot off the back of his head. You could see parts of his brain scattered throughout the boat. Harrison showed the pictures to Julio, and everything went back to normal—if you can call this normal. The camera might be in Harrison's house. I don't know if he's deleted the photos yet."

The interrogator leaned forward and placed his forehead in the palms of his hands. With his eyes closed, he asked, "So, Ian Anderson is dead, and Hunter Harrison killed him?"

"Yes."

"Do you know where Harrison is right now?"

"He told me he was going to his mountain house. But I've never been there, and I don't know where it is."

"Do you have a way to contact him?"

"No. He rarely calls. And it is always from a different number."

"When was the last time you talked to him?"

"Just over a week ago."

The interrogator continued questioning the man for several hours. As time passed, they learned more about the mysterious La Mangosta—the man who managed one of the largest drug empires like a ruthless **despot (#232).** While the interrogation continued, another agent called Agent Stadler to relay the bad news.

***

Jack burst onto the deck and placed his hand on Chief McKinney's shoulder. "What happened?" The chief and Agent Stadler were too **despondent (#233)** to speak. They both just looked at the ground and shook their heads. "He's dead, isn't he?"

"Apparently so," said the chief, his eyes beginning to tear.

Jack felt as if someone had punched him in the stomach. He stood motionless for a moment while he tried to comprehend what had happened. "Who? How?" He was so upset that he could not form coherent sentences.

Again, the chief looked at the ground and shook his head.

The three men stood side by side, leaning against the railing and staring off into the distance. No one talked for several minutes. Chief McKinney eventually broke the silence when he placed his arm around Jack's shoulders. "Come with me." While the two walked through the house, the chief explained the fate of Ian Anderson.

CHAPTER TWENTY-SEVEN

The gravel crackled with each step as Jack climbed the long winding driveway to his Explorer. By the time he opened the door, he was both mentally and physically exhausted. After he took off his sweatshirt, he slid into the driver's seat, placed the key in the ignition, but he did not start the engine. In his mind, he reenacted the events of Ian's abduction and murder. His eyes started to tear. He could not **fathom (#234)** what the boy must have endured. And even though he didn't know Ian well, his grief was very intense.

With his stare fixated on a cardinal perched on a tree branch, Jack held his phone to his ear while he waited for his father to answer his call.

"Did they find him?"

Jack sighed. "No. Dad, I don't think they're going to."

There was a pause before his father asked, "What happened to him?"

"Harrison killed him."

"What! Are they sure?"

"Yeah. According to some guy who works for Harrison's, Ian saw someone get murdered. So, they kidnapped and killed him to shut him up."

Mr. Graystone was at a loss for words. "How could somebody do that to a kid?" Jack could sense his father's empathy in his **lugubrious (#235)** tone, but he too was at a loss for words. "Robert and Christina will be devastated. Have they told them?"

"Not yet. Agent Stadler wanted to talk to Harrison first, but they can't find him."

"Where are you now?"

"I'm just about to leave Harrison's mountain house. Why?"

"I want you to ride home with Chief McKinney. We can pick the Explorer up later."

"Dad, don't worry. I'll be all right. If I have any problems, I'll call you."

"I don't know, Jack."

"I'm serious. Don't worry."

"Okay, but call me in an hour to let me know how you're doing."

"I'll talk to you in an hour." Jack hung up the phone, started the truck, and then made his way toward the interstate. He drove in silence down the winding mountain road thinking of Mr. and Mrs. Anderson and imagining their reactions to the news. Images of Agent Stadler sitting next to them explaining what happened to their son raced through his head. He tried to **efface (#236)** these thoughts by thinking of Courtney. But it didn't help. He tried thinking of next year's football team. That didn't help either. He even tried thinking of some of the **hilarious (#237)** things that Ollie had done. But no matter what he thought about, the image of Mrs. Anderson fainting into her husband's arms kept repeating in his head.

The engine groaned as he accelerated up the on-ramp. Jack set the cruise control and headed toward Worthington. He had only traveled a mile when the low fuel indicator started to glow. *Why didn't you get gas at the truck stop, you dumb ass?* Knowing he could not wait very long, he decided to get gas at the next exit.

The exit had only one gas station. It was an old building with two gas pumps. Jack inserted the nozzle and then leaned with his back against the Explorer. He looked across the road at the only other building around, Parker's Antiques. With his mind wandering, he stared at the **quaint (#238)** building. On its side was a mechanical sign consisting of an old man sitting in a rocking chair with his feet resting on a wood-burning stove. The old man appeared to be rocking back and forth. After a few seconds, a chill ran up Jack's spine. He grabbed his iPhone, scrolled through his emails, and found the transcript from Harrison's office. While the gas continued to pump, he scanned the email for the conversation about the mountain house. After locating it, he read it aloud hoping to **decipher (#239)** the **esoteric (#240)** message. "Hello. No, I'll be at the mountain house for two weeks. Yeah, deliver it there. I need everything on that list. That's correct. No, the first one. Yeah, you'll see the old man in the rocking chair. Second driveway on the right, past the old bison barn. Yes. Right. About four point six. See you then." Jack heard a click when the gas dispenser stopped pumping. He removed the nozzle and walked, as if in a daze, into the store. After receiving his change from the weathered old woman behind the counter, he headed for the door. Before he exited, he turned to her and asked, "By any chance, have you seen a fancy orange sports car driving around here?"

Without hesitation, the woman said, "Funny you should ask. Right at closing around a week ago, a sports car stopped to fill up. I didn't pay any attention to it. All cars look the same to me. But there were three high school boys in here that were going crazy over the car. They said it costs over four hundred thousand dollars. I didn't know a car could cost that much."

"Do you remember if it was orange?"

"It was dark outside, so I couldn't exactly tell. It could've been orange or red. I'm not sure."

Jack thanked the woman and then jumped into the Explorer. With the chance that Harrison might be close by, he picked up his phone to call Chief McKinney. "Dammit, there's no signal," he muttered. He figured he would have a better chance of getting a signal farther up the mountain, so he decided to do a bit of reconnaissance.

The conversation mentioned an old bison barn and the number four point six. Assuming this number was how many miles from the interstate to the driveway, he reset his odometer and headed down the twisty, two-lane road. He had not traveled very far when a large lake came into view. *That must be the lake I could see from the mountain house.*

Jack continued to look for signs of a bison ranch while he kept an eye on his odometer. It clicked to four point four as the road made a sharp curve to the left. When he rounded the corner, he saw an old barn just off the edge of the road. Mounted to it was a historical plaque that read, "Old Bryson Barn, Est. 1893."

"This is it," yelled Jack, as if someone could hear him. "It was

Bryson, not *bison.* That's why they couldn't find it."

Jack continued slowly down the road. He came across the first driveway after the barn. Its mailbox had the name of Moore painted on the side. This driveway was well worn, and he assumed someone lived there permanently.

Just after the odometer hit four point six, there was another driveway. This one had a metal farm gate secured by a lock and chain. The driveway looked unused. It was overgrown with native grasses that showed no signs of traffic.

Thinking aloud, Jack said, "This has to be it."

Jack reached for his cell phone. Again, he did not have a signal. He held the phone out the window and pointed it in several different directions. But this proved fruitless. He scratched his head while he tried to think of a plan.

I should probably turn around and go find Stadler. But, what if I'm wrong? And what if he comes all the way over here and it's a waste of time? Also, I'll have to explain how I got this information. Stadler doesn't know about the recordings. Jack stared out the window and shook his head. *What if they have to get a search warrant? How long will that take? Maybe I should walk down the driveway and see where it leads first. If I see anything suspicious, then I'll go get him.*

Jack **vacillated (#241)** between going in for a closer look or going to find Stadler. In the end, he decided to get a closer look. He parked the Explorer down the road, hiding it behind a stand of trees next to a large field. Then he walked the hundred or so yards along the edge of the road toward the locked gate. As he approached, he looked for signs of surveillance cameras. With none in sight, he went closer. His examination of the driveway indicated no signs of any recent vehicular traffic.

Jack stared at the ground for a moment while the **quandary (#242)**, should I, or shouldn't I, raced through his head. *Agent Stadler said I shouldn't take matters into my own hands. He also said he'd arrest me if I do. But all I'm doing is walking down a driveway. How can he arrest me for doing that? He could probably find a way. I really get the impression that he doesn't like me.* The agent's **edict (#243)** was clear. Do it again and go to jail. Jack contemplated the situation for a few more seconds and then raised his head. "Screw it. I'll take my chances," he mumbled. He quickly looked to his right and to his left before he jumped over the gate.

The forest along both sides of the driveway was dense with foliage. Trees of various sizes and wild blackberry bushes, with their sharp stickers, made it impossible to traverse. With no other choice, Jack meandered along the forest's edge and tried to leave as few footprints as possible. After a long, slow descent, the driveway came to an opening. He peered from behind a tree to survey the **desolate (#244)** topography. Ahead of him was an open field of tall grass. To the right was a small cabin set in a clump of trees. It overlooked the lake that he could see from the mountain house. To the left, on the other side of the field, was an old barn. It was in a sorry state of disrepair.

Jack worked his way through the woods and headed toward the cabin. With his eyes darting in every direction, he looked for signs of Harrison or his henchmen. He stopped about one hundred feet from the structure and crouched behind a tree. The cabin appeared to be abandoned. From what he could see, no one had been there for a while. The surrounding vegetation was overgrown and showed no signs of being disturbed.

As Jack formulated his plan, he searched for surveillance cameras. With none in sight, he made one last scan of the area and then bolted toward the back of the cabin. The trunks from several large trees provided his cover along the way. He eased along the back side of the cabin and stopped at a window covered by two old wooden shutters. When he peeped through the cracks in these shutters, he could examine most of one-half of the structure. The small room contained old furniture consisting of a couch, two chairs, and a couple of tables. As far as he could tell, there were no signs of a current inhabitant. He crept to the next window. Inside this room, he saw two perfectly made single beds, both covered with old pink and white quilts.

Jack stood with his back to the cabin and wiped the sweat from his forehead. *What do I do next?* After a moment, he mustered enough courage to scurry around to the front of the house. The front porch's old wooden planks squeaked with each step he made toward the first window. When he looked inside, he could re-examine the bedroom.

Again, he saw no signs of personal belongings such as clothes or shoes. He then maneuvered around two rocking chairs covered with cobwebs and continued along the porch. At the second window, he peered inside and resurveyed the living room. From this vantage point, he saw no dishes in the sink or any other items that would indicate the cabin was occupied.

Jack stood on the front porch and gazed at the barn. He had to decide whether to walk across the open field or follow a protected route through the forest. Not wanting to take any chances, he backtracked through the trees and brush to the driveway. He then ran along the driveway for several hundred feet before he disappeared into the forest and made his way to the back side of the barn.

There were no doors or windows on the rear of the dilapidated building, so he walked through the knee-high grass to the far side. On this side, there was only one door. He pressed his ear against it and listened for signs of life. He heard nothing. Again, should I or shouldn't I, raced through his head. *I've come this far. I can't turn back now.* With a deep breath, he twisted the doorknob and pushed. The door creaked as it slowly opened. When he poked his head inside, he felt a rush of cool air.

The barn was dark. Besides the open door, cracks in the walls and roof provided the only light. These small beams illuminated random portions of the barn. Jack took a few steps and then stopped to let his eyes acclimate. After blinking several times, he saw an old John Deere tractor with two flat tires directly in front of him. Behind it was an old Cadillac limousine. The large old car, which was originally black, was now brown from a thick blanket of dust and dirt. Jack continued into the barn. He walked around the back of the limo and came across a third vehicle. This vehicle was much smaller and covered by an old tarp. Intrigued by the sight, he knelt to the ground and removed the rear portion of the cover. What he discovered made his heart pound. Parked in front of him was a new, orange Lamborghini Aventador with a New York license plate that read HII3.

Jack was scared, nervous, and excited at the same time. He scratched his head while he paced back and forth. *What do I do now?* He looked at his phone but did not have a signal. Thinking aloud, he said, "I'll go back to the Explorer and drive toward the mountain house. When I get a signal, I'll call Stadler and tell him that I found Harrison's car."

Jack scurried back to the door, poked his head outside, and looked around before he exited. He was jogging when he rounded the back corner of the barn; however, he was stopped short in his tracks. Now filled with **consternation (#245)**, he did not know what to do. His body trembled as standing before him was Hunter Harrison pointing a gun at his head.

"Stop right there, boy," Harrison said with a piercing stare.

Jack froze. He wanted to bolt but knew he could not outrun Harrison's bullets. He thought about going for the gun but knew he was no match for Harrison.

"What are you doing in my barn, boy?"

Without hesitation, Jack said, "I'm looking for my dog. He got loose. I thought I saw him go into your barn."

"Oh, really? Then why were you hiding behind trees and snooping around my house? I've been watching you ever since you got on the driveway."

Jack stammered.

"That's what I thought. You have no answer. Give me your wallet and phone, boy."

Jack reached into his pockets and removed his wallet and phone. He passed them to Harrison with a trembling hand. Harrison extracted Jack's driver's license, examined its information, and then looked at Jack with suspicious eyes. "Jack Graystone from Worthington, your dog sure has traveled a long way."

Jack stood motionless and said nothing. *Remember what Chris told you. Stay calm.*

Harrison tossed the wallet to Jack. "You're the kid who was snooping around my house in Worthington on your paddleboard. I recognize you from my surveillance videos. Sticking your nose in places where it doesn't belong can get you killed, you know."

Jack had no response. For fear his words would anger Harrison, he thought it best to remain quiet.

Harrison waved the end of the gun, indicating for Jack to move. "Turn around and head for the cabin." Jack **capitulated (#246)**, and as soon as he turned, he felt the barrel of the gun in his back.

While Harrison escorted him by gunpoint through the knee-high grass, Jack's mind raced. *He's too big. I'll never get his gun away from him. Maybe I can reason with him.* With his adrenaline pumping, he quickly formulated a plan. Jack placed his left hand on his stomach, discreetly reached over with his right hand, and unscrewed the antenna on his Breitling watch. After extending the antenna, which in turn activated the electronic locating transmitter, he unclasped the band, removed the watch from his wrist, and held it in his right hand. Knowing that structures or tree cover would disrupt the transmitter's signal, he had to leave the watch in the open field. Harrison continued to nudge him with the gun. And when they reached the middle of the field, Jack pretended to trip, landing face down in the tall grass.

"Get up," Harrison said with a swift kick to Jack's feet.

With his back toward Harrison, Jack hid the watch in the grass and then jumped to his feet. He increased the pace of his steps as he headed toward the cabin in hopes that Harrison would not discover what he had done. He had taken only a few steps before Harrison said, "Stop."

Jack froze and closed his eyes. He could hear Harrison's footsteps moving through the grass. *Please don't let him find the watch. If he does, I have no other choice than to go for the gun. I'll jump on him when he bends over to pick it up.* Jack opened his eyes and was about to turn around when he felt the gun in his back.

"Slow down." Harrison nudged Jack with the gun. "Head over to the cabin."

Jack slowly climbed the steps to the cabin's front porch. His heart was pounding in his chest. "Take a seat, boy." Harrison pointed to one of the cobweb-covered rocking chairs with his gun. He stared into Jack's eyes for a moment and then shook his head. "You're a day early. Why couldn't you've come tomorrow?"

"Why tomorrow?"

Harrison leaned against the porch railing. "Because tomorrow morning I'm going to disappear forever. I'm taking my 852 million dollars and will vanish into thin air."

Not knowing what to say, Jack sat in the chair gently rocking back and forth. *Keep making eye contact with him. That should make it harder for him to shoot you.*

Harrison squinted his eyes and tilted his head. "Jack Graystone, how did you find this place? Only one other person knows of it. I'm sure the cops don't know about it, or they would've raided it this morning."

After a pause, Jack said, "Lucky guess?"

"Yeah, right. Try again."

Jack was unsure of what to say. He could not think of a story and did not know whether to tell him the truth. Harrison was correct. The cops did not know about the cabin. And, until someone detected his distress signal, they won't. Although he did not know if Harrison had already determined his fate, Jack decided he had nothing to lose by telling the truth.

"Well, I overheard a conversation when I bugged your house. That and the old woman at the gas station led me here."

Harrison stood straight up and gasped. "You bugged my house? That's impossible. The place is like Fort Knox."

With a hint of **arrogance (#247)**, Jack replied, "The guy you have watching your house doesn't set the alarm when he leaves to meet the seaplane. The man in the Mercedes can't see the front door from where he parks. So, if you swim underwater to the south end of your property, you can climb up the rock face and crawl into your house without being detected by the outside cameras."

Harrison looked **incredulous (#248)**. "Are you serious? I spent almost four hundred thousand dollars on surveillance equipment, and it's beaten by a kid."

Jack raised his eyebrows and nodded slowly in response.

"I don't ever remember saying the address to this place. So, how'd you find it?"

"The old man in the rocking chair. You told someone they'd see an old man in a rocking chair. When I stopped to get gas, I saw him on the side of Parker's Antiques. I followed the road searching for a bison farm. But, when I found the Old Bryson Barn, I knew it had to be the second driveway."

"Wow! How observant for a kid." Harrison rubbed his cheek. "I assumed you tried to call the cops, but had no luck?"

"Yep, I did."

Harrison shook his head. "You can't get a signal around here, thanks to the terrain and several well-placed cell phone jammers."

Jack paused for a moment before he spoke. He remembered Chris saying you should humanize yourself to your captor. Let them know that you're a person with a life and that you don't want to die. "So, Mr. Harrison, what are you going to do with me? I don't want to die. I haven't even made it out of high school yet."

"Well, I'm going to..." Harrison's phone vibrated and he stopped talking. When he looked at the screen, his demeanor changed. "Get inside," he said, waving the gun.

Jack opened the door and walked into the dark cabin. It smelled like an old person's house. Harrison pointed to a chair. "Take a seat."

Jack sat while Harrison walked over to what appeared to be a set of closed curtains covering a window. He reached behind these curtains and tugged on a cord. When they opened, Jack saw nine video monitors. Harrison flipped a flick of a switch that turned them all on. Their images showed several locations throughout the property.

Harrison pointed to a monitor. "Just a deer." Noticing a confused look on Jack's face, he continued, "I have motion sensors all over this place. They send a signal to my phone when they're tripped."

While they both sat in silence and viewed the monitors, Jack's legs started to tremble from an intense sense of fear. "Are you going to kill me, like you did Ian?" Jack asked in a squeaky voice.

Wrinkles formed on Harrison's forehead. "Who told you I killed Ian?"

"When they raided your house in Worthington this morning, the guy they arrested made a deal and told the FBI everything they wanted to know."

"Really? What exactly did he say?"

"He said Ian saw everything and you kidnapped him. Then La Mangosta made you kill him."

"You know about La Mangosta?"

"Yes."

"Interesting. Continue."

"Well, the guy said you took Ian fishing, and he never came back. He also said he saw a picture of Ian dead on the back of the boat. Mr.

Harrison, if you let me go, I'm sure you can get away without being caught."

The **intransigent (#249)** Harrison became agitated. He appeared **impervious (#250)** to Jack's pleas. "Get up," he said with a wave of his gun. Jack slowly stood. Harrison pointed his gun toward a door in the middle of the room. "Go over there and open it." Jack took several uneasy steps toward the door. Harrison followed closely. With his hand trembling, Jack reached out and grabbed the doorknob. He opened the door and saw a set of stairs leading to a basement. Harrison gave him a nudge with the gun. "Go down." The stairwell was dark. After Jack took his first step, Harrison flipped a switch that turned on a light. Jack continued. His apprehension grew greater with every step. About halfway down, Harrison placed his hand on Jack's shoulder and said in a **phlegmatic (#251)** voice, "I'm going to do the same to you as I did to Ian."

Harrison's emotionless words filled Jack's entire body with fear. He grabbed the handrail as his knees went weak. With almost every part of his body trembling, he fought back the urge to throw up. He stepped onto the basement floor and stood in front of a metal door. He was too **debilitated (#252)** to make an attempt at the gun.

"Step aside," Harrison calmly said. He inserted a key into the locked door. Tears started to flow from Jack's eyes while he waited for his impending doom. The door opened with a soft screech. Jack closed his eyes in fear of what he might see. "Go in," said Harrison with another nudge from the gun. With his eyes closed, he took three steps into the room knowing that at any second a bullet might pierce the back of his head. When he came to a stop, Jack heard a familiar voice.

"Jack, what are you doing here?"

Jack opened his eyes to see Ian Anderson sitting in a chair playing a video game. He stood frozen for a moment and stared at his friend. "Ian, you're supposed to be dead."

Ian stood, his face pale and withdrawn. "No, I'm still alive."

Jack tried to regain his composure. "I have been looking for you ever since you went missing." He wiped the tears from his face with his hands and then turned to Harrison. "What's going on?" he demanded.

"Sit down and I'll explain."

Besides Ian's chair, the only other place to sit was a single bed placed against the back wall. Jack walked over and sat on its edge. He leaned forward with his elbows on his thighs and his hands folded. He then glared at Harrison, eagerly waiting for his explanation.

Harrison stood with his back against the door jamb while holding the gun in his right hand. He let out a long sigh before he told his story. "A while back, I was approached by a man who wanted to invest money in my company. At first, the transactions were all **legitimate (#253)**. Then one day, this man told me he had money that needed laundering. Meaning it was money obtained illegally and he wanted it to become legit. He offered huge profits if I could succeed. At the time, my business wasn't doing very well. So, against my better judgment, I devised a way to launder the money. I knew I shouldn't have done it. But I had payroll to meet, investors to keep happy, and an out-of-control lifestyle to support. I laundered about eighty million dollars, of which I kept half. This **infusion (#254)** of money got me back on my feet. I told the man . . ."

"Was this man La Mangosta?" interrupted Jack.

"Yes, it was. So, I told La Mangosta, who went by the alias Ricardo Lopez, that I was finished. I could no longer launder any more money. He looked at me, laughed, and said I didn't have the choice of whether or not I wanted to stop laundering the money. He explained how I was already in too deep. He said he would crush me if I tried to get out. So, getting out meant either death or a long time in prison." Harrison looked at the ground and frowned. "I never saw it coming. I didn't realize he had an **insidious (#255)** plan to take over my business until it was too late." Harrison looked up and shook his head. "Over the next several months, he forced me deeper and deeper into his operation. And, before I knew it, he was running drugs through my house in Worthington."

Jack interrupted Harrison. "I guess that's what my dad means when he says, 'If you lie down with dogs, you'll get up with fleas.'"

Harrison nodded. "Yes, this is a prime example."

Jack pushed himself backward on the bed and rested against the back wall. He looked cautiously at Harrison and waited for him to continue.

"When he abducted Ian and told me to kill him, that was the final straw. I'm not a murderer. I'm not a drug dealer either. I'm a businessman under the control of a very **nefarious (#256)** person. So, for the last month, I've been secretly diverting most of La Mangosta's money to an offshore account. The final **embezzlement (#257)** will happen at midnight tonight. And in the morning, La Mangosta will be broke, and I'll be gone."

"What about the picture of Ian with the back of his head blown off?"

Before Harrison could answer, Ian blurted out, "We staged that!"

Harrison nodded, "Yes we did. I explained the whole situation to Ian. I let him know that if he escaped and went home, La Mangosta would find him, then kill him and his whole family. I asked Ian to be patient and told him I'd figure out a way to protect him. That's when we decided to stage his death. As long as La Mangosta thought he was dead, he'd be safe. So, boys, tomorrow morning when my girlfriend arrives, she and I are leaving for good."

"Well, what about us?"

"Tomorrow evening, when we're long gone, I'll send an email to the FBI explaining where you're located. I have written a letter explaining everything that has happened. It also explains that La Mangosta believes Ian is dead. And, for Ian's protection, it needs to stay that way. Ian knows where I have hidden the letter and can get it for the FBI when they arrive. So, boys, by tomorrow night, you should be on your way home."

"I can't wait to see my parents and Reilly."

Harrison took a step backward through the open door. "I have a few things to do. Play your video games, and I'll bring some food down later."

Jack kept a constant eye on Harrison while he closed and locked the metal door behind him. Jack jumped up from the bed and glanced the room. He saw no windows. And the only other door led to a small bathroom, which contained a toilet and a sink.

Ian placed his video controller on the table. "What are you doing?"

The stress from being locked in a basement caused Jack to panic. "I'm looking for a way to escape." Ian stood and followed Jack around the room. Jack used the knuckle of his index finger to knock on each wall. He was listening for any signs of hollow space. Unfortunately, they all sounded solid. He paused to scratch his head, then removed a dime from his pocket and unscrewed the covers to several electrical outlets. After looking inside each outlet, he found every wall was constructed from solid concrete.

Jack closed his eyes and rubbed his forehead with the fingertips of his right hand. He was trying to formulate an escape plan, but he came up with nothing.

"He said he'll let us go tomorrow. Why do we need to escape?" whispered Ian.

"Because a lot can happen between today and tomorrow," Jack barked, acting like an impatient father. "And don't forget, no matter what he says, we're still dealing with a drug dealer."

Ian's demeanor quickly changed. A look of fear came over him, and his body started to tremble.

Jack realized he should not have made this impetuous remark. He should have kept his mouth shut. "You're right. If he were going to harm us, he would've done it already. Come over here. Let's play some of these games. Do you have *Call of Duty*?"

"Sure do."

Jack grabbed a controller and sat next to Ian. Before they started, Ian turned to him and asked, "How are my parents doing?"

Jack was unsure of what to say. *Do I tell him the truth, or do I sugarcoat it?* He looked at Ian. "Your dad is trying to remain strong, but I can tell he's having a real hard time. And your mom, well, she had to go to the hospital because she stopped eating."

"Jack, do they think I'm dead?"

"I don't think so. I don't think they've given up all hope just yet."

"What about Reilly?"

"Your parents didn't have the strength to walk him. So, for almost every night since you've been gone, I took him for a walk. While we went around the Ocean Walk, he constantly sniffed the ground. I knew he was searching for you."

"Jack, where am I? And how did you find me?"

"You don't know where you are?"

Ian shook his head. "Mr. Harrison must have given me a sleeping pill when we went out on the boat. All I remember is drinking a can of

Coke, and when I woke up, I was in this room."

"You're in the mountains about four hours north of Worthington."

"Really?"

"Yeah."

"Does anybody know you're here?"

Jack frowned and shook his head. "It's a long story." He then spent the next twenty minutes explaining the events of the past several weeks. At no time, however, did he mention his watch in the field. He could not take a chance that there was a listening device in the room.

"So, Ian, if you hadn't put your initials on the basement window, I would've never found you. What possessed you to do that?"

"Well, I thought if I wrote something like 'Help me, I'm being held hostage' or 'Ian Anderson was here,' they would've seen it and then cleaned the window. If they saw the letters *I. A. C.*, they most likely wouldn't know what they stood for and would leave them alone. I figured if the cops ever came snooping around, they'd see my initials and understand what they meant. I also put my handprints all over the bedroom door. This way, if they dusted for fingerprints, they'd have proof I was held in the room."

Jack smiled. "That's smart thinking."

"You ready to play?"

"Yeah, but let me asked you one more thing. Did you read Harrison's letter?"

"No."

"Are you sure he wrote one?"

"Well, I saw him put an envelope between two books on the mantel."

"I'd sure like to read this letter," mumbled Jack.

"Why do you want to read it?"

Jack's forehead wrinkled. "I'm just curious about what it says."

The pair played video games into the evening. The entire time, Jack noticed the smell of body odor wafting off Ian. Finally, he had to ask, "Does Harrison let you take a shower?"

Ian paused the game and looked at Jack. "Yeah, he does. I can take one whenever I want. Why?"

"Well, when was the last time you took one?"

"Uh, it's been about four days since I showered or changed my clothes. He doesn't make me take one, so I don't."

"Ian, I hate to tell you this, but you kind of smell."

Ian had become **inured (#258)** with his body odor. He lifted his right arm and sniffed his armpit. "You get used to it," he said. Then he unpaused the game and continued to play.

Around seven o'clock, the metallic sound of Harrison inserting a key into the door lock got their attention. When the door opened, Harrison entered the room with two cooked, frozen pizzas and two cans of soda. With a constant eye on Jack, he placed the items on a TV tray and then slowly backed out of the room.

Dinner was followed by more video games and talking. Around ten o'clock, after both kids had yawned several times, Jack suggested they get some rest. He wanted to have plenty of energy for whatever was going to happen the following day. After making Ian wash and change his clothes, they were sound asleep on the tiny single bed by ten thirty.

CHAPTER TWENTY-EIGHT

While Ian slept in his contorted positions, he occasionally woke Jack with a kick or a nudge. The room was pitch black and quiet. The **sporadic (#259)** drips from the faucet, and Ian's breaths were the only sounds Jack heard. As he dozed in and out of sleep, he became more **apprehensive (#260)** of how the following day's events would unfold.

Around two in the morning, both boys woke to the sound of four gunshots from a semi-automatic rifle. Seconds later, bursts from several machine guns responded. The sounds of bullets piercing the cabin's walls and glass breaking resonated throughout the basement.

Jack grabbed Ian's arm. "This can't be good." He ran to the door, placed his ear against the cold steel, and listened. He heard nothing.

"What's going on, Jack?"

Jack shook his head. He knew this gunfire was a **presage (#261)** that they might not make it out alive. He began to pace back and forth. "It's probably the FBI."

Throughout the night, Jack had anticipated their arrival. He hoped the FBI would subdue Harrison before he could harm either of them. Jack was **cognizant (#262)** of the fact that Harrison would use them as hostages if he had a chance. He had come to the realization that Harrison would do whatever it takes to save himself.

Just as Jack anticipated, Harrison was at the door a few moments later. The boys could hear him inserting the key into the lock.

"Get behind me," Jack said, standing only a few feet from the door. "When I get a chance, I'm going to overpower him. Stay away from the barrel of the gun and do whatever you can to help."

Harrison entered the room, blood-soaked. It appeared he had taken a bullet to the left shoulder. "They're here!" he said, waving his gun in the air.

"Mr. Harrison, just let us go. I'm sure you can work a deal with the FBI if you help them catch La Mangosta."

Harrison paused and then looked at Jack with eyes full of worry. "The FBI isn't here. It's La Mangosta."

Jack's stomach instantly tied in knots. All night long, he had made plans for several scenarios, but he had not planned for this.

"Put any sign of Ian in this bag." Harrison removed a plastic garbage bag from his back pocket and handed it to Jack. "They think Ian is dead, and we need to keep it that way." The two did not question their captor. Jack grabbed the video games. Ian gathered what few clothes were scattered around the room. "Is that everything?" Both boys nodded. "We don't have much time. Follow me."

As they followed Harrison out of the bedroom, Jack's mind raced. *Why would Harrison care if La Mangosta knew Ian was alive? I wonder what he plans on doing with us?*

Harrison went into the small hallway and stopped at the base of the stairs. He inserted the gun into his pocket, bent over, grabbed the bottom stair, and then pulled. With relative ease, the bottom half of the staircase pivoted upwards, revealing a hidden room. He ducked as he entered the concealed space, then reached for a chain from an overhead light fixture and pulled. The light revealed a round, metal hatch on the far wall.

"Turn that handle and open it," Harrison said with a glance toward Jack. Jack did as told. "Now, listen to me. We don't have much time. This tunnel will take you to the barn. It comes out under the floor drain in the back room. Look for the latch underneath to open the grate. When you're sure everyone is gone, go behind the barn. You'll see an old well that's next to a potting shed. Behind the potting shed, you'll find a path that leads to the field where you hid your truck. Got it?"

Jack said, "Yes." Ian nodded.

"Okay. Take this iPad. You should have a signal at the end of the tunnel and be able to view the video feeds. Be quiet and watch what's going on. Remember, stay in the tunnel until you're sure the men are gone. I'll stay here and hold them off as long as possible."

"Jack, you first." Harrison handed him a mechanic's dolly. "There's a rope in there. Pull yourself along until you get to the end of it. You'll then be twenty feet from the opening."

Before Jack climbed into the tunnel, Harrison looked into his eyes, then shook his head and sighed. "I'm sorry for what I put you two through. I'll figure out a way to make things right." Jack could sense the **compunction (#263)** in Harrison's voice.

Jack climbed headfirst into the tunnel. He grabbed a flashlight from Harrison and inspected his escape route.

"Ian, you're next." Harrison handed him a dolly.

Ian shimmied into the tunnel. "Mr. Harrison, can I take the letter with me?"

"Ian, we don't have time. I'll leave it on the mantel. Now, remember to make the least amount of noise as possible. And turn off the light when you get close to the end. Now, go!"

The background light faded as Harrison closed the hatch. Jack pointed the flashlight's beam throughout the tunnel. At closer examination, it appeared to be made of thirty-six-inch-diameter concrete pipe.

The metal wheels from the dolly made a grinding sound as the boys pulled themselves through the cool, damp pipe. The air inside had a musty smell, which made Jack want to sneeze. He knew he had to be quiet, so he pinched his nose and held back each one. With every jerk of his head, he thought, *That's another day off my life.* Occasionally, Jack swatted at a spiderweb that blocked their passage. After he crushed the spider with the end of the flashlight, the two would continue through the darkness.

The boys methodically worked their way toward the barn with the **disquieting (#264)** sounds of gunfire echoing through the tunnel. The exchanges happened several times and were always the same. Harrison shot five or six times and then La Mangosta's men countered with their machine guns. Jack could only imagine what was happening above them.

The farther Jack traveled into the tunnel, the more claustrophobic he became. Couple this with the thought of being shot, and he started to panic. His chest tightened and his breathing became shallow. Trying not to show his fear, he persevered, knowing that shortly they would be at the tunnel's end. "How are you doing back there?" he whispered.

"Okay. Can you see the end yet?"

"No, not yet."

After a few more minutes of pulling, Jack came to the end of the rope. "Stay here. Let me go ahead and check things out." Jack turned off the flashlight and eased toward the end of the tunnel that was now **devoid (#265)** of light. He listened for any activity in the barn while he waited for his eyes to adjust to his surroundings. Moments later, the bottom of the grate slowly came into view. "Ian, come over here."

Ian rolled next to Jack who had removed the iPad from underneath his shirt. To their surprise, they had a signal and could view the nine surveillance cameras. As far as they could tell, two of the cameras covered the driveway and three were located throughout the woods. Of the remaining four, one looked from the house to the lake. Another watched the front and one side of the barn. The remaining two were set at an angle and covered the front, back, and both sides of the house.

There was no gunfire for almost a minute. Jack enlarged the video feed that covered the front of the house. "Look." Jack pointed at the screen. "Harrison killed two of them."

"Maybe he got them all."

Jack glanced at Ian. "Or maybe they got him." He switched from screen to screen but saw no one or any activity of any kind.

"Jack, do you think we should make a run for it now?"

"Not just yet. I'm sure his men are still out there."

"Do, do you think Mr. Harrison is dead?"

Jack shook his head. "I don't know. You think we would have heard him get into the tunnel by now."

An eerie calm had settled within the tunnel. It was so quiet that any sound seemed amplified. Jack continued to tap on the iPad screen, switching from camera to camera. Each tap appeared to get louder and louder. And as the sounds increased, so did Jack's fear.

It had remained quiet for several more minutes—the proverbial calm before the storm. Then an all-out assault began. From the camera covering the front of the house, they saw several smoke canisters land on the front porch. The smoke quickly engulfed the structure. Within seconds, two men wearing gas masks and body armor ran toward the porch and disappeared into the smoke. Moments later, there was a bright flash and a bang that the boys could feel and hear in the tunnel. Then, there was silence. Since there were no interior cameras, they could only imagine what was happening.

"That's not a good sign," Jack said after scrolling the through the camera feeds twice.

"Why's that?"

"There were no gunshots. Harrison either gave up or is dead."

Jack's and Ian's eyes were riveted to the iPad. They saw several men emerged from the trees and walk in and out of the house. As far as Jack could tell, there were five of them.

The two boys watched the camera that covered the house for several minutes but saw no signs of Harrison. Jack began to scroll through the different video feeds. When he got to the camera that covered the barn, he saw two men walking toward the side door. He pointed at the screen. "Someone's coming. We need to move back a few feet."

The two retreated farther into the tunnel and waited for their visitors. They heard the side door open, followed by the men entering the barn. Several silent minutes later, the door to the back room opened, and they saw the beam from a flashlight flickering in the room above. Shortly after, the light disappeared. They remained huddled in their hiding place and did not hear any further commotion for several more minutes.

"Maybe they're gone," whispered Ian.

Jack shook his head. "I don't think we'll be that lucky."

The two men eventually started a conversation in Spanish. Jack listened closely. Unfortunately, his two years of Spanish proved **futile (#266)**. He might have understood if they had said they were going to wash the car or study in the library. But their dialect and speed of speech were too much for him to comprehend.

The boys continued to listen as a third man entered the conversation. Although Jack could not understand what he said, he knew this man was angry by the tone of his voice. When the conversation stopped, the men began ransacking the barn. Jack and Ian heard them tossing objects throughout the building. The old Cadillac limo screeched as each door opened. One by one, they heard a loud *thunk* when the men slammed each door closed.

The noises grew louder as the men worked their way toward the back room. After several long minutes, the two saw the flashlight again. This time, they heard a clink of a chain and the room filled with light. Paint cans rattled, and several glass jars broke while the men rummaged through the shelves that lined the walls.

Jack deciphered three distinct voices. One man, clearly in charge, fired all the orders. Lying just feet from the floor grate, Jack watched a set of hands grab hold of it and pull. The grate rattled but did not open. After more conversation, the shadow of a head appeared when someone made a closer examination of the space. Within seconds, a brief whiff of a man's cologne came through the entrance to the tunnel. The **evanescent (#267)** scent caused Ian's body to tremble. Jack looked at him. Through the dim light, he could see Ian's eyes were the size of golf balls, and his mouth was open. With the fear of God in his face, he turned to Jack and mouthed, "La Mangosta."

Another attempt was made to open the grate. This time, two sets of hands grabbed hold. Just as before, the grate rattled but did not budge. The men eventually gave up but continued to search the room. After a few more minutes, which seemed like an hour, the noises stopped.

Jack waited before making any moves. When he thought the time was right, he eased back toward the grate and turned on the iPad. Before he scrolled through the images from the cameras, he looked at Ian and asked, "How'd you know that was La Mangosta?"

Still visibly upset, Ian replied in a shaky voice, "His cologne. After they kidnapped me and took me back to Harrison's house, he was there. When he got close to me, I smelled his cologne. I'll never forget that smell."

"Let's see where he's gone." Jack placed the iPad between them.

On a few of the video feeds, they saw several men walking around the house. Ian gasped and pointed at the screen. "That's him, the man with the hat and bandana." La Mangosta's disguise made it impossible to see his face. Ian was positive; however, this was the same man he had seen in Worthington. He recognized him by his outfit.

The boys stared at the video screen and watched the **omnipotent (#268)** La Mangosta instruct his men from the front porch of the cabin.

The men obeyed his every order while they continued their search throughout the property. Occasionally, La Mangosta would point or yell at them. Then, without saying a word, he disappeared into the woods.

Jack frantically scrolled through the video feeds but found no trace of La Mangosta. After numerous attempts to locate him, he appeared to have vanished.

The activity, centered mostly on the house, continued in La Mangosta's absence. Several men walked in and out, while others examined its exterior.

Jack switched from camera to camera. When he viewed the camera covering the barn, he noticed someone walking toward it.

"What's he carrying?" asked Ian.

Jack shook his head. "I have no idea."

The two stared at the screen, and when the man arrived at the front of the barn, the object came into view. Jack panicked and grabbed Ian's arm. "It's a gas can! They're going to burn this place! We have to get out!"

The two scrambled toward the end of the tunnel while the man doused the barn with gasoline. He started along the front and worked his way around the perimeter.

Jack inspected the underside of the grate and found two latches. He quickly released them, pushed the grate aside, and then wiggled through the opening. He then lay on the ground and extended his hands toward Ian. "Hand me the flashlight and iPad." Jack placed the items next to the opening. "Now, give me your hands." He grabbed Ian's hands, and from a crouched position, yanked him out of the hole.

The smell of gasoline was overwhelming. The two hesitated at the side door as they heard the man splashing the final wall. Jack grabbed Ian's shoulder, stared directly into his eyes, and whispered, "When he goes around the corner, I'm going to open the door, and we're going to creep toward the back of the barn. I'll make sure nobody's there. Then we'll go to the potting shed, find the path, and run like hell. Got it?"

Ian replied with a nod.

With their eyes fixed on the iPad, the two waited for the man to walk out of sight. When he got to the front corner of the barn, he stopped, dropped the gas can, and then reached into his pocket for a lighter. After several attempts, the lighter ignited, and he placed it against the front of the building. The flames quickly spread along the barn's front side and then followed the man's path around the building. With the barn's old wooden structure being so dry, the flames quickly reached the roof. Within a matter of seconds, the second side started to blaze and the barn filled with **noxious (#269)** black smoke.

"We have to run for it before it gets to this last wall," Jack said in a panic. It was getting harder to breathe by the second. Jack knew if they inhaled too much of the poisonous smoke it would be **deleterious (#270)** to their health. The boys watched the iPad with great intensity. Just as the **conflagration (#271)** approached the last wall, the man walked around to the front of the burning barn and the two bolted. By the time Jack poked his head around the back corner of the barn, flames had engulfed the entire structure.

With no one in sight, he motioned for Ian to follow, and the two scrambled into the woods for cover. Jack looked around and spied the old well and potting shed. They were about a hundred feet away in a small clearing. Methodically, they forged through the thick growth and approached the shed. The two crouched on the edge of the clearing while Jack scanned the area for any signs of La Mangosta's henchmen. Seeing no one, he grabbed Ian's arm. "Let's go." They ran to the shed and stopped when they rounded the back corner. With a glance to his right, then left, Jack found the path. "Follow me," he said, grabbing Ian's shoulder.

The two started to run down the path. They had only taken a few steps when they heard the door to the shed open. Jack's entire body filled with fear. Not knowing if they had been detected, the two continued their escape. Unfortunately, Jack's worst fears were realized when a man with a Colombian accent yelled, "Stop or I'll shoot!"

"Keep running!" Jack gasped in between breaths. He then let Ian take the lead. Although the dense tree cover blocked most of the light from the night's moon, the two could still make out the narrow path. The thicket scraped against their adrenaline-filled bodies as they bolted through the woods.

With a hundred-foot lead, the boys were pulling away from their pursuer. Again, they heard the man yell, "Stop or I'll shoot!" This time, however, shots from a silenced handgun followed. *Ffft-pop* was all they heard as a bullet whizzed by, and bark exploded off a tree to their left. Another *ffft-pop* and a bullet ricocheted off a rock by their feet.

Ian was a few feet ahead and was doing an excellent job negotiating the pathway. When they reached the top of a small hill, he stopped and pointed into a gully that had a small stream running through the middle. "Look! Now, what do we do?"

"Follow me." Jack dropped to his butt and slid down the embankment. Ian quickly did the same. Dirt ground into their clothes as they skidded down the muddy slope.

The boys stomped through the small stream and approached the far side of the ditch. Since a recent rainstorm had washed away the portion of the path that went up this embankment, they were confronted with a six-foot earthen wall to climb. Ian grabbed Jack's arm. "What do we do?" Jack did not hesitate. He bent down, wrapped his arms around Ian's thighs, and then hoisted him upward. Ian scratched at the ground and pulled himself over the edge.

The boys could hear their pursuer getting closer. Jack clawed and kicked his way up the barrier. Ian grabbed Jack's shoulder and gave a tug that brought him over the edge. Starting from a crawl, Jack ran just as another bullet pierced the adjacent foliage.

They continued down the dark, narrow path. Water from the stream had filled their shoes, and it squished between their toes. The terrain was difficult to maneuver. Occasionally, they would have to jump over a fallen tree or duck under a low branch. Although the air was cool, sweat started to cover their bodies. The two were quickly running out of breath, but Jack knew they had the **fortitude (#272)** to continue their escape.

In mid-stride, Jack placed a hand on the outside of his pocket and felt for his keys. He made sure they were still there while he formulated a plan. For fear of dropping them, he would not extract the keys until he was within operating distance of the keyless entry system. At that time, he would tell Ian to jump in the back seat and lie down. After getting into the truck, starting it, and putting it in reverse, he would back out of his hiding place as fast as possible. If necessary, he would run over their pursuer.

Jack caught a glimpse of moonlight in the distance. In anticipation of entering the field, he regained the lead, ran up the last knoll, and then stopped. After glancing right, then left, he bent over, hands on his knees, and tried to catch his breath. He looked around in the attempt to get his bearings.

With Ian behind him, Jack said, "Follow me." He had only taken a few steps when he saw the Explorer about two hundred yards away. It was located on the far side of the field. Knowing they did not have enough time to reach it, he decided not to bisect the field. His plan was to run along its perimeter, and when their pursuer entered the field, they would dart into the trees for cover. Subsequently, they would crawl through the forest until they reached the truck.

As planned, the two jumped into the thicket when the man entered the field. Ian crouched behind Jack, and the two watched him walk aimlessly in circles. With the gun in his hands extended out in front of him, the man looked for any signs of the pair. After a minute, he appeared to have given up and started to walk toward the path. The boys breathed a sigh of relief. But their freedom was ephemeral. The man stopped at the path's entrance and looked toward his feet. He then turned and ran in their direction.

There was one fatal flaw in Jack's plan. The man could see their footprints in the dew. And before Jack realized this, it was too late. The man stood only ten feet away.

"Come out, come out, wherever you are," the man said in his thick accent.

Not knowing what to do, Jack panicked. His heart was pounding and his breathing was shallow. All he could think about was how close they were to escaping. And after a month of searching for Ian, it would end this way.

Jack realized there was no way to **elude (#273)** the man. They could not go deeper into the forest. The brush was too dense. He also knew that they could not run out into the field, as their pursuer would surely shoot them. Their only hope was to give up and somehow try to escape later.

Jack glanced toward Ian and frowned. "We're caught. I'll try to talk our way out of this. But if that doesn't work, we're going to have to overpower him somehow and get his gun. Follow my lead." Jack hid the iPad in thicket before the two crawled out of the woods. They emerged to find their pursuer's large handgun pointing at them. The man, who was breathing heavily, appeared shocked when he saw the two boys in front of him. "What are you boys," he took several deep breaths, "doing around here?"

Realizing that the assault team was only expecting to find Harrison, Jack made up a story hoping to **dupe (#274)** their captor. "We were camping in the woods and heard a bunch of noise. So, we went over to see what was going on. That's when we saw the barn on fire and a bunch of men with guns. We got scared and decided to get out of there. That's when you chased us. We'll go ahead and leave right now if that's okay with you."

The man shook his head. "No, I need to take you back. I'll let the boss deal with you. Let's go." He pointed to the path with the end of his gun.

The three walked back to the path with Ian in the lead. Jack followed closely behind, keeping one hand on Ian's shoulder. Their captor stayed back about five feet and never let the two out of his sight.

With every step, Jack had a steadily escalating sense of **foreboding (#275).** He knew they had to make a move before they arrived at the house. La Mangosta would not want any loose ends and would most definitely have them killed. Running away would not be good enough. He would have to disarm and disable the man. *If I could find a large stick, I could pretend to trip and then knock him over the head as I got up. Or I could try to go for the gun. But that's risky.*

Jack kept a watchful eye for a large stick on his march down the path. He constantly scanned the ground but found nothing suitable for the job. As they approached the gully, he thought maybe an opportunity would present itself when they crossed the embankment. He moved close to Ian and whispered, "I have to do something soon. Help me any way you can."

The man made the boys go first. The two sat at the edge of the small bluff and then jumped. Jack watched their captor prepare to do the same. He was ready to pounce on him if he made a mistake. In the seconds before the man jumped, Jack contemplated whether he could actually shoot him if he got a hold of his gun. *I guess I won't know until it happens.*

With a constant eye on Ian and Jack, the man jumped. When he landed, he momentarily lost his balance. *Here's my chance.* Jack summoned every ounce of his **indomitable (#276)** courage. He dove at the man and knocked him to the ground.

All he could think about was getting the gun. He remembered what Chris had told him and put one hand on the man's wrist and the other on the barrel of the gun. They struggled on the ground. Dirt scraped against Jack's face and arms. Ian joined in by kicking the man every chance he had. They exchanged no words, only grunts. Jack watched the barrel of the gun point in every direction and knew he had to keep it away from Ian and himself. The struggle continued, and several times, Jack felt parts of the gun rubbing against his body. Ian now jumped in and had his hands on the man's forearm. Jack kept a close eye on the gun, and when it was pointing toward the man, he yelled, "Bite him!"

Ian didn't hesitate. He clamped down on the man's right forearm, just above a tattoo of a snake. This caused enough pain to make the man loosen his grip, which gave Jack a chance to slip his finger onto the trigger of the gun and pull it twice. The first bullet hit the man's upper left arm; the second grazed his shoulder. He screamed in pain and released the gun.

Jack snatched the weapon out of the man's hands, then rolled to his right and onto his back. He lay motionless with the gun pointing toward the man's head. "If you move, I'll kill you." The man lay still, moaning in pain. Jack looked at Ian who had jumped to his feet. Jack pointed toward the small bluff. "Go over there."

Ian scurried over as Jack got to his feet. With the barrel of the gun pointed at the man, Jack moved next to Ian, reached down, wrapped his left arm around Ian's legs, and then lifted him over the edge.

Jack continued to stare at the man; the gun still pointed at his head. With his hands slightly trembling, he thought, *What do I do now? If I let him go, I'm sure he'll tell La Mangosta. And if La Mangosta finds out that it was Ian and me, which he probably will, we'll both be in danger for the rest of our lives.* Jack's mind raced. *I have shot so many people in Call of Duty, but I can't do it.*

Jack tossed the gun to Ian. "If he comes after me, shoot him." Ian stood wide-eyed, holding the gun with both hands. Jack kicked and clawed his way up the embankment. He took one last look at the man before he grabbed the gun from Ian. "Come on. Follow me."

The two ran down the path. When they got to the open field, Jack said, "My truck's over there." They continued running. The whole time Jack kept thinking this would all be over soon. Twenty feet from the truck, he reached into his pocket, removed his key, and pressed the unlock button. "Jump in the back seat and lie down." They both were in the Explorer in a matter of seconds. Jack's hands were shaking so much that he could barely get the key into the ignition. After he started the engine and put it in gear, he glanced at Ian. "We're almost in the clear."

Jack's next problem was whether to turn right or left at the road. *If I turn left, I go past the entrance to the cabin. What if La Mangosta's men are there and they come after us? If I turn right, I don't know where the road leads. What if it's a dead end?"* The wheels spun, and the Explorer fishtailed in the dew-covered grass. "Screw it," he mumbled. "I'm going left." When the tires hit the pavement, they let out a squeal. He accelerated quickly, and when he passed the entrance, nobody was there. Instantly, his body relaxed. He had a huge smile on his face when he turned and looked at Ian. "We made it. You can sit up now."

They continued down the road, and Jack did not slow down until he approached the sharp right-hand curve by the Old Bryson Barn. He went around the curve with the tires screeching and was about to accelerate when the light from several high-powered spotlights blinded him. Without the ability to see where he was going, he had to slam on the brakes. Jack panicked, and before he could figure out what to do, he saw three red dots from laser sights on his chest. "Oh, shit," he mumbled.

"Jack, what's happening?"

"I don't know. I thought we were home free."

Before Jack could say any more, the figures of four men surrounded the Explorer. The blinding light kept their appearance concealed. Simultaneously, all four doors opened, and the men pulled Ian and Jack from the vehicle. One man threw Jack to the ground and handcuffed him within seconds. When he looked up, he saw the barrel of an FBI sniper's rifle and Agent Ralston staring at him. His body went limp and his eyes began to tear. *Now I know we're safe.*

"Jack?"

Jack breathed a sigh of relief. "Yes, it's me."

"Is this who I think he is?"

"Yeah, it's Ian Anderson."

Agent Ralston had a huge smile on his face. "Robin plus one are in the nest," he said into his headset. After a short pause, he replied, "No, it's not Harrison."

Within seconds, the sounds of machine gun fire filled the air. Shortly after, two helicopters flew overhead, and it sounded like a small war raging.

"I need to get you boys to safety," Agent Ralston said with a serious demeanor. "Agent Stadler has set up a command center down the road." He helped Jack to his feet and uncuffed him. "Get in. I'll drive."

Jack jumped into the backseat with Ian. He glanced at his friend and let out a long sigh. "Now I definitely know we're safe." Ian started to cry.

Agent Ralston stopped the Explorer next to Stadler's surveillance van. Within seconds, the van's sliding side door flew open, and Agent Stadler stepped out. He stood with his arms crossed and glared at Jack.

Man, he looks pissed. I guess he's going to arrest me. I don't care. It's worth it, now that Ian is safe. Jack slowly climbed out of the backseat, approached the agent, and held out both wrists.

At first, Stadler did not move. Then he slowly started to shake his head. "I don't know whether to arrest you or thank you."

"I would prefer the latter."

The normally poker-faced man smiled and extended his hand. Jack reached out to shake, but the agent could not contain his excitement. He grabbed Jack and gave him a bear hug that lifted him off his feet. "I don't know how you did it," Agent Stadler repeated several times. The **ebullient (#277)** agent walked over and put his arm around Ian's shoulder. "How are you doing? Are you all right?"

"I'm okay, but I'd really like to see my parents."

Agent Stadler patted Ian's back. "You'll see them soon. First, I want the paramedics to give you a quick examination. Jack, you'll come with me. I need you to debrief me on what you know."

Agent Stadler motioned to a paramedic. When the paramedic arrived, he said, "Take Ian and give him a quick examination. Then bring him back to me."

Agent Stadler and Jack went into his van to continue monitoring the action at the house. Once inside, another agent informed them of the most recent events. Jack listened and then spent the next ten minutes recounting everything he knew. By the time he had finished, eight of La Mangosta's men were shot and killed. Jack was not sure if he had seen eight men plus La Mangosta, or he had seen eight men including La Mangosta. Since La Mangosta wore a hat and a bandana, Jack would not be able to identify him amongst the pile of bodies.

"He was wearing a pair of khaki pants and a khaki shirt," explained Jack. "He looked like he was going on a safari. Also, he was wearing a very strong-smelling cologne." Jack paused. "What about the man I shot? Have you found him? Look for a man with a bite mark on his right arm. It's just above a tattoo of a snake."

Agent Stadler listened in his earpiece while he relayed the information to his men. After examining each of the corpses, they found the man with the bite mark but no one matching La Mangosta's description.

"I saw him walk into the woods. Then I lost him. Maybe he's still out there."

Agent Stadler's forehead wrinkled. "So, you think he's still out there? We've covered a mile radius with the infrared cameras on the helicopter, and we can't find anyone else. I'll have them expand the search." He paused for a moment while he listened to someone in his earpiece. "You left Harrison in the house, right?"

Jack shook his head. "Yes, why?"

"And you didn't see him leave or be carried out of the house?"

"No. Why?"

Agent Stadler leaned backward in his chair and let out a long sigh.

"Because my men can't find him or his body anywhere. They looked throughout the house and even in the tunnel. But they can't find him." He paused and stared at the van's floor in contemplation. "Jack, how long ago did you last see La Mangosta?"

Jack thought for a moment. "Around an hour ago. Why?"

"My men found blood splatter on the wall and a partial blood trail. It looks like Harrison has lost a **prolific (#278)** amount of blood. My guess is La Mangosta captured him and took him away. If you last saw him an hour ago, I'm sure they're long gone by now."

CHAPTER TWENTY-NINE

The command center was full of activity. Both uniformed and plainclothes personnel scurried about performing a variety of tasks. Occasionally, someone made an announcement over a loudspeaker. The words echoed off the adjacent forest.

Jack and Ian sat with Agent Stadler in the FBI van and told their stories. In turn, Agent Stadler explained how they had arrived at the property. "Jack, two planes reported the distress signal from your watch yesterday evening. It would've most likely been disregarded. But your friend Chris called the FAA and told them to be on the lookout for your signal. Once it was detected, we sent the whole team back up here. To our surprise, La Mangosta's men were at the house. They'd just set the barn on fire when my first men arrived. We didn't know where you were. And when we saw your truck speeding down the road, we weren't sure who was driving."

Over the next hour, the two tried to call their fathers but never made contact. They were on Mr. Anderson's private jet and were out of reach from Jack's cell phone. "They'll be here soon," assured Agent Stadler. "Why don't you two try to get some rest."

Before they knew it, the morning sun peeked over the mountaintop. Ian had fallen asleep in the van's driver seat while Jack sat in the back answering more questions from several of the agents. Around seven o'clock, the van shook from a helicopter landing in the field. At the same time, the van's sliding side door opened, and Agent Stadler stuck his head inside. "You boys need to get out here."

Jack helped Ian, still half-asleep, out of his seat. Ian rubbed his eyes while he exited the van. The two stared at the helicopter, and after the blades came to a stop, the side door opened. Chief McKinney jumped out first. Chris, Mr. Graystone, and Mr. Anderson followed him. The last passenger to exit was Reilly.

Jack and Ian waved their arms while the men ran toward them. As soon as Reilly caught a glimpse of Ian, he bolted to him. He jumped on Ian at full speed, knocking him off his feet. Ian's best friend jumped all over him and licked his entire face. The two wrestled on the ground until Mr. Anderson arrived, then Ian sprang to his feet and wrapped his arms around his father. Mr. Anderson, who cried **profusely (#279)**, could barely stand. His tears and shaking body **evinced (#280)** his overwhelming joy.

Mr. Graystone hugged his son, then put both hands on his shoulders and looked him in the eyes. "You're incredible."

"The other agents and I nicknamed him Robin," said Agent Stadler.

"Robin? Why Robin?" asked Jack.

"Robin was Batman's young sidekick that he called 'The Boy Wonder.' We thought that fit you perfectly."

Everyone laughed and then headed over to a large RV with the words 'Mobile Command Unit' written in big letters on its side. Agent Stadler opened the door and directed everyone to take a seat. For the next two hours, they discussed what had happened and what was going to happen.

"As far as La Mangosta knows, Ian is dead and Jack doesn't exist," explained Agent Stadler. "We need to keep it that way. Jack, we'll keep your name out of all the reports. We will also **emend (#281)** any previously written correspondence that mentions your name. Mr. Anderson, you need to act as if Ian is dead. We can place you in witness protection if you like. Right now, though, you can't take Ian back to Worthington. At least not until we catch La Mangosta."

"I planned on taking Ian to our apartment in Manhattan. My wife is there recovering from a nervous breakdown."

"That's perfect. I'll provide protection until we get everything settled."

With the meeting adjourned, the men stepped out of the mobile command unit and into the field. The plan was for Ian, Reilly, and Mr. Anderson to fly to New York City. Chris, Chief McKinney, Mr.

Graystone, and Jack would drive back to Worthington in the Explorer.

Jack walked with the Andersons to the helicopter. When they were a few steps away, the pilot opened the side door. Jack shook Mr. Anderson's hand first. "Will I see you at work this week?" asked Jack.

"Well, no, because I am giving you the week off with pay. I'll see you next week." Before Mr. Anderson climbed into the helicopter, he put his arm around Jack's shoulder. "Jack, thank you so much. I don't know how I'll ever repay you." He patted him on the head before he jumped aboard.

Jack turned to Ian. "Now that all this is over, hopefully, we can hang out sometime."

"That'd be great. Maybe you can come to New York."

"I'll try," Jack said while he bent over to pet Reilly's head. Reilly licked a tear running down Jack's cheek. "I told you I would find him, little buddy," he whispered.

"Come on, Reilly. Let's go." Ian slapped his knee, and then the two jumped onboard the helicopter. Before Ian sat, he turned and gave one last wave. "Thanks, Jack," he said just before the pilot shut the door.

Jack walked away from the helicopter. When he was sufficiently clear of the blades, he turned and waited for the pilot to start the engine. The blades turned slowly at first and then picked up speed. The faster they rotated, the more sand blew up from the ground and filled the air. Jack shielded his eyes from the stinging sand with one hand and waved to Ian with the other. While he watched the helicopter fade into the distance, a strange feeling overcame him. He had the feeling he would never see Ian or Reilly again.

Jack remained in the field for a moment. He stared off into the distance while random thoughts about the past few days raced through his head. Finally, he smiled and ran toward the three men who were waiting for him.

Mr. Graystone, grinning ear to ear, placed his arm around his son. "Come on, Robin. Let's go home."

CHAPTER THIRTY

Over the next two days, Jack relaxed. It was a much-needed **respite (#282)**. The past **enervating (#283)** weekend had drained him both physically and mentally. He went to the beach with Courtney and hung out with Ollie at the shed. He did all the things a typical teenager would do during their summer break. The entire time, however, he never said a word about what had happened over the weekend. He wanted to, but he was under **stringent (#284)** orders from the FBI to remain silent. Until they found Harrison and La Mangosta, he had to keep it a secret. People's lives depended on it.

Jack slept in on Wednesday morning. At ten o'clock, a knock on his bedroom door broke his slumber. "Jack, your father's been trying to reach you all morning. Give him a call. He needs to talk to you."

Still half asleep, Jack sat on the edge of the bed and called his father. "Mom said you needed to talk to me," he said in a raspy voice, rubbing his eyes.

"Yes. Mr. Anderson called. He wants to meet with you and me at four o'clock at his office in the dealership. Can you make it?"

"Yeah, sure. Why does he want to see us?"

"I think it's about the situation over the weekend. He said he couldn't speak about it on the phone. Come to my office and we'll drive together."

"Okay." Jack ended the call, then collapsed back onto the bed and returned to sleep.

***

The two Graystone men arrived at the dealership fifteen minutes early. Jack did this on purpose. He wanted to show his father around the dealership and introduce him to his coworkers. After a brief conversation with Mr. Barrini, Jack directed his father to the showroom. "I'll show you the car you need to buy." His father followed him through the large glass door, but to Jack's dismay, his favorite Porsche was not there.

"Mr. Russo, where's my car?"

Mr. Russo looked up from his desk. "Someone bought it the other day."

Jack smiled. "Darn, I was going to buy it today."

"Oh, I can get another one," Mr. Russo replied without skipping a beat.

Jack countered with, "Well, I left my checkbook at home. I'll have to come back tomorrow."

While they waited for their meeting, Jack showed his father a few of the other cars and explained why he needed to buy each one.

After the third car, Mr. Graystone looked at his son and shook his head. "Jack, you realize if I bought each of the cars you say I need, they would cost more than your mother and I paid for our house."

Jack put his hand on his father's shoulder. "Well, maybe we should sell the house."

His father grinned. "I think we need to talk about your priorities."

It was not long before the receptionist called over to the two. "Mr. Anderson's ready to see you. He's in the conference room."

The two entered the room to find Mr. Anderson sitting with another well-dressed man. After a brief introduction, they found out his name was Harold Peterson. He was one of Mr. Anderson's many attorneys.

Mr. Anderson took his seat at the head of the conference table. Jack sat next to his father, toward the middle. "We're waiting for two more people," Mr. Anderson said. He looked like a different person. The raccoon eyes were gone, and he had a permanent smile on his face.

"Mr. Anderson, how's Ian doing?"

"Better than we expected. His psychiatrist suggested extensive counseling over the summer break to make sure he's not traumatized for the rest of his life. So far, everything seems to be going well."

A knock on the door stopped the conversation.

Mr. Anderson stood. "Come in."

To Jack's surprise, it was Chris and Agent Stadler. After they all exchanged greetings, Agent Stadler updated them on the search for the **elusive (#285)** La Mangosta and Hunter Harrison. From the other end of the table, he explained, "As of now, we can't find either of them. We don't know if La Mangosta took Harrison, dead or alive, or if they went separate ways. I say this because, when we examined the cabin, we found another tunnel that went from the back of the cabin into the bottom of the lake. Therefore, it's possible that Harrison had a scuba tank and swam underwater to safety. But there was no blood in this tunnel. With the amount of blood Harrison lost, surely there would've been a trace of it in there."

"Jack, are you sure Harrison was shot in the shoulder?"

Jack paused for a moment and thought. "There was a hole in his shirt, but he had a towel wedged under it. I never saw the actual wound. Why do you ask?"

"Well, several things don't make sense. When we opened the envelope from the mantel, it was empty. We think Harrison never planned to let Ian go. Only three other people; being the security guard at the Worthington house, Julio the driver, and La Mangosta, knew about Ian's abduction. Unless the police caught one of them, they wouldn't say anything if Harrison killed Ian. So, once Harrison **absconded (#286)** with all of La Mangosta's money and was out of the country, Ian would be nothing but a liability. He would've served his purpose as an insurance policy and would then be expendable."

"Hmm," Jack said. "Then, why did he let us go?"

"We think you **foiled (#287)** his plan when you told him that the security guard we arrested in Worthington confessed about the whole operation. Harrison wouldn't want murder added to his charges if he were caught. That'd be one reason to let Ian go. The other reason is if you two told everyone that he had been shot, it would appear as if La Mangosta abducted him or possibly killed him. Harrison probably believed that it would throw us off his trail. Appearing to be dead would be the perfect cover for him to start a new life. So, if he were pretending to be shot and could remove the bloody clothes, it'd be possible for him to escape through the other tunnel leaving no traces of blood. After he swam underwater to safety, he could've driven off without anyone seeing him.

"Then there's the other option. He was actually shot, and La Mangosta abducted him to get his money back. If that's the case, La Mangosta will surely kill Harrison when he's done with him."

Agent Stadler paused before he reached into a file folder and removed a piece of paper. "There's one other puzzling item." The agent scratched his head. "On the outside of Ian's envelope was a handwritten note. Harrison must've written it just before he disappeared because the envelope was covered with blood. The note read, '*Guys, whatever happens, I hope you two do well in life.*'" Agent Stadler displayed the piece of paper, which was a photocopy of the envelope. "It seems like an odd thing to say and doesn't make sense. We think he may have become delirious from the loss of blood and was remorseful." The agent replaced the piece of paper into the file folder. "There are still many unanswered questions; however, we have every government agency looking for them. If they're in the country, which I expect by now they're not, they won't be able to move around freely or continue to conduct business. Especially La Mangosta. Between losing all his money and the collapse of his drug empire, I don't think he will be able to survive this **maelstrom (#288)**. My gut feeling is that they'll both lie low for a long time."

Mr. Anderson shook his head. "Hopefully, you can find them sooner, rather than later. I'd sure like to get my life back to normal. Is there anything else, Agent Stadler?"

"No, that's it. We'll keep you and the Graystones up to date with whatever information we get."

"Thanks, I'd appreciate that. Now before we all leave, there's one last item I'd like to go over." Mr. Anderson looked at Jack. "I told you that I didn't know how I could ever repay you for what you've done. I thought about it and decided to set up a trust fund for you. Mr. Peterson has prepared the documents and arranged for Chris to be your trustee. It'll help you get a good start in life."

Jack turned to his father with his forehead wrinkled. Mr. Graystone, whose eyes were wide open in surprise, had placed one end of his reading glasses in his mouth and was holding it between his teeth. The room was silent. Mr. Graystone looked at Mr. Anderson for a moment before he turned his gaze toward Jack. Both Graystone men were at a loss for words. Jack leaned forward and placed his elbows on the table. "Mr. Anderson, you didn't have to do that. I'm just happy Ian's all right."

"It's the least I could do. Oh, and there's one other thing." Mr. Anderson grabbed a large envelope from under the table and placed it in front of him. He reached inside and removed a small black and silver object. With the flick of his wrist, he slid it down the table to Jack. Jack caught it just as Mr. Anderson said, "Here's the key to your new car."

With his hand trembling, Jack picked up the key. He immediately recognized it. It was a key to a Porsche Carrera. *This can't be happening.* He stared at it for a moment and then tried to speak. But he couldn't get any words out of his mouth. He looked at his father and passed him the key from his shaking hand. Mr. Graystone inspected the key and never said a word. Jack could not tell if he was happy, angry, or in shock.

"Th, th, thanks, Mr. Anderson, but I can't accept this."

"I insist, Jack. If it weren't for your determination and **valor (#289)**, I would've lost my son."

"There's only one problem, Robert," Mr. Graystone interjected, his glasses still dangling from his mouth. "The cost of insurance for a sixteen-year-old would be **prohibitive (#290)**. We won't be able to afford it."

"Don't worry about that. The trust fund will pay for it."

Mr. Graystone placed his glasses and the key on the table and then leaned back in his chair and clasped his hands. "Just how much money's in this trust account?"

"A million dollars. But, other than school and car-related expenses, Jack can't touch it until he's twenty-five."

A million dollars! Did I hear that right? Did he say a million dollars?

"What!" exclaimed Mr. Graystone who jumped in his seat when he heard the amount of this **munificent (#291)** gift. "That's too generous. You shouldn't have done that."

"Thomas, that's a small price to pay for my son's life."

Jack was **flabbergasted (#292)**. Not knowing what to do or say, he looked at his father for guidance. Mr. Graystone appeared just as bewildered. He stared at Mr. Anderson with his mouth partially opened.

Mr. Anderson slid the envelope to Jack. "Here's the owner's manual, your extra keys, and some other paperwork. Chambers knows I bought you the car. He also knows not to ask any questions or tell anyone at the dealership. If anyone asks, he's to say it's your dad's car."

Jack looked inside the envelope. When he glanced through the items, he saw his new car's window sticker. His heart pounded as he removed it. At the top of the paper, it read, *Porsche Carrera 4S, GT Silver Metallic with Black Leather Interior.* At the bottom, right corner, the final sticker price was $146,800. This was the car that had sat on the showroom floor since his first day of work. Jack could not believe what was happening.

The meeting ended and everyone walked into the hallway. Jack tapped his father's shoulder. "Dad, can I keep it?"

"I don't know. That's too much car for a sixteen-year-old."

"I'll, I'll be careful. Please?"

Mr. Graystone shook his head. "I don't know." He then turned toward Mr. Anderson. "Robert, can I speak to you in your office?"

"Sure. Follow me."

Mr. Graystone glanced at his son. "Stay here. I'll be right back."

Jack took two steps backward and leaned against the wall. He then closed his eyes and bowed his head. He knew his **pragmatic (#293)** father was not going to let him keep the car.

"Jack, what's the matter?"

Jack opened his eyes and saw Chris standing in front of him. "I don't think he's going to let me keep the car. I just know he's going to say it's not practical for a sixteen-year-old to drive a Porsche."

"That is a very expensive and powerful car for a kid to be driving."

"I'll be careful," Jack said wide-eyed.

Chris laughed. "You don't have to convince me. It's your dad you need to convince."

"Well, if I were your son, would you let me keep it?"

Chris's smile quickly faded. He looked toward the ground for a moment before he said, "Yeah, if you were my son, I'd let you keep it."

"Good. I may need your help to convince my dad."

"Have him call me. I'll see what I can do. I have to go now. Stadler and I want to play a few holes of golf before it gets too dark. Text me later and tell me how it goes."

Jack walked down the hall and stood outside of Mr. Anderson's office. He could hear the men talking, but the closed door and the soft music playing over the intercom muffled their voices. He caught the occasional word. "Porsche." "Insurance." "Expensive." "Teenager." *I know he's not going to let me keep it.*

Fifteen minutes had passed. By now, Jack sat on the floor with his back against the wall. His mind raced with thoughts of how he would convince his father to let him keep the car. When the door opened, he sprung to his feet.

"I'll talk to you later, Robert." Mr. Graystone shut the office door behind him.

"Dad, can I keep it?"

Mr. Graystone shook his head. "I don't know."

I don't know? Why do you keep saying that? You're killing me. Just make up your mind. Jack wanted to press the issue but thought it best not to do anything that could upset the man who would determine the fate of his new Porsche.

Before Jack could say any more, Mr. Chambers walked around the corner and approached the Graystones. "Thomas, I'm Burt Chambers," he said, extending his hand.

"Thomas Graystone, nice to meet you. You know my son, Jack."

"Yes. I see him running around here. He's a good worker. The car's outside. Follow me."

"Does this mean I get to keep it?" Jack asked while he followed his father into the parking lot.

Again, his father shook his head. "I don't know."

Jack now felt nauseous. *I don't know? Make up your mind.*

For the next twenty minutes, Burt Chambers explained all the car's features. *Maybe he's just screwing with me. Maybe he's going to let me keep it.* Twice during the demonstration, Jack asked, "Does this mean I can keep it?"

Both times, his father replied, "I don't know."

Burt Chambers finished his demonstration and shook hands before he walked away. By this time, Jack did not know what to think. He was about to ask the question one more time when his father tossed him the keys to the Buick. "I'll meet you at home."

"Does this mean I get to keep the car?"

"We'll discuss it when we get home."

Well, at least he didn't say no.

The trip home in the Buick seemed to take forever. The anticipation of finding out the fate of his car was killing him. While he drove, he thought of what he would say to convince his father. *I'm a good kid and I never get in trouble. I get good grades. I don't drink or do drugs. I'm a hard worker, just ask Mr. Chambers. It's not that much more expensive than Ollie's BMW.*

When they arrived home, Jack was ready. His plan was not to let his father have the first word. As soon as he got out of the car, he would plead his case.

Jack followed his father into the driveway. His mother was standing on the back porch, her right hand on her cheek. Jack was the first out, his father shortly after. He took a deep breath and was about to speak when his dad looked at him and said, "Jack, there are going to be two rules with this car. First, you can't drive it to work or school. Second, the first time you get a ticket or your grades drop, the car goes into storage until you graduate from high school."

Jack's body went numb. *Did I hear him correctly? I hope he's not screwing with me.* "Does that mean I can keep it?"

"Yes, but you can't drive it to work or school and the first time you get a ticket or your grades drop, the car goes into storage until you graduate from high school. Do you understand these two rules?"

Jack thought for a moment. *Technically that's three rules, but I'm not about to tell him that.* "Yes, I understand," he said with great **alacrity (#294)**. He then ran over and hugged his father. "You're the greatest!"

When Jack let go, Mr. Graystone put both hands on his son's shoulders and stared into his eyes. His father then said four words. "Jack, don't disappoint me." They were words his father used sparingly. But Jack knew when he said them, he was serious.

"I won't."

Jack's mom had not yet said a word. Jack could not tell what she was thinking. Finally, she shook her head. "Mr. Anderson shouldn't have done this. This is too nice of a car for a sixteen-year-old to drive. How much did this car cost?"

Jack turned his head away from his mother, and mumbled, "A hundred and..." He then turned toward her and said, "Forty-six thousand."

Dr. Graystone gasped and put both hands on her cheeks. "Forty-six thousand dollars! That's just too much money for a teenager's car. Mr. Anderson shouldn't have spent such an **exorbitant (#295)** amount on a car for you."

Jack looked at his father but did not say a word.

Mr. Graystone smiled and shook his head.

"Dad, can I go now?"

"No. Not yet."

I hope he's not having second thoughts. I hope she's not going to change his mind.

Mr. Graystone looked at him and tilted his head. "What are you going to tell your friends when they ask how you got this car? They'll know I didn't buy it for you."

"Oh, yeah. That's a good question. I can't tell them the real reason. It might jeopardize Ian and his parents."

They both thought for a minute before Jack said, "The news reported that Harrison killed Ian. I'll tell Courtney and Ollie that when I found the binoculars, it helped the FBI solve the case. I'll say Mr. Anderson bought the car for me to show his gratitude. I'll also tell them that he doesn't want anyone to know he bought it for me, so they can't say anything. If anyone else asks, I'm going to say it's your car."

Mr. Graystone nodded. "I guess that'll work. Maybe I should drive the car to work a couple of days a week to keep up appearances."

Jack laughed. "How about once a month?"

"Okay, once a month it is."

"Can I go now?"

"Yes, but remember the rules."

Jack jumped into his new Porsche, grabbed the steering wheel, and inspected each button and switch. He closed his eyes and sniffed the air while he ran his hands over the **supple (#296)** leather seat. The new car smell made him smile. It took a minute to adjust the seat and rearview mirrors and then several more to pair his iPhone and set the radio stations. His body filled with adrenaline when he finally reached for the gear shift to put the car in reverse. Before he backed out of the driveway, he glanced toward the house. Both parents stood by the back door watching him. His father had a smile. His mother still had one hand on her cheek.

Jack drove down Maple Avenue with both windows open. He could hear the Porsche's engine rumbling. "What a great sound," he mumbled to himself. Freddie, the twelve-year-old neighbor, stopped his bike and stared as Jack passed. Jack gave him a nod. Freddie just stared in disbelief.

With his heart pounding, Jack turned onto Main Street and headed for Courtney's house. He had his hands wrapped tightly around the steering wheel and the muscles in his arms tensed. He constantly scanned the road ahead and checked his rearview mirrors for fear that something bad might happen. The Porsche quickly accelerated to thirty-five miles per hour with just a slight press on the pedal. He had driven many Porsches at the dealership, but never for more than a couple hundred yards. This was the first time he drove one over ten miles per hour. The steering was precise. The brakes were tight. *This is nothing like driving the Explorer.*

When he pulled into Courtney's driveway, she was sitting on her front porch steps. All she knew from an earlier text was that he needed to talk to her. She stood and stared at the car for a moment before she approached. "Whose car is this?"

"It depends."

Her forehead wrinkled. "What does that mean?"

"Get in. I'll explain when we get to Ollie's house."

Courtney jumped into the passenger seat and buckled her seatbelt. She sat silently for a moment while her eyes scanned the interior. "Is this your dad's car?"

"Kind of."

She shook her head. "Kind of? What does that mean? Why won't you tell me whose car it is?"

"It's mine."

"Yours? Your dad bought you this car?"

"Not exactly. It's a long story. Just wait 'til we get to Ollie's."

"Okay," she said, her eyes still inspecting the interior.

Ollie was waiting in his driveway when they drove up. He had the same reaction and asked the same questions. While Ollie walked around the car, Jack told his story. He felt terrible that he had to deceive his friends, but he knew the potential consequences if he told them the truth. With a straight face, he explained how finding the binoculars helped to solve the mystery of Ian's disappearance. He also explained how Mr. Anderson bought him the car to show his gratitude, and for some unknown reason, he did not want anyone to know.

"So, guys," said Jack, "if anybody asks, it's my dad's car. I'm serious about this. You can't tell anyone it's my car. Okay?" His eyes went back and forth between the two. They both agreed. "Ollie, I'm serious."

"You have my word. I won't tell anyone." Ollie walked to the passenger door and looked at Jack. "Well, come on. Take us for a ride."

The three jumped into the car. Courtney scrunched in the back. Ollie sat in the passenger seat. And Jack was behind the wheel. They drove around for an hour before they stopped to eat at the Worthington Diner.

After their meal, they decided to drive by the beach club to see if anyone was hanging out in the parking lot. When they pulled up, they ran into Edward and Lip. Edward was standing next to his car wearing a white polo shirt with a BMW crest on the left side of his chest. Several of his friends were gathered around him. By the time Jack came to a stop, everyone had swarmed his car. That is, everyone except Edward. They peppered Jack with questions. "Whose car is it? How fast is it? What did it cost?" Jack could not keep up with the answers. Lip walked over and added his two cents. He looked at Jack and shook his head. "That sure is a small backseat."

For the next hour, they hung out in the parking lot. Jack was the center of attention. Most of the kids were happy for him. Some he could tell were envious. And Edward, of course, was jealous. Jack knew this because Edward never acknowledged him or his car. He stood in the background talking to anyone who would listen. On this night, he had few listeners.

The sun faded and the air grew cooler. Jack stood behind Courtney with his arms wrapped around her, but the chill in the air still made her shiver. "Are you ready to go?" he asked. She replied with several exaggerated nods. "Come on, Ollie," he yelled across the parking lot. "Let's go."

While Jack helped Courtney into the backseat, Edward opened the driver side door and looked inside the car. He glanced at Jack. "I bet it's pretty fast."

It took everything Jack had not to say, "No, it's really slow," and then turn and walk away. But he **abstained (#297)**. He refrained from being just as big of a jackass as Edward. Instead, he said, "I assume it is, but I'll probably never know. If I get a ticket, I can't drive it again." Edward cracked a smile, if only for a second.

After another lap around Oceanside Drive, Jack dropped his friends off and headed home. He found his father in his study shuffling through a stack of papers. Mr. Graystone glanced at his son and then his watch. "It's only eleven. What are you doing home this early?"

Jack walked into the study and stood next to his father. "It's been a crazy day and I'm really tired. What are you doing up so late?"

"I'm preparing for court tomorrow."

"Is there anything I can do?"

Mr. Graystone shook his head. "No, I'm almost done. So, how do you like your new car?"

"It's great. I still can't believe it's mine." Jack started out of the office. When he got to the door, he turned and looked at his father. "Dad." Mr. Graystone looked up from his papers. "It's hard to believe that I woke up this morning a regular kid, and now I'm a millionaire with a new Porsche."

"It's funny how life can change so quickly. But, remember, it can change just as quickly the other way."

"I just hope I don't wake up tomorrow and this was all a dream."

Mr. Graystone laughed. "Yeah, that would really suck."

That night, before he fell asleep, Jack lay in bed contemplating the events of the last several weeks. He thought about how sad he was when he thought Ian was dead and how exhilarated he was when he knew he was alive. He remembered the fear he felt when—not only once, but three times—he had a gun stuck in his back. Laughing to himself, he recalled the time when the man at Overton's Jewelers wanted him arrested for having a stolen watch. Then it dawned on him. His six-thousand-dollar watch was still in the field by the cabin.

The next morning, Jack called Agent Stadler who informed him that the crime scene unit was no longer at the cabin. He gave Jack the combination to the padlock on the gate and said he could look for himself. So, after getting permission from his parents, Jack planned to drive up on Friday. He would use Ollie's metal detector in hopes of finding the watch.

CHAPTER THIRTY-ONE

The journey began at seven o'clock on Friday morning. Just like last time, the **monotonous (#298)** four-hour drive up the interstate was uneventful. Remembering the rules, Jack set the cruise control at two miles an hour under the speed limit. He was not going to lose his car in the first week of ownership.

After getting several disapproving looks from older men in lesser sports cars, Jack arrived at his exit. He pulled the Porsche into the parking lot of Parker's Antiques, opened the sunroof, lowered both windows, and cranked the volume. With his favorite songs blaring from the speakers, he drove the four point six miles along the twisty mountain road to Harrison's cabin.

Jack didn't speed. He didn't need to. The fifty-five-mile-an-hour speed limit was sufficient—especially if you didn't slow down for the curves. He could not stop smiling. *Man, this is the most fun I have ever had.* Unfortunately, the trip did not take very long. And before he knew it, he was at the metal gate that secured the driveway.

The lock on the gate proved difficult to open. After several attempts, Jack was about to give up and make the long walk to the field. But then he realized something. He had written down the combination in a hurry, and what he thought was a nine was actually a four. He let out a quick sigh. "Graystone, you're an idiot," he mumbled.

The driveway looked completely different. The multitude of vehicles going in and out of the crime scene had left it well worn. Jack drove the Porsche down the long, slow descent toward the cabin, being careful to avoid any potholes or stirring up too much dust. When he reached the opening to the field, he stopped. With his eyes wide and mouth partially open, he looked over the property. He could not believe the sight in front of him. The cabin looked nothing like when he first saw it. The doors and windows were boarded up with sheets of plywood, and the entire structure was surrounded by yellow police tape. The barn was a pile of ashes, and most of the tall grass in the field had been flattened or burned. *This place looks spooky.*

Jack parked the Porsche by the burnt barn and then walked over to inspect the **vestige (#299)** of Harrison's Lamborghini. All that remained was the shell of the car amongst the ash and partially burnt timbers. He shook his head and thought, *What a waste.* He then grabbed Ollie's metal detector and began the search for his watch. The search took only five minutes. He found it buried within a tire track of a large vehicle, most likely a fire truck. Besides being dirty, there appeared to be no damage. *It's nothing my friend at Overton Jewelers can't fix.*

After he stowed the metal detector in the Porsche's trunk, he reached for the door handle but did not open the door. The two Cokes he had consumed on the drive up were now putting pressure on his bladder. Realizing he could not wait until he got to the old country store, he decided to walk to the edge of the woods and a take a leak.

Jack looked around while he relieved himself. He peered into the field and watched the remaining patches of tall grass sway back and forth in the breeze. A strange sense of calm had settled over Harrison's property, and for some reason, it made Jack uneasy. He could not believe that less than a week ago, gunfire, helicopters, and nauseous smoke filled the air. This place was a horrible scene of death and destruction. Now, birds chirping, leaves rustling, and fragrant honeysuckle filled the air. It was quite the opposite.

The sound of dried leaves crackling and twigs breaking startled Jack. *I hope that's not La Mangosta.* He snapped his head to the left and saw a mother deer and her two babies walking through the forest. The mother made eye contact and froze. The three deer scattered when Jack reached for his zipper.

Being a city dweller, it was a rare opportunity to see a wild deer. The sight of them bounding past the potting shed and the old well was mesmerizing. The deer were gone in a flash, but Jack continued to stare into the forest. His gaze was set on the old well. Its image reminded him of the bizarre note written on Ian's envelope, which read, "*Guys, whatever happens, I hope you two do well in life.*" Knowing that Harrison claimed he was going to "figure out a way to make things right," he thought, *Maybe there's a hidden message in the note.*

Jack walked over to the well. It was your typical old-fashioned well. It had a stone wall base extending three feet above the ground. On two sides of this base were seven-foot-tall wooden posts that supported a small wood-shingled roof. Between the posts was a metal pipe with a crank, which raised and lowered a bucket tied to a rope.

Jack leaned over the stone wall, turned on his iPhone's flashlight, and looked inside. At the bottom of the well, which appeared to be about thirty feet deep, he saw something shiny. He stared at the object but could not determine what it was. With curiosity getting the better of him, he decided to descend into the well.

Along one side of the stone wall were rusty metal ladder rungs embedded into the mortar that held the stones together. They led all the way to the bottom. Jack slid his phone into his back pocket and then, feet first, made his way, rung by rung, toward the bottom of the well. The air grew cooler, and it became darker with every step. He stopped halfway to let his eyes acclimate. After they adjusted, he continued his descent, examining the walls along the way. *I sure hope I don't find Harrison's dead body down here.*

Jack did not pay attention to how close he was to the bottom of the well. Before he knew it, his right foot plunged into the cold water. "Oh, great," he mumbled as he shook the water from his shoe. He looked toward the shiny object. It was a new stainless-steel chain attached to the bottom ladder rung. He slowly pulled on the chain, which was fastened to something heavy. When he came to the last links, he was amazed at what he saw.

***

The drive between the cabin and the interstate was just as much fun the second time. With the gas tank almost on empty, Jack stopped to fill up at the old gas station. The same weathered old woman took his money with the same toothless smile.

Even at two miles an hour under the speed limit, the drive home was a blast. Jack flipped through his music playlist listening to some songs three or four times in a row. When no one was looking, he sang along at the top of his lungs. About halfway home, the phone rang. The display on the dashboard indicated it was Chris.

Jack depressed the hands-free button on the steering wheel. "Hello, Chris."

"Mr. Graystone, where are you?" Chris asked in a very serious tone.

"I'm driving back from the cabin. I left my watch there. What's up?"

"Well, we need to have a little talk. Is now a good time?"

Jack could tell by the tone of Chris's voice he was not happy about something. Slowly, Jack replied, "Yeah, it's as good as any."

Chris's first words were, "Well, son," and Jack knew right then he was in trouble. "When you came to my house the night you found the money and the drugs, you had twenty thousand dollars. I was just talking to Chief McKinney, and he made a comment about the drugs and the ten thousand dollars. I remember you handing him the money. Thinking back, it was only ten thousand. So, ten thousand dollars are missing. I'm not going to tell you what to do, but you have to realize that you stole money obtained through illegal means. Those illegal activities most likely destroyed many lives. I won't tell anyone about this. I'll leave it to you to do what's right. Think about it on the way home, then come to see me tonight."

"Okay," was all Jack could say before he hung up the phone. For the rest of the way home, he thought about his conversation with Chris and what to do with the money. He understood that drugs can have a **pernicious (#300)** impact on society. And how they can slowly take over and destroy whole families. He also understood why you should not capitalize from this.

***

Jack parked the Porsche in Chris's driveway and sat in the driver's seat until he gathered enough nerve to walk to the door. Stomach churning, he climbed the steps to the front porch. He took a deep breath before ringing the doorbell. He could hear Sherlock and Mycroft before he could see them. Within seconds, they were barreling toward the front door. Allison arrived shortly after that. She greeted him with her usual smile and sent him to the study.

Chris was at his desk reading a magazine when Jack entered the room. "Hey, Chris," he said with a slight tremble in his voice.

Chris looked at Jack with a skeptical eye. He did not return the greeting. "Take a seat. Have you thought about what you're going to do with the money?"

Jack sat in one of the slippery leather chairs, and as his butt slowly slid toward the end of the seat, he let out a long sigh. "Ikndspntit," he mumbled.

"What?"

Again, he mumbled, "Ikndspntit."

"Speak up. I can't hear you."

Jack leaned forward, put both elbows on his knees, and looked at the ground. "I kind of spent it."

Chris's eyes widened. "You did what? Jack, that was drug money."

"I know it was drug money. But what if I did something good with it?"

Chris squinted his eyes. "Well, what did you spend it on?"

"I donated it to my mother's clinic."

Chris shook his head. "And nobody said anything when you handed them ten thousand dollars?"

"I went to the bank and said Ollie's grandfather wanted to donate it to the clinic. I told the teller he was out of checks, and he wanted me to get a cashier's check. Since Grandpa Culver is involved with so many **philanthropic (#301)** endeavors, she never questioned me." Jack paused and glanced at Chris. Chris still looked angry. "And he's getting forgetful in his old age. So, if someone thanks him for the donation, he'll probably assume he made it."

Chris leaned forward, put his elbows on the desk, and rested his chin in the palms of his hands. He stared at Jack for an uncomfortably long time, not saying a word.

This is worse than being in the principal's office, he thought while Chris's eyes pierced through him.

Chris leaned back in his chair and then stared at the ceiling. "What did you do with the receipt from the cashier's check?"

"I have it here in my wallet." Jack handed the receipt to Chris. "I planned on slipping it into the top drawer of Grandpa Culver's desk the next time Ollie and I were at his office."

Chris shook his head. "If you had **pilfered (#302)** a couple hundred dollars, I probably wouldn't have said anything. But if you would've **squandered (#303)** the money on yourself, I would've been really upset with you. And I, I don't know what I would've done. At this point, though, I don't see how trying to return the money to the Worthington Police would help anything." Chris glanced at Jack and cracked a slight smile. "I don't think we should call you Robin, The Boy Wonder. I think we should call you Robin Hood."

Jack looked up from the ground. "Uh, Chris. I have another problem."

"What is it?"

Jack stood. "Follow me." He walked out of the room and to his car. After he removed the key from his pocket and pressed the button that unlatched the front trunk, he opened it and then looked at Chris. "So, what should I do with this?" He reached into the trunk and unzipped a backpack. Inside were stacks of bundled hundred-dollar and fifty-dollar bills. Jack said nothing else. He just stared at Chris.

Chris's eyes lit up. He staggered to the trunk and examined the money. Sherlock followed and sniffed the backpack. "Jack. Where did you get this? And how much is here?"

"A million dollars. I counted it on the way home." Jack stopped talking and continued to stare at Chris.

Chris paced back and forth. He looked worried, confused, and excited all at the same time. "Where'd this money come from?"

"When Ian and I were leaving in the tunnel, Harrison shook his head and said, 'I'm sorry for what I put you two through. I'll figure out a way to make things right.' I didn't think any more about it until I was leaving the cabin. I had drunk two cokes and I had to go. I mean, really go. I couldn't wait until I got to the old country store. So, I walked over to the woods. When I was going, I saw three deer run by the old well, and it made me think. I remembered the strange note written on Ian's envelope that said, '*Guys, I hope you two do well in life.*' I thought that maybe Harrison was trying to relay a **cryptic (#304)** message. So, I climbed down the well. At the bottom, attached to the last ladder rung, was a new stainless-steel chain. When I pulled on it, I found this backpack sealed in a plastic container. I guess he wanted Ian and me to have it."

Chris continued to pace back and forth. "Jack, this is a whole different story. There are people who'll kill you for this money." Chris walked over to the front porch steps and sat. He stared at the ground in deep contemplation before asking, "So, what are you thinking?"

"Well, I understand your point that this money could be profits from illegal drug sales. And those drugs could've ruined lives or even killed people. But what's done is done. I don't know how giving this money to the cops will undo anything. I think this money could be put to better use at my mother's dental clinic. This money would help them reach their goal."

"But, Jack, it's drug money."

Jack took a seat on the front steps next to Chris. "How do you know that? Harrison has made a lot of money legally through his investments. What if this is some of that money? Does that change anything?" He tapped Chris on the shoulder with the back of his hand. "What if it isn't even Harrison's?"

Chris shrugged his shoulders. "I guess we'll never know."

Jack glanced at Chris. "Unless Harrison is alive and he gets caught."

Chris nodded.

"So, Chris, what do you think I should do with it?"

Chris let out a long exhale. "You make some good points. I agree that the money could be put to better use at the clinic. But still, it's most likely drug money. I think you need to tell the FBI." He paused for a moment and then looked at Jack. "You're not a boy anymore. You know right from wrong. But, as an adult, I can't let you drive around with a million bucks in your trunk. I'm going to take this money and lock it in the spy room. Then, I'll give you three options. One, we call Agent Stadler and tell him about the money. Two, we find a way to give it to the dental clinic. But you have to remember that technically half of this money is Ian's."

"Yes, I know that. I was going to talk to Mr. Anderson before I did anything with it." Jack looked at Chris. "What's option three?"

"Option three is we get in the Range Rover, drive to the cabin, and put the money back in the well. Like you said, what if it isn't even Harrison's money?"

Jack's forehead wrinkled. "I never thought of that."

"So, Jack, what are you going to do?"

Jack stood, walked over to the Porsche, looked at the money in the trunk, and then turned toward Chris. "I have decided I'm going to…"

What should Jack do with the money? Leave your comment at: jackgraystone.com.

ACKNOWLEDGMENTS

I want to thank my editors and friends who helped me in so many ways. I would especially like to thank James "Jay" Carney whose knowledge and support was essential to the completion of the Freshman Trilogy.

SAT VOCABULARY WORDS

1. **Barrage:** A large volume or quantity of something happening all at once. **Noun**

2. **Antediluvian:** Made, developed, or evolved a long time ago: Very old. **Adjective**

3. **Enthusiastic:** Having or showing great excitement or interest. **Adjective**

4. **Crestfallen:** Feeling of shame or humiliation: Dejected. **Adjective**

5. **Warped:** 1. Having ideas that most people think are strange or unpleasant. **Adjective**
2. Bent or curved, usually because of damage by heat or water. **Adjective**

6. **Elite:** 1. Selected as the best. **Adjective**
2. The upper levels of society. **Noun**

7. **Anthropology:** The study of the origins and social relationships of human beings. **Noun**

8. **Affluent:** Having an abundant supply of money or possessions of value: Wealthy. **Adjective**

9. **Prosperity:** The condition of being successful or thriving, especially economic well-being. **Noun**

10. **Irreverence:** A mental attitude showing a lack of respect or veneration. **Noun**

11. **Idiosyncratic:** Peculiar to the individual. **Adjective**

12. **Vacuous:** 1. Devoid of thought or intelligence. **Adjective**
2. Empty of or lacking content. **Adjective**

13. **Embodiment:** An individual or thing that serves as a role model. **Noun**

14. **Diffident:** Reserved or shy and lacking self-confidence. **Adjective**

15. **Aspire:** To seek to obtain or accomplish a particular goal. **Verb**

16. **Miffed:** To be irritated and upset. **Adjective**

17. **Concur:** To agree or approve of something. **Verb**

18. **Facetious:** Joking often inappropriately; not serious. **Adjective**

19. **Procrastinate:** Delay or postpone action; put off doing something. **Verb**

20. **Sarcastic:** A mental attitude showing a lack of respect or veneration. **Noun**
    Sarcastically: **Adverb**

21. **Negligent:** Characterized by neglect and undue lack of concern: Careless, Irresponsible. **Adjective**

22. **Cosmopolitan:** Reflecting the influence of numerous cultures and countries: Sophisticated, Urbane. **Adjective**

23. **Convivial:** Friendly and making you feel welcome. **Adjective**

24. **Brevity:** Shortness of duration. **Noun**

25. **Explicit:** Specific about rules or what is required. **Adjective**
    Explicitly: In an explicit manner. **Adverb**

26. **Irreproachable:** Free of guilt; not subject to blame; without fault: Impeccable. **Adjective**

27. **Inconsequential:** Of no significance: Unimportant. **Adjective**

28. **Foster:** To encourage or promote something. **Verb**

29. **Subtle:** Hard to notice or see. **Adjective**

30.	**Acrimonious:**	Angry and bitter. **Adjective**
31.	**Impudent:**	Very rude: not showing respect for other people. **Adjective**
32.	**Spartan:**	A situation that is plain and not luxurious. **Adjective**
33.	**Corroborate:**	To support with evidence or authority. **Verb**
34.	**Presumptive:**	Having a reasonable basis for belief or acceptance: Probable. **Adjective**
35.	**Scour:**	1. To make a thorough search to find what you are looking for. **Verb** 2. Rub hard or scrub. **Verb**
36.	**Preclude:**	Keep from happening or arising; make impossible. **Verb**
37.	**Proximity:**	The nearness of one thing or person to another: Closeness. **Noun**
38.	**Nonchalant:**	Relaxed and calm in a way that shows you do not care or are not worried about anything. **Adjective**
39.	**Impugn:**	Attach as false, wrong, or questionable. **Verb**
40.	**Recalcitrant:**	Stubbornly resistant to authority or control. **Adjective**
41.	**Irascible:**	Quickly aroused to anger. **Adjective**
42.	**Insolence:**	The trait of being rude and improperly forward or bold: Disrespectful. **Noun**
43.	**Exasperation:**	A strong degree of annoyance or irritation. **Noun**
44.	**Equivocate:**	To use unclear language especially to deceive or mislead someone. **Verb**

45. **Incorrigible:** Not reformable, not manageable: Delinquent, Unruly. **Adjective**

46. **Tenuous:** Weak and likely to change; having little substance or strength: Flimsy, Weak. **Adjective**

47. **Aroma:** A distinctive, typically pleasant smell. **Noun**

48. **Altruism:** Unselfish concern for the welfare of others. **Noun**

49. **Empathy:** To understand and share the feelings of another. **Noun**

50. **Frugal:** Careful in spending money or avoiding waste. **Adjective**

51. **Abdicate:** Give up a position. **Verb**

52. **Torrid:** 1. Extremely hot and dry. **Adjective**
2. Characterized by intense emotion. **Adjective**

53. **Onerous:** Involving great effort and difficulty. **Adjective**

54. **Disaffected:** Discontented and resentful especially against authority. **Adjective**

55. **Sustenance:** That which gives nourishment or support. **Noun**

56. **Augment:** 1. Enlarge or increase. 2. Grow or intensify. **Verb**

57. **Pretentious:** Acting as though more important, valuable, or special than is warranted. **Adjective**

58. **Condescending:** Showing or characterized by a patronizing or superior attitude toward others. **Adjective**

59. **Disdain:** Lack of respect accompanied by a feeling of intense dislike. **Noun**

60. **Aspersion:** A false or misleading charge meant to harm someone's reputation. **Noun**

61.	**Disparaging:**	Expressive of a negative or low opinion: Belittle. **Adjective**
62.	**Tirade:**	A long and angry speech. **Adjective**
63.	**Pejorative:**	Expressing disapproval; belittling the importance of something. **Adjective**
64.	**Mercurial:**	Subject to sudden or unpredictable change. **Adjective**
65.	**Impute:**	Attribute or credit to. **Verb**
66.	**Haughty:**	Being arrogant, talking down to people. **Adjective**
67.	**Substantiate:**	To prove the truth of something; Verify. **Verb**
68.	**Fallacious:**	1. Intended to deceive. **Adjective** 2. Based on an incorrect or misleading notion or information. **Adjective**
69.	**Zephyr:**	A gentle breeze. **Noun**
70.	**Mellifluous:**	Pleasing to the ear. **Adjective**
71.	**Pert:**	Highly spirited, lively, or cheerful; attractive or stylish in appearance. **Adjective**
72.	**Tremulous:**	Shaking or quivering from weakness or fear. **Adjective**
73.	**Peripheral:**	1. On or near the edge; constituting the outer boundary. **Adjective** 2. Related to the key issue but not of central importance. **Adjective**
74.	**Purportedly:**	Believed or reputed to be the case: Allegedly. **Adverb**

75. **Solicitous:** Full of anxiety and concern. **Adjective**

76. **Indiscernible:** Difficult or impossible to see, notice, or hear. **Adjective**

77. **Docile:** Easily handled, led, or managed. **Adjective**

78. **Equitable:** Dealing fairly and equally with all concerned. **Adjective**

79. **Fatuous:** Devoid of intelligence. **Adjective**

80. **Adversity:** Hardship, Misfortune. **Noun**

81. **Ameliorate:** To make better or more tolerable. **Verb**

82. **Transitory:** Lasting only a short time: Temporary. **Adjective**

83. **Complement:** Something that fills up, completes, or makes perfect. **Noun**

84. **Raiment:** Especially fine or decorative clothing: Clothing, Garments. **Noun**

85. **Compliment:** A remark or act expressing praise and admiration. **Noun**

86. **Decorum:** Propriety in manners and conduct; proper and polite behavior. **Noun**

87. **Unequivocal:** Unquestionably clear. **Adjective**

88. **Torpid:** Sluggish in functioning or acting: Lazy. **Adjective**

89. **Apathy:** Lack of interest, enthusiasm, or concern. **Noun**

90. **Diffuse:** To spread out over a large area. **Verb**

91. **Noisome:** Offensive to the senses, especially the sense of smell. **Adjective**

92. **Grimy:** Thickly covered with ingrained dirt or soot. **Adjective**

93. **Eclectic:** Something that is made up of various sources or styles. **Adjective**

94. **Quell:** To calm or reduce. **Verb**

95. **Comely:** Very pleasing to the eye. **Adjective**

96. **Congenial:** 1. Pleasant and enjoyable (suitable to your needs.) 2. Sociable. **Adjective**

97. **Irate:** Feeling or showing extreme anger. **Adjective**

98. **Discomfit:** To make a person feel uncomfortable. **Verb**

99. **Ascendancy:** The state that exists when one person or group has power over another: Domination. **Noun**

100. **Erudite:** Having or showing profound knowledge. **Adjective**

101. **Preeminent:** Greatest in importance, degree, significance, or achievement. **Adjective**

102. **Indecorous:** Conflicting with accepted standards of good conduct or good taste: Inappropriate. **Adjective**

103. **Puerile:** Displaying or suggesting a lack of maturity: Juvenile. **Adjective**

104. **Contravene:** To go against a rule or law: Violate. **Verb**

105. **Neophyte:** Someone who is just learning to do something. **Noun**

106. **Phobic:** Suffering from irrational fears. **Adjective**

107. **Surreptitious:** Kept secret, especially because it would not be approved of; marked by quiet, caution and secrecy. **Adjective**

108. **Amiable:** Friendly, sociable, pleasant. **Adjective**

109. **Furtive:** Done in a quiet and secretive way to avoid being noticed. **Adjective**
   Furtiveness: **Noun**

110. **Plausible:** Something appearing reasonable or probable. **Adjective**

111. **Purveyor:** Someone whose business is to supply a particular service or commodity. **Noun**

112. **Supercilious:** Behaving in a way that suggests you are superior to others. **Adjective**

113. **Juxtaposition:** The fact of two things being seen or placed closed together with contrasting effect. **Noun**

114. **Officious:** Assertive of authority in an annoyingly domineering way, especially with regards to petty or trivial matters: Meddling. **Adjective**

115. **Umbrage:** A feeling of anger caused by being offended. **Noun**

116. **Pugnacious:** Having a quarrelsome or combative nature. **Adjective**

117. **Conciliatory:** Intended to gain goodwill or favor or to reduce hostility. **Adjective**

118. **Mollify:** To soothe in temper or disposition: Appease. **Verb**

119. **Obtrusive:** Obvious in an unlikable way: Undesirably noticeable. **Adjective**

120. **Mawkish:** Being overly sentimental or emotional to the point it comes across as fake or silly. **Adjective**

121. **Dearth:** A scarcity or lack of something. **Noun**

122. **Disposition:** The way that someone normally thinks and behaves. **Noun**

123. **Impetuous:** Acting without thinking, done impulsively: Sudden decision. **Adjective**

124. **Penurious:** Desperately in need; not having enough. **Adjective**

125. **Bilk:** Cheat somebody out of what is due, especially money: Defraud. **Adjective**

126. **Charlatan:** A flamboyant deceiver. **Noun**

127. **Multifarious:** Having great variety; numerous: Diverse. **Adjective**

128. **Dubious:** Fraught with uncertainty or doubt: Causing doubt. **Adjective**

129. **Dispel:** 1. Make (a doubt, feeling, or belief) disappear. 2. To drive away or cause to vanish by or as if by scattering: Dissipate. **Verb**

130. **Debunk:** To reveal inaccuracies associated with a belief. **Verb**

131. **Construe:** 1. To make sense of. 2. Assign a meaning to. **Verb**

132. **Burgeon:** Grow or expand rapidly: Flourish. **Verb**

133. **Pedestrian:** 1. A person who travels by foot. **Noun**
2. Lacking wit or imagination: Boring, Commonplace. **Adjective**

134. **Placid:** 1. Free from disturbance by heavy waves (body of water). **Adjective**
2. Not easily irritated or excited. **Adjective**

135. **Relinquish:** 1. Turn away from; give up: Abandon. **Verb**
2. To part with a possession or right. **Verb**

136. **Robust:** Having or exhibiting strength or vigorous health. **Adjective**

137.	**Plethora:**	An abundance or excess of something. **Noun**
138.	**Acumen:**	Insightfulness. **Noun**
139.	**Bashful:**	Socially shy or timid: Self-conscious. **Adjective**
140.	**Emulate:**	1. To imitate and copy. 2. Strive to equal or excel. **Verb**
141.	**Inane:**	Lacking sense: Stupid. **Adjective**
142.	**Predilection:**	A preference or special liking for something; a strong liking. **Noun**
143.	**Convoluted:**	Extremely complex and difficult to follow: Involved, Intricate. **Adjective**
144.	**Gratuitous:**	Uncalled for; unnecessary: Unwarranted. **Adjective**
145.	**Capricious:**	1. Changeable. 2. A person or thing that is impulsive and unpredictable. **Adjective**
146.	**Portent:**	A sign of something about to happen. **Noun**
147.	**Inchoate:**	Beginning to develop or form. **Adjective**
148.	**Espoused:**	To support an idea, belief, or principle. **Verb**
149.	**Trite:**	Repeated too often; overfamiliar through overuse. **Adjective**
150.	**Hubris:**	Exaggerated pride or self-confidence. **Noun**
151.	**Duplicity:**	Contradictory doubleness of thought, speech, or action. **Noun**
152.	**Nadir:**	Point of greatest adversity or despair; all-time low; rock-bottom. **Noun**
153.	**Resolute:**	Marked by firm determination: Persistent. **Noun**

154. **Concomitant:** Happening at the same time as something else: Accompanying. **Noun**

155. **Serene:** Peaceful; not agitated. **Adjective**

156. **Intuition:** An impression that something might be the case: Instinctive knowing. **Noun**

157. **Compliant:** Disposed or willing to comply. **Adjective**

158. **Dalliance:** A relationship, usually romantic, that is taken lightly. **Noun**

159. **Adept:** Thoroughly proficient: Expert. **Adjective**

160. **Knack:** A special way of doing something. **Noun**

161. **Sophistry:** A subtly deceptive reason or argument that sounds correct but is actually false. **Noun**

162. **Prospectus:** A preliminary printed statement that describes an enterprise and that is distributed to prospective buyers, investors, or participants. **Noun**

163. **Copious:** Large in number or quantity. **Adjective**

164. **Ostensible:** Appearing as such but not necessarily so. **Adjective**

165. **Paucity:** An insufficient amount or number. **Noun**

166. **Disillusioned:** Disappointed after not having expectations met: Dissatisfied. **Adjective**

167. **Reconnaissance:** A preliminary survey to gain information. **Noun**

168. **Astute:** Marked by practical hardheaded intelligence: Mentally cleaver or sharp. **Adjective**

169. **Allocate:** Assign, portion: Distribute. **Verb**

170. **Adamant:** Not yielding: Insistent. **Adjective**

171. **Intimation:** A sign or suggestion that something is likely to happen. **Noun**

172. **Intermittent:** Stopping and starting at irregular intervals. **Adjective**

173. **Arduous:** Hard to accomplish or achieve: Difficult. **Adjective**

174. **Deft:** Skillful in physical movements; especially the hands. **Adjective**

175. **Vulnerable:** Exposed or in a position that cannot be completely defended. **Adjective**

176. **Exigent:** Requiring immediate aid or attention: Urgent. **Adjective**

177. **Palliate:** Lessen or try to lessen the seriousness or extent of; provide physical relief. **Verb**

178. **Buoyant:** Capable of floating. **Adjective**

179. **Exacerbate:** To increase the severity or worsen. **Verb**

180. **Resilient:** To recover from damage quickly. **Adjective**

181. **Fortuitous:** Happening by accident or chance: Fortunate, Lucky. **Adjective**

182. **Digression:** 1. Wandering from the main path of a journey. 2. A temporary departure from the norm. **Noun**

183. **Chagrin:** Distress of mind caused by humiliation, disappointment, or failure. **Noun**

184. **Rife:** Excessively abundant; in a great quantity. **Adjective**

185. **Currency:** 1. Anything used to purchase goods and/or services.
2. General acceptance or use. **Noun**

186. **Ephemeral:** Lasting a very short time. **Adjective**

187. **Tenacious:** Not readily letting go of or giving up. **Adjective**

188. **Attenuate:** To lessen the amount, force, magnitude, or value of: Weaken. **Verb**

189. **Ballast:** Any heavy material used to improve stability and control. **Noun**

190. **Empirical:** Derived from experiment and observation rather than theory. **Adjective**

191. **Incoherent:** 1. Unable to express yourself clearly or fluently. **Adjective**
2. Not logical or easily understood. **Adjective**

192. **Articulate:** Express or state clearly. **Verb**

193. **Parched:** Deprived of natural moisture; thirsty. **Adjective**

194. **Elucidate:** To make clear or easy to understand. **Verb**

195. **Incontrovertible:** Impossible to deny or disprove: Indisputable. **Adjective**

196. **Rehash:** To go over something again. **Verb**

197. **Oration:** An elaborate speech delivered in a formal and dignified manner. **Noun**

198. **Egotistical:** Believing oneself to be better, more talented, and more important than others. **Adjective**

199. **Hypothesis:** An assumption or concession made for the sake of argument. **Noun**

200. **Promulgate:** To make something recognized or known: Proclaim. **Verb**

201. **Advocate:** One who pleads for a person, cause or idea. **Noun**

202. **Trenchant:** Having keenness or sharpness in thought, expression, or intellect: Keen, Sharp. **Adjective**

203. **Deliberation:** A careful or thorough consideration. **Noun**

204. **Dissent:** To differ in opinion. **Verb**

205. **Concordance:** Accord: Agreement. **Noun**

206. **Erroneous:** Containing or characterized by error: Wrong or Incorrect. **Adjective**

207. **Collaborate:** Work together on a common enterprise or project. **Verb**

208. **Ambiguous:** Having more than one possible meaning. **Adjective**

209. **Callous:** Emotionally hardened: Insensitive. **Adjective**

210. **Cacophony:** An unpleasant mixture of loud sounds. **Noun**

211. **Maverick:** Someone who exhibits great independence in thoughts and actions. **Noun**

212. **Qualification:** A special skill or requirement that makes a person eligible for a position or activity. **Noun**

213. **Admonish:** Take to task: Warn strongly. **Verb**

214. **Pellucid:** Easy to understand. **Adjective**

215. **Perusal:** Reading carefully with the intent to remember. **Noun**

216. **Foolhardy:** Marked by defiant disregard for danger or consequences. **Adjective**

217. **Exotic:** 1. Not native; foreign. 2. Strikingly strange or unusual. **Adjective**

218. **Dispassionate:** Unaffected by strong emotion or prejudice: Unemotional. **Adjective**

219. **Irrefutable:** Impossible to deny or disprove. **Adjective**

220. **Vicissitude:** A change of circumstances or fortune, typically one that is unwelcome or unpleasant. **Noun**

221. **Enervated:** Lacking physical, mental, or moral vigor. **Adjective**

222. **Assuage:** To lessen the intensity of something. **Verb**

223. **Apprehension:** Fearful expectation or anticipation. **Noun**

224. **Sedate:** Keeping a quiet steady attitude or pace: Unruffled. **Adjective**

225. **Envision:** Imagine; conceive of; see in one's mind. **Verb**

226. **Bereft:** Deprived of or lacking something, especially a nonmaterial asset. **Adjective**

227. **Intrigue:** 1. Caused to be interested or curious. **Verb**
2. A complex scheme devised to gain something in a sneaky way. **Noun**

228. **Amass:** To collect or gather: Accumulate. **Verb**

229. **Coerce:** To compel to an act or choice. **Verb**

230. **Perfidious:** Not able to be trusted: Underhanded, Treacherous, Deceitful. **Adjective**

231. **Flagrant:** Conspicuously and outrageously bad and reprehensible. **Adjective**

232. **Despot:** A brutal ruler who controls everything. **Noun**

233. **Despondent:** Very sad and without hope. **Adjective**

234. **Fathom:** Come to understand: Comprehension. **Verb**

235. **Lugubrious:** Looking or sounding sad and gloomy: Excessively mournful. **Adjective**

236. **Efface:** To cause something to fade or disappear: Erase. **Verb**

237. **Hilarious:** Very funny, causing great merriment and laughter. **Adjective**

238. **Quaint:** Appearing old-fashion in an appealing way. **Adjective**

239. **Decipher:** 1. Decode 2. To make out the meaning of despite indistinctness or obscurity. **Verb**

240. **Esoteric:** Known about or understood by very few people. **Adjective**

241. **Vacillate:** Waver between different opinions or actions: Be indecisive. **Verb**

242. **Quandary:** A state of doubt about what to do in a certain situation. **Noun**

243. **Edict:** An order made by a person or body of authority. **Noun**

244. **Desolate:** Devoid of inhabitants and visitors: Deserted. **Adjective**

245. **Consternation:** Fear resulting from the awareness of danger. **Noun**

246. **Capitulate:** 1. To give in. 2. To surrender under certain conditions. **Verb**

247. **Arrogance:** Overbearing pride evidenced by a superior manner towards inferiors. **Noun**

248. **Incredulous:** Unwilling to admit or accept what is offered as true: Unbelievable. **Adjective**

249.	**Intransigent:**	Impervious to pleas, persuasion, requests, or reason: Uncompromising. **Adjective**
250.	**Impervious:**	1. Not capable of being affected or disturbed. 2. Not allowing entrance or passage. **Adjective**
251.	**Phlegmatic:**	Not easily upset, excited, or angered: Showing little emotion. **Adjective**
252.	**Debilitate:** **Debilitated:**	Make weak or feeble. **Verb** **Adjective**
253.	**Legitimate:**	In accordance with recognized or accepted standards or principles. **Adjective**
254.	**Infusion:**	The act of adding one thing to something else in order to make it stronger or more successful. **Noun**
255.	**Insidious:**	Something that is slowly and secretly causing harm. **Adjective**
256.	**Nefarious:**	Extremely evil and wicked. **Adjective**
257.	**Embezzlement:**	The fraudulent taking of funds or property one has been entrusted to keep. **Noun**
258.	**Inure:**	To become immune or accustom to unpleasant events or situations. **Verb**
259.	**Sporadic:**	Recurring in scattered and irregular or unpredictable instances: Occurring occasionally. **Adjective**
260.	**Apprehensive:**	In fear or dread of possible evil or harm. **Adjective**
261.	**Presage:**	A sign that something bad is about to happen. **Noun**
262.	**Cognizant:**	Knowledge of something, especially through personal experience. **Adjective**

263. **Compunction:** Anxiety arising from awareness of guilt; a feeling of deep regret. **Noun**

264. **Disquiet:** A feeling of anxiety or worry about possible developments. **Noun**
　　Disquieting: Causing mental discomfort. **Adjective**

265. **Devoid:** Entirely lacking: Empty **Adjective**

266. **Futile:** Serving no useful purpose; completely ineffective. **Adjective**

267. **Evanescent:** Lasting only for a short time: Fleeting or Temporary. **Adjective**

268. **Omnipotent:** Having virtually unlimited power or influence. **Adjective**

269. **Noxious:** Physically or mentally harmful or destructive to humans. **Adjective**

270. **Deleterious:** Causing harm or damage. **Adjective**

271. **Conflagration:**
1. A very intense and uncontrolled fire.
2. Conflict/war. **Noun**

272. **Fortitude:** Strength of mind that enables one to endure adversity or face challenges with courage. **Noun**

273. **Elude:** To avoid something or somebody: Evade. **Verb**

274. **Dupe:** To deliberately mislead someone. **Verb**
A person who is easily used or tricked. **Noun**

275. **Foreboding:** A feeling something bad is going to happen. **Noun**

276. **Indomitable:** Impossible to subdue or defeat. **Adjective**

277. **Ebullient:** Joyously unrestrained. **Adjective**

278.	**Prolific:**	Present in large numbers or quantities: Plentiful. **Adjective**
279.	**Profusely:** **Profuse:**	To a great degree: In large amounts. **Adverb** **Adjective**
280.	**Evince:**	To show or express clearly; to make plain. **Verb**
281.	**Emend:**	Make improvements or corrections to (in reference to text.) **Verb**
282.	**Respite:**	A pause from doing something; a pause for relaxation. **Noun**
283.	**Enervating:**	Causing one to feel drained or energy or vitality. **Adjective**
284.	**Stringent:**	Demanding strict attention to rules and procedures. **Adjective**
285.	**Elusive:**	Difficult to find, catch, or achieve. **Adjective**
286.	**Abscond:**	To run away, usually taking something or someone along. **Verb**
287.	**Foil:**	To prevent from obtaining an end. **Verb**
288.	**Maelstrom:**	1. A situation in which there is great confusion, violence, and destruction. **Noun** 2. A powerful whirlpool. **Noun**
289.	**Valor:**	Courage in the presence of danger. **Noun**
290.	**Prohibitive:**	1. Excessively high (of price or charge); difficult to pay. **Adjective** 2. Forbidding or restricting something. **Adjective**
291.	**Munificent:**	Very generous. **Adjective**

292.	**Flabbergasted:**	Overwhelmed with shock, surprise, or wonder. **Adjective**
293.	**Pragmatic:**	Concentrating on practical results and facts instead of speculation and opinion: Practical, Sensible. **Adjective**
294.	**Alacrity:**	Liveliness and eagerness. **Noun**
295.	**Exorbitant:**	Exceeding the customary or appropriate limits in intensity, quality, amount, or size. **Adjective**
296.	**Supple:**	Flexible, easy to bend: Pliant. **Adjective**
297.	**Abstain:**	To choose not to do something. **Verb**
298.	**Monotonous:**	Dull, tedious, and repetitious; lacking in variety and interest. **Adjective**
299.	**Vestige:**	The last small part of something that existed before. **Noun**
300.	**Pernicious:**	Excessively harmful; working or spreading in a hidden and usually injurious way: Deadly. **Adjective**
301.	**Philanthropy:**	Voluntary promotion of human welfare: Generosity. **Noun**
	Philanthropic:	Of or relating to or characterized by philanthropy; generous in assistance to the poor. **Adjective**
302.	**Pilfer:**	To take illegally in small amounts. **Verb**
303.	**Squander:**	Spend thoughtlessly; to waste. **Verb**
304.	**Cryptic:**	Having a secret or hidden meaning. **Adjective**

Made in the USA
Lexington, KY
11 December 2019